D0894456

Vulture au Vin

Also by Lisa King

Death in a Wine Dark Sea

Vulture au Vin

LISA KING

THE PERMANENT PRESS
Sag Harbor, NY 11963

For information, address:
The Permanent Press
4170 Noyac Road
Sag Harbor, NY 11963
www.thepermanentpress.com

Library of Congress Cataloging-in-Publication Data

King, Lisa—
Vulture au Vin / Lisa King.
page cm
ISBN 978-1-57962-357-9
1. Wine—Collectors and collecting—Fiction. 2. Wine and wine making—Fiction. 3. Wine tasting—Fiction. I. Title.

PS3611.I58335V85 2014
813'.6—dc23 2014014225

Printed in the United States of America

To the memory of my dear friend Tomás Villalobos,
the warmest, funniest, most creative man
I've ever known.

Acknowledgments

For their ongoing love and support, I thank my children, Irina, Anton, and Lex, and my mother, Georgianne King. Special thanks to my sister, Margaret King, for her editing help, and to David Gadd for his wine expertise. I am also indebted to friends who read my early drafts and gave invaluable input: Cat Georges, Kathy Morrisson, Donna Morris, Bill Tracy, and Mark Lupher. Thanks also to my agent, Sally van Haitsma, and my publishers, Martin and Judith Shepard.

Chapter 1

Three vultures soared and dipped in the early morning light, riding silently on broad dark wings. Katharine Murdoch observed them from her kitchen window—she had always found them among the most beautiful raptors in flight.

She brought her tea out onto the deck to watch the canyon wake up, moving carefully, making sure of every step. If she fell and broke a hip, her twenty-five-year idyll at this wonderful house likely would be over.

Katharine settled into a deck chair and sniffed the breeze, scented with chaparral and the faint spicy aroma of pepper trees. Below her, a roadrunner with a lizard clamped in its mouth dashed along the canyon floor. Two brown rabbits nosed among the oleanders and geraniums planted just off the deck. A bobcat used to come around most mornings, but she hadn't seen him since construction began on her neighbor's house, nearly three years ago.

She scowled at the imposing structure across the canyon, the only false note in the wild world outside her deck. The huge compound, a California-Spanish pile with the requisite orange tile roof, ran along the entire opposite ridge, 10,000 idiotic square feet for two people.

Katharine could never fathom why Theodore Lyon and his wife had come to this remote corner of San Diego County when they could afford to live anywhere in the world. They certainly didn't appreciate or understand the area—workers had torn up acres of chaparral, cut down a dozen live oaks, flattened the top of the ridge, dug a gigantic basement, and, worst of all, planted things that needed a lot of water, when

Valle de los Osos was lucky to get ten inches of rain a year. There was a rose garden, a bamboo thicket, a pond full of koi, even a putting green. Katharine snorted. Next they'd be terracing the hill to grow rice.

They were draining the aquifer, the well man had told her, filling their pools and oversized bathtubs, watering their thirsty plants. If they continued consuming water at this rate, she'd have to dig a new well. She could sue them—existing users had priority in water rights—but she didn't want to spend her last few years fighting a billionaire in court.

At least the couple slept late, giving her a few peaceful hours before their gardeners started blowing leaves or chipping branches or mowing lawns. She preferred the cool mornings anyway—it would be another hot July day, and the dryness took its toll on her parchment-thin skin.

The canyon ran nearly north-south, and as the sun came up over the sprawling stucco monstrosity, Katharine looked at the brightening sky; now there were nine vultures. What had they found? She searched along the canyon floor—maybe a possum or skunk had died during the night. Moving shadows along the opposite hill caught her eye. Downslope from the flagstone terrace and Olympic-sized infinity pool, two men worked, partly obscured by a dense stand of manzanita. They were darkly tanned and on the short side, perhaps from Guatemala or Oaxaca, she surmised. As she watched, they loaded large, shaggy black things into the back of a green pickup.

Katharine made her way to the deck's corner bench and picked up the binoculars she kept there, next to a well-thumbed copy of *Peterson Field Guide to Western Birds*. Although her hearing worsened every day, her eyesight was remarkable for a woman of ninety-two. She could still tell the difference between a red-tailed and red-shouldered hawk from quite a distance.

Shielding herself behind the magenta bougainvillea that cascaded over the railing, she focused her binoculars near the truck and realized the black things scattered about were dead vultures. The men were picking up carcasses by the feet and swinging them into the truck bed. She counted more than a dozen bald pink heads flopped over a heap of tangled wings.

Katharine spotted two rifles on the gun rack mounted across the truck's back window. She scoured her memory of the last twenty-four hours. Maybe the vultures had been slaughtered during her nap. Or perhaps while one of those infernal landscaping machines was running. With her poor hearing, Katharine easily could have missed the gunshots. She felt a sudden flush of rage, but just as quickly took a few deep breaths. Anger was bad for her blood pressure.

The men drove the truck north along the canyon floor until they came to a sandy area near a large prickly pear cactus. They grabbed shovels out of the truck bed and started to dig. Katharine continued watching them for the next half hour as the sun rose, filling the canyon with warmth and light. They finally unloaded the vultures into the deep mass grave.

Katharine lowered her binoculars. Not deep enough, she thought as the men covered the pit with dirt. Just wait until the Department of Fish and Wildlife office opened. After tending to her own birds, she'd call a friend who worked there. The fine for killing a raptor anywhere in the United States was $5,000.

Mr. High and Mighty, with his noise and lights and his ignorant, arrogant ways, always maintained that he could do what he wanted on his private property. Well, not this time. This time he would pay.

On a warm Monday morning a few weeks later, Katharine came in from feeding her birds just in time to answer the phone. She inserted one of the hearing aids she kept in a small dish nearby. She hated wearing them unless she absolutely had to.

"Katharine, you crafty old witch, you got him!" It was Bob, her exuberant young friend from fish and wildlife. "Lyon decided not to appeal. His lawyer probably told him he didn't have a chance. The son of a bitch is going to pay the full amount—$70,000."

"Bob, that's wonderful."

"It'll be all over the news. Nice work, lady. Next time I'm in town, I'll buy you a drink."

"I look forward to it. Thank you so much for the call." Katharine hung up, went to the living room window, and gazed at the big white house with satisfaction. Last night there had been a party across the canyon, the music so loud it bothered even her. Of course it would be better if the vultures were still alive, but at least Lyon would make restitution. This time his selfish, destructive actions would have harsh consequences.

Katharine decided to celebrate by having lunch at Big Tom's, her favorite of the three restaurants in town. Just before noon she put in her other hearing aid, took a wooden cane from the closet, got into her old green Isuzu Trooper, and drove down the hill. She'd have the bacon, lettuce, and tomato sandwich on white toast with iced tea, and then some of that nice apple pie from Julian, a town in the mountains to the northeast where it was cool enough to grow apples.

Katharine would try to sit in Doris's station. She was the older, more sensible of the two daytime waitresses. The little flirty one, Pilar, was friendly and talkative, but tended to ignore Katharine when male customers were around.

She pulled the Isuzu into the nearly empty parking lot. Leaning on her cane as she got out of the car, she noticed a kettle of vultures overhead. They circled above a small grove of eucalyptus trees bordering the asphalt lot, and now and then a few descended. Katharine did a quick appraisal of the route through dry grass and decided she could manage it. She was curious to see what the vultures were scavenging—last year she had followed a large flock at the edge of town and found the carcass of a mountain lion, unusual so close to civilization. Fish and wildlife had been very interested in that find.

Katharine worked her way toward the grove and stepped into its scented shade. Behind one of the trees, several vultures hopped about, pecking at a mound covered with leaves. Whatever lay beneath was the wrong shape to be a mountain lion. In any case, why would anyone camouflage an animal carcass? She moved closer and saw a slender human leg protruding through the leaves, female by the look of it. The vultures had ripped through suntan-colored hose, bloodying the leg, but the foot still wore a white, rubber-soled shoe.

Katharine recoiled in horror, nearly falling, but caught herself on a tree trunk. She knew she shouldn't touch anything, but she had to see who it was. She gently brushed leaves away from the body's head with the tip of her cane. It was a young woman lying on her side, her black hair tied back with a red ribbon, her pretty brown eyes staring vacantly at nothing. Katharine knew the face well—Pilar.

Katharine backtracked to the restaurant, willing her heart to stop pounding. Inside the old-fashioned diner-style establishment, a plump woman in a red and white uniform poured coffee for one of the half-dozen patrons, all of whom Katharine knew by sight. "Hi, Katharine," Doris said, smiling over her shoulder and tucking a strand of lank brown hair behind her ear. "You want your usual table?"

"Doris, call the sheriff. It's Pilar. She's dead."

A chorus of gasps and exclamations rose through the dining room. Doris blinked. "Dead? What happened?"

"I don't know. She's lying in those trees." Katharine gestured. She sat down in the nearest chair, too upset to stand any longer.

"Oh my God." Doris put the coffeepot back on its burner and hurried toward the phone next to the cash register. "Are you sure she's dead?"

"I'm sure. There are vultures. They only eat dead things."

Later that afternoon, Katharine and Doris sat together at a window table in the empty restaurant. Outside they could see two sheriff's cars, an ambulance, and a few curious people peering past yellow crime-scene tape into the clump of trees. Deputy Sheriff Matt Baeza, a tall, overweight man in a tan and green short-sleeved uniform, stood just inside the tape, talking to another officer. Doris blew her nose on a tissue. Her eyes were red from crying.

"I feel so bad," Doris said, tearing up again. "I had to cover the whole place during the breakfast rush, and I was so mad at her. And now look at her." She covered her face with her hands and cried harder.

Katharine patted Doris's hand. "There, there, you didn't know."

"Who would want to hurt her?" Doris's eyes grew wide. "Did they—was she—"

"The deputy told me she has all her clothes on," Katharine said gently.

The two women watched as the paramedics emerged from the trees carrying a gurney. Strapped to it was a slender shape in a plastic body bag. They descended the slight incline to the parking lot and lifted Pilar into the waiting ambulance.

Deputy Baeza came into the restaurant. He took out a blue bandanna and wiped his forehead and the back of his thick neck. Katharine knew his mother was a Native American, which showed in his straight black hair and strong profile. "Mrs. Murdoch, Doris, you can go now," he said. "We have your statements. If I need to ask you anything else, I'll give you a call."

"Thank you, Deputy," Katharine said. "Can they tell what happened to Pilar?"

"Don't know yet, but Dr. Crawford says it looks like she was stabbed. Probably killed on her way to work this morning. Somebody went through her purse, so maybe it was a robbery."

Katharine closed her eyes. It always hurt so much when young people died, especially by violence. What a terrible thing that a sweet, vivacious girl like Pilar should be killed for the pathetic sum of money she'd probably been carrying. She wouldn't even have had her day's tips yet. "Have you told her folks?" Katharine asked.

"Sheila's over there now," the deputy said. Sheila was the only woman deputy in the small department, and Katharine had heard her complain that she always got the job of conveying bad news to relatives.

Katharine said good-bye and got back into her Trooper, her appetite gone. With a heavy heart, she drove toward Pilar's parents' house. She knew the dead girl's mother well—Rosa Ochoa came in twice a month to clean Katharine's house. The family would need friends now.

As she drove, Katharine thought about who in the world could have stabbed Pilar. Robbery seemed awfully farfetched to her—Pilar was not an obvious target for someone who needed money. Could it have been a lovers' quarrel? She didn't know if Pilar had a boyfriend. The girl had flirted with customers but was always lighthearted about it. Illegal immigrants camped out in some of the nearby canyons, but they rarely caused trouble. In fact they tried hard not to be noticed by the authorities. What about the methamphetamine cooks who supposedly worked in the area? Perhaps someone on drugs had done it.

In the twenty-five years Katharine had lived here, there'd been fatal car wrecks, deadly fires, farm equipment accidents, and the like, and sometimes criminals from the city dumped bodies in the canyons, but there had been very few murders of local people. She shook her head. It occurred to her that a lot of things had changed since the Lyons had arrived.

Chapter 2

There was nothing wrong with Jean Applequist's appetite. Her stomach growled as she contemplated the prospect of a four-star lunch at the Fairmont instead of the boring cheese sandwich she'd brought from home. She and her boss, Owen Partridge, editor and publisher of *Wine Digest*, rode in the back seat of their host's black and silver Maybach Zeppelin, a make of car Jean knew nothing about. That was unusual for her—she had an unhealthy interest in high-performance automobiles. This one had a cream-colored leather interior and little curtains on the windows that you could close if you wanted to elude the paparazzi. Jean kept the curtains open, hoping someone she knew would see her.

Jean had no idea why Theodore Lyon, oil billionaire and wine collector extraordinaire, had invited her to lunch instead of Kyle, the managing editor. Owen had asked her along at the last moment at Lyon's behest. The minute they were alone, she was going to grill Owen about what was going on. Fortunately she looked good today, in a gray matte jersey dress with a sash belt that she'd made from a Donna Karan pattern. The outfit went well with hematite hoop earrings. She ran a hand over her prematurely silver hair, liking the feel of her new very short cut.

"This is the life," Owen said. He was in his early forties, running to fat, with a professorial tweed jacket and graying beard. He glanced at Jean. "I don't have to tell you to behave, do I?"

"What, you think I'm going to dance on the table with a lampshade on my head?"

He chuckled. "One never knows with you."

They drove to the top of Nob Hill and pulled up in front of the Fairmont Hotel, a stately Beaux-Arts edifice completed in 1907. Colorful flags from around the world surmounted the squared-off portico. The driver, a stocky young Latino named Chencho, jumped out and hurried to open the passenger door. He wore khaki slacks and a windbreaker with the Lyon Oil logo on the back. He smiled, showing a deep dimple on one side. "Here we are," he said.

He tossed his keys to a valet and led the way into the enormous lobby. The décor was an elegant blend of neutral colors and gold accents, with massive pillars of heavily veined beige marble. Tall potted palms and extravagant flower arrangements broke up the seating areas. It was a busy morning, and many of the gray velvet sofas and cream-colored chairs were occupied. Jean had been here a few times with her friend Lou, who loved the mai tais in the Tonga Room bar.

As Jean and the two men waited before a bank of elevators, a loud voice at the registration counter caught their attention. They turned to look.

A dark, grizzled man in his fifties argued loudly with a harried young woman behind the counter. He held a battered straw cowboy hat in his hands.

"I told you, I gotta see Theodore Lyon," the man said. In jeans, a Western-style shirt, and well-worn cowboy boots, he looked distinctly out of place among the well-dressed tourists and business people who surrounded him.

"I'm sorry, sir, but he is unavailable," the clerk said.

"This is important. I gotta warn him." Jean thought the man was probably Latino or Indian. He was definitely drunk.

"I'd be happy to take a message and have him get back to you."

"How the hell's he gonna do that? I got no phone."

"Perhaps you could write him a note."

"No! I wanna talk to him face to face. Right now!"

To the young woman's obvious relief, two large men in dark suits approached the yelling man, one on each side, and escorted him from the hotel.

The express elevator arrived and Chencho, Jean, and Owen got on. "What was that all about?" Jean asked.

Chencho shrugged. "That sort of thing happens now and then. Crazies trying to get to Mr. Lyon. He's had to take out restraining orders a few times against people bothering him or the rest of the family."

"Do you know that man?" Owen asked.

"Nah. He must be a new one."

They got off the elevator and entered the Penthouse Suite. Jean had looked it up on the Internet—it covered the entire seventh floor, comprised six thousand square feet, including its own billiard room, and cost $15,000 a night.

Their host approached them with a welcoming smile. Chencho made introductions. "Pleased to meet you both," Ted Lyon said as they shook hands. "That'll be all for now, Chencho. Thank you." The young man moved off to another part of the vast apartment.

Jean had of course seen Ted Lyon in the media many times. She had read that he was sixty-four, but he looked younger. He was about six feet tall, with a compact build and honey-blond hair shot with white. He had the good haircut and perfect teeth Jean expected to see in the very rich. He wasn't conventionally handsome, but his long jaw and broad nose made for an appealing face. His camel sport coat, navy trousers, and pale blue open-necked shirt fit him perfectly. The jacket looked to Jean like Zegna—way out of her price range.

"We'll dine on the patio," Ted told them. He led the way through high-ceilinged rooms that oozed luxury. The colors were on the cool side and the décor looked like an *Architectural Digest* spread—expensive and tasteful, but somewhat impersonal. Every window framed a spectacular vista of the city.

A table for three was set up outside on the patio, which had a breathtaking view of the San Francisco skyline, the Transamerica pyramid dominating, and the Bay Bridge and Treasure Island beyond. A waiter worked at a table nearby, arranging salad on three plates, and a sommelier opened a bottle of white wine.

Jean, Owen, and their host ate spinach salads with blue cheese, roasted pears, and candied walnuts, accompanied by a smooth and spicy Merry Edwards Sauvignon Blanc. The conversation was mostly about wine, and Jean was impressed with Ted's thorough knowledge of the subject.

After the salad course, the sommelier presented a bottle of red wine with a simple black-and-white label Jean had seen before. "I've brought a bottle from my own cellar," Ted explained. "It's a 1996 Domaine de la Romanée-Conti La Tâche."

Jean knew the wine—it was a rare red Burgundy that usually brought at least $1,500 a bottle at auction. After Ted had tasted the wine and pronounced it lovely, the sommelier filled their glasses and a waiter served them Kobe flat iron steak sandwiches with sautéed mushrooms and onion rings.

Jean sipped her wine carefully—she had a tendency to dribble on her shelf, and besides, she didn't want to waste a drop. She didn't know whether the wine was worth half a month's pay, but it was damn good. On the nose she detected black cherries, toasty oak, and something elusive that reminded her of Chinese five-spice powder. The aromas carried through on the palate. It was full-bodied and intense, with a long, long finish. She thought it would be even better in five years.

As Jean ate her sandwich with a knife and fork, striving to keep meat drippings off her dress, Ted focused on her. "Now Jean," he began, "as you know, I'm hosting a very important Sauternes tasting in early October, and *Wine Digest* will be covering it exclusively. Owen and I have been discussing which writer should be there, and I've decided to offer that honor to you." Owen smiled at her and nodded his agreement.

Jean opened her eyes wide, genuinely surprised. "I'd love to cover it—thank you," she exclaimed. Exclusively? How had Owen managed that? For a moment she wondered if Ted had a prurient interest in her—she was in her early thirties, five ten and fit, and her hourglass figure meant she often had to consider this possibility in her interactions with men. She dismissed the thought—she wasn't getting the right vibes from Ted, and besides, she'd seen photos of his wife. Covering the tasting also meant she would get free meals and good wine for an entire weekend, not an unimportant consideration given the state of her finances.

"Are you familiar with the wines I'll be pouring?" Ted asked.

"Owen showed me the list." It had made her groan with longing.

"Owen tells me you have a good grasp of sweet wines in general, but that won't be enough for my purposes," Ted said. "I expect you to do some serious research on Sauternes before the tasting."

Jean didn't like his lecturing tone, but under the circumstances she figured she could put up with it. "Of course," she said politely. "I'll be well prepared."

The three of them discussed the logistics of the tasting as they finished their sandwiches. "One more thing," Ted added as they drank coffee. "I'm aware that you wrote about those murders you were involved in earlier this year. There was a murder in Valle de los Osos a couple of months ago, but I don't want any mention of it in your article. Is that clear?"

Again the lecturing tone. Ted was shaping up to be kind of a prick. "Sure," she said. "Who was killed? Did you know the victim?" Another thing she had an unhealthy interest in was murder.

"A local girl. I didn't know her." Ted glanced at his watch, a complicated gold timepiece with four smaller dials on its white and blue face. Jean strained to read the brand name—Vacheron Constantin. Never heard of it. But then Jean wasn't into watches. She wore a black and white plastic Swatch.

"Well, this has been delightful." Ted stood up. "Right now I have another appointment. Chencho is waiting downstairs to take you back to your office." He walked Owen and Jean to the elevator, and they shook hands. "It's been a pleasure to meet you, Jean," Ted said. "I'm sure I won't regret choosing you for this assignment."

"I look forward to it," she said.

She and Owen got into the elevator. "So what's up?" she demanded as soon as the doors closed. "I thought Kyle was covering that tasting."

"He was, but Ted asked to meet you," Owen said. "It seems he liked your coverage of the TBA tasting in Los Angeles."

Jean thought that made sense. TBA—Trockenbeerenauslese—was the finest German dessert wine, just as Sauternes was the finest from France.

"Anyway, the least I can do is send the reporter he asks for, since he's letting us cover the tasting exclusively," Owen said.

"How the hell did you swing that? Doesn't he want Parker and *Wine Spectator* and the rest of the big guns to be there?"

Owen looked away uncomfortably. "I'm letting Ted have final say on the articles and photos," he muttered. "The other editors wouldn't agree to that."

"You *what*?" Jean exclaimed. "That means the story will say whatever he wants, no matter how the tasting comes out."

"Get a little perspective, Jean. This tasting is historic. We can sell a lot of ads against that article. I'd advise you to get off your high horse and think about the wines you'll be drinking."

Jean sighed. He was right. She'd have to put up with a lot more editing than usual and possibly wholesale rewriting, but it was worth it to try the wines. She ran through the list in her head. This tasting was going to be better than sex—almost.

As they exited the hotel, a tall black man in a red doorman's uniform with gold epaulets directed them around the corner to Mason Street, and Jean spotted the Maybach pulled up next to the building's service gate. Chencho got out to open the back door.

It was a cool, clear day, and Jean gazed out over her adopted city, struck once again by its ever-changing beauty. As they came abreast of the car, she glanced up. A large dark shape hurtled toward them from above. "Whoa!" she exclaimed. She stepped back quickly, instinctively pulling on Chencho's sleeve and forcing Owen back with her other arm. A moment later the falling object slammed into the roof of the Maybach with a horrific crashing thud, crumpling the top of the car and spraying them with glass. Several airbags deployed with muffled explosions.

It was the body of a man, face down. Jean recognized the cowboy boots of the stalker they'd seen earlier in the lobby. One of his mangled legs hung down over the rear passenger door, right where Chencho had been standing. A woman screamed and people ran toward the Maybach.

"My God," Owen said, gripping Jean's arm. "Are you OK? Is anybody hurt?"

"I think I'm OK," Jean said. She realized she was trembling and took a few deep breaths. Owen edged over to the man on the roof of the car. "Is he dead?"

"Has to be," Jean said. "Look at the angle of his head." She brushed small crumbs of safety glass off her clothes; the two men did the same. "Where did he come from?" She looked up at the side of the building, but could see nothing out of the ordinary.

Chencho, pale and shaken, ran his hands over his face. "Jesus, that was close," he said. "I owe you one, Ms. Applequist."

A small crowd gathered around the car. "Are you three all right?" asked the tall doorman. His nametag said "William."

"Yeah, we're fine," Owen said. "More or less."

William walked over to the crushed car and searched for a pulse on the man's bloodied wrist. "Yeah, he's dead," he said after a few seconds. "I called the police. You should stay put until they get here."

"I need to sit down," Jean said. "I think we all do."

"OK, go back into the lobby," William said. "I'll stay here and keep people away."

The three of them walked slowly back to the hotel entrance and went inside. Jean felt cold and disoriented, as if she were in shock. The two security men who had thrown the stalker out hurried past them, headed for the Maybach. Sirens grew closer as they sat in a deserted corner of the lobby.

"I need to tell Mr. Lyon what's happened," Chencho said.

"What *did* happen?" Owen said. "Did he fall? Did he jump? Did someone push him?" He took out his cell. "I have to call my wife. What a hell of a thing. I've never seen a dead body before."

"Me neither," Chencho said.

Jean said nothing—she'd seen more than one.

Chencho walked toward the elevators and Owen went outside. Jean pulled her new cell from her purse. She hated cell phones, but had finally broken down and bought one. It wasn't a smart phone, but it did the job. It was just after two o'clock. Jay "Zeppo" Zeppetello, her current boyfriend, was a student at the University of California at Davis. He would be in class now—she'd call him later. She phoned her office and asked for Kyle, the managing editor.

"Look at the local news online," she told him. "We were about to get into Lyon's car when somebody fell on it. He's dead."

"No way!" he exclaimed. "You OK?"

"Yeah, we're fine. But don't expect us back any time soon."

"Who was it?"

"Don't know. Some guy who was trying to see Lyon earlier today." Jean saw two uniformed officers enter the lobby and look around. "I have to go. The cops are here."

"OK. Keep me posted."

Jean stood and approached the policemen. She could feel an adrenaline rush as she remembered the dead man's words: He'd wanted to warn Ted Lyon. Warn him of what?

Chapter 3

The homicide inspectors let Jean and Owen take a cab back to the office around five. Jean had managed to have a brief conversation with Zeppo, who was suitably alarmed by what had happened. Since it was Friday, he was due to arrive in San Francisco that evening. She couldn't wait to see him.

The police had asked plenty of questions but hadn't answered many of hers. Jean thought she knew who would. Last March she had met homicide inspector George Hallock during the investigation of a murder that she'd helped solve. Back in her cubicle, she dug his card out of her purse and called his cell.

"Hallock," he barked.

"Hi, Inspector. This is Jean Applequist. Do you remember me from the Wingo investigation?"

"How could I forget?"

"I witnessed the death at the Fairmont today," she said. "I was about to get into the car he fell on."

"You're kidding. Am I in for another wild ride?"

"I hope not. The officers I talked to wouldn't tell me much. Is there any chance you'd answer a few questions?"

He paused. "Like what?"

"Like who the guy was. Did the fall kill him or was he already dead? Was it suicide or murder? He said he wanted to warn Ted Lyon. What about?"

She heard him sigh. "Let me talk to the investigating officers. I'm not promising anything."

"Thanks." Jean hung up and signed off her PC, anxious to get home. Zeppo would arrive in a couple of hours, and her apartment was a mess.

She put on the loose black Chinese jacket she often wore on mass transit to discourage male harassment and left the office, on the second floor of Opera Plaza. She passed Max's café, which was filling up with the Friday happy-hour crowd, and walked briskly along Van Ness, past San Francisco's green-domed City Hall and through the Civic Center. She dodged feral pigeons and aggressive homeless people as she made her way to the BART station.

Jean waited with the other commuters on the underground platform, thinking about the dead man. Whether it was murder or suicide, was the targeting of Lyon's car random or deliberate? The timing had been lucky. If it was murder, whoever pushed the man could have done it when Chencho was alone in the car or when she and Owen and Chencho were all in the car. As it was, if she hadn't noticed the falling body, Chencho might have been injured, but probably not killed. Had the man gone off the roof or out of a window? She thought of calling George Hallock again, but didn't think he'd respond well to nagging. A train arrived and she pushed on, not bothering to find a seat since it was a short trip.

Jean felt a flutter of anticipation as the train neared Mission and Twenty-Fourth. She saw Zeppo nearly every weekend, and he was always so glad to see her, so warm and funny and full of energy. He was only twenty-four, eight years her junior, and sometimes his youthful, unsophisticated ways irritated her, but she had no complaints about their physical relationship. In fact he kept her so busy that she'd been reasonably faithful to him. It wasn't that she'd reformed; there just hadn't been the time or opportunity for any outside flings. And on the few occasions when an old lover had come through town, Zeppo hadn't complained. That was another thing she liked about him.

Jean walked up the Twenty-Fourth Street hill, across Dolores and Church, then turned uphill again for a few blocks to her studio apartment. It was small, but there was a nice view out the bay window, a handsome old red and black Afghan rug on the floor, and an expensive sewing machine under the clutter.

Once the apartment looked reasonably neat, Jean took a shower and put on her red silk robe with a dragon on the back. She curled up on the sofa to wait, and soon heard his key in the lock.

Zeppo—tall, skinny, and redheaded—came in carrying an overnight bag and balancing his bicycle; they planned to go riding this weekend. He dropped his bag and leaned his bike against the wall next to hers as she shut the door. "Jeannie," he said, gathering her in a fierce hug. "I'm so glad you're OK." They kissed—he tasted faintly of coffee. "I heard some of it on the radio. What the hell happened?"

They sat together on the sofa, sipping wine, and Jean told the story again, including her thoughts on whether the dead man or his murderer had aimed for Lyon's car and had deliberately done it when there was no one inside, or if the target and timing were random.

"Whew," Zeppo said when she was through. "If it was planned, then he only wanted to kill himself. Or his killer didn't want any collateral deaths or serious injuries. But why would he pick Lyon's car?"

"No idea. The cops told me the dead guy had no ID, so they're running his prints. I'm hoping George Hallock will call back and tell me what's up." She poured them more wine. "Hey, I almost forgot. The reason Ted Lyon fed me lunch is that he wants me to cover the Sauternes tasting I told you about."

"In San Diego County, right? Tell me the name of the town again."

"It's a small unincorporated area called Valle de los Osos—valley of the bears."

"Yeah, that's it. I heard on the news about a murder there. First one in years." He looked into his glass. "The reason I remember is that it was a young woman and she was stabbed."

As a teenager, Zeppo had been tried and acquitted in the stabbing of his sister-in-law.

"That must be the murder Ted mentioned," Jean said. "He told me not to write about it. Who stabbed her?"

"Unknown. Haven't seen a follow-up story." He cocked his head at her. "Going down there seems like a really bad idea. I mean, this guy Lyon just had two violent deaths right near him, and you said on the phone that the dead guy was trying to warn him about something."

"But I really want to taste the wines, and it'll mean a cover story for me. Don't worry, I can take care of myself." Jean squeezed his hand. "I'd bring you along, but I don't think Lyon would go for it."

"When is it?"

"Second weekend in October."

"I couldn't go anyway. I've got a paper due that Monday and a big chemistry test on Tuesday. Seriously, Jean, you have no idea what's going on with Lyon. He's a billionaire. Probably has lots of enemies. You don't know what you're walking into."

Jean was getting annoyed. One of her big complaints about her last boyfriend was how overprotective he was. This was atypical behavior for Zeppo—he usually trusted in her abilities. "Stop being so paranoid," she said a bit more sharply than she'd intended. "The woman who was killed was just from the same town. Ted says he didn't even know her."

Zeppo sighed. "Will you at least listen to what Hallock has to say before you make up your mind?"

Jean hesitated, aware that Zeppo might actually have a point. "All right. If he finds out something scary I'll reconsider."

"Thanks. Who else gets to go? A photographer?"

"Yeah. Not sure who yet."

"Roman's pretty good with a camera, and he'd be much better protection than I could be," Zeppo said. "I'd feel a lot better about it if he was there. Anyway, he's a Sauternes freak."

Roman Villalobos was a good friend of them both. "That's a great idea. I'll work on it." Jean looked closely at Zeppo. "Hey, where are your glasses?"

He blinked his pale blue-green eyes at her. "I finally got the contact lenses. They bother me some, but I like them."

"I like them, too." She kissed him, and as his hands roamed over her she felt the heat of desire that his touch always brought. He stood and pulled her up, backing her onto the bed, taking off her robe as she helped him out of his shorts and UC Davis T-shirt. He paused for a moment to look at her. "You're even more gorgeous when you're in focus."

"Stop gawking and come here," Jean ordered. She'd been looking forward to this moment all week. Zeppo was always passionate, but their first encounter after a separation was especially intense.

AFTERWARD ZEPPO sprawled on the quilt, eyes closed. Jean rolled onto her side, feeling languid and dreamy, stroking his pale freckled skin, playing with his ringlets—he was growing out his coppery red hair.

She touched the ugly pink scar on his right shoulder over his clavicle; there was a bump where the bone had healed crookedly. He'd been shot during the Wingo investigation, and he had another scar on his back, from the exit wound. His physical therapist had him lifting weights, and Jean could see the results in his shoulders and arms. "Are you hungry?"

"Always. What's for dinner?"

"I have ravioli from Lucca's deli and some antipasti." Jean loved to eat but wasn't much of a cook, especially on work nights. "And I splurged on a bottle of Amarone."

Zeppo chuckled. "What's that, a fifty-dollar bottle of wine? No wonder you never have any money."

After a while they got up and Jean put her robe back on. In the small kitchen she started a pot of boiling water while Zeppo, in boxers and T-shirt, rooted through the refrigerator and pulled out containers of antipasto, looking into them, setting it all on the kitchen table—cheeses, pickled eggplant and mushrooms, red pepper and artichoke salad, Italian cold cuts. "It looks like you got a little of everything," he said.

That particular speech pattern of his was starting to irritate her. "'Like' can be a preposition, a verb, or an adjective, but you can't use it to introduce a clause."

He closed the fridge and gave her a strange look. "I know that. I'd never write it in a paper that way."

"Sorry." Jean put marinara sauce into a pan to heat and opened the bottle of red wine, pouring them two glasses. She dumped ravioli into the boiling water, stirred them around, and sat with him at the table, both of them eating antipasti with their fingers and sipping the wine. It was rich and concentrated, tasting of ripe fruit. "So what's your paper about?"

"It's for bonehead English, where we read novels and write a paper. Mine's on *The Great Gatsby*."

Jean grinned. "Now you know what to name your daughter."

"Daisy?"

"Zelda."

He laughed. "Zelda Zeppetello. Perfect."

They ate at the kitchen table, discussing Zeppo's classes and Jean's week at work. When they'd finished, Zeppo cleared the table. "I'll do these dishes," he said.

Jean pulled him away from the sink. "Later. Come sit for a while." They took their wine into the living room and sat back on the sofa.

"So what wines has Lyon got that you're so hot to try?" Zeppo asked.

"Sauternes from as far back as the early nineteenth century. I've never had any of it older than the 1920s."

"How come the wines are still drinkable? I mean, I thought a couple of decades was about the limit for most of the great reds, and aren't they as good as it gets?"

"It's different with sweet wines. The sugar acts as a preservative and makes them last a lot longer. I've read about Sauternes from the late eighteenth century that were still pretty good two hundred years later."

"What kind of grapes do they use?"

"Sémillon mostly, with a little Sauvignon Blanc blended in. They leave the grapes on the vine until they get really ripe, and then if conditions are perfect, a fungus called *Botrytis cinerea* attacks the grapes and dehydrates them, making the sugar and acid and the other flavor components really concentrated. Another name for the fungus is noble rot. It's very costly to make wine that way—rain or an early frost can ruin your crop while you're waiting. At the top châteaux, the pickers make several passes through the vineyards to pick each grape at the right time. They don't get much juice, either—only about a glass of wine from one vine. It's like making wine from raisins."

"But they charge a lot for it, don't they?"

"You bet. The current release of Yquem, the best Sauternes, goes for more than six hundred dollars a bottle."

"What about your pal René Chatouilleux? I thought he made great Sauternes."

"Château d'Yquem is the only *premier grand cru*, first great growth, in Sauternes. The next level is *premier cru*, first growth, and that's what Château Chatouilleux is. René is campaigning to have the family château elevated to *premier grand cru*."

"Can he do it?"

"I'll be amazed if he pulls it off. It has only been done once before in Bordeaux, and never in Sauternes."

"So what does Lyon have to do with it?"

"He has the world's largest collection of old Chatouilleux, and this tasting will put it head to head with Yquem, supposedly proving that Chatouilleux measures up. Of course the people who'll be at the tasting don't have anything to do with the French ranking system, but René is hoping the publicity will help his cause." Zeppo was getting more and more interested in wine, and Jean was tired of these endless question-and-answer sessions. "I don't want to talk about wine anymore," she said impatiently. "I'm tired of it."

"Don't be cross, Jeannie. Next quarter I'm going to take an introductory enology class so I won't have to ask you so many dumb questions, OK?"

"Oh, Zeppo, I'm sorry. It's been a rough day."

"Well, it's not over yet." He put their wine glasses on the coffee table and knelt in front of her, parting her robe, dissolving her bad mood and making her gasp. The dishes sat in the sink until morning.

Chapter 4

The opening bars of Harry Lime's theme music from *The Third Man* woke Jean from a deep sleep at eight fifteen the next morning. She groped for her cell phone on the bedside table.

"Hello?"

"Ms. Applequist? George Hallock."

She sat upright and tried to shake the sleep out of her head. "Hi. Thanks for calling back."

"Sure. So the deceased was a guy named Domingo Huerta, age fifty-three. He had a few priors for drunk and disorderly and check fraud, a couple of DUIs. Lived in a converted garage in Valle de los Osos. He was part Luiseño Mission Indian and got a little money from the tribe's casino."

Jean struggled to process all this information. "What was he doing in San Francisco?"

"Took a Greyhound up two days ago. He was spotted by the doormen hanging around the Fairmont and finally went in yesterday. No one on the staff saw him after he was tossed out of the hotel. He went off the roof. No indication of how he got up there. His blood alcohol was twice the legal limit. That's about all they have so far."

"Well, thanks. Do they have any idea what he wanted to warn Ted Lyon about?"

"Not yet. But he was apparently known as a serious drunk with a rich fantasy life. Liked to hang around local bars and tell tall tales."

"Do they think he jumped or was pushed?"

"There was no sign of a struggle, but he may have already been dead. Autopsy is in a week or so."

"Will you please let me know what they find?"

She could hear Hallock coughing, a loose, wet sound—he was a heavy smoker. "OK," he said finally, "if you promise to stay out of this case."

"I promise to try."

"Have a good day, Ms. Applequist."

"Call me Jean."

Later, as they ate scrambled eggs and wheat toast, Jean told Zeppo what Hallock had said.

"It sounds li. . . as if this guy Huerta might be a random crazy person who killed himself," Zeppo said. "I guess we won't know anything for sure till the autopsy. But if someone pushed him, then there's something else going on. Something dangerous."

"Look, I want to go to this tasting no matter what. It's really important to me."

"I realize that," he said. "You know I'm not trying to be an asshole. I just don't want anything to happen to you."

She put her hand on his. "Yes, I know. If Roman comes with me, will you relax?"

"I guess so. Hey, let's call him and ask if he can go."

After breakfast Jean called Roman Villalobos. Jean's Uncle Beau Reed, her only relative west of Indiana, owned a Queen Anne Victorian in the Castro District, and behind it was a pre-earthquake cottage that Roman had rented for nearly twenty years. She'd met him while she was still in high school, when she'd come out to look at universities with Beau, and had thought Roman the best-looking man she'd ever met, and one of the smartest. She still thought so. It had been a great disappointment to discover that he, like Beau, was gay. She'd never been able to seduce him, but he had become one of her best friends. He and Zeppo had grown close as well.

Roman, a freelance book editor, had refined tastes in art, music, furniture, clothes—and wine. He was fond of the deep golden dessert wines of California, Germany, and especially France's Sauternes appellation. Jean planned to talk the art director into letting Roman shoot the tasting so he could have the once-in-a-lifetime chance to try the rare old wines. And if Zeppo's fears had any basis in reality, Roman would come in handy—he taught martial arts. As far as passing for a professional photographer, Roman took great photos, but his camera wouldn't be good enough for magazine work, and he'd need professional lights.

The three of them had planned to go biking later, but Roman had begged off; he was in the middle of a big editing project with a tight deadline, a biography of Howard Hughes. He answered his phone sounding distracted.

Jean explained that she'd be covering the Lyon tasting. "If I convince my art director that you can handle the photography and you offer to do it for free, she'll go for it. We're in a real budget crunch these days."

Roman made a dismissive noise. "I have a lot of work to finish," he said in his soft baritone, "and I don't want to spend a weekend in hundred-degree weather with a collection of rich, supercilious fools."

"Too bad. There'll be several Sauternes from the nineteenth century, including an Yquem and a Chatouilleux from the comet vintage. The 1811 comet vintage."

"Indeed." Roman was silent for a few moments. "And exactly how am I going to pass myself off as a professional photographer?"

"Leave that to me. I've got a friend who can lend you some equipment." Never mind that the last time she'd seen that particular friend, they'd had a loud screaming fight that had prompted the neighbors to call the police.

Zeppo gestured for the phone and she handed it over. "Hiya, Roman. What Jean isn't telling you is that she may be in some danger. You hear about the body that fell on a car outside the Fairmont yesterday? It was Lyon's car and Jean was about to get in it. They don't know if the guy jumped or was pushed, but he was from the town in SoCal where Lyon has a house." Jean could hear Roman's voice but couldn't make out the words. "Yeah," Zeppo said to him. "I can't go, but you could if you pull off the photographer thing. One of us has to keep an eye on her." He handed the phone back to Jean, who made a face.

"Zeppo's being a little paranoid," she said to Roman. "But I'd love it if you'd come along."

"Under the circumstances, I suppose I'd better make the time. When were you thinking of leaving?"

ON SUNDAY night, after Zeppo left for Davis, Jean decided to do some research on the woman who was stabbed in Valle de los Osos. She'd always been fascinated by murders, both real and fictional, especially since she'd helped solve three of them. She had to admit that in spite of the danger she and Zeppo had been in, she'd loved the adrenaline rush and the sense of accomplishment from figuring it all out.

She booted up her computer and typed "Valle de los Osos" and "murder" into Google. There it was, on the *U-T San Diego's* website.

Two months ago, Pilar Ochoa, twenty-two, was found stabbed to death in a stand of trees near her place of employment, Big Tom's Diner. It had happened early in the morning as she was on her way to work. There was no evidence of sexual assault, and robbery was the assumed motive. A woman named Katharine Murdoch had discovered the body. The young woman was survived by her parents, two brothers, and various aunts, uncles, and cousins. There was a photo of a dark, pretty girl that looked like a high school yearbook shot.

Jean scrolled through the article. It seemed the night before her death, Pilar had worked as a server at a party at Ted Lyon's estate. So there *was* a connection. Interesting.

She'd have to tell Zeppo—he shared her fascination with murder.

Jean found two more references on a small local newspaper's website over the following two weeks, then nothing. So the murder still hadn't been solved. She'd have to ask about it once she got to the scene of the crime. There were several Pilar Ochoas on Facebook, but none was the right one. Her page had probably been taken down by now. Jean checked for updates on Domingo Huerta, but there was nothing new.

She also looked up the Maybach Zeppelin and Vacheron Constantin watches. Ted's car, which she figured was probably totaled, had cost nearly a million dollars, and his watch, one of only seven Tour de l'Iles ever made, had cost half again as much as the car. Holy shit.

THE NEXT morning at work, Jean cornered Carol, the art director, and coaxed and cajoled her into letting Roman shoot the tasting. She exaggerated her friend's skill and experience, making it sound as if he were practically a professional. The clincher, as she'd expected, was that he'd pay his own way and do it for free.

She went into an empty conference room and closed the door so no one could hear her conversation. Now for the hard part: She was going to call Clive Deegan to beg equipment. Jean had met Clive, an Australian photographer, when he'd shot a few events for *Wine Digest* as a freelancer. He'd still be working for them if he hadn't been hired full-time by the *San Francisco Chronicle*—he was a very good photographer, fast and flexible, able to get flattering shots of half-drunk wine snobs in poorly lit tasting rooms or under bright Napa sunshine. She'd been attracted to him, and he to her. Sex with him had been fun in a rough-and-tumble way, but he was controlling and pig-headed and his temper was as bad as hers, so they'd usually wound up yelling at each other. She hadn't seen or spoken to him since their final spectacular blowup.

As for getting Clive to help, it was doubtful he'd do it for old time's sake. But he had a special fondness for vintage Port, and Jean had a few bottles left over from a tasting at the magazine a few months ago, including three from 1977, a great vintage that was drinking beautifully now.

As Jean looked up his phone number in her contacts, she tried to remember what she'd said to him during that last fight. It had probably been really insulting—she had a tendency to say things in the heat of the moment that she later regretted. Maybe he'd forgotten, too. She found his number and dialed.

"Deegan." He always answered his cell as if he were sitting in a newsroom.

"Clive, it's Jean Applequist."

"What in hell do you want?"

Jean smiled; she loved his Russell Crowe accent. "I need a favor."

"Ha! You've got balls, I'll give you that."

"Look, I'm sorry for whatever I said during our last fight."

"Don't you remember? You called me a witless, dickless Neanderthal. That was after you threw the clock, but before the cops came."

Jean laughed. "I'm sorry, Clive. I know you're not dickless. And don't forget, you called me a blood-sucking, ball-busting bitch."

"I'm sure you're still all those things, and proud of it."

"Now Clive, I'm not asking you to do anything for free. I happen to have half a case of vintage Port in my possession, including a Fonseca and two Dows from 1977. I'll let you have it if you help me out."

There was a pause. "What exactly do you want?"

"I want you to lend a friend of mine the equipment he'll need to shoot a tasting. He's not a professional, but he takes good pictures."

"Who's the guy? Your current boyfriend?"

"No, an old friend named Roman."

"You know, Jean, what I do requires skill and experience. It's not something just anybody can pick up in a few hours."

"I know that. He doesn't have to be as good as you are—he just has to take some usable shots of people at a couple of tastings at Theodore Lyon's spread in San Diego County. It'll be relentlessly sunny and hot, and there's a big fancy tasting room. We'll need shots of the bottles, head shots of the participants, candid shots of the group tasting and hanging out, like that. And Roman's a fast learner."

Clive thought about it. "OK. I'll meet him and see if I want to do it. I'm not making any promises."

"Thanks, Clive. I'll talk to Roman and phone you. And I really am sorry I called you dickless."

"Yeah, that hurt. I thought that was the one part of me you appreciated."

AFTER WORK on Tuesday Jean headed for Il Castrato, a bar on Eighteenth Street near Diamond that she and Roman frequented. Here she could get a glass of good wine instead of the usual Castro bar plonk, and Roman could listen to Italian opera instead of club dance music. It was a lively spot, full of a mixed after-work crowd, male and female, gay and straight. Vintage opera posters hung on the walls.

Roman was already there, chatting with the bartender. Jean watched her friend for a few moments, admiring him. Several patrons had noticed him as well, and not only because he was something of a celebrity in the gay community. He was almost fifty but looked ten years younger, tall and muscular, covered with sleek black hair nearly everywhere except the top of his head. Across his bald pate was a white scar he'd gotten from a police baton in a bar down the street thirty-some years ago, when it was called the Elephant Walk. His fringe of hair was cut short and his goatee neatly trimmed, and he sported a single gold hoop earring. He wore jeans and a blue Hawaiian shirt Jean had made. She came up behind him and pinched his butt.

Roman turned and smiled. There were circles under his beautiful dark eyes and he looked tired and stressed out. "Hello, Jean. Good to see you." He gave her a kiss.

Jean ordered a glass of Sangiovese, Roman picked up his Bourbon on the rocks, and they sat at a table along the wall. She liked the music, a lighthearted aria, but couldn't tell if the singer was male or female. "What's that?" she asked Roman.

"Orsini's drinking song from *Lucrezia Borgia* by Donizetti."

"Sung by a countertenor?"

"No, a mezzo-soprano. It's a pants role—a woman singing a man's part. She's saying something like 'I know the secret of happiness. I joke and drink and laugh at fools.' "

"Sounds like my kind of gal. Or guy."

"Unfortunately, the wine is poisoned and everyone dies."

"Opera's such fun." Jean reached into her purse. "Speaking of wine, I brought you a list of the wines Lyon's going to pour."

"Just a minute. Zeppo told me there was a murder recently in Valle de los Osos, a young woman. I looked it up online—she worked at Lyon's house the night before she died. And then there's the man who fell on the car. Zeppo says you're not taking the two deaths seriously."

"The guy at the Fairmont could be a suicide or an accident. He was a well-known drunk."

"And the waitress?"

"I know you both mean well, but look at it from my perspective," Jean said. "This tasting is a really big deal in my world. It's a major career coup that I get to cover it. You think I should skip it because of some vague possibilities of danger? Ted Lyon asked for me. If I refuse to go, I might lose my job."

Roman smiled at her. "I knew you'd go no matter what. We'll just have to stay on our toes. Let's see the wines." He took the list and put on his reading glasses. He raised an eyebrow as he looked down the list, then glanced at her over his glasses. "OK, these wines are worth a couple of days of bodyguard duty. What do I have to do?"

"Clive Deegan is a friend, a photographer at the *Chronicle*. I'm going to give him some vintage Port so he'll lend you lights and whatever and tell you what to do with them."

Roman nodded, putting his glasses into his shirt pocket. "Sounds reasonable. But if he's a friend, why are you paying him?"

Jean sipped her wine. "We parted on bad terms."

"Ah. So he's one of your discarded lovers."

"The discarding was mutual, believe me."

Just then Clive came through the door carrying a large, well-used camera case. He was of average height and burly, with a craggy, masculine face and blue eyes. His dark hair was buzz cut. He wore a battered leather bomber jacket—evidence of his Indiana Jones complex.

Jean waved to Clive, who got himself a draft beer and joined them. She introduced him to Roman.

"So you're an old friend of Jean's, eh?" Clive said. "Based on what I've seen, I wouldn't think she'd have many of those." Jean made a face at him but kept quiet.

"The trick is don't get into bed with her," Roman said.

Clive sighed. "That's the trick, all right. You're looking great, Jean."

"You too, Clive."

A slender man with dark shoulder-length hair came over to their table. He wore a tasteful woman's blouse tucked into tight jeans, and for once his makeup and jewelry were understated.

"Good for you, Jean," he said. "Roman hasn't been out of the house in weeks."

The last time Jean had seen Lou Kasden, he'd been a blond. "Hi, Lou," she said. "Your hair looks nice."

"Thanks, honey. I think people take me more seriously as a brunette." He looked at Clive. "Who's your hunky friend?"

Roman did the honors. "Clive Deegan, this is Lou Kasden."

Clive stuck out a big paw. "Pleased to meet you."

Lou held on to Clive's hand. "Oh, you're Australian! I love Australians. And they usually love me, too. How about buying a girl a drink?"

"No thanks, mate," Clive said, gently extricating his hand. "I'm a strict vagitarian myself."

"What does that make me?" Lou asked coyly. "A carnivore?"

"I'll bet you're a regular Tyrannosaurus."

"Oh, honey. You have no idea what you're missing," Lou giggled. "Well, see you all later. I'll go find somebody who appreciates me. Jean, give my love to Zeppo." He moved across the room to talk to friends at another table.

Clive gazed after him. "He one of those pre-op fellows?"

Roman shook his head. "No, he doesn't want to be a girl. He simply enjoys dressing like one."

"Looks good on him." Clive turned back to Jean. "Now don't get me wrong. Roman here seems bright enough, but why not hire a professional?"

"Roman's crazy about Sauternes and he really wants to try the wines, and even if Lyon won't give him his own pours, he can taste mine."

"Got a sweet tooth, have you?" Clive said to Roman.

Roman grinned. "Absolutely."

"Ever try any of the Australian stickies? We make some great dessert wines, even get noble rot on the grapes sometimes. Pretty good quality for the money."

"Some of them are quite good. But there's nothing like Sauternes for depth of flavor and complexity."

Jean laughed at them. "You guys sound just like the geeks I work with. I can't get away from it."

"She's never happy, is she?" Clive drank some beer. "OK, Roman, let's do it. I agree to the bargain. The first rule is, shoot a lot of photos, ten times more than you think you'll need. Delete the ones that aren't great, but save most of them. Get vertical and horizontal shots of the same scenes. The main thing to remember at a tasting is to shoot the people early, before they get drunk and sloppy and there's wine spilled all over the tablecloth. After half an hour or so, there's nothing new happening anyway. Then afterward get shots of the empty bottles with the labels showing. Jean will tell you if you need to shoot a specific bottle. And if there's food to shoot, do it before people start on it, right after it's set up."

"That all sounds logical," Roman said.

"I've brought along a couple of DSLR cameras for you, a few collapsible softbox lights with light stands, and a tripod." He zipped open the camera bag at his feet. "If you've got time this evening, I can show you a few things."

"That would be fine. We can go to my house—it's just a few blocks away." Roman pulled another, much smaller DSLR camera out of Clive's bag. "What about this one?"

"That's the one I always carry with me in case my luck ever changes."

"How do you mean?" Roman asked.

"I have a history of missing the main event. I was set to fly to New York on September 12, 2001, I left Phuket three days before the tsunami hit in 2004, and I changed my plans and went to Bangkok instead of Tokyo the day before the earthquake."

Roman sipped his Bourbon. "I'd call that extraordinarily good luck."

As they left the bar, Roman stopped to speak to a friend, so Clive and Jean waited outside for him. Clive looked her over, shaking his head. "You may be a hellhag, Jean, but you're put together better than any other woman I know. It's a damn shame."

"It was nice to see you, too, Clive. And thanks."

When Roman came out of the bar, he and Clive turned uphill toward Beau's, and Jean walked down to Castro and waited for a bus to take her home. As she walked up the hill to her apartment, her cell phone rang. It was George Hallock.

"They just got the autopsy results on Huerta," the inspector said. "He was dead when he hit the car. Broken neck. Also had cirrhosis and a few other alcohol-related conditions."

"So it was murder."

"Yep. No suspects yet. Roger Belnap got the assignment, and he'll keep me in the loop. Now remember, you're staying out of it."

"Yes, sir."

"I mean it. The last thing we need is you meddling in this."

Jean hung up, glad that Hallock felt he owed her enough to satisfy her curiosity. She felt trepidation about Zeppo's and Roman's reactions to this news, but also excitement for what was to come. Valle de los Osos was going to be exciting—she couldn't resist the combination of world-class wine and two unsolved murders.

Chapter 5

Ted Lyon and Owen decided that Jean and Roman should arrive a couple of days before the Saturday tasting so the story could include the event preparations. Jean owned a red Porsche Carrera, a gift from a rich friend, and she wanted to drive it to San Diego County—the long, empty stretch of Interstate 5 through the Central Valley was one of the few places she could get the car up to high speed and still have a good chance of eluding the highway patrol. But since Roman resisted getting into any car she was driving, they decided to fly out Wednesday morning.

Roman picked her up in his Prius, which they left in long-term parking. Jean loved to travel and had done a lot of it. She packed light and never checked luggage. They boarded the plane after lengthy security delays, put their bags and Clive's camera case into the overhead compartment, and settled into the too-small seats, their long legs cramped.

Roman leaned back on the headrest and rubbed his eyes. "Pardon my yawning," he said. "I've been up all night."

"Did you get everything finished?" Jean asked.

"Yes, just barely. I sent the damn thing off right before I left for your house. I never want to read another word about Howard Hughes as long as I live."

"I'll try to get your mind on something else." Jean pulled out her notebook. "I did a little research on the Lyons this week since I knew you wouldn't have time. Want to hear it?"

"Certainly. If I doze off, poke me."

"OK. This is mostly from an interview Ted gave last year, plus a few other articles I found online. You probably know a lot of it already. Lyon's ancestors came from Maine, and in 1849 they sailed around Cape Horn to California looking for gold. They didn't find any, but a couple of generations later, his grandfather Bernard Lyon struck oil near Long Beach and founded Lyon Oil. Ted got an MBA from Harvard and went to work for the family firm, learning the ropes and getting ready to run the company one day. Meanwhile, his wife, Anne, felt bored and neglected, so she ran off with some soap-opera actor she met in a bar. Ted divorced her, of course."

"Pretty standard scenario," Roman said.

"Yeah, but here's where the story gets interesting: Less than a year after Anne left, she and her boyfriend went skiing in the Swiss Alps and got killed in an avalanche. Ted and Anne had two little kids, a boy and a girl. Since he didn't have to work for a living, Ted resigned from the firm to stay home and take care of his kids, figuring otherwise they'd feel totally abandoned."

"Speaks well for him."

"Yeah. Supposedly he raised them by himself, no nannies. Makes me think better of him—he comes across as really controlling." She looked at her notes. "Bernard is now forty and Lydia is thirty-seven. Ted is an active member of the board of directors. He didn't remarry until three years ago."

"He was probably a little wary of women after the first debacle. And imagine what dating is like for billionaires. You're never really alone with anyone—all that money is a constant presence."

"He solved that problem by marrying someone almost as rich as he is. His wife's the daughter of a Taiwanese microchip tycoon. He met her when he was in Taiwan shopping for art. She's younger than his kids. I'm sure you've seen her picture—she's really beautiful."

"Of course. She was all over the media when she was dating that Brazilian soccer star. She looks like a Tang princess."

"How do you pronounce her first name? It's spelled M-e-i-d-e."

"May-duh, I think."

"So a couple of years ago Ted moved to the middle of nowhere because he and Meide like the dry heat and they want to be away from urban evils when they have kids. Built a huge house called Phoenix Garden, where they have a fabulous collection of Chinese art in an underground gallery."

"How do Bernard and Lydia feel about sharing Dad's fortune with half siblings?"

Jean shrugged. "None of the articles I read mentioned family dynamics. They were all puff pieces. The press really worked Ted over when his wife ran off and got killed, so he's wary of reporters. He only talks to them if they agree to give him final approval. My boss is going to let Ted read my article before it runs, which sucks, but what can I do?"

"Do the children work?"

"Oh sure. Lydia is an animal rights lawyer, of all things. She's involved with PETA, fighting the property status of animals. Bernard is some sort of screenwriter-director wannabe in Hollywood."

"I don't think people in his income bracket can be called wannabes. They simply write a big enough check and presto: They become what they claim to be."

"Apparently the kids don't have access to much money yet. Ted's trying to teach them fiscal responsibility."

Roman chuckled. "I'm sure no one ever denied little Ted anything. It always amuses me when people who've inherited vast fortunes get self-righteous with their children."

"Yeah, as if withholding their allowance would make them think they're growing up middle-class. If you ask me, when you have that much money, there's nothing you can do to make life normal for your kids."

"I agree." Roman stifled a yawn. "So who else will attend the tasting?"

Jean pulled out the list of guests Owen had given her. "OK, let's see. René Chatouilleux, of course, and his wife, Monique. Jasper Oliphant, a professor of finance at New York

University and a member of the Lyon Oil board of directors, and his wife, Sissy. Wang Yuan, a friend of Meide's who's an art expert and museum consultant. Angus MacKnight, retired from the military. Carl Schoonover, the interior designer who did their house. And Anthony Feola, the football player."

Roman perked up. "Really? I look forward to meeting him. I was quite a 49ers fan in the eighties, when he played for them. But I lost interest when Montana left, and Feola had retired by that time. Running backs don't last nearly as long as quarterbacks."

"We're supposed to include brief bios, so get head shots of everyone."

"Not to worry. Clive has given me my marching orders." Roman yawned again. "Was there any inkling of the kind of trouble that could explain the two murders?"

"Not at all. I even checked the tabloid press. The Lyon family is either squeaky clean or really good at hiding things."

In San Diego they picked up a rental car, a green Taurus with GPS. Roman was so drowsy that he let Jean drive, but only after she promised not to exceed the speed limit by more than twenty miles per hour. She drove away from the harbor and took the freeway heading toward Escondido, about thirty miles northeast of San Diego. She couldn't have driven over the speed limit if she'd tried—traffic was heavy through the parched, hilly terrain.

They exited the freeway near a gigantic mall and headed east, past prosperous suburban neighborhoods, less affluent tracts, strip malls, and schools. As they left Escondido, the landscape grew more rural; horse corrals and citrus orchards surrounded many of the houses. Roadside produce stands offered oranges, melons, avocados, even ostrich eggs. They finally climbed through a narrow mountain pass and drove down into Valle de los Osos. A flashy casino, the Valley View, stood on the right side of the road at the edge of town.

The main street was lined with businesses offering groceries, feed, hardware, real estate. There was a working dairy in the middle of town. Jean counted three restaurants and two traffic lights before they were out in the country again. The widely scattered homes they passed ranged from trailers and small bungalows near the road to imposing houses on the ridges above. She turned off the main road onto Lyon Way. As they rounded a curve, the Lyon home loomed above them, a huge white structure perched on top of the mountain.

"Turn onto that road," Roman ordered. "I'll get a few shots of the castle."

Jean drove slowly down a narrow gravel road for a few hundred yards, until Roman liked their view of the house. Jean pulled over and killed the engine. On the other side of the road sat a small beige prefab house in a grove of oak trees. Roman pulled a camera from Clive's bag, got out, and took several shots of the Lyon compound. Jean rolled down her window and a blast of hot air filled the car. She checked out the unassuming house, which was surrounded by a bare earth yard and an eight-foot chain-link fence. An old Chevy Nova and a red Ford pickup were parked inside the fence.

When he was done, Roman turned toward the small house. He pointed to a handmade wooden sign hung on the gate announcing "The Jone's." "Look at that sign, Jean. I've never seen so many usage errors in so small a space." He snapped a few pictures of the sign. A big, lean, fierce-looking dog jumped off the porch and loped over to the fence, staring at them with pale blue eyes. Jean could hear his low, rumbling growl.

Roman put the camera away. "Just a minute," he told Jean. He walked back to the fence and looked past the house to a shed visible beneath the trees. A pile of rubbish next to the shed drew his attention. The dog followed him along the fence, still growling.

A fifty-something woman in a short denim skirt and dirty blue T-shirt came out of the house. She was as thin and scary as the dog, but much less healthy-looking, with bad skin and graying hair tied back in a ponytail. Cradled in her arm was a hunting rifle. "What do you want?" she demanded.

Jean sat as still as she could, glad to let Roman handle things. "I was admiring your dog," he said in his most soothing, unthreatening tone. "Is he part wolf?"

"Half wolf," the woman said, eyeing Roman with suspicion.

"What's his name?"

"None of your goddamn business." The woman looked at Jean, then back at Roman. "You're going up the hill, aren't you? To the Lyon place."

"That's right."

She spat into the dirt. "Asshole thinks he owns this mountain."

A scraggly blond man came out the front door and stood next to her on the porch. He wore shorts and a tank top, and his arms and legs were as thin as sticks. "What's up, Honey?"

"We stopped to admire your dog," Roman said, smiling.

"Go back inside, Farron," the woman told him. "I'll handle this."

"Don't get all bent out of shape," Farron said. "He's just looking at Mojo."

"He's a fine animal," Roman said. "Seems to be a great watchdog."

"Yeah, he is." The man smiled; he was missing several teeth. "But we don't really need him—most folks around here are scared shitless of Honey."

Honey glared at Roman. "And that includes Farron here."

"Well, we'd better get going." Roman turned and walked back to the car. "Good meeting you." He got in and Jean sped away up the hill.

"Nice neighbors Lyon has," Jean said. "What in the world was she so hostile about?"

"Did you see the setup there? The gun, the fence, the dog, the canisters near the shed in back?"

"What about them?"

"I'll bet money the Jones family is running a meth lab. I'll notify the sheriff. In this dry heat, it's an incredible fire hazard."

Jean knew that the fire danger wasn't the only reason Roman was going to bust the Joneses. Meth was one of his hot-button issues—its rampant use in the gay community was fueling a new increase in HIV infections.

They continued along the steep, narrow road, which climbed a hill strewn with huge granite boulders, each winding curve revealing a dramatic vista across the valley.

"It's quite beautiful in an austere way," Roman said. "Reminds me of where I grew up in New Mexico."

"What do people do out here, anyway?" Jean asked. "I mean, the nearest city is San Diego, forty-five miles away, and that's not much of a city."

"People ride horses and cook meth, I suppose."

"How in the world did they get construction equipment and moving vans up this road?"

"Good question," Roman said. "I can't imagine a fire truck could make it."

As they reached the mountain's crest, a vast orange tile roof came into view, surrounded by lush green plantings and a high white stucco wall. Jean turned into the driveway. Two life-sized stone lions reproducing the Lyon Oil corporate symbol flanked the entry. A thin balding man in a short-sleeved uniform sat reading a book in a booth just outside the wrought iron gate. Jean gave their names and flashed her driver's license, and he waved them through. She drove up a curving lane lined with tall, graceful palm trees. The house was a sprawling white Spanish-style structure embellished with arches, carved wooden doors, and black wrought iron flourishes.

Roman took off his sunglasses. "Lovely. Father Junípero Serra meets Walt Disney."

"It's fucking enormous," Jean said. "Maybe they're planning to have twelve children."

"Quite a contrast to the Jones spread. Have I ever expressed my views on the distribution of wealth in this country?"

"Many times."

They got out of the Taurus into searing dry heat. A purple Plymouth minivan and three older cars were parked at the far end of the driveway—they probably belonged to the help.

A six-car garage built in the same faux-Spanish style faced the house across the circular driveway. Four of the doors were closed, one was open and the space empty, and the last one held a wicked-looking, low-slung, gunmetal gray car that made Jean gasp. She hurried over to it. The vanity plate read "NOIR."

"Look, Roman. It's a Lamborghini Murciélago. I've never seen one up close. Isn't it beautiful?"

"That's the one from *The Dark Knight*, isn't it?"

"Yeah. It has a twelve-cylinder engine, four-wheel drive, and scissor doors. I wonder if I'll set off an alarm if I touch it."

"Don't chance it. Come on, let's get out of this heat." Jean followed him toward the ornate wooden front door. Chencho, the young Latino who had driven Ted's Maybach, came out to greet them. He wore a short-sleeved white polo shirt and khaki slacks.

Chencho introduced himself to Roman, grinning and showing his dimple. He shook Jean's hand as well. "Good to see you again, Ms. Applequist."

Roman chatted briefly with the young man in Spanish, the conversation lost on her.

"Come on, you'll be in the cabins," Chencho finally said in English. He gestured to his left and they followed him along a brick path around the side of the house, through a courtyard dominated by a white tile fountain. The landscaping was beautiful, even though the flowers were all white: Jean saw roses, daisies, lilies, and others whose names she didn't know. A Mexican gardener pushed a wheelbarrow past them. The heat was intense; Roman's shirt was already damp, and Jean felt sweat trickling between her breasts.

"The Lyons aren't home tonight," Chencho explained as they walked. "They said to tell you they'll see you tomorrow. When you're ready, come into the main house and find the kitchen so you can meet our chef, Laszlo."

They passed a large rectangular swimming pool. "Now that looks inviting," Jean said.

"There's an Olympic-sized pool on the other side of the house," Chencho said. They came to a row of eight small white cabins connected in pairs, and he unlocked the door of one. "But this pool gets afternoon shade," he added. "You can use either. And there are two tennis courts on the south side of the house and a putting green." He showed Jean into the cabin, unlocking the adjacent door for Roman. "If you need anything, just call me on the white house phone. The extensions are listed on each one. Also, cell phone service is really bad up here, so feel free to use the land line."

After Chencho left, Jean dropped her suitcase and looked around. The cabin was like a large, impersonal hotel room, icy cold from the air conditioning, with a queen-sized bed, a desk holding a phone and Internet hookup, a cluster of sofas and chairs, everything white and vaguely Southwestern in style. The walls were adorned with Chinese scrolls and museum posters; the overall effect was somewhat schizophrenic. She knocked on the connecting door and Roman let her in. His room was exactly like hers, with different Chinese art on the walls.

"What did Chencho say to you in Spanish?" she asked.

"We talked about the weather. Apparently we're in the middle of a Santa Ana right now, with no relief in sight." Roman stepped out of his sandals, took off his damp shirt, and lay back across the bed, an arm thrown over his eyes. "God, I'm tired. There was a time when I could stay up all night and still function the next day. I must be getting old."

Jean sat down on the bed and looked at him, at his broad shoulders, slim waist, flat muscular stomach, the pelt of black hair on his chest. "Oh Roman," she said with a sigh, seizing a handful of chest hair and making him yelp, "I wish I could have Zeppo's brain in your body for two hours."

He pushed her hand away, chuckling. "I doubt my aging shell could survive two hours with you and Zeppo's brain."

"I'd be willing to risk it."

"I wouldn't. Go out and rub against that Lamborghini. Or call Zeppo and have him come down."

"Nah, he's working on a paper. I'm not worried; something will turn up."

He frowned at her. "You've got a good thing with Zeppo. Why not try hanging on to it for once?"

"Don't lecture me. Other men don't bother Zeppo."

"Of course they bother him, you idiot. He thinks you'll throw him out if he complains, so he doesn't."

"Is that what he told you?"

"Yes. We talk about you a lot. Mostly it concerns how he can stay in your good graces and still retain a shred of self-respect."

This was news to Jean. She knew she had the upper hand, but she hadn't realized Zeppo was actually suffering. Lately she'd been correcting his grammar and getting annoyed with his endless wine questions—he probably thought she was tired of him. Nothing could be further from the truth. She just got cranky sometimes. It hurt to think of him walking on eggs, trying hard not to say the wrong thing, afraid she'd dump him if he griped about anything. "I'm glad you told me, Roman. I'll be more appreciative next time I see him."

"He deserves it. You're a fool if you sabotage this one. And if you push him too far, remember that he goes to school with thousands of attractive women his own age."

"I know. I worry about that sometimes." Roman and Zeppo had become good friends and often went cycling together. Jean could imagine them talking about her, Zeppo complaining, Roman sympathizing and giving advice. "You know, Zeppo no longer has a father figure," she said. "You seem to have stepped into the role."

"He doesn't need a father figure. He needs a lover who recognizes his worth. Now go away and let me sleep."

"Not yet. Put on a dry shirt—we have to meet the chef."

Roman sighed and sat up. "Very well."

Jean went into her room and washed her face with cold water. Her black travel dress was sweaty, so she changed into shorts and a red T-shirt. She examined her chopped hair in the mirror. It looked pretty much the same whether she combed it or not.

She and Roman walked to the main house and let themselves in a side door. They passed through a foyer into a vast living room with high ceilings. The furniture was an eclectic mix—Chinese, French, overstuffed modern—all of it blond wood or white upholstery. Chinese rugs in neutral shades covered the white marble floors. A huge, dramatic arrangement of white roses and bamboo sat on a low table. The only color came from the Chinese art scattered around the room—scrolls covered with calligraphy, landscapes, or fanciful animals; statues of horses and camels splashed with green and orange glazes; a cabinet of ceramics in pale celadon, deep blue and white, and bright yellow.

All-white rooms irritated Jean, whose favorite color was red. "You know what this place needs?" she whispered to Roman. "A few cans of spray paint in primary colors."

"Those twelve children are going to be hard on the furniture," he whispered back.

They followed sounds of laughter and rock music to a big restaurant-style kitchen at the back of the house, all gleaming white surfaces and stainless steel appliances. A short, stocky man in an unbuttoned white chef's coat and loose trousers in a chile-pepper print sat on a stool at a counter, smoking a cigarette and speaking Spanish to a young Mexican woman in a white uniform. She leaned on the counter near him, laughing at what he was saying. The music on the iPod dock behind him was early Bruce Springsteen.

"Hey," the chef said, putting out his cigarette and jumping up when he saw them. "You must be the press."

"That we are," Roman said. "And that's the worst Spanish I've ever heard."

The short man spread his hands. "Whadaya want? My parents were Hungarian." He had a broad New Jersey accent.

The chef offered a hand. "You Jean Applequist? I'm Laszlo Harady. Welcome to Hearst Castle South."

"Glad to meet you." She introduced Roman.

Laszlo gestured to the young woman. "This is Tina, my assistant," he told them. She shook hands shyly. "You can go on home now—see ya tomorrow," he said to her, switching off the music as she went out the back door.

Laszlo had a round face covered with smoker's wrinkles and thinning hair somewhere between blond and brown. He looked to be in his late thirties. "It's way past happy hour. You guys wanna try the house apéritif?" He took a pitcher out of the huge stainless steel refrigerator and poured three tall drinks over ice. They were a deep rusty red somewhere between the colors of oranges and fresh blood. "Here ya go. A little something of my own. I call it a cannibal's kiss." He held one out to Jean.

"There's a forgettable novel by Odier called *Cannibal Kiss*," Roman said, taking a drink.

"When I get famous he can sue me."

Jean sipped hers. It was tart and complicated, tasting of citrus, mint, and things she couldn't identify. "It's wonderful. What's in it?"

"Blood orange, lime, rum, and a few secret ingredients," Laszlo said. "Let's go outside. There won't be much of a sunset, but it'll cool off soon." He led them out the back door to a table and chairs in the shade near the pool. Jean could still feel the heat, but it was abating. Laszlo put his drink on the table and went back inside, whistling to himself, a full, musical sound. He returned in a moment with a tray of cold appetizers: tiny heirloom tomatoes stuffed with a green and white substance and thin slices of baguette holding slivers of meat and a dab of sauce.

"What are these?" Jean said, popping one of the baguette slices into her mouth. The meat was very tender and the sauce garlicky. "Mmm, delicious."

"That's poached lamb's tongue and a little aioli."

"What about these?" Jean ate a tomato, surprised by how spicy it was.

"Stuffed with serrano chiles and a Mexican cheese I like."

She noticed Laszlo's hands as he served her; they were chef's hands, strong and gnarly, covered with scars and calluses from years of cuts, burns, and scrapes.

They devoured the appetizers as the sun began its slide behind the big house. Roman craned his head back to watch several huge dark birds soaring above them. "Look, *Cathartes aura*," he said. "Must be a corpse nearby."

"Nah, this is just the evening patrol," Laszlo said. "If they'd found something, there'd be twenty of them."

Jean watched the vultures ride the thermal currents, gliding effortlessly in wide, swooping circles. "I know they're ugly close up, but they're really lovely in the air."

Laszlo grinned. "Don't mention vultures to the Lyons. It's a real sore point between them."

"I read about something involving vultures," Roman said. "Lyon shot a few, didn't he? Had to pay a big fine."

"He paid, but he didn't shoot them. See, there are a lot of vultures around here, and Meide hates them. They always sit in those big trees by the pool and shit on the terrace, hang out on the cliffs down the canyon, fly around overhead. Drives her crazy. So a couple months ago, she had the gardeners shoot a bunch of them. As if that would stop the rest from coming around. The old lady across the canyon saw the gardeners burying them and called fish and wildlife. Teddy hadda shell out seventy grand."

"Wow," Jean said. "That's a lot of money, even for a billionaire."

"Lyon must have been furious," Roman said.

"Sure was. Usually he's a mellow guy, but that set him off. I've never seen him so mad at Meide. She slunk around all quiet and sorry for a couple weeks, and he finally forgave her. He's still pissed at the old lady."

"We met another of your neighbors on the way up," Roman said. "The Jones family."

"That Honey Jones is crazy," Laszlo said as he refilled their glasses. "Her granddad owned this whole mountain forty years ago, but they sold it off piece by piece. They've only got a few acres left, and Ted's been trying to buy it since forever, but she and her low-life husband won't sell."

Roman ate a canapé. "I think they have a meth lab in their shed."

"Yeah? I'll mention it to the sheriff."

A warm breeze stirred Jean's hair. There wasn't much color in the cloudless sky, just a pink glow to the west as darkness fell. "You had a murder here recently, didn't you?" she said.

Laszlo's animated face grew sad. "Yeah. Pilar Ochoa. Hell of a thing. Some piece of shit stuck her with an ice pick for ten dollars and change."

"Did you know her?"

"Oh, sure. She was a waitress at a restaurant in town, and sometimes she'd come up here for big parties. In fact, she worked Meide's birthday party the night before she died. She was a good waitress, could handle cocktails, buffets, sit-down dinners too, and she was always cheerful about it. She talked too much and flirted with everything male, but I liked her."

"So they didn't catch the killer?"

"Nah, they just rousted the illegals camping east of here. Now you can't find a crew to wash dishes or clear brush."

"Who do you think killed her?"

"I couldn't tell you. I figure it was just some random shithead who needed money." He sipped his drink. "You know, where I grew up in Newark, you always heard about somebody cut or shot or OD'd. That's one of the things I like about living out here in the sticks—that kind of crap usually doesn't happen. And you can bet the terrorists don't even know this place is on the map."

"What about the man who was dumped onto Lyon's car up in San Francisco?" Jean asked. "Did you know him?"

"Domingo Huerta? I've heard of him. A bartender I know told me he was a real lowlife. He was always making big plans that didn't work out. Spent most of his time losing money. Slots and tequila."

"How was he connected to Lyon?"

"I got no idea. I doubt if they ever met."

In a little while, they moved into the kitchen where Laszlo fed them a light supper of seared diver scallops, roasted potatoes, baby artichokes, and Chardonnay as they discussed the logistics of the next few days. Jean was impressed not only with his cooking, but with his easy confidence in the face of all the meals and tastings he'd be responsible for.

After dinner Roman took out his cell and fooled with it. "Apparently my cell provider doesn't know this place is on the map, either."

"Yeah, service sucks up here," Laszlo said. "It comes and goes. Sometimes if you stand out by the big pool, it works. Ted's gonna get one of those cell boosters but hasn't done it yet."

As Laszlo put away the leftovers, Jean could hear his musical whistling again, but she couldn't make out a tune. "I'm the busboy tonight," he told them. "I gave everybody the night off, since the Lyons are gone till tomorrow and we're all gonna be working overtime this weekend." He piled their dishes in a sink. "Tina will take care of these in the morning. Hey, Jean, you wanna go to town with me tomorrow and get supplies? I need to pick up fresh fish and some produce."

"Sure. That would be fun."

"Meet me here about ten o'clock. Well, I gotta turn in early. I'm baking tomorrow, have to get up at five A.M. You oughta go find the theater. Teddy's got a great setup and lots of good movies. Go through the main living room and down the hall into the south wing—you can't miss it."

Roman went back to his cabin to get some sleep, and Jean went in search of the theater.

Chapter 6

Jean prowled around in the deserted house, wishing Zeppo were with her. She'd have to phone him tomorrow. She poked her head into several rooms, mostly bedrooms, all with white furnishings, Chinese art, and fresh-cut white flowers, ready for the guests who would start arriving tomorrow afternoon. The door of each guest room was identified with a Chinese character and the name of an animal in English—Jean recognized the signs of the Chinese zodiac.

She found the theater at the end of a long hall. Laszlo was right—it was a great setup, twenty plush off-white chairs with little tables in between, on carpeted risers. The chairs faced the biggest flat-screen TV Jean had ever seen. There was a wet bar off to one side.

Against the back wall were shelves holding dozens of DVDs. Jean perused the titles. Most were popular movies tending toward melodrama, big-budget action, cutesy romance, and infantile comedy, with way too many teen vampire romances and Judd Apatow movies. Jean sighed, disappointed. But off to the side she found a separate shelving unit that held DVDs of crime movies, with the emphasis on film noir: classics like the original *Scarface* with Paul Muni, *Rififi*, *Out of the Past*, and neo-noir like *Croupier*, *The Last Seduction*, and *Devil in a Blue Dress*. There were films she'd seen a dozen times—*Chinatown*, *The Third Man*, *L.A. Confidential*—and rare films she'd only read about. All the movie versions of Chandler and Hammett books were here. Jean made delighted noises as she read the titles; Ted's movie collection was almost as great as his wine collection. She crouched down, checking the bottom shelf.

"Hey, buddy," a voice said behind her. "Can I help you find something?"

Jean stood and turned around. It was a man a few years older than she, about six feet tall, trim and nice looking, in cutoff jeans and an old Zoetrope T-shirt. "Buddy, huh?" She put a hand on each of her breasts. "What do these look like? Grapefruit?"

He grinned. "Gladys to Marlowe, *The Big Sleep*. And no, they don't look a thing like grapefruit. Sorry. The short hair fooled me." He stuck out a hand. "I'm Bernie Lyon."

Jean should have known—he shared Ted's long jaw and broad nose, and his honey-blond, blue-eyed coloring. "Jean Applequist from *Wine Digest*."

"So you're here for the tasting."

"I wouldn't miss it. You, too?"

"Yeah. Dad taught me to love Sauternes."

She gestured at the shelves behind her. "I'll bet you're the film noir buff."

"Guilty."

"These are all my favorites—what a fantastic collection."

"The best that money can buy, like everything else here," he said with a wry grin.

"That must be your Lamborghini with the 'NOIR' plates, right?"

"Yeah, that's mine, too. I've been wanting to meet you, Jean. You were involved in a crime of your own, weren't you?"

"It was self-defense," Jean said automatically.

"I don't mean shooting that man. Anyone would fight to defend herself. I mean figuring out who killed Wingo after the police arrested the wrong guy. I followed the story closely. I'm a big fan of yours."

Jean laughed. "Well, thanks. I didn't realize I had any fans."

"I'm a screenwriter, and the Wingo case gave me some great ideas. I was thrilled when Dad said you'd be here for the tasting. You can tell me what wasn't in the papers."

"What sorts of screenplays do you write?"

"Modern noir, mostly."

"Have you had anything produced?"

"Not yet. But there's an investor who's really interested in my current project, *Night Sweat*. I'm trying to keep creative control and I want to direct as well, which isn't easy. Would you like a drink?"

"You bet."

Bernie went to the wet bar and opened the small refrigerator. "Have you tried these?" He held up a pitcher of a familiar red concoction.

"Oh yes, a cannibal's kiss. I had one this afternoon. They're great."

Bernie poured two tall drinks. "I always watch movies when Dad's not around, so Laszlo sets things up." He pulled a plate of assorted hors d'oeuvres out of the fridge and put it on a small table. "Laszlo takes good care of me."

Jean smiled, sipping her drink. "Very cozy. Now we just have to pick a movie."

They sat next to each other in the big white chairs and watched their favorite parts of several movies—the fiery climax of *White Heat*, the meeting at the ferris wheel and the chase through the Vienna sewers in *The Third Man*, the shoot-out in a hall of mirrors in *The Lady From Shanghai*. Bernie worked the remote, fast-forwarding to just the right point, pausing on well-composed frames. He was funny and insightful and knew the films well. They finished the snacks and worked their way through the pitcher of cannibal's kisses, laughing at each other's jokes, touching each other's arms. Jean was in hog heaven, discussing all the film trivia that bored most of her friends. Zeppo loved film noir, too, but hadn't seen enough of the classics to talk about them in such depth.

"Just brilliant," Bernie exclaimed as he ejected *Kiss Me Deadly*. "That's what I aspire to. *Night Sweat* will be an homage to film noir conventions. I want to shoot in black and white with high-contrast lighting, using chiaroscuro, vertiginous camera angles, shots featuring spiral staircases and Venetian blinds, the whole German Expressionist look. And my plot is full of the requisite uncertainty and deception and betrayal."

"I'd love to read the screenplay."

"I'll get you a copy. It's great to have an appreciative audience."

Jean gave him an appraising look. She really liked him and could tell it was mutual, but his vibes were strictly non-sexual. A few offhanded remarks he'd made, particularly his reaction to the young Burt Lancaster in *The Killers*, completed the message. "Bernie," she said, leaning toward him, "the next logical step would be for us to go back to my room and have some fun. But something tells me you wouldn't be interested."

He smiled apologetically. "I'd only disappoint you."

"And I'd disappoint you." Jean hadn't read a word about his being gay and thought he might be closeted. "Don't worry," she said, patting his hand. "I won't out you in my article."

He chuckled. "My father wouldn't let you anyway. As far as I'm concerned I'm already out, but he's in denial."

"Do you have a partner?"

"I did, but we broke up a few weeks ago. That's why my movies are here—I'm staying in a hotel while I look for a new apartment."

"I'm sorry. How long were you together?"

"Six months, which is a long time for me." He gave his wry, self-deprecating grin. "My love life is problematic. There's always the question of whether he loves me for myself or for my family's money. I tend to ask too often."

"Tell me, does *Night Sweat* have an *homme fatal*?"

"Yes, it does. That's why I have to go independent. None of the producers I've talked to want anything to do with gay noir. The last big studio honcho I pitched it to said, and I quote, 'That's not a genre—that's straight to DVD.' But I'm optimistic about that investor I mentioned."

"Why not get the money from your dad?"

"He's holding out until I come to my senses and start dating girls. I keep telling him it's going to be a long wait. That's why he gave me the Lamborghini—he thought it would be a babe magnet."

Jean yawned and looked at her watch. "Damn. It's after one A.M.—I'd better get to sleep. I'm supposed to go to town with Laszlo in the morning when he's done baking so I can write about the preparations. I asked him why he didn't get everything delivered, and he said he likes to schmooze with his suppliers."

"Laszlo's amazing. He's buddies with all the purveyors, so they go out of their way, get him anything. Dad's lucky to have an operator like him out here in the middle of nowhere."

Bernie shut things down and they walked along the hall to the back door. Once outside, they were buffeted by a gust of wind. "Feel that?" he said. "One of those hot dry Santa Anas that curl your hair and make your nerves jump and your skin itch."

"'Meek little wives feel the edge of the carving knife and study their husbands' necks.' Raymond Chandler, *Red Wind*. Too bad they never made a movie of it." She gave him a kiss. "Good night, Bernie. This was big fun."

"For me, too," he said. "Sweet dreams."

Jean walked out under bright moonlight to her cabin, hearing coyotes in the distance, smiling to herself, full of plans. She deliberately hadn't mentioned Roman to Bernie. One of the secrets of successful matchmaking was not to let the victims know they were being set up, and Roman was particularly resistant. He'd seen so many friends and lovers die from AIDS that he'd withdrawn from that part of life, and had been celibate for over a year now. It wasn't just simple grief; he also felt guilty for being HIV negative when so many others had perished. After the Wingo investigation, he seemed to be recovering, but then another close friend who'd been doing well had died of pneumonia, sending him back into his depression.

She thought he must be terribly lonely. Bernie was just the kind of intelligent, funny, sexy man he liked. The two would inevitably cross paths, but getting them alone together during a crowded party weekend might be tricky. Jean fell asleep, confident she could manage it.

JEAN WOKE early with a hangover and decided to swim some laps in the big pool to clear her head. She paused at the connecting door; Roman was still snoring. Thinking about him and Bernie made her smile. She'd get to work on it this morning.

Jean put on her black racerback swimsuit and a gray and white striped caftan and slipped past the cabins and the main house toward the Olympic pool. Besides Laszlo and Tina moving around in the kitchen, there were no other signs of life. Jean opened a heavy wrought iron gate in the high stucco wall surrounding the compound; Chencho had given her the security code to get back in.

The infinity pool was set into a flagstone terrace on the edge of the canyon, with two huge sycamore trees providing shade at one end. No vultures lurking about this morning, Jean was happy to note. Phoenix Garden was only two years old, not nearly enough time to grow trees this size. Jean couldn't imagine how they'd gotten the trees up the winding road to the house. Maybe they'd been brought in by helicopter—there was certainly enough room to land on the lawn. She was amused to see the Lyon coat of arms in mosaic tiles at the bottom of the big pool.

The morning was still and clear, the cool of night lingering. Jean heard mockingbirds and the distinctive call of quail. The day smelled of chaparral and creosote, rich and resinous. Across the canyon, a beautiful old adobe house the color of milk chocolate seemed to grow out of the ridge, surrounded by mature pepper trees, oleanders, a few bright flowers. An enormous magenta bougainvillea covered the deck. It all looked very inviting. Maybe Jean would introduce herself to the owner—she must be the woman who'd reported the dead vultures. If she were friendly, maybe Roman could take some shots of Phoenix Garden from her deck. He'd love checking out the adobe house, too.

Jean slipped off her sandals and caftan and dove into the cool, ice-blue water. She swam slowly for a long time, loosening up, stretching her muscles, crossing back and forth over the coat of arms. As she finished her laps and paused to rest, she heard a faint rustling nearby. It sounded as if a large animal was behind one of the bushes just off the terrace. Jean frowned—coyotes were supposed to be nocturnal, but she didn't know about bobcats or cougars or bears. This was bear valley, after all. Then she heard a muffled sneeze. Definitely Homo sapien.

Jean got out of the pool and wandered over to a green coil of hose next to the cabaña. She found the nozzle and turned on the water, pretending to wash off the terrace. Once in range, she shot a hard spray at whoever was hiding in the bushes.

"Hey!" A thin, pimply teenage boy jumped up.

Jean screwed the nozzle off. "What the hell are you doing there?"

"Nothing. Just watching." He pulled at his soaked Little Wayne T-shirt and baggy shorts. "Now I'm all wet. My mom'll be pissed."

"Sorry. But you can get into a lot of trouble spying on people like that."

"I wasn't spying. Just watching." He eyed her boldly. "You ought to be used to it. Got any tattoos?"

Jean laughed. "No, and the only things pierced are my ears. You?"

"My mom won't let me. Just wait till I turn eighteen, though."

"Do you live over there?" Jean gestured toward the adobe house.

"Nah, that's the bird lady's house. We're helping her out, my mom and me." He shook his head vigorously, spraying water from his short spiky hair. There was a scatter of dark freckles across his nose.

"Why is she the bird lady?"

"She fixes up gimpy birds. If they break a wing or get shot or whatever. She's got four of them now." He grinned at Jean. "You want to see them? I could show you."

Jean thought about it. She really did want to see the house up close, and this cocky kid seemed harmless. In any case, she was bigger than he was. "I'd like that. How do we get across the canyon?"

"There's a path. You need shoes, though."

She retrieved her sandals. "Are these OK?"

"Sure. Just watch out for rattlers."

Jean wasn't afraid of snakes, so she stowed the hose and put on her sandals and caftan. "What's your name?"

"Ethan Wexler."

"Nice to meet you, Ethan. I'm Jean Applequist."

Ethan led her to a narrow but well-beaten path that ran down into the canyon and back up the other side. Jean pulled her caftan up so it wouldn't catch on prickly chaparral. Ethan's high-tech sneakers made wet squishing noises as he walked.

"What's this path for?" Jean asked. "Don't tell me—does Mrs. Lyon swim a lot?"

Ethan glanced back, then looked away. "Yeah, and so does Lydia, the daughter, when she's here." He smirked at her again. "Although they're both kind of skinny compared to you."

"You're kind of skinny yourself."

"Hey, give me time. I'm only sixteen. I'll bulk up." He pumped his scrawny arms to make biceps.

They followed the path along the top of the ridge and then down into the canyon until they came to the adobe house. The hill wasn't as steep here, and below the house was a long narrow green building. Beyond that stood another long low structure made of wire and netting.

Ethan pointed. "That's the birdhouse and the other one's a flight cage, so they can practice before she lets them go."

A woman of about forty was watering potted plants on the porch. She was slightly overweight, wearing a loose yellow sundress. When she spotted them, she put her watering can down and came over. She had Ethan's straight auburn hair, freckles, and greenish-brown eyes.

Ethan gestured awkwardly at the woman. "This is my mom."

The woman smiled and extended a hand. "Hi, I'm Bonnie Wexler."

Jean introduced herself. "Ethan offered to show me the birds."

Bonnie examined her son. "Ethan, how'd you get wet? Are those your new sneakers?"

Ethan shrugged and looked at his feet.

"I accidentally sprayed him," Jean said. "Sorry."

"Were you over there spying again?" Bonnie shook her head in exasperation. "Honey, if you're not careful, one of the gardeners is going to shoot *you*."

"I wasn't doing any harm."

"Well, I suppose you'll dry off by the time we leave, in this heat. Go ahead, Jean, have a look at the birds. Katharine's getting ready to feed them."

Ethan led her around the house to an open garage door. "You have to talk loud," he told Jean. "She's kind of deaf."

Inside the garage a small, thin woman in loose slacks and a white blouse took something out of a refrigerator. Ethan came up quietly behind her and tapped her on the left shoulder, then moved quickly around to her right. She looked left and then right, her expression affectionate when she saw him. "There you are, Ethan. Would you like to feed them today?"

"You bet," he said. "Katharine, this is Jean, from across the way. She wants to see the birds."

Katharine turned with the slow, careful movements of great age. "How do you do?" The old woman's smile faded. She was older than Jean had thought at first, close to ninety, with crisply permed white hair and pale blue eyes that still looked sharp and youthful. She wore a hearing aid in each ear.

"Glad to meet you." Jean spoke in the loud, clear tones she'd used with her grandmother. "Your house is lovely."

"Are you a friend of the Lyons?"

"Not at all," Jean said, sensing that this was the source of the woman's cool manner. "I'm a reporter for *Wine Digest*, a magazine in San Francisco, covering a tasting of old wines. Just doing my job."

Katharine's expression warmed. "Well, in that case, you're welcome to have a look." She picked up a wooden cane that leaned nearby.

"Come on, Jean." Ethan took the white bundle Katharine had removed from the fridge, unwrapping it as he walked. Jean fell into step as they followed Katharine's slow pace to the birdhouse. To Jean's surprise, the bundle contained several dead mice.

"Yow," she said. "What kind of birds are these, anyway?"

"Nothing but raptors here on Farmer Murdoch's spread," Ethan said. "Now we gotta slop the hawks."

Katharine smiled indulgently at him as she opened the door. "Move slowly," she told Jean, "and keep your hands down."

The birdhouse consisted of eight pens against one wall. Sitting on a wooden perch in the first cage was an animal Jean recognized—a great horned owl. "What's wrong with him?"

"He was hit by a car and injured his wing. He's been here nearly two months, but I'll release him this week."

Jean stared at the huge, beautiful bird. She'd never been this close to a raptor before, and it was breathtaking. She admired his striking plumage and feathered horns, powerful talons, sharp curved beak. His most dramatic feature was big round yellow eyes, piercing and unblinking.

"Blink when you look at him," Katharine said. "If you don't, he'll think you're a predator."

Jean did as she was told. "Won't you feed him?" she asked as they moved away.

"Owls eat at night."

The next cage held a smaller owl. "This is a barn owl," Katharine said. "He was probably a pet, which is illegal, by the way. Someone cut off his major flight feathers with scissors. Even after they grow back, I don't know if I can release him—the poor fellow is practically tame."

"We're trying to teach him to catch his own live mice in the flight cage," Ethan said. "He has to realize, 'Hey, I'm a killing machine.'"

They passed two empty cages and came to a smaller bird, a hawk. It flew to the topmost perch, nervous and skittish. "This is a Cooper's hawk," Katharine said. "She's a bird eater. She flew into a restaurant window chasing a pigeon. The pigeon broke its neck, but I think I'll be able to release the hawk soon." Ethan gave the hawk two mice.

A beautiful big hawk sat two cages down. "This is a red-tailed hawk that I think was poisoned," Katharine said. "He probably ate rodents that had eaten rat bait. That's one of the major causes of death for raptors—that, and lunatics with rifles." The big hawk got four mice. "Now, we can't stay long or they'll get too used to people." Katharine led them out of the birdhouse.

"That was fascinating," Jean said. "When Ethan said gimpy birds, I imagined injured quails and jays. I'll bet you root for the cheetahs instead of the gazelles on nature shows."

Katharine smiled at her. "Of course."

"So do I. Do you know Lydia Lyon? She's an animal rights lawyer."

"Oh yes. She's very interested in my work, very supportive with both money and time. She's a fine young woman, but a bit strident about her beliefs. It's hard to grow up sensible with so much money."

"How about Bernie?"

"He sometimes comes over with Lydia to see the birds, but I don't know him well. The children seem a good deal more reasonable than their father and stepmother."

Bonnie, carrying a big canvas purse, came around the side of the house. "Come on, Ethan, time to go. We've got to get you to school. Katharine, see you on Saturday."

"Thank you, Bonnie," Katharine said. "And you, too, Ethan."

"You going to be around all weekend?" Ethan asked Jean.

"Yes, until Sunday."

"Maybe I'll see you again. Hey Mom, can I drive?" Bonnie tossed him the keys; they got into a blue Hyundai and left.

Jean noticed a trail leading away from the dirt driveway toward a higher ridge to the west. "Where does that trail go?" she asked Katharine.

"Nowhere really. It just meanders around in the mountains. It's a beautiful walk. I'm too unsteady to take it anymore, but you're welcome to go hiking. Would you like some tea?"

"That would be nice. Thank you."

Katharine led the way into the milk-chocolate house. Inside the thick adobe walls it was cool and dim, with comfortable old furniture and Kilim tribal rugs. The art was mostly bird-related—ceramic statuettes of soaring eagles, an Audubon falcon print, framed photographs of hawks and vultures, a San Diego Zoo Safari Park poster advertising an exhibit of live

California condors. There were several photos of Katharine at various ages with a thin, balding man in glasses. The books were mostly about birds, with a few reference works and, surprisingly, romance novels.

Jean went around the room looking at everything. "These condors are amazing. They look just like big vultures, don't they?"

"They're closely related."

"I understand you're the one who caught Ted Lyon's workers burying some vultures. Cost him a lot of money."

"I try to keep an eye on those people so they can't do too much harm," Katharine said with a gleam in her eye.

"I also read that you found Pilar Ochoa's body."

Katharine sighed. "I didn't find her, the vultures did. It was dreadful. I'd prefer not to discuss it."

"OK." Jean reluctantly changed the subject. "How'd you get interested in birds of prey?"

"My late husband was an avian veterinarian. I met him when I went to work as his assistant. In those days there was no question of my becoming a vet myself." Katharine put a kettle on the stove. "We did quite a bit of work for the San Diego Zoo, and raptors were our specialty."

"When did your husband die?"

"Just over twenty-five years ago. That's when I moved from San Diego to this house, and later I joined Project Wildlife and began caring for injured birds. Bonnie and Ethan have been helping me out. I couldn't go on doing this otherwise. Ethan has a real gift for the work."

"Do you have any children?"

Katharine smiled at her. "Are you interviewing me for your story?"

"No, I'm just nosy," Jean said, smiling back. "And I find you fascinating."

"You flatter an old woman. To answer your question, no, we never had children, Harold and I. He always said our children had feathers. What about you, Jean?"

"I'm not married, never have been. I don't think I'll ever marry or have children. But I have fourteen nieces and nephews, so the Applequists are well represented in the gene pool. I'm too selfish for motherhood."

"We're not selfish, we're independent." Katharine poured hot water into a ceramic teapot with a bald eagle painted on the side. "I was quite a radical in my day—I thought I'd never marry, that I would travel around the world helping wounded animals, until I met Harold. We had a good marriage for thirty-nine years."

"That's more than most people get."

Jean sat at the kitchen table and Katharine brought out a plate of muffins. "Would you care for a blueberry muffin?"

Jean selected one, unwrapped it from its paper liner, and took a big bite. "Mmm, these are delicious. Did you make them?"

"Yes. I'm lucky to be able to indulge my sweet tooth at my age."

They chatted as Jean ate a muffin and drank strong black tea. Listening to Katharine reminisce reminded her of conversations with her beloved grandmother, who'd died several years ago. Jean still missed her. She was startled when she looked up at the kitchen clock—it was nearly ten.

"Katharine, I have to get back. I'm supposed to go to town with Laszlo, the chef. May I visit you again soon?"

"Anytime, my dear. I've enjoyed meeting you very much."

"Thanks for breakfast. Bye!" Jean pulled up her caftan and ran across the canyon along Ethan's path to Phoenix Garden.

CHAPTER 7

Jean stuck her head into Roman's cabin to say good morning. He stood at the bathroom mirror in briefs, shaving. She phoned Zeppo, catching him on his way to the library. She told him how much she missed him and described meeting Katharine, and he wished her luck playing matchmaker. She also assured him that she and Roman had encountered no dangerous characters, with the possible exception of Honey Jones.

After rinsing off in the shower, Jean examined the few clothes she'd hung in the closet. Wearing the right designer was never an issue since she made most of her clothes—her height and figure didn't conform to ready-to-wear sizes. It was also a lot cheaper to dress well that way. Opting for comfort, she put on a sleeveless cobalt blue knit dress that matched her eyes. Jean usually wore Opium or Black Cashmere, but not this weekend—perfume and serious wine tasting didn't mix. She slipped on her sandals, added lapis earrings, and dropped a notebook and a couple of pens into her shoulder bag.

As she walked toward the house, Jean spotted a Maybach Zeppelin parked in the garage. It looked just like the one she'd ridden in—Ted had either had it repaired or bought an identical one. She gazed longingly at the Lamborghini. Maybe Bernie would let her take it for a spin if Roman kept mum about her driving record. Jean sighed, wondering if she'd ever have enough money to support a really good car. She was struggling to pay the insurance on her Porsche, and every speeding ticket she got jacked up the premiums. But what was the point of owning a Porsche if you couldn't drive fast?

Jean noticed a lot more activity around the place today. Gardeners pulled weeds, clipped hedges, and mulched flowerbeds. Once inside, she saw maids dusting and vacuuming, keeping the white rooms white.

In a side room, Jean heard two people arguing and looked in. A slim black-haired woman in a white sundress stood with her back to Jean. "You'll use the spray if I tell you to use the spray," she said to a stocky, middle-aged maid. "It's the only thing that works!" Her Chinese-inflected English told Jean this must be Meide.

"It's bad poison," the sullen maid said. "Too strong."

"Wear gloves when you use it. I won't have ants in my house."

The maid sniffed and left the room, brushing past Jean on her way out. Jean stood in the doorway. "Mrs. Lyon? I'm Jean Applequist from *Wine Digest*."

Meide walked over and lightly touched her hand. "Oh yes. I'm sorry we weren't here to greet you yesterday. Please call me Meide. Have you been comfortable?"

"Yes, very." Meide was the most beautiful woman Jean had ever seen in person. She was willowy and small-boned, with flawless pale skin and jet-black hair in a loose stylish cut around a perfect oval face. Her delicate, classic features really did make her look like a Tang princess, full lips adding a sensuous element. She wore green jade and gold earrings and a matching pendant. Even her hands were perfect, long and delicate, with nails painted a pale peach. Her wedding ring was an elaborately carved dark green jade band. Her light floral perfume smelled expensive. She was about five four, but Herve Leger sandals made her three inches taller. So this was what a billionaire's trophy wife looked like.

"Have you any ants in your room?" Meide asked.

"I don't think so," Jean said. "Why, are they a problem here?"

"Yes, tiny black ants are everywhere in Southern California. Very hard to kill. Well, I must freshen up and unpack. I'll see you at six o'clock in the gallery." Meide walked away on slender, well-shaped legs, her movements unselfconsciously seductive. Jean, who almost always wore flats, marveled that the woman could balance on such idiotic shoes.

She found Roman at the kitchen table with Laszlo, having fruit and yogurt for breakfast. The room smelled of baking, and several loaves of bread rested on racks near the oven. Laszlo smoked a cigarette and drank coffee.

"Morning, Jean," he said. "What can I get you?"

"Nothing, thanks," she said, fanning away smoke. "Katharine fed me."

"So you met the old lady? She's something, huh? Ninety-two years old and she can still eat anything. Did you see the birds?"

"Yes, they're amazing. Roman, she's in the adobe house across the canyon. She takes care of injured raptors. You have to check them out."

"I'd like to." Roman finished his coffee. "Meanwhile, the sommelier is going to bring up the unopened bottles so I can shoot them in natural light."

"That sounds good. I just met Meide—what a knockout."

"If you like the type," Laszlo said. "She's a real pain in the ass to work for."

"I got that impression. She lets you smoke indoors?"

"Just in the kitchen. Smoking isn't such a big deal in Asia."

A Latina about Laszlo's age came into the kitchen. "Good morning, Laszlo," she said in faintly accented English. She was short and full-figured, with a Mayan profile and thick black hair held back in a white scrunchie. Her white shirt and khaki slacks were a woman's version of Chencho's attire.

"*Hola*, Gloria." Laszlo introduced Jean and Roman. "This is Gloria Guzman, the sommelier. She'll show you around the tasting room and help you set up the photos."

Roman greeted the woman in Spanish.

"Later on I'll give you the grand tour, Jean," Gloria said. "Come down when you have a chance."

"Hey Roman," Laszlo said, "be careful with those old bottles. Remember, you break it, you bought it, and I don't think you can afford it."

"I'll keep that in mind," Roman said, as he and Gloria went out the door.

"OK, let's go get our supplies," Laszlo said as he led Jean out to the purple minivan. "Meide let me pick out the color. Looks like a fucking eggplant on wheels, doesn't it?"

"Now that you mention it, yeah." Jean got in; the middle seat had been removed.

Laszlo drove fast toward Escondido, through the pass and down into the valley, where a faint brown tint was already visible in the warming air. "It's gonna be smoggy today," he said. "But it'll all blow away by this afternoon. The Santa Ana's good for something."

"It's like living in an oven," Jean complained. "I'm used to the fog in San—"

"Whoa!" Laszlo exclaimed. He pulled sharply onto the dirt shoulder and braked to a halt, startling the driver behind him, who honked as he sped past through the dust clouds billowing around the minivan.

"What?" Jean looked for some explanation. All she could see was a dead possum a few feet ahead, lying prone across the centerline.

"Road kill," Laszlo explained, jumping out of the car and jogging around to the back. "For my vultures."

Jean got out and followed him. She could smell the strong, minty scent of the eucalyptus trees that lined the road. The air was already quite warm, and so dry her skin itched. "You mean to tell me you feed the vultures?"

Laszlo opened the tailgate and pulled a large red cooler toward him. "Sure. Drives Meide bat shit." He opened the cooler, which contained several cold packs and a folded plastic bag. Laszlo shook the bag out and laid it aside. "I see something prime, I pick it up, take it back home. Then after it gets dark, I put it out on one of the hills to the south, so in the morning there they are, a whole flock of ugly black vultures." Next to the cooler was a box of plastic food-handling gloves. He pulled out a pair, grabbed the plastic bag, and walked toward the possum, glancing along the road for traffic. "This won't take a minute."

"So you're creeping around the hills at night carrying dead animals. Aren't you afraid of coyotes or bobcats?"

"If I met something big, I'd just give up the road kill." Laszlo lifted the limp animal by the tail and lowered it into his bag. "Same result. Next day you got a carcass, you got vultures all over the place, and her screaming at Teddy to do something about it." He trotted back to the car and dropped the varmint into the cooler along with the plastic gloves, then closed it and slammed the rear door shut. "It's a panic—you'll see."

"How long have you been doing this?"

"Since right after fish and wildlife dug up the dead ones and Teddy hadda pay the big fine. I got the idea from the old lady, Katharine. One day I was driving through town and I saw her pulled over. I thought maybe she was having car trouble, so I stopped. But she was picking up fresh road kill to feed her birds. She told me only vultures like it aged. And I thought, hey, if I put some out in the hills, I'll have Meide going nuts." They got in the car and Laszlo pulled back onto the road.

"Why do you dislike her so much?"

"Cooking for her makes me crazy," Laszlo said with feeling. "She's the weirdest fucking Chinese I ever met. Usually those people will eat anything, and I mean anything. A Chinese dude I knew in New York once served me fried scorpions. But not her. She only eats chicken breast. No fish, no shellfish, no lamb, no game birds, not even pork or beef. And forget tofu. Just fucking chicken, with plain rice or potatoes and really boring salads. I grill a steak for Teddy now and then, but he's almost as bad as she is. 'Nothing too spicy, nothing too weird,' she tells me. Weird to her is I use some wild mushrooms."

"So you hate her because she's a picky eater."

"Don't get me started. Picky eaters are the lowest form of life. I mean, down here I can get fourteen kinds of chiles, tortillas made fresh every day, all your Latin and Asian ingredients, not to mention local citrus and avocados. But I gotta make chicken. And God forbid I should stuff it with kasha or marinate it in sake. The only time I get to cook normal is when they have company, like now. I don't know how much more I can take."

"Laszlo, you're ranting," Jean said, laughing.

"Yeah, I guess I am. But you know what? I think you can tell a lot about a person if you watch them eat. You see someone won't try anything new, eats the same stuff every day, you know they're gonna be uptight, boring, set in their ways, probably a lousy lay. Someone who likes to eat, tries new things, well, they're gonna be more relaxed, more interesting, and a whole lot sexier." He winked at her. "You know, when you put that lamb's tongue in your mouth without knowing what it was, I knew we were gonna get along."

Jean smiled, thinking how well the omnivorous and always ravenous Zeppo fit this stereotype. "I'm glad I measure up. How long have you worked here?"

"Since they moved in, about two years. I live over in one of the cabins."

"Why do you stay? You're a good chef. I'm sure you could get a better job."

Laszlo shifted uncomfortably and looked out the window. "I had some trouble back East, owe some people money. I'm trying to keep a low profile. So I hide out here, feeding the vultures and cooking chicken."

Jean wanted to pump him about his debts, but decided she didn't know him well enough, so they rode in silence for a while. "Did you eat the fried scorpions?" she asked.

"No, I couldn't do it. It's the only food that ever gave me the willies in my whole life."

When they got back to Phoenix Garden with a van full of supplies, Chencho came out to greet them. "Ms. Applequist, Mr. Lyon wants to see you. He's in the library."

"Sure. See you later, Laszlo." She followed Chencho to the north wing of the house, into a big, high-ceilinged room lined with bookshelves and filled with cozy-looking white chairs, blond wood tables, and reading lamps. More pale Chinese rugs covered the floor. Roman was already there, standing with Ted Lyon at the fireplace. Ted wore white slacks, a pale blue linen shirt, huaraches, and his obscenely expensive watch.

"The Villalobos family's Mexican, from the Mexico City area by way of New Mexico," Roman was saying.

"But you look Spanish, not Indian or mestizo," Ted remarked.

"Oh yes, my family's very proud of our Castilian heritage." There was a note of contempt in Roman's voice that was apparently lost on Ted.

"Ah, here's our reporter," he said, advancing toward Jean with his hand extended. "Good to see you again, Jean. We were just discussing genealogy. Applequist—that's Swedish, isn't it? From *apelkvist*, apple tree."

Genealogy was a subject that bored Jean to tears. She had a tiresome aunt on her father's side who had, in all seriousness, traced the Applequist lineage back to Adam and Eve. "I'm an American mongrel," she said politely, shaking his hand. "Swedish, English, Scottish, Irish, French, Danish, a little of everything."

"I was just showing Roman our family trees." Ted gestured to three panels on the wall above the walk-in sandstone fireplace. Each was an elaborate and convoluted family tree, beautifully hand lettered and decorated. The middle one, Lyon, was topped by the Lyon coat of arms; on the right, Liu, Meide's family, featured Chinese designs in the borders;

and on the left, MacNaughton sported Gaelic patterns and symbols. Jean remembered that was the maiden name of Ted's first wife, Anne.

"Very nice," Jean said neutrally.

Roman examined a chessboard set up on a table near the fireplace with a game in progress. "Whose game is this?" he asked.

Ted turned away from contemplating his ancestors. "Bernie's and mine. I'm white."

"You'll win," Roman said.

"I always do. Oh, one more thing, Roman. We'll be serving cocktails in the underground gallery later this afternoon, and I realize you'll take photos of the guests. But I don't want any pictures of the art. There are several priceless pieces on display, and even though we have an excellent security system, I'd rather not advertise their presence here."

"No problem," Roman said. "We're only interested in the people and the wine."

"Chencho, take Mr. Villalobos to the art gallery so he can see the lay of the land," Ted called toward the door. After the two men left, he smiled at Jean. "Now that you've had time to think it over, what will your approach be in writing up the tasting?"

"Pretty straightforward. I'll describe how René is trying to upgrade Chatouilleux and give some background and history on the château, relating it to Yquem. The conclusion will depend on the outcome of the tasting, of course. Then I'll run detailed tasting notes."

"I'm confident we'll prove once and for all that Chatouilleux is Yquem's equal. What about the Burgundy tasting?" he asked. Ted was also pouring white Burgundy for his guests over the course of the weekend.

"I plan to cover it as a sidebar," she said. "We may be able to run those notes as well, depending on space. I'll also include brief profiles of the guests."

"That sounds fine," he said, nodding sagely. "I hope it goes without saying that you are not to mention the death of that man who fell on my car."

"Of course. Did you know him? Do you know what he was trying to warn you about?"

"Never met the man in my life. I understand that he was a drunkard who was often delusional." He made a dismissive wave. "By the way, have you met my son, Bernie?"

"I ran into him last night in the theater."

"What do you think of him?"

"I like him," Jean said, not sure where this was going. "We got along fine."

"Good. Since you'll be here such a short time, I'll be blunt. As you see, genetic continuity is very important to me. Nothing means more to me than carrying on the dynasty my ancestors founded. But I am unable to realize my dream. My son is a fine young man, but he has trouble relating to women. He believes that he's gay, but I know better. There have never been any homosexuals in our family. He has many women friends, but can't go beyond that because he fears betrayal and desertion due to his mother's abandonment and early death. His interest in film noir is symptomatic of his problem—they're full of women who lie, betray, even kill. There are very few positive female images in that genre."

"That's just a reflection of male anxieties during a time when sex roles were changing," Jean said, quoting Bernie from the night before. "Anyway, there aren't many positive images of either sex in that genre."

Ted continued as if she hadn't spoken. "I believe there is hope for Bernie, that he can overcome his self-imposed limitations with the right intervention. What it all boils down to is that my son needs an alluring, experienced woman to put him on the right path." He turned and looked at her. "Someone like you."

Jean blinked in astonishment. This was one explanation for her invitation to cover the tasting that had never occurred to her. "I see," she said carefully. "I was invited here to cure your son of his sexual dysfunction."

"Not entirely. I also genuinely admire your work for the *Digest*. You wouldn't be here otherwise. The tasting is important to me as well."

Jean was fighting hard against her anger, reminding herself over and over again about her job, the wines she and Roman wanted to taste, her plan to set up Roman and Bernie. It wouldn't do to lose her temper and get thrown out. She took a deep breath. "What put this bright idea into your head?"

"It was René. He told me you were the most exciting woman he'd ever been with, that if anyone could help Bernie, you could. So I came to San Francisco to meet you and found you to be a remarkably attractive young woman."

Jean resolved to strangle René with her bare hands when she saw him.

"Obviously there's no obligation on your part," Ted continued. "If you find the idea repugnant, stay and enjoy the tasting, write it up. No harm done. I'm merely asking you to consider it. Get to know him. He's a wonderful person. You'll be doing me a great favor, and Bernie as well." Ted turned and gazed at the Lyon family tree, his hands clasped behind his back. "I have a second chance to continue the Lyon line. Meide is pregnant, due in June. I couldn't be more pleased. But I'm no longer a young man. I'd like to see my grandchildren before I die, and Bernie is my only chance to do that. My daughter is philosophically opposed to children."

"I'll, uh, do what I can," Jean said, not knowing what else to say. She felt a wave of sympathy for Bernie now that she saw what he was up against.

"Thank you. That's all I can ask." He turned back to her. "I'm not the only one who was interested in meeting you. Sissy Oliphant wasn't going to attend until she learned you'd be here."

"So I'm supposed to cure her sexual dysfunction as well?"

Ted laughed heartily. "Oh no. She's a prominent literary agent from New York. She wants to talk to you about doing a book on the Martin Wingo murder."

Jean groaned inwardly. She'd already dealt with dozens of similar vermin by ignoring their calls and e-mails and letters. Now she'd have to be polite to an annoying agent for an entire weekend.

"One other thing, Jean. Roman is very nice looking, very fit for a man his age. Is he gay?"

"Oh no," Jean said quickly. "Roman's a real lady's man. He always says he's a strict vagitarian." She regretted her choice of words instantly, but it didn't seem to bother Ted.

"Good," he said. "I don't want Bernie to face the wrong kind of temptation."

Jean saw an angle she could use. "Will you do me a favor in exchange, Ted? Roman has quite an interest in Sauternes and he's very knowledgeable on the subject. Will you pour him his own tastes?"

"I'd be glad to. I'll make sure we have enough places set."

Chencho came back into the library. "Mr. Lyon, Deputy Baeza is here to see you."

Ted scowled at him. "What does he want now?"

"He heard that some of the people who were at Mrs. Lyon's birthday party will be here this weekend. He wants to question them again about Pilar."

"Question my guests! He isn't even assigned to this case."

Chencho didn't answer.

"Very well, I'd better set him straight. Miss Applequist was just leaving. Show him in, will you?" Chencho went off on his errand and Ted turned to Jean. "He's here about that girl from town who got herself stabbed the morning after Meide's birthday party. Remember, you're to stick to wine in your article."

"No problem," Jean said. "By the way, you should tell the deputy that Roman thinks the Joneses have a meth lab behind their house."

"Do they?" There was something like satisfaction in Ted's eyes. "I'll let him know."

As Jean left the library she passed Chencho and a big Native American man in a green and beige uniform, holding a beige hat. She paused, her curiosity getting the better of her. She slipped behind a tall cabinet full of Chinese porcelain in the hall, waiting until Chencho went off on another errand to creep toward the library door.

". . . aren't coming here to be badgered by the police," Ted was saying.

"I realize that, Mr. Lyon," the deputy said in a low, soothing voice. "But the homicide unit has made no progress, and this is another chance to question some of the people who were the last to see Pilar alive."

"But why question them at all? None of them had anything to do with that girl. She was a *waitress*, for God's sake."

Jean, who had paid for a substantial part of her college education by waitressing, was really starting to dislike Ted.

"Nonetheless," the deputy said calmly, "Pilar spent several hours here the night before she died. One of your guests might have seen or overheard something that they don't realize is significant. I'm sure if you explain that the killer is still at large, they'll be eager to cooperate."

"We'll see about that. By the way, one of my guests is doing your job for you—he thinks there's a meth lab behind the Jones place."

"I'll take a look, but I'd be surprised if there is. Farron's still got three months left on his parole."

Jean heard footsteps coming along the corridor and scurried down the hall out of sight. She found a house phone and buzzed Gloria to see if Roman was finished shooting; he was. Next she called Bernie. "This is Jean," she said when he answered. "Can you come to my cabin? I have something wild to tell you."

"I'll be right there."

Jean smiled. Introducing the two men and leaving them alone was going to be a piece of cake now. She liked the irony that Bernie's controlling, manipulative father had provided her with the means to pull it off. She got to her cabin just as Bernie arrived wearing shorts and a *One False Move* film promo T-shirt.

"The deputy's here," she told him. "Apparently he wants to interview the guests about Pilar's murder."

"Oh, great," Bernie said. "Dad'll hate that."

Jean called Roman's name through the connecting door. "Come in here," she said. "I've solved the mystery of why I was invited here."

Roman stepped into her room, looking handsome and furry in black linen shorts and a white camp shirt. She introduced them.

"I've seen you before," Bernie said. "You're involved with Bash Back, right? Self-defense for gays and lesbians?"

"That's right. I'm one of the founders."

"I saw you give a demonstration in LA last winter. It was very impressive."

"Thanks." Roman took one of the overstuffed chairs and Bernie the other. "All right, Jean," Roman said. "Why did Ted want you instead of Kyle?"

Jean sat on the bed near Bernie's chair. "You're going to love this—he thinks I can cure Bernie of being gay. It's all René's fault. He told Ted I was so hot in the sack that I'd have Bernie turned around in no time."

The two men glanced at each other and laughed. "Well, Bernie, I suppose it's worth a try," Roman said. "Jean is a very enthusiastic proponent of heterosexuality. And who wants to go through life as a despised pervert?"

"Some of my best friends are despised perverts," Bernie said. He sighed, shaking his head. "I'm sorry you've gotten caught in the middle of our family problems, Jean. Dad's done this before, invited good-looking women to visit while I was staying here and then attempted to set up a romantic tryst. Some of them actually tried hard to seduce me. It's very embarrassing. I've asked him to stop, but he's incredibly obstinate. He's used to getting his own way."

"What are his grounds for objecting to your homosexuality?" Roman asked. "Moral, religious, philosophical?"

"Dynastic. My father isn't really a homophobe, but he wants grandchildren more than anything else in this world, and my sister is a dead loss there. Lydia's a true eccentric as only the filthy rich can be: She eats raw foods exclusively, is a rabid animal-rights activist, and believes reproduction is irresponsible. She thinks we should turn the earth over to the animals." He shrugged. "I'm a dead loss, too, but my father won't accept it. I am the first-born son, after all."

"Only raw foods?" Jean said. "She must drive Laszlo crazy."

"That she does. It's a real struggle whenever she visits. He practically goes on strike. But she seldom comes here. I usually see her in LA—she and Meide don't get along. In fact they haven't spoken since the vulture incident. Do you know about that?"

"Yes, Laszlo told us," Jean said.

"Meide's pregnant now, and I hope that'll take some of the heat off me. But even if she has triplets, there's still a strong financial reason for me to go straight. Do you know what a family incentive trust is?"

"Sure," Roman said. "A trust with strings attached that pays out according to performance. It's usually tied to getting good grades or finishing graduate school or something like that. Don't tell me he's tied it to reproduction."

"Yes, exactly. The payout is enough to live on comfortably now, but if I get engaged it goes up, if I marry it goes up again, and if I have a child I get access to the principal. It drives me nuts, because other than this one area, Dad and I get along great. I really do love him. I'll be a wealthy man when he dies, but I hope that won't happen for another thirty years."

"Bernie, that's brutal," Jean said. "Why don't you just make an arrangement with a female friend? Use the turkey-baster method."

"I've considered that, of course. Do you know about my mother?"

They both nodded.

"After she left we rarely saw her—she lost interest in us. And then there was the divorce and her death. All of it was incredibly hard on Lydia and me. I don't know what would have happened if Dad hadn't quit work to stay home with us. I'd never want to put children through that kind of hell, and if I married, a breakup of some sort would be inevitable. How can you raise kids in a family where Mom and Dad each have a man on the side? And what happens when the kids learn about Daddy's other life from the tabloid press? Being a Lyon complicates matters, as it always does. I don't want to get mixed up with some money-hungry surrogate. All that aside, I want to live out in the open, not pretending to be something I'm not." He gave his self-deprecating grin. "Why am I telling all this to a couple of reporters?"

Jean patted his knee. "We won't tell anyone, I promise. *Wine Digest* isn't a tabloid. Anyway, we've got a secret, too—Roman's not a professional photographer. He's a good friend of mine who loves Sauternes, so we gave him a quick course in how to shoot tastings and here he is."

"A party crasher, eh? Roman, what do you do in real life, besides teach queers to kill with their bare hands?"

"I'm a freelance book editor. Jean tells me you're a screenwriter."

"Currently struggling to finance my first picture."

"But all you have to do is make a baby and your troubles will be over."

Bernie slapped his forehead. "Why didn't I think of that?"

"Hell, all you have to do is pawn Dad's watch and you're nearly there," Jean said. "Roman, Ted's watch is worth a million and half."

"Is it indeed?" Roman raised an eyebrow.

Bernie laughed. "That goddamned watch. He bought it to hand down to his grandson."

"Bernie's interested in the Wingo case," Jean said. "Thinks he might use parts of it for a screenplay." She turned to Bernie. "Roman was involved in the whole thing, too. He knows as much about it as I do."

"Where were you when she was getting her wrist broken and shooting the bad guy?" Bernie asked.

"I was unavoidably detained. It's a long story."

"I'd love to hear it sometime."

Jean noted their body language; they were leaning slightly toward each other. This seemed like a good moment to disappear.

"Well," she said, standing up, "I have to strangle René. See you guys later." She put her pen and notebook into a small evening bag that she could sling over her shoulder and closed the door behind her, immensely pleased with herself. They were obviously attracted to each other, and Roman didn't have to start taking pictures for a couple of hours. If this didn't work, nothing would.

Jean thought she'd better tell Laszlo about Meide, so she went to the kitchen. He and Tina arranged canapés on platters as Gloria, the sommelier, set up glassware on trays. Laszlo was whistling again.

"Laszlo," she said, "can I talk to you for a minute?"

"Sure thing, Jean." He wiped his hands on a towel and stepped out into the courtyard with her. "What's up?"

"Look, maybe you should cool it with the vultures for a while—Meide's pregnant."

"No shit. I didn't know that." He pursed his lips. "OK, you're right. I'll give the possum to Katharine."

"Good. I'm sure Meide doesn't need any more stress right now."

"Hey, you know what? When my sister was pregnant, she hadda have weird shit like tabouleh and fish tacos and avocado ice cream. Maybe Meide will start craving normal food." He brightened visibly.

"Avocado ice cream? Where in the world did she get that?"

"I made it for her. It's one of my specialties."

"Will you make me some? I'm not pregnant, but I'd love to try it."

"I'm serving it tonight. It's great cooking for people who like to eat." He lowered his voice. "Bernie says you're OK, so if you get the urge for any recreational chemicals, you just let me know. I can get anything you want for a good price."

"Thanks, Laszlo. I'll keep it in mind." Laszlo certainly seemed to be making the most of his exile in this remote outpost. Jean wondered briefly if he ever bought crystal meth from the Joneses, but decided not to get into that; she had to kill René first. "Do you know what room René Chatouilleux is in? I need to talk to him about the tasting."

"Sure. René got here a couple of hours ago and he's resting on account of jet lag. Come on." He led her back into the kitchen and consulted a list pinned to a corkboard. "He's in the rat room." Laszlo looked at her. "Can you believe it? The Chinese have a fucking rat as part of their zodiac."

"In René's case, it's appropriate," Jean said. She walked along the hall looking for his room, recalling their one encounter, on a *Wine Digest* trip to Bordeaux. As part of their tour of Sauternes, she and her boss had spent the night at Château Chatouilleux and she'd taken a liking to the proprietor. After Owen went to sleep, she and René had returned to the seventeenth-century wine cellar for more tasting. They'd ended up finding new uses for a plastic tarp and a bottle of 1983 Chatouilleux. Afterward they'd rinsed off the sticky Sauternes residue in the swimming pool under a full moon and had finished the evening in the château's tower room in René's antique four-poster bed. It had been a memorable night, but she couldn't let these pleasant thoughts distract her from the good screaming rage she was working on.

Jean found his door and went in without knocking, slamming it behind her. René, who lay on the bed barefoot in slacks and an open-necked shirt, leapt up when he saw her. He was tall and thin, in his early forties, with a fine Gallic nose and a perpetual five-day growth of beard. Physically he reminded her a little of Zeppo, but dark.

"Jean!" He broke into a grin and came toward her, arms wide. "I'm so glad to see you." He stopped short when he saw her expression.

"René, you asshole. You told Ted that I'm some sort of traveling sex therapist who could turn Bernie into a happy heterosexual with one fuck. How dare you!"

"Jean, let me explain—"

"The man's gay. That never changes!"

"I know, I know. Jean, listen: Bernie has nothing to do with this. When I learned your magazine would cover the tasting, I told Ted about you so he would ask for you to come here, so I could see you again." He took a wary step toward her. "I must have you once more."

She wasn't sure if this admission mollified her or made her angrier. "I seem to recall that you're married now."

"But Monique will not be here until tomorrow. She is visiting a friend in Los Angeles. She knows about you, and that it's over between us, but since Ted extended the invitation, she's not suspicious."

"Oh for God's sake, René. I can't believe this. All these elaborate machinations just to get me into bed. And for nothing—I never mess with married men."

"Just once! Monique will never know."

"Forget it. It's not going to happen."

"Jean, you are breaking my heart."

She laughed. "You old goat, this has nothing to do with your heart."

He shook his head sadly. "American women are so conventional."

"Ha! French men are such *cochons*."

"First I am a goat, and now a pig. Jean, I know you will change your mind. We have three days. Just tell me when and we will find a way."

She smiled at him, softened by his accent, which she loved, and flattered by his enthusiasm in spite of everything. "I had a great time, too, René, but it won't happen again. Work it off with Monique. She'll appreciate it." She went out, closing the door quietly this time.

Chapter 8

Jean didn't want to go back to her cabin and disturb the boys, so she decided to see who else had arrived. She looked out onto the driveway; besides the Lyons' cars and the rolling eggplant, she spotted a BMW sedan, a new Bentley, and a big gray limo. A uniformed chauffeur came out of the house and drove off in the limo.

Jean glimpsed a tall man in shorts and a yellow polo shirt walking toward the terrace, limping slightly. As she followed him around the house, a hot wind assailed her. The fronds of the palms lining the driveway made dry rustling sounds and dust stung her eyes.

The man stood beyond the Olympic pool, hands in pockets, looking across the canyon. He had the hard, no-nonsense physique of a serious athlete. Jean recognized him immediately—Tony Feola, former 49ers running back and owner of two Super Bowl rings.

As she walked toward him, he turned and smiled at her. He'd definitely kept in shape since retiring; the only changes Jean saw were a lot of gray in his thick black hair and a few new lines on his homely face. Below his shorts, both knees were scarred from surgery.

"Mr. Feola? I'm Jean Applequist."

He extended a huge hand. "Pleased to meet you. And call me Tony."

Jean grinned as she took his hand. "I've always wanted to shake a hand that's slapped Ronnie Lott's butt."

He laughed. "Well, I don't think I've ever slapped his butt. I've showered with him and had a few beers with him, though."

"That's good enough for me." Jean had seen pictures of Tony's wife, a pretty blonde woman who did a lot of volunteer work, and his two strapping teenage daughters. "Is your wife here?"

"No, she's busy with the girls. My oldest has an important soccer game this weekend. I'm sorry I'll miss it."

"She takes after you, does she?"

"Sure does," he said with a proud grin. "Her time in the hundred meters is close to what mine was in high school. It's a good thing she can never play pro football—I hope her knees will last a lot longer than mine."

"I'm here to cover the tasting for *Wine Digest*. What brings you here?"

"Ted and I are old drinking buddies. Met at a wine auction in Napa. We were both bidding on the same bottle of 1974 Heitz Martha's Vineyard. When we were the final two bidders, he suggested we split the cost and share the bottle."

As he spoke, Jean flipped open her notebook and took notes. "I'd like to ask you about your wine collection. Do we have to stand out here in the sun?"

"Hot as hell, isn't it? Let's go inside."

They went into the cool living room. Jean interviewed Tony about his cellar, which ran heavily to California Cabs and Rhône varietals. "How'd you get interested in wine?" she asked him.

"My family's Italian, so we always had wine at dinner. When I got drafted by the Niners and moved to San Francisco, I started going up to wine country a lot. Before I knew it, I was a collector."

"Do you collect as an investment?"

"No, I drink everything I buy. Wine's the disposable collectible—you've got to destroy it to enjoy it."

A painfully thin woman in her fifties emerged from the hallway. She was artfully made-up, dressed in a black knit tunic and skirt, with stylish heavy shoes and lots of earth-toned ethnic jewelry. She looked hot and uncomfortable. Jean thought she must be the New York agent.

"God, this heat is murder," the woman said, running a hand through her chin-length red hair, dyed a few shades darker than Zeppo's. "Tony, how are you?" She had a deep, rough voice and a strong New York accent.

Tony stood up. "Hello, Sissy. Where's Jasper?"

"He's lying down. All those martinis on the plane, and then this heat—he needed a nap. Who's your friend?"

"Sissy Oliphant, this is Jean Applequist."

"Jean!" Sissy exclaimed, gripping her hand. "I didn't recognize you—your hair's longer in the news photos. I've been dying to meet you. I've left God knows how many messages on your machine."

"Sorry. I hear from a lot of agents."

"But I'm the one you need. I'm the one who can get you the best deal."

Jean flipped a page in her notebook. "Tell me, what wines do you and your husband collect?"

"All sorts of wines." She pulled a chair over and sat down. "Listen, Jean, the real story behind the Martin Wingo murder would sell big. It's obvious that a lot went on that was never in the news. I read *Wine Digest*, so I know you can write. And look at you—you're a publicist's dream. If you work with me, I can get you a six-figure advance and a national book tour, all the talk shows—Letterman, Conan O'Brien, maybe even Jimmy Fallon."

Jean couldn't deny that the money was tempting, but the murdered man had been a systematic blackmailer, and she'd promised her friend Diane, Martin's widow, never to reveal the details. Jean thought she'd better put a stop to this now. "Thanks, but I'm really not interested. The things that didn't make the news are secrets, and they're going to stay that way."

"Come on, Jean. Don't play hard to get."

"I never do."

Tony watched the interchange with amusement. "I advise taking a hard line with Sissy," he said to Jean. "She's about as sensitive as a goddamn toilet seat, to quote Holden Caulfield."

Sissy raised her waxed eyebrows. "Why, Tony, I didn't realize you'd actually read a book."

"Just the one." He winked at Jean.

"Thanks for the advice," Jean said. "I can get tough if I need to, but I'm sure Sissy will take no for an answer."

"Don't bet on it," Tony said.

Sissy tossed her head, making her long earrings jingle. "You'll change your mind, Jean. Let me know when you do."

Jean sighed. She'd already heard that once today, and she knew she wouldn't change her mind in either case.

Jean announced that she was due for a tour of the wine cellar and excused herself. With relief, she made her way to the busy kitchen where Laszlo and his crew were in high gear getting ready for cocktails and dinner. Laszlo directed her through a door just off the kitchen to stairs that led down to the cellar.

The room was cold and dimly lit. Gloria, who'd put on a blue cardigan sweater, sat at a desk in an alcove to the right, working on a MacBook. She turned and smiled when she heard Jean.

"Hi," Jean said. "Is this a good time for a tour?"

"Sure." Gloria closed a file and stood. "I was just updating the inventory. We're making quite a dent this weekend." She guided Jean around the extensive cellar, which was cleverly laid out, divided into storage areas for each of the world's major wine regions. The beautiful, high-tech shelving was made of different woods put together in intricate geometric patterns. But the most impressive aspect was the wine: Ted had cases and cases of virtually every top vintage of every great producer Jean could think of, from cult Napa Cabs to German Eiswein to *tête de cuvée* Champagne. She'd seen less impressive cellars in three-star restaurants.

Jean paused at a neat pile of wooden boxes, eight cases of a red Burgundy she loved but couldn't afford. One of the cases was open and several bottles stood on a nearby counter. "Do we get to drink some of this?" she asked.

"Yes, with dinner tomorrow."

"Nothing like being rich."

"That's funny," Gloria muttered to herself as she eyed the stack of cases. "I thought we ordered ten cases."

Jean looked through her notes. "Gloria, how did you learn about wine?"

"I started out waiting tables at my uncle's restaurant in LA and decided wine and liquor service was a lot easier than food service, and wine was pretty interesting, so I worked at learning about it."

"What are you doing out here in the middle of nowhere?"

"I took this job to get my boys away from the gangs in LA—they're thirteen and sixteen."

"How do they like it here?"

"They complained a lot when we first moved, but they're getting used to small-town life. My youngest has discovered horses, and the older boy gets to play first base on the varsity team, which he never would at a big school. And it's so much safer—except we did have a murder here recently."

"I heard about it. Did you know the victim?"

Gloria nodded. "Pilar worked events up here fairly often. She loved coming here—she had a crush on Bernie."

"I suppose he looked like the area's most eligible bachelor to her." Jean wondered if the staff knew he was gay.

"Yes, he did." Gloria looked at Jean speculatively, and Jean realized the woman was wondering if she knew.

"I didn't know Pilar, but having met Bernie, I think it was hopeless," Jean said.

Gloria smiled in understanding. "Definitely. I tried explaining that to Pilar, but she thought true love could move mountains. She was always trying to talk to him. Poor thing. I'll miss her."

"What do you think happened to her?"

"I have no idea. It must have been a robbery or a random killing. Pilar wasn't the kind of person who made enemies. She was silly and not too smart, but she didn't have a mean bone in her body. Her family is devastated."

"I overheard the sheriff's deputy telling Ted that he wants to question the guests who were here that night."

"Yes, I know. Matt thinks one of them may have heard Pilar say something about where she was going or who she was meeting. He's taking it hard. This is the first murder he's dealt with here, and he's getting nowhere."

"I can't imagine he's had much experience with homicide."

"Oh, but he has. He used to work homicide with the Phoenix police department. He took this job to get away from the big city. Matt's from around here, and he loves the area."

"Sounds as if you two are good friends."

"Yes, we are," Gloria said, smiling.

"What about Domingo Huerta, the guy who fell on Ted's car? Did you know him?"

"No, I didn't know him. I'm not much of a barfly."

Chencho came through the cellar door. "Hey, Gloria. Come show me which wines are for cocktails and which are for dinner."

Gloria looked at her watch. "OK." She turned to Jean. "Sorry. Duty calls."

"Thanks. It's been a pleasure." Jean climbed the stairs to the kitchen. She noted that it was nearly five o'clock, so she went into the library to kill time and hide from Sissy. The walls of books made the library restful despite the room's lack of color. Jean walked around reading the titles and admiring the art. Besides the family trees and a few Chinese textiles, several framed black-and-white photos were hung on the walls. They were urban landscapes, dark and gritty, looking so much like sets from old movies that she thought Bernie must have taken them. She was amazed at how good they were—maybe he did have a future in film.

Just before six o'clock, Jean went in search of the gallery, dying to find out what had happened with Roman and Bernie. At the end of the guest hallway she followed stairs down to heavy double doors that stood open. There was an elaborate security panel on the wall next to the doors. The underground gallery was a big, open room carpeted in off-white, with a group of overstuffed white chairs and sofas at the near end. It was as cold as the wine cellar, and a rack of sweaters and jackets and even a long chinchilla coat stood near the door—for chilly guests, no doubt. Jean, always on the warm side, didn't take a jacket.

The art was displayed at the far end of the room in blond wood and glass cases. Jean was amazed at the size and scope of the collection: beautiful scrolls, porcelain, furniture, statues, and small delicate treasures. Low benches covered in butterscotch leather faced the cases of art. Soft music played in the background, something annoyingly New Age.

Roman and Laszlo were already there, Laszlo in his chef's whites. Roman had set up Clive's softbox lights and was shooting the gorgeous appetizer table along the far wall as the chef watched, kibitzing. Gloria stood ready behind the wood and zinc bar.

"Hey, Jean," Laszlo said when he spotted her. "Come have a drink."

"Thanks, I will. Everything looks great."

"Doesn't it? I got dinner to do. See you later." Laszlo dashed up the stairs.

Gloria served Jean a glass of vintage rosé Champagne from the array of rare and costly bottles behind the bar. It was going to be tough to stay sober with so much great wine tempting her, but Jean knew she had to, at least until she was off duty. She ate a few delicious tidbits from the buffet as soon as Roman had finished shooting the food.

She was about to take Roman aside and ask him what had happened when Ted and Meide arrived hand in hand, Meide managing to look ethereal and wanton at the same time in a peach-colored silk dress with no back. Pale green jade jewelry graced her neck and wrists, and she balanced on another pair of delicate high-heeled sandals. Sissy and her husband, Jasper, a heavy white-haired man who would have looked distinguished if it weren't for the burst capillaries covering his cheeks and nose, arrived on the Lyons' heels. Sissy took a black cardigan sweater from the rack and put it on. A handsome Chinese man Jean took to be Wang Yuan, the art expert, came in and gave Meide a friendly kiss; he was followed by Tony Feola and two men Jean didn't know, presumably Carl Schoonover and Angus MacKnight.

The dress was casual, the men in lightweight jackets without ties and the women in summer dresses. The guests seemed to know each other, and Jean hung back while they embraced, shook hands, caught up on gossip. From their solicitous remarks to Meide, Jean could tell they all knew she was pregnant. Ted introduced Wang Yuan to a few people—apparently he was new to the group.

Jean repeatedly tried to catch Roman's eye, but he was busy taking photos. She didn't wonder for long—the moment Bernie walked in, he and Roman exchanged an unmistakable look. Jean couldn't help grinning.

As soon as Roman was alone for a moment, she sidled up to him and nudged him. "No need to thank me."

Roman put his arm around her shoulders and spoke into her ear. "Thank you," he said softly. "I see René still lives. What did he have to say?"

"His motives were purely selfish. He wanted me here so we could have one last fling before his wife arrives tomorrow."

"I hope you controlled yourself."

"Of course. I don't want that kind of trouble."

"You're showing uncharacteristic good judgment. Now let me work, you conniving bitch."

Jean went over to Bernie, who held a glass of brut Champagne. "You're quite an operator," he told her. "A little obvious, but very effective. One thing, though—if my father finds out, he'll ask Roman to leave, and I'd hate for that to happen."

"Your secret is safe with me." Jean noticed Ted looking at them, smiling. She kissed Bernie on the cheek. "He's watching now, so act entranced. Did Roman tell you he hadn't been with anyone in more than a year?"

"No, he didn't. Well. That explains . . . that explains a lot."

"I'm so glad it worked out," she said, squeezing his arm.

"I'm glad, too."

"By the way, did you take those black-and-white photos in the library?"

"Yes. I'm always finding great locations around LA, so I immortalize them until I can use them in my film."

"They're really good. Well, I have to mingle. See you later." As she walked toward Wang Yuan, René intercepted her.

"Jean, I love you in blue," he said in a half whisper.

"You fool, stop staring at me like that. People will notice."

"I can't help it—you look so alluring. Why do you torture me this way?"

"Oh, give it a rest."

Jean felt an icy hand on her arm and turned to see Sissy Oliphant, clutching a martini with two olives in her other talon. She wondered why anyone would have a martini when she could drink Ted's wine.

"René, how are you?" Sissy said. She spoke again before he could answer. "Jean, do you remember when that woman in East Hampton with the botched facelift shot up her surgeon's office and took hostages? I got a three hundred grand advance for one of the nurses who survived, but she had to share it with a ghostwriter. You'd keep the whole amount. Minus my commission, of course."

"Excuse me. I have to meet the other guests." Jean moved away as quickly as she could, leaving René and Sissy together. They deserved each other.

Tony stood alone sipping a glass of red wine, so Jean went over to him. "God save me from agents," she said.

"It's going to be a long weekend if you let her get to you."

"She's pretty hard to ignore."

"And impossible to insult or embarrass."

Roman shot a picture of her and Tony, and Jean introduced them. "I was a fan of yours," Roman said. "It was always a pleasure to watch you play." At six two and just over two hundred pounds, Roman was almost as big as Tony.

"Thanks," Tony said. "You ever play any football yourself?"

"Not since high school."

Ted approached them, glass in hand, smiling. "Excuse me, gentlemen. I'm going to steal Jean and introduce her to my other guests." He took Jean's arm and led her away. "You and Bernie seem to be getting along well."

"We have a lot in common," Jean said.

"I'm very pleased. I see you've already met Sissy."

"Unavoidably."

He steered her to Wang Yuan. He was about her height and slender, with pronounced cheekbones and beautiful brown eyes. He looked a well-preserved forty-five.

"Delighted to meet you." His hand in hers was smooth and cool, his voice soft, his accent slight. "I very much enjoyed your article on the Burgundy tasting in New York. It's nice to see a little humor in a subject that is usually taken much too seriously."

"Thanks. Are you a Burgundy lover?"

"Oh, yes. In fact I expect to enjoy the white Burgundy tasting as much as the main event."

Ted excused them, guiding her over to where Jasper Oliphant and another man stood talking. Jasper held a martini and already seemed half lit. Carl Schoonover was a fit man in a black raw silk jacket and tight pants. Jean eyed his hairline suspiciously; his wavy brown hair looked surgically implanted.

"Good to meet you," he said, holding on to her hand as he spoke. "There's nothing like a beautiful woman wearing a thin dress in a cold room. I'll bet that's why Ted keeps it so chilly in here."

Jasper chuckled. "Don't be vulgar, Carl."

"The cold keeps the art from deteriorating, Jean, as he well knows," Ted explained. "Just like a wine cellar."

Jean fought the urge to cross her arms over her chest. "Are you a wine collector as well?" she asked Carl, trying to sound businesslike.

"Sure am. We'll be tasting a few bottles from my cellar on Saturday."

"I'll need the details for my article. And you, Jasper?"

"Sissy's in charge of our wine cellar—you'll have to ask her. I'm in charge of martinis."

Jean wondered if Jasper's presence here had anything to do with corporate politics. What a waste to pour 1811 Sauternes for such a know-nothing lush.

Ted took her arm again. "Excuse us, but Jean still has one more person to meet."

"Later, Jean." Carl winked and shot at her with an index finger.

Ted and Jean found Angus MacKnight at the bar, waiting while Gloria poured him a glass of single-malt Scotch neat. His age was hard to guess—his body was muscular and sinewy, but his skin was leathery and freckled, ruined by the sun. He had close-cropped reddish blond hair and was missing the top part of his right ear. Jean recalled that he had some sort of military background.

She shook his hand. "Hello, Angus. How do you know Ted and Meide?"

"Ted and I met online. 'MacKnight' is a variation of 'MacNaughton,' his first wife's name, and we were both researching ancestors. 'Lyon' is Scots as well. We finally met in person on a trip to Scotland."

"So you're practically related," Jean said.

"We're in-laws about five generations back." Angus gave a crinkly grin. "But I don't expect to be remembered in his will." Despite his mild words, something in his manner put Jean on her guard. He stood very still and didn't seem to blink. His pale blue eyes, cold as ice, made her think of Mojo, the wolf dog. Jean tried not to blink either, remembering what Katharine had told her about predators.

"I see you prefer the drink of your ancestors. Do you collect wine?"

"Yes, especially dessert wines from Germany. Ted thinks he's going to convert me to Sauternes."

"Now Angus," Ted said, "I want to ask you about some MacNaughtons I've uncovered who lived in British Columbia in the eighteenth century. Jean, why don't you have a look at the art before dinner? I don't want you to write about it, but you can still enjoy it."

"Thanks, I will." Jean was glad to be dismissed; she'd already had enough genealogy to last her for months.

Wang Yuan gazed into one of the glass-front cabinets. She walked over and stood next to him. The cabinet contained a dozen small animals carved from deep green jade—the Chinese zodiac again, displaying the classic Chinese combination of whimsy and exquisite workmanship. Jean especially liked the coiled snake, the intricately scaled dragon, and the playful monkey. Even the rat was beautiful. "How wonderful," she exclaimed. "Ted should put little cards on the cabinets as they do in museums for the unenlightened among us."

"These are from the Han Dynasty, carved from the most precious kind of jade," Yuan said. "They were commissioned by a high official who was a renowned poet and calligrapher in his own right. If they had been carved yesterday they would be museum pieces. As it is, they're priceless."

"How old are they?"

"The Han Dynasty was contemporary with the Roman Empire, so they're about 2,000 years old."

"Amazing." She took out her notebook. "Can I ask you some nosy questions?"

"Of course."

"How do you know the Lyons?"

"I was a friend of Meide's brother Kede. He was killed in a plane crash five years ago—one of his hobbies was stunt flying. He always spoke warmly of his baby sister, so when she and I were in Taipei at the same time a few months ago, I looked her up."

"Have you been here before?"

"I have visited their Taipei home, but this is my first time in Valle de los Osos. I rather like it. I spend most of my time in cities, so it's very pleasant to be out in the country where one can see animals in the wild."

"You can see owls and hawks close up right across the canyon." She told him about Katharine.

"I would enjoy that very much. But Meide explained the incident with the vultures—isn't Katharine the woman responsible for Ted's paying the fine?"

"Well, technically Meide's responsible. She ordered them shot."

"Nonetheless, if Ted is angry with his neighbor, it wouldn't do to socialize with her. He is very possessive of his friends and unforgiving of his enemies." He smiled and inclined his head toward the next cabinet. "Come, let me show you some other exceptional pieces."

They walked around the gallery examining Ming furniture made from an extinct golden-brown wood, Song porcelain and rare silk scrolls, and fanciful bronze animals. The Lyons' collection was on a par with those in the Asian art museums Jean had been to around the world, and Yuan's knowledgeable commentary added a new dimension of enjoyment.

Jean especially liked a stocky rhinoceros about eight inches long that reminded her of a Dürer etching. "This is my favorite," she said. "Is he gold?"

"Yes, solid gold. Isn't he splendid? He and these bronze animals are from the Shang Dynasty, which lasted roughly from 1711 to 1066 B.C. This fellow was made about 1600 B.C."

Meide came over to join them. She wore the long chinchilla coat over her flimsy dress and carried a Champagne flute of mineral water. "Jean, you must share Yuan with me," she said with mock petulance, slipping her arm through his. "I see him so seldom. What are you two talking about?"

"I'm getting a course in Chinese art history," Jean said.

"Sometimes I think he knows more about our collection than Ted or I."

"I ought to—that's my business. I consult to museums on Chinese art," he explained to Jean.

Jean sensed Meide didn't want her there, so she excused herself; they switched to Mandarin as she moved away. She went over to the bar for another glass of wine, planning to try something different this time. "Gloria, I feel like a kid in a candy store," she said, eyeing the bottles. "What do you recommend?"

Gloria smiled. "I've got something special you might want to try." She reached into a small refrigerator behind her and brought out a distinctive bottle of white wine. "Do you like Viognier?"

"Oh, Château-Grillet. I love it."

Carl Schoonover came over, empty glass in hand. "I'll have some of that, too, honey."

"Yes, sir," Gloria said formally, setting to work with a corkscrew.

"So you're the decorator," Jean said to him. "How did you meet the Lyons?"

"Interior designer, please. Ted and Meide liked what I did for friends of theirs and asked me to work with them on Phoenix Garden. What do you think of the result?"

"It's boring. I prefer more color." She felt no obligation to stroke Carl's ego.

He smiled smugly. "A neutral, unintrusive backdrop is essential for art of this caliber. I doubt if you have any Song porcelain or Ming furniture to complicate your decorating decisions."

"You're right about that. But white's such a pain to keep clean."

Gloria poured them both some of the rare white Rhône. Carl swirled his on the bar and sniffed it deeply, then tasted it, rolling it around on his tongue. "Ah, perfect," he announced, looking at Jean. "Great legs, full-bodied and round, luscious and succulent, mature, yet with youthful vigor. This is my kind of wine." He leered at her.

Jean glanced at Gloria, who rolled her eyes. "You know what's amazing, Gloria?" she said. "Every man who says that kind of shit to me thinks it's original."

Carl chuckled. "René said you had a smart mouth."

"You know another thing I don't understand?" Jean said. "Why do men torture and mutilate themselves to get a full head of hair? The best-looking man I know is almost completely bald."

Gloria grinned. "That would be Roman."

"Say, what's Roman's last name?" Carl asked, oblivious to Jean's barbs. "I think I recognize him."

"Uh, Villalobos," Jean answered reluctantly.

"Hmm. I don't know the name, but I've seen him before. I never forget a face—I have a phenomenal visual memory. Well, catch you later." He drifted off.

"Poor man was born too late," Gloria said. "I can see him in gold chains and bell-bottoms."

Jean laughed. "With a shiny polyester shirt unbuttoned down to here." She sincerely hoped Carl didn't recognize Roman from some Bash Back event, as Bernie had.

Gloria got busy serving wine to Sissy and another martini to Jasper, so Jean moved away fast. She saw Roman rummaging in his camera bag behind a chair. "Roman," she said, "you have to look at the art. It's unbelievable."

"All right. I'm done taking pictures for now—we're reaching what Clive calls the red-nosed, wine-stained phase of the evening."

Roman got himself a glass of rosé Champagne and they walked through the gallery. Jean told him what she could remember of Yuan's discourse. She pointed out the gold Shang rhinoceros, the piece she'd most like to take home with her. Soon Roman was scowling.

"What's the matter with you?" she asked as they stood before the jade zodiac figures.

"These pieces should all be in a museum. It's unconscionable for a single individual to own them."

"Lighten up, you Bolshevik. We still have two days to go."

Bernie joined them, a glass of Champagne in his hand. "Hey, baby, what's your sign?" he said to Jean.

"I'm a snake and Roman's an ox. You?"

"Dog. I'm loyal and sincere, rare qualities in Hollywood."

"Rare qualities anywhere," Roman said.

"I was lucky to find an exotic hunk like you who appreciates a sterling character."

"And who has a weakness for all-American boys."

"I overheard you telling Tony you played football in high school," Bernie said. "I'll bet you had a crush on the quarterback."

"I was the quarterback. I had a crush on the president of the chess club."

As they bantered, Jean watched their expressions with alarm. "Hey," she said, nudging Bernie. "If you two keep grinning at each other like that, Dad's going to figure things out."

Bernie put his arm around Jean. "Fortunately, you're a very convincing beard."

Chencho came through the double doors and announced dinner. People drifted toward the stairs; Yuan hung up Meide's fur coat as they led the way out. Jean waited for Roman to gather his equipment.

As she and Roman moved to the stairs behind Ted, Jean saw Carl outside the double doors, looking put out. "Ted," he said, "I've told you many times you shouldn't leave the gallery open like this. What did we install that expensive security system for?"

"I only leave it open when I have guests. Meide and I want our friends to be able to drop in whenever they get the urge, and I certainly trust our friends." He patted Carl's shoulder. "Don't worry, it's locked up tight the rest of the time. Come to dinner."

CHAPTER 9

Dinner was to be alfresco, served on two long tables set up on the flagstone terrace. The theme was Southwestern—brightly colored linens, straw placemats, centerpieces of gourds and dried flowers. The wind had died down and the evening was pleasantly warm after the chill of the gallery.

Everyone gravitated to an elaborate outdoor kitchen built into the high wall near the pool. A beehive wood-burning oven, a refrigerator, and a sink were set into the stone counters. On the oversized restaurant grill, two headless animals the size of cocker spaniels rotated on a spit under Laszlo's supervision. Jean sniffed deeply; it smelled heavenly, rich and garlicky. The guests gathered around, asking what it was.

"*Cabrito*," the chef answered. "Kid in my special marinade." He carved neat slices from the animals with a long sharp knife. A plain chicken breast grilled to one side, presumably for Meide.

People drifted over to the bar, where Gloria and Chencho served wine. Jean leaned on the bar, smiling at Chencho. "Hey, are you old enough to drink?"

"Just barely," he said. "What can I get you?"

Jean had a glass of a rare dry German Riesling. When she saw Carl coming, she started to move away, but he stopped to speak to Jasper and Sissy.

"Jasper," Carl said, poking the man's belly, "looks like you've put on weight since Meide's birthday."

"I wax and wane like the moon, depending on the caliber of the dinner parties I've been attending."

"You ought to try this liquid diet my doctor put me on." Carl poked him again.

"He's practically on a liquid diet now," Sissy muttered.

"I used to be a whale," Carl continued. "Lost a hundred and forty pounds in a year, and that was nearly ten years ago. You'll look better, feel better, and live a lot longer. Besides, it'll do wonders for your sex life."

"Liquid diet indeed," Jasper said with a snort. "I'd rather eat broken glass. And Sissy claims to like my generous proportions." He patted her skinny butt.

"Say, have you been out to your place in the Hamptons this summer?" Carl asked. "That was one of my favorite projects. The old house has great bones."

Jasper cleared his throat and looked sideways at Sissy. She raised an eyebrow at him. "The bank foreclosed on it," she said to Carl. "Jasper's been managing our real estate holdings."

"That's a tough break," Carl said. "I'll bet it's no fun living on a professor's salary, huh?"

"Thanks to me, he doesn't have to," Sissy said coolly.

"But still, it can't be easy keeping up with the Lyons." Carl punched Jasper playfully on the arm.

Jasper drank the rest of his martini and said nothing.

In a few minutes, the guests sat down and Laszlo's crew served the *cabrito*, along with a creamy corn and green chile pudding, grilled portobello mushrooms and squash, and a salad of mixed greens, tomatoes, and roasted red peppers with a chipotle dressing. The food was superb, flavorful and imaginative, but not too spicy. It all went beautifully with the dry California rosé Gloria poured. Jean, seated at one end of the table between Bernie and Tony, quickly forgot her vow not to drink too much. She was delighted to see Sissy at the other table, next to Carl.

Jean leaned toward Bernie. "That Carl's a real asshole," she whispered.

"He's not a bad person, but he's a straight man in a field dominated by queers," Bernie said, his voice low as well. "He wants to make sure no one thinks he's a fairy."

"So he's definitely straight?"

"Oh yes, and he has two or three beautiful young ex-wives and a current fiancée to prove it. Dad says he's paying phenomenal amounts of alimony."

"Do you like his decorating?"

"Not much. I'm more into dark colors and art deco furniture."

"That figures. What about Yuan? What's his story?"

"I don't know him well, but I like him. Meide's crazy about him because he's a connection to her big brother, whom she worshipped. He died a few years ago."

"Yuan told me." Jean glanced at Tony, who was deep in conversation with Angus on his left. "I like Tony, too."

"Yeah, he's a great guy, but not a great businessman. Dad invested in his chain of restaurants—you know, Tony's Chop Houses—and they're not doing well. Dad says he needs more capital." Bernie shook his head. "They should never have gotten involved financially. It's putting a strain on their friendship."

Halfway through dinner, Ted, seated at the head of the other table, waved an arm in the air. "Bernie," he called, "come over here and settle an argument."

Bernie grinned at Jean. "Excuse me." He grabbed his wine glass and got up.

"Jasper says Gloria Graham played the moll in *The Big Heat*," Ted explained. "I say it was somebody else."

Yuan, seated near Ted, stood and offered Bernie his chair. "Bernie, please sit here. I'm quite lost in this conversation—I know nothing about American cinema." He took Bernie's seat next to Jean. An alert waiter switched the two men's plates and cutlery.

Meide, seated next to Ted, craned her head. "Oh Yuan, come back. You don't have to pay so much attention to our reporter—you'll get your picture in the magazine anyway."

Yuan said something soothing in Mandarin and Meide went back to her dinner, giggling. He smiled at Jean, who made a face. "Forgive Meide. She's a trifle spoiled. She is many years younger than her other siblings and was always treated like a little princess."

"And I'm sure being incredibly beautiful doesn't hurt."

"There is an Italian proverb that says, 'With the very rich and the very beautiful, a little patience.' In any case, I would much rather sketch you."

Jean laughed. "Now there's a line if ever I heard one."

"Not at all. In the Musée Guimet in Paris, there is a twelfth-century stone statue from southern India that I have always regarded as the perfect female shape—long-limbed and voluptuous, strong yet sinuous. You are that statue made flesh."

"Well, thank you," Jean said, disarmed by the wine, his words, his gentle tone. "Are you an artist?"

"Not really. I'm a good technician and can copy almost anything, but I lack my own . . . fire, I suppose you would call it."

Jean and Yuan talked about cities they'd visited, museums they'd toured, works of art they loved. Jean was well traveled, but Yuan made her feel like a homebody. He regaled her with first-hand descriptions of Angkor Wat, the cave paintings at Lascaux, the Dazu Buddhist grottos in Sichuan Province, and several other places she hadn't yet managed to visit. At the end of dinner, as Laszlo's crew cleared the tables and served an exquisite dessert of blood orange sorbet and avocado ice cream, Jean realized she'd barely said a word to Tony.

Over the course of the evening, she watched Bernie interact with his father. There was genuine affection between them, which made Ted's attempts to change his son even more inexplicable to Jean. Bernie and Meide seemed fond of each other as well.

As the guests rose from the table, Meide kissed Ted and Bernie goodnight and retired, pleading fatigue.

Jean caught Bernie's arm. "Dad doesn't seem bad at all tonight."

A tired, bitter look crossed Bernie's face. "I've scored a lot of points by nuzzling you."

The group moved to the seating area near the pool, Tony limping just ahead of Jean.

"Tony," Carl called. "Go long!" He heaved a dinner roll in an uneven arch toward the big man. Tony moved nimbly to catch the roll with one hand.

"Not bad," Jean told him.

"Have to earn my keep as a sideshow freak," he said with a grin.

As Gloria poured Cognac and liqueurs, Chencho brought out a beautiful antique humidor covered in embossed leather. Ted supervised the distribution of cigars, which he said were Montecristo No. 2s, a name Jean had heard before. She noted that the cellophane was brown, which meant the cigars were aged. Everyone but she and Yuan took one, even Sissy. Jean disliked all forms of tobacco, but at least they were outside this time, so she wouldn't have to shower tonight to get the smell out of her hair.

Jean sipped Cognac as she watched Roman clip and light his torpedo-shaped cigar. He'd quit smoking cigarettes years ago but had been known to backslide. He breathed out a puff of fragrant smoke. "Mmm, this is the real Cuban article. No doubt rolled by an elderly woman making pennies a day."

"You'll stink if you smoke that thing," she told him.

"Nonsense. I'll smell like very expensive tobacco, and so will Bernie."

Jean moved away from the miasma of smoke. She sat on a chair near the edge of the canyon, enjoying the stars and soft warm night. A single light burned in a window at Katharine's house. Soon Yuan, holding a glass of Port, pulled up a chair and joined her. "You don't like cigars either?" she asked him.

"No. I believe smoking dulls the senses."

"I'm with you. I want to be sharp for the wine tastings." Jean set her Cognac down and pulled out her notebook. "Speaking of which, I might as well take advantage of having you to myself. What types of wines do you collect?"

"I move around so much for my job that I don't have a large wine collection, but I occasionally buy favorites at auction. I was able to provide a bottle of 1945 Yquem for this tasting, from an auction in Paris last year. I drink a lot of white Burgundy." And they were off again, talking about the Burgundy domaines they'd visited and the wines they'd especially enjoyed. Jean had taken a bicycle trip through Burgundy with Roman a few years ago, which Yuan found fascinating.

When the smokers had finished their cigars, Angus stood. "Who's up for a card game?" he asked.

"No more of that Chinese poker for me," Tony said. "I can't figure the hands fast enough."

"I'll give you a break this time, Tony," Angus said. "We'll play Texas Hold 'em or stud instead of *pai gow*."

"Now that I can handle," Tony said, and he, Carl, and René followed Angus into the house.

"Don't you like poker?" Jean asked Yuan.

"I limit myself to bridge—it's a more elegant game, and much less expensive." He stood, stifling a yawn. "Your excellent company has enlivened me in spite of jet lag, but now I must finally succumb." He took her hand and kissed it. "Good night, Jean."

"Sweet dreams," she said. She watched him walk into the main house.

By prior arrangement, Roman left first while Jean and Bernie waited; they went back to her cabin together. She could see Ted looking on with approval.

Jean, tired and tipsy, kissed Bernie good night, closed the connecting door after him, and fell into her lonely bed. The muffled sounds of passion from the next room made her long for Zeppo. She considered going to René's room, but quickly ruled it out; even if she didn't have a strong moral objection to screwing married men, she knew that in a place like this, it would be common knowledge by morning, and someone would tell Monique. Jean didn't want to hurt Monique and didn't need that kind of psychodrama when she was working. And if she did end up bedding someone, Roman would scold her about cheating on Zeppo, as he always did.

She ran through the single prospects: Carl Schoonover and Angus MacKnight were out of the question. She also nixed Laszlo—she liked him, but there was no chemistry. That left Yuan. He was definitely handsome and interesting, and he seemed several cuts above the others in terms of sensitivity and intelligence. He'd also made his interest in her very clear. And if she worked things right, Zeppo would never find out. She'd see what happened tomorrow.

VOICES OUTSIDE her cabin woke Jean early. She parted the blinds and took a quick look, then knocked lightly on the connecting door. There was no answer, but she went in anyway and stood next to the bed. The two men slept nestled like spoons, Roman curled around Bernie.

"Hey, guys," she said softly, "are you awake?"

Roman made a snoring noise and rolled onto his back. Jean looked them over—they were half uncovered and tangled in the white sheets. Bernie's sparse body hair and pale skin made a nice contrast with the dark, hirsute Roman. Jean grinned. "Roman," she said. "You look like a tarantula on a slice of angel food."

"Marlowe, internal monologue," Bernie mumbled. "*Farewell, My Lovely*."

"Sorry to disturb you," Jean said, "but Chencho is outside with the pool man. Why don't you leave through my door, Bernie? We don't want Daddy to eighty-six Roman."

"OK, sure." Bernie turned onto his stomach and buried his face in his pillow.

"Go away, you annoying woman," Roman said.

Jean went back to her cabin and took a shower. She heard Bernie leave through her room as she toweled off. The day was already hot, so she dressed in black capris and a blue T-shirt. She spent some time reviewing her notes from yesterday, expanding them where needed and writing down odds and ends she hadn't had a chance to add last night. She called her office and talked to Kyle, the managing editor. A lengthy phone call to Zeppo only made her miss him more; he was thrilled to hear about Roman and Bernie.

Jean went in search of breakfast. As she walked across the yard toward the kitchen, René intercepted her and pulled her into an alcove near the pool.

"Jean!" he exclaimed, hurt and indignant. "Ted told me Bernie came out of your room this morning. You would rather be with a man who is gay than with me?"

"Don't even go there, René. I need some coffee." Jean pushed past him and went into the house.

She found the breakfast room off the kitchen, a sunny, pleasant room that actually had touches of yellow in its white décor. Roman sat at one of three round tables with coffee and his usual Spartan breakfast of fruit and yogurt, reading a newspaper.

"Good morning, you devil," she said as she took coffee and some of Laszlo's nut bread from the heavily laden buffet against the wall. "It's a good thing Bernie went out my door—René has already heard about it."

"You know I dislike this sort of duplicity."

"It's only for a couple of days." She sat down. "Besides, Bernie's worth it."

"Yes, he is." He pushed the newspaper toward her.

In a few minutes Tony joined them, serving himself eggs and hash browns. He and Roman talked football while Jean read the paper. To her annoyance, their pleasant interlude was interrupted by Sissy's arrival. She looked sleepy and hung over, and her black sundress emphasized her scrawny arms, which were nearly as thin as Farron Jones's.

"Good morning, all. Jean, I knew I'd catch you if I got up early." She visited the buffet table and sat down next to Jean with black coffee and dry toast. "So," she said, "how much do you make at *Wine Digest*? Forty thousand? You could make five times that much for a few months' work. And you'd be famous."

"No thanks," Jean said as politely as she could. "Let's drop it."

"I'm offering you a shot at the big time." She looked Jean over. "Somebody did a really nice job on your tits. Have you ever thought of having your nose done?"

"The tits are mine, Sissy. And I like my crooked nose." Roman and Tony watched the two women with amusement.

"You could even make a workout DVD," Sissy said. "How do you keep in shape?"

"Cycling and sex."

"And you're so witty. Do you ever wear makeup?"

"Only on Halloween."

Tony shook his head. "Sissy, don't you ever give up?"

"Never. That's what makes me so good at my job."

"Excuse me." Jean finished her coffee and hurried out the back door, anxious to get away before she said something rude. She decided to visit Katharine's island of sanity across the canyon, and to hell with what Ted thought about it. Up in the cloudless sky, several vultures circled an area past Katharine's house, beyond the far ridge.

As Jean went out the gate and past the big pool, she could see a man in blue trunks swimming laps—Ted himself. She tried to sneak by, but he noticed her and stopped to rest, pushing his goggles onto his head. "Jean, good morning," he said.

"Morning."

"You lied to me, young lady," he said sternly. "Last night after you retired, Carl told me that he recognized Roman—he's part of a gay and lesbian group that promotes self-defense. Carl saw his picture a few months ago in the *Los Angeles Times*. I should be angry with you, but it appears to be beside the point."

"Uh, that's right." Jean knew she shouldn't say too much—she was a very poor liar. "Bernie seems perfectly normal to me." At least that was true.

"I owe you a debt of gratitude, Jean, and I don't forget my debts."

She noted that he'd carefully avoided mentioning money—René had probably told him that she'd get angry if he tried to pay her for servicing his son. But the offer was there. She wondered briefly if she could get the price of Bernie's movie out of him.

"Well," Ted announced, "I have fourteen laps to go. Where are you off to so early?"

"Going for a walk." Jean waited until he was swimming again before she ducked behind the bushes and started across the canyon. As she walked along Ethan's path, she looked up at the vultures again. There were so many that she thought they must have found breakfast. She hoped Meide could see them from her bedroom. Jean was feeling less and less sympathy for the woman.

Katharine wasn't on the porch or in the yard, so Jean rang the bell, knocking and calling after a few moments. She tried the knob; the door was unlocked. Thinking Katharine might not have heard her, she searched the house. No one was home, but there was an empty bowl and spoon in the sink and a half-full mug of tea and two hearing aids sitting on the kitchen counter.

Katharine's green Trooper sat in the driveway, so she hadn't left that way. Jean looked into the birdhouse and flight cage, but no Katharine. Maybe a friend had taken her somewhere. Jean glanced toward the far ridge; she'd never before seen so many vultures in one place. Maybe Katharine had gone to investigate what the birds were eating. That's how she had found Pilar's body, after all. Jean set out along the narrow trail that led away from the house. Despite the heat, it was a beautiful morning, clear and still, the only noise her sandals slapping against the rock-hard ground. She called Katharine's name a few times, but realized the old woman probably couldn't hear her.

Jean had gone a couple hundred yards along a precarious trail around the side of a granite cliff when she saw what the vultures had found—at the bottom of the steep slope, Katharine's small, frail body sprawled against a boulder.

Chapter 10

"Oh my God," Jean said aloud. Three vultures pecked at Katharine's face, and Jean could see bloody holes where her eyes had been. A wooden cane rested on an outcropping halfway down the cliff face. Jean paced frantically back and forth along the path, trying to figure a way down so she could protect Katharine from the vultures. She could probably slide down on her butt with minimal risk, but getting up to the path again would be impossible. She looked around for help, but Phoenix Garden was too far away and there were no other houses or roads in view—just empty, rocky hills and vultures.

While she was deciding what to do, two more vultures landed and hopped over to Katharine's body. Jean yelled and waved her arms, but they ignored her. She threw a stone and hit one of the birds, scaring it into the air, but only for a moment. She would have to move fast. Jean ran along the path to Katharine's house and dialed 911 on the kitchen phone. A dispatcher told her they'd send an ambulance at once.

As she sat in the lovely old house, imagining what horrible things the vultures were doing to the body, a wave of sorrow washed over her and she sniffled and wiped her eyes. What had possessed Katharine to take that dangerous path? Was she losing it? She had seemed so together for a woman her age. Another explanation crossed Jean's mind: Someone had pushed Katharine. What were the odds of three unrelated deaths of people from the same small town? There had to be a connection. Was Katharine's death somehow connected to her finding Pilar's body? But then how would Domingo Huerta's murder tie in?

A tattered leather-bound address book lay near the phone. Even though Katharine had no children, there must be lots of people who should know what had happened. Jean flipped through the book and dialed the only person she knew: Bonnie Wexler, Katharine's friend who helped with the birds. Bonnie answered.

"This is Jean Applequist. I met you and Ethan at Katharine's."

"Yes, of course."

"Bonnie, I have really bad news. Sometime this morning Katharine fell from the trail near her house. She's dead."

Bonnie gasped. "I'll be there as soon as I can."

A few minutes later, Jean heard a siren and went outside to greet the ambulance pulling into the driveway. Two paramedics in dark blue uniforms got out, a skinny Latino youth and a blonde woman about Jean's age.

"We got a report of a fall," the woman said. "Is it Katharine?"

"Yes, she fell off the trail. I couldn't get down, but I know she's dead. I'll show you."

"Just tell us where. You wait here for the deputy."

Jean gestured toward the cliff. "Follow the vultures."

The two paramedics took a stretcher out of the ambulance and trotted along the trail. Deputy Sheriff Baeza arrived soon after and Jean directed him to the body.

In a little while, he came back alone, walking slowly, examining the bare ground and the brush on both sides, snapping photos of the area. "I've called the medical examiner and the search-and-rescue people to retrieve the body," he told Jean. He put the camera into the trunk of his car and wiped his neck with a blue bandanna. "You're one of the Lyons' guests, right?"

"I'm a journalist covering the wine tasting tomorrow." She stuck out her hand. "Jean Applequist."

"Matt Baeza." He shook her hand; his was big and sweaty. "I saw you sneaking around in the hallway when I was talking to Mr. Lyon."

Jean shrugged. "Hey, I'm a reporter."

"What are you doing over here?"

"I met Katharine yesterday and preferred her company to the crowd over there. I came to visit."

"How'd you get here?"

"There's a trail across the canyon that comes out near the big pool."

"Oh yeah. The one Ethan Wexler uses to spy on the Lyons. Did you see anyone?"

"No, not a soul. Just vultures." She told him how she had found the body.

"I'm assuming you phoned from the house. Did you touch anything else?"

"I walked around looking for her, but I just touched the phone. And her address book to call her friend Bonnie."

"How about on the trail?"

"I threw a stone at the vultures. I didn't touch anything else."

A blue Hyundai came up the narrow driveway and braked to a halt. Bonnie Wexler emerged, her eyes tearing up, and walked over to where they stood in the shade of a pepper tree. "She's really dead, isn't she? The ambulance is still here."

"I'm so sorry, Bonnie," Jean said.

The deputy put his arm around Bonnie's shoulders as she sobbed into a tissue. "The EMT says she probably died quickly," he said. "Looks like she went for a walk and lost her footing on the cliff."

"Matt, what in the world was she doing out there?" Bonnie said. "You know she never took that path anymore. She was afraid of falling and going to a nursing home." Bonnie blew her nose. "I'd better see to the birds. She may not have fed them." Bonnie moved off toward the birdhouse.

When she was gone, Jean squinted up at the vultures, still circling in the hot, cloudless sky. She looked at Matt. He was heavyset and had sweated through his beige uniform, but she liked his strong features and calm, intelligent manner. "What do you think happened? Did you see any tracks or anything on the trail?"

Matt shook his head. "No, but then you don't get much in the way of tracks on ground that hard, and whatever was there got obliterated when you and I and the paramedics went through."

"Do you really think she just took a walk and fell?"

"That's what I aim to find out. Katharine was really sharp, but you never know with someone that old."

"Could her death be connected to the other two? Could it be murder?"

He shrugged. "No way of knowing yet. But I'm definitely considering that possibility."

They were interrupted by Bonnie walking up from the birdhouse. "They haven't been fed. That means Katharine went out early, before eight A.M."

"Do you need help?" Jean asked.

"No, thanks. The birds are a little spooked anyway, with their schedule thrown off." She went into the garage and soon emerged carrying a white package of dead mice.

Jean waited on a bench in the shade while Matt looked around in the house. In a little while Bonnie sat next to her.

"I have to call my husband," she told Jean. "He'll be so upset. So will Ethan." Bonnie sniffled. "With a friend this old, you expect her to die at any time, but I always thought she'd be sick first and we'd get to say good-bye."

"Does she have any relatives?" Jean asked.

"No one close. But she has hundreds of friends."

Matt came out of the house and Bonnie left, promising to keep Jean posted.

"The forensics people will go over the house thoroughly, so stay out of there," Matt said. "I'm going to ask some questions at the Lyons' place. Come on, I'll give you a lift. I don't want you walking on that path again until we've had a chance to check it out."

Jean got into the squad car. She'd been in police cars a few times, but never before in the front seat. "Are you going to question the guests?" she asked, relishing the thought of Matt facing off with Ted Lyon again.

"I'll talk to them, but I'm mostly interested in the help." He started the car and drove out the driveway. "They're up and around much earlier. If anything did go on this morning, a gardener or maid may have seen it."

"Did you question the guests about the other murder? The waitress?"

"I know you're an amateur detective, but I can't discuss an ongoing homicide investigation, especially with the press."

He drove to a side road and along the main street to Lyon Way. Partway up the hill, he took the gravel road that led to the Jones's trailer. He slowed as they drove by the house. Mojo, lying on the porch, raised his head as they passed.

"Are you looking for evidence of a meth lab?" Jean asked.

Matt glanced at her. "Why do you ask?"

"My photographer is the one who gave Ted Lyon the idea."

The deputy turned back to his examination of the neat prefab house. "He may be right. Honey's fixed the fence, and that shed has a new lock. I'll have a closer look later on."

"I heard you say Farron is on parole. What did he do?"

"He did time for assault with a deadly weapon, and before that for arson. Recently he did some short time for possession of crystal meth. His next serious bust will be strike three, and he'll spend the next thirty years in prison."

"That guy won't live thirty years. He must be pushing sixty."

"He's forty-three. Honey's a couple years younger."

"Seriously?" Jean said in amazement. "They look really old."

Matt snorted. "There are no old meth cooks."

"When we first drove up, we stopped here for a minute and Honey came out with a rifle."

"That doesn't mean anything—the woman's mean as a snake," Matt said as he accelerated past the house. "She always waves a gun at uninvited visitors, but she hasn't shot anyone yet."

Jean's curiosity got the better of her. "Gloria told me you used to be a homicide detective in Phoenix. What brought you back to Valle de los Osos?"

"I like the area. I grew up around here. My mother's a Luiseño Mission Indian."

"I've heard of them. Don't they own that casino as you come into town?"

"No, they own the one just east of town." He made a face. "It's a great idea: the poor stealing from the poor. Those two casinos have created a lot of traffic and crime problems here."

"So you're opposed to Indian casinos?"

"Yeah, but I'm definitely in the minority. It's hard to argue with all that easy money." He pulled into the Lyons' driveway. "Thanks for your help, Jean." He handed her a business card. "Let me know if you think of anything else."

Chencho let them in the front door, shaking Matt's hand warmly. In answer to Jean's question, he told her Bernie and Roman were playing tennis and directed her to the courts, then led Matt along the hall to see Ted.

Jean followed Chencho's directions away from the canyon to two green tennis courts inside a high chain-link fence. She spotted the guys on the far court, shaded by a couple of bushy palm trees. Bernie was in fashionable tennis whites, Roman in gray shorts, a plain white T-shirt, and a Giants baseball cap. She watched them for a few moments; Roman had a stronger serve but Bernie was a better player. They were laughing, and neither of them was trying very hard to win. Jean sighed. At least one potentially great thing had come from this horrible weekend. She waited until they were switching serves to let herself in.

"Jean!" Roman called when he saw her. "Where have you been? We were afraid Sissy scared you back to San Francisco."

"Oh, Roman. I went over to see Katharine, the woman who lives across the canyon. She's dead. I found her body. The vultures were all over it." Jean swallowed a lump in her throat. "She fell off the trail near her house. Or maybe she was pushed."

The two men came over to her, setting their rackets on a bench. Roman put his arms around her and hugged her tight. He was hot and sweaty, but she didn't care.

Bernie put his hand on her back. "That's terrible news," he said softly. "What bad luck for you to be the first one there."

They sat on the bench and Jean told them what had happened.

"Do you think it was murder?" Roman asked.

"I don't know," Jean said. "If there is something suspicious about her death, the deputy will realize it. He seems pretty sharp. He's questioning the people up here right now. He'll probably want to talk to you two. Bernie, you can tell him you were with me all night if it comes up. I think that qualifies as a white lie."

"It qualifies as a felony," Roman said. "This charade is getting out of hand."

Bernie reached across Jean to pat his knee. "Don't worry, I'll tell Matt the truth. He's very close-mouthed, and he and my father aren't exactly pals." He shook his head. "What a shame. She was a great lady. I'll have to call my sister, Lydia—she and Katharine were friends."

"I feel like shit," Jean said. "I need a swim."

"Good idea," Roman said. "It's getting too hot for tennis."

They walked slowly back to the cabins in the intensifying heat, Roman's arm around Jean's shoulders, Bernie carrying the tennis gear. Jean sighed again. "I suppose dying quickly at ninety-two isn't so terrible. It could have been worse—Katharine's friend said she was worried about ending up in a nursing home."

"A quick death is always a better death," Roman said, and Jean knew he was thinking of all his friends who had died slowly from AIDS.

Bernie continued up to the main house as Jean and Roman went to their cabins to change. Jean called Zeppo and told him what had happened.

"Now you've got three bodies," he said.

"There's no obvious connection among them except that Katharine found Pilar's body. And Angus, the guy I like best for the killing in San Francisco, wasn't even here when Pilar was killed."

"I don't suppose I could talk you into coming home right now."

"I know you're worried, but I really don't feel threatened. The only people who are bothering me are Sissy and René, and they're harmless. And the Sauternes tasting is tomorrow. No way I'm missing that unless there's an 8.0 earthquake. I'll be home soon."

They said their good-byes. Jean put on her swimsuit and met Roman and Bernie at the big pool. In spite of her dark mood, Jean couldn't help smiling at them—Bernie looked cute in Hawaiian-print trunks, and Roman, in a black Speedo, looked good enough to eat.

Roman and Bernie horsed around at one end of the pool while Jean swam laps. She always found comfort and escape in physical exertion, whether exercise or sex, and she quickly lost herself, pushing hard, concentrating on the rhythm of her strokes, forgetting everything but movement, breathing, and the cool, cleansing water.

Finally she paused to rest, feeling breathless and exhausted, and looked around. The two men lay side by side on chaise lounges they'd pulled into the shade, talking in low tones. Sissy, wearing huge sunglasses and a black straw hat, sat at a table under an umbrella, a pile of paperback books beside her. Jean thought about doing more laps but was too tired, and hungry as well. She got out of the pool and plopped down near Roman in a chair at one of the umbrella tables.

"I hope you three realize you're not fooling anyone but Ted," Sissy rasped.

"We don't need to fool anyone but Ted," Bernie said.

Sissy got up and moved to Jean's table, carrying her books. "Jean," she said, "I just talked to the deputy. He says you found another body. You seem to have a genius for this sort of thing."

"What sort of thing?" Jean asked, gritting her teeth.

"Why, getting involved with unnatural death, of course. Unnatural death sells. That's why you need an agent who understands the market." She put a hand on the pile of books. "I've brought you some books. They'll give you an idea of what true crime writing's all about. I'm assuming you've already read *In Cold Blood*." She picked the books up one at a time. "Here's *The Billionaire Boys' Club*, Sue Horton's book about Joe Hunt, and here's Maureen Orth's thing about Andrew Cunanan, and one about the Menendez brothers. And this is the best book on OJ. Look these over."

Jean couldn't remember the last time she'd been forced to exercise so much self-control over such a long period of time. It went against her nature. Finding Katharine had shaken her, and she desperately needed to blow off some steam. Pushing Sissy in the pool would be gratifying, but then she would never taste those wines.

"Sissy, Jean just found a body being eaten by vultures," Bernie said. "Can't you let up even for a minute?"

"Oh Bernie, what do you know about business?" Sissy said, pushing up her African leather bracelets.

"Why are you so thin?" Jean demanded, feeling nasty. "Do you have an eating disorder? Anorexia, or maybe bulimia?"

"Don't change the subject, Jean. I've got a copy of my standard contract in my room. You can look it over later."

Jean was at the end of her limited patience. She stood, gathered up the paperback books, and flung them into the pool. "Listen, you vulture. This is getting really tiresome. I'm not writing a fucking word about Martin Wingo for any amount of money, and that's absolutely final."

Sissy smiled, calmly watching the books bob on the surface of the water. "You'll change your mind."

Jean picked up her caftan in disgust and stomped into the house.

Chapter 11

"There you are, Jean," René said as he came out of the library. "The deputy told me what has happened. I'm very sorry, *ma pauvre petite*."

She let him give her a comforting hug. He smelled good, and his bony embrace made her think of Zeppo. "Oh Jean," he said softly into her ear, "how can you be this near to me and not feel as I do?" She felt his hands slide down to her butt, pulling her closer.

Jean pushed him away. "Leave me alone, you old satyr."

They heard a car pull up outside. Jean opened the front door; a tall brunette got out of a white limo, looking cool, chic, and thoroughly French in well-cut navy slacks and a navy and white striped T-shirt. This had to be René's wife.

Jean glanced back at René, who stood out of Monique's line of sight behind the door; the imprint of her wet swimsuit was clearly visible on his shorts and batik shirt. He looked down at himself and saw it, too. She decided to throw a scare into him.

"Welcome," Jean said, stepping outside. "I'm Jean Applequist. You must be Monique." Behind her René gasped. She heard him scurrying down the hall toward his room.

"Oh yes. René has spoken of you. I'm happy to meet you." Monique offered her hand and smiled, revealing a network of fine laugh lines, and Jean realized the woman was probably René's age. Still, she looked like the kind of gorgeous, empty-headed clotheshorse he'd marry. The driver unloaded several leather suitcases in the foyer and drove off. "Why is there a police car here?" Monique asked.

"There was an accident at the neighbor's. An old woman fell to her death hiking in the canyon." Jean was glad to discover that Monique was not the jealous type.

Monique shook her head. "That's so very sad. Usually I am more nervous in American cities, but the countryside is dangerous in its own way."

"I'm starting to agree with you." Jean led her inside. "Funny. René was here a minute ago. I think he said he was in the rat room. Let's go find him."

"I'm so glad you're covering this tasting," Monique said pleasantly as they walked down the hall. "It means so much to René, and we always enjoy your pieces in the *Digest*."

"Are you in the wine business, too?" Jean asked.

"No, I'm a cardiologist."

"Oh." Maybe she had underestimated René. But that didn't mean she'd let him off the hook. She pretended to find his room for the first time. "Here we are." She knocked lightly and opened the door to find René coming out of the bathroom tucking in his shirt—he'd managed to get into dry clothes.

"Ah, Monique!" he exclaimed, gathering her into his arms, looking daggers at Jean over her head. He gave his wife a kiss, and there followed a torrent of French and more kissing. Jean left them alone.

Jean's stomach growled, so she slipped on her caftan and headed toward the back of the house, which smelled delightfully of tomatoes and seafood. In the kitchen, Laszlo and Tina were hard at work on lunch.

The chef stood at the stove stirring something in a big stainless steel pot that was the source of the aromas. "Hey, Jean," he said when he saw her, setting the spoon down and walking toward her. "Matt Baeza was just here. He told me what happened to Katharine. Poor old gal. Finding her must have been rough."

"It was a lot rougher on her. Did your staff see anything this morning?"

"Nah, we couldn't help much. The canyon was pretty quiet when we came on at seven thirty. Matt's thinking her death might be tied to the other murders. But who would want to hurt a great old lady like her?"

"Good question."

Laszlo took her arm. "Here, have a taste of this cioppino. It'll give you a reason to live." He led her to the stove, dipped a fork into the big pot, and fed her a fat shrimp dripping with dark red sauce.

Jean smiled at him as she chewed. It was wonderful. "Thanks, Laszlo. When's lunch?"

"Half an hour."

"I'll go change." Jean went to her cabin, showered, and put on capris and a T-shirt. As she walked back to the house, Chencho came up to her. "Excuse me, Miss Applequist?"

"What can I do for you?"

"Mr. Lyon would like to see you for a minute before lunch, OK? In the library."

"Sure." As she went along the hall, male voices drifted out to her—Ted and Tony arguing. She paused to listen just outside the library door.

". . . responsible for your mismanagement," Ted was saying.

"You cut me off now and that's the end," Tony said, a pleading note in his voice. "I don't need much—just enough to pay my vendors for a month or two, until the new ad campaign is ready. That'll turn things around."

"No. I'd be throwing good money after bad. Now let's drop the subject. I told you I didn't want to talk business this weekend."

Tony made an exasperated noise, and Jean heard his footsteps on the marble floor. She pretended she'd just arrived as he went out past her, scowling. "Hi, Tony," she said warmly. She pitied anyone who was at Ted's mercy. Tony gave her a distracted smile but said nothing.

In the library, Ted was once again contemplating his family tree. He turned when she came in. "Ah, there you are. I've spoken with the deputy. Apparently he has a new reason for bothering my guests."

The man's self-absorption was impressive. "So you think Katharine fell just to annoy you?"

"You presume too much, young lady. It was regrettable that you found the body, but you had no business over there in the first place. Do you pretend not to know there were bad feelings between us?"

"*You* presume too much, Ted," she said, trying to keep her tone cool. "I'm here to cover this tasting for my magazine, period. Anything else I do is none of your business, and that includes whatever is between Bernie and me."

Ted gave her a patronizing smile. "I was told that you're prickly."

"Told by whom? René?"

"By your boss, as a matter of fact." He waved a hand, dismissing the matter. "Since there's no chance of your repeating this particular error, I'll let it slide. Now let's go have lunch."

Jean bit her lip. What did he think he was going to do if she misbehaved again, spank her? This weekend was turning into one long pain in the ass. Only acute hunger and the prospect of Laszlo's cooking made her follow Ted through the house to a dining room.

They were the last to arrive. The guests, sipping drinks, had gathered around an array of appetizers on a sideboard. A large, intricate Chinese tapestry of a dragon in shades of blue on a peach-colored ground was hung against one wall.

As the guests turned to greet the newcomers, Ted cleared his throat. "For those of you who don't already know," he said when the talking had died down, "the deputy is here again and wants to have a brief word with those of you he hasn't spoken to yet, after lunch. The neighbor across the way has died in a fall. Jean found her body this morning."

There were gasps and subdued exclamations from the group. "How dreadful for you, Jean," Yuan said, a compassionate frown on his face.

"I'm starting to see a pattern, Ted," Sissy said. "Every time we visit you, one of your neighbors dies."

Jasper, sipping a martini, winked at Jean. "You seem to have a real nose for news, young lady. You were there when that body fell on Ted's car, weren't you?"

Ted snorted. "This death hardly counts as news. The woman was ninety-two, and she fell."

Jean glowered at Ted but said nothing.

In a few minutes everyone sat down. Chencho and one of the maids served the cioppino—besides shrimp, it contained scallops, crab, clams and fish—and, on the side, a big green salad and French bread. Jean noticed a plain chicken breast on Meide's plate. Apparently she wasn't craving normal food yet.

Gloria poured Italian wines, Tignanello and a Gaja Chardonnay. Jean sat between Bernie and Roman, who were beginning to seem far too friendly in public. Across the table from her, Tony was quiet and glum. As the great food and wine relaxed her and lifted her spirits, she made an effort to cheer Tony up, and eventually had him smiling. At one point Jean noticed someone was missing. "Hey, where's Carl?" she asked Bernie.

He looked around. "Dad, isn't Carl joining us?"

Ted, at the next table, swallowed. "Apparently he got a call early this morning from his Beverly Hills office. There's some sort of crisis he has to deal with personally. He left me a note saying he'd try to be back for the tasting tomorrow."

"Let's hope he makes it," Jean said, winking at Bernie. She really hoped she had seen the last of Carl. Now if Sissy would only be called back to her office in New York.

After lunch, as the guests drifted out of the dining room, Chencho caught Jean's attention. "Ms. Applequist," he said in a low voice. "I have a friend who wants to talk to you. Could you please come outside for a minute?"

Intrigued, Jean followed him down the hall and out the back door into the heat to a late-model Lexus parked at the far end of the driveway, behind the old cars and purple van. The windows were rolled up and the engine running. The woman who leaned across and opened the passenger door was an attractive Latina in her mid-forties, wearing a pink T-shirt and shorts. A diamond tennis bracelet glittered on her brown wrist. She smiled nervously at Jean. Her lipstick was pink, too.

"This is Maria Esposito," Chencho said, as they both leaned down to look into the car. "She's a friend from my church. She wants to ask you something."

Jean, puzzled but curious, got into the car. The cranked-up air conditioner made the beige leather seats cool.

"*Gracias*, Chencho," Maria said. He shut the door and waved as he walked back across the drive.

"Thank you for coming," Maria said as they shook hands.

"No problem." Jean waited for the woman to speak. Maria hesitated, working her hands together. There was a gold band and a diamond solitaire on her left ring finger.

"My maiden name is Ochoa," she said finally. "I'm . . . I was Pilar's aunt."

"The girl who was killed?"

"Yes. That's why I'm here. I read about that other murder you solved, up in San Francisco. Chencho told me you were here." She stopped, and then said in a rush, "I want you to find out who killed Pilar."

Jean sighed. "I'm not a detective. In that case I knew the victim, and I got lucky."

Maria picked up a Coach purse from the floor of the Lexus and pulled out a wallet. "I want to show you something." She took out a photo and handed it to Jean. "Here's Pilar's senior picture from high school."

Jean looked at the face in the photo. It was the same photo she'd seen on the Internet—a pretty young woman with wide-set brown eyes and a small Cupid's-bow mouth. Her dark hair had been carefully styled and she wore a lavender sweater and a pearl necklace. She had the same lively eyes and heart-shaped face as Maria.

"She was beautiful," Jean said, handing the picture back. "I'm so sorry about what happened, but I don't see how I can help."

"You can help because you're here with the people who last saw her alive. The investigators in San Diego don't care about a poor Mexican girl like her. They've forgotten Pilar. No one from homicide has been here in weeks. I'm asking you because Chencho says you're not like the Lyons. He says your photographer is Latino and that you're good friends."

"I hope I'm not like the Lyons," Jean said. "What about Matt Baeza? He hasn't forgotten Pilar."

"I know, but he's brown-skinned, too. The Lyons' friends won't talk to him like they'll talk to you." Maria frowned, showing a deep furrow between her eyebrows. "There's another reason I'm asking, besides for Pilar herself. Her father, Salvador, is my oldest brother. My mother brought us north from Mexico when I was six years old. Our father died young. Salvador took care of all five of us kids, worked two or three jobs, never got past the tenth grade so we could all finish school. Now he runs a landscaping business with his two sons.

"My husband's trucking company has done very well and I have a successful bridal shop, so I try to help Salvador's family when I can. But he and my husband don't get along, and he's very old-fashioned. He doesn't want money from a woman.

"My brother's life has been hard, and it's made him hard. But Pilar was special. She was his youngest, and so lively and pretty. He was a harsh man, except with her. She could always get away with anything, always make him laugh." Jean could see Maria's emotions rise as she spoke. "When she was killed, it broke him. Now he won't go to work, won't eat or get out of bed. I think he wants to die, too." She fought back tears. "Rosa, his wife, is a devout Catholic, and that's brought her some comfort, but Salvador has nothing. His boys are trying to keep the business going, but they can't do it without him. I want to help him. I'll pay you." Maria took a tissue out of her bag and wiped her eyes.

"Finding the killer won't bring her back," Jean said gently.

"I know. But it might bring Salvador back."

Jean put her hand on the woman's arm, wanting to give her something, but not false hope. "I'm not going to promise that I'll find out who killed her, but if I do learn anything that would help solve her murder, I promise to tell Matt. And you don't have to pay me."

"Thank you." Maria took a breath, composed again. "Let me tell you a little about her. Pilar was a good daughter. The boys have their own apartments, but she still lived at home because her daddy didn't want her to move out. She was very outgoing, very friendly. I know she must have talked to some of the Lyons' friends that night. She came home late after the party, and Salvador and Rosa were already in bed. They heard her come in but didn't speak to her. And they were both gone to work by the time she got up to go to her job at the restaurant. So they feel like they let her down, like they should have stayed up to see her or say something to her." She sighed deeply. "That's a sad house, and I don't know what to do to help them."

"They're lucky to have you," Jean said. "You should hire a professional investigator."

"That's what I'm going to do if you don't find anything out, hire a detective. But those people will be more likely to talk to you because you're one of them."

"I'm not so sure about that. But I'll try."

Maria gazed out the car window. “It’s the worst thing that can happen to a person, to lose a child.”

“Do you have children?”

She turned back to Jean. “Yes, a boy and a girl. Younger than Pilar. She used to babysit for me. I always thought I’d plan her wedding. There’s a dress in my store she loved.” She shook her head. “I just don’t understand what could have happened to her.”

“Did she have enemies, jealous boyfriends, anything like that?”

“No. She dated a few local boys, but Matt has already checked them out. He’s very good at his job. That’s why I think those people must know something.”

“Maria, give me your phone number and I’ll let you know if I find out anything useful.”

She handed Jean a pale pink business card that said “Brides by Maria.” They shook hands again and Jean got out of the car. The Lexus backed out and went slowly down the hill.

Jean walked to the house and went into the kitchen; Laszlo was smoking a cigarette on his stool at the counter while two maids loaded the big dishwasher. “Laszlo, can I ask you something? At Meide’s birthday, were all the same people here?”

“Lemme think.” He took a pull on his cigarette. “Yeah, the same gang, plus a few friends from Long Beach and a couple of relatives from Taiwan. But not Angus or Yuan. Angus has been to the Long Beach place, but this is the first time I’ve seen those two here. Why?”

“Just curious. Thanks.” She went down the hall, finding most of the guests in the library. Jasper, Sissy, Meide, and Yuan were playing bridge. Bernie and Ted sat at the chessboard, and Roman browsed the bookshelves. René and Monique were nowhere to be seen; Jean hoped he’d leave her alone now that his wife was here. Tony and Angus were missing, too.

She walked over to the chess game. "You know what Raymond Chandler said about chess?" she asked Bernie.

"That it's the most elaborate waste of human intelligence outside of an advertising agency."

"Hmph." Ted moved a knight. "He probably wasn't very good at the game."

Jean gazed out the big window, thinking about Pilar and her heartbroken father, wondering who in the world killed her and what the motive could have been. She wanted to help Maria, but as she looked around the room she couldn't imagine any of them stabbing a woman with an ice pick under any circumstances. Well, maybe Sissy if a book deal was involved. And how were Domingo Huerta and Katharine connected to Pilar? She needed to talk to Zeppo. What was he doing now? Midafternoon on Friday—he'd be in chemistry class. She imagined him taking notes in a big lecture hall, getting bored, maybe thinking of her. Suddenly a series of loud sharp noises outside made her jump. They sounded like gunshots.

Her heart pounding, she looked out and saw two figures below her on the terrace—Tony and Angus firing shotguns into the air. Her alarm subsided when she realized they were shooting at orange clay pigeons arcing past them from the left. Tony wore shorts and a polo shirt, to which he'd added a Panama hat. Angus sported a long, loose white garment with some sort of Arab headdress. "Oh, skeet shooting," Jean said. "They scared the hell out of me."

Bernie looked up. "Angus is really good, old soldier that he is."

Roman joined Jean at the window as Tony missed a shot. "Roman," she said. "Get a load of Angus's outfit."

"He has been in Afghanistan, I perceive."

"Holmes to Watson, *A Study in Scarlet,"* Jean said. Come on—I want photos of that."

"I'll get a camera."

Jean went out into the blistering heat, and soon Roman, in sunglasses and Giants cap, met her on the terrace with his equipment. He set his case in the shade and took several frames of the men shooting.

"Going to run a picture of Angus of Arabia in the magazine?" Tony asked when his turn was done.

"That headdress is Afghan, not Arab, isn't it?" Roman said to Angus.

Angus lowered his gun. "Yeah. Got the outfit in Kabul a few years back."

"What were you doing in Kabul?" Roman asked. "Helping out the Mujahideen against the Soviets?"

"Something like that." Angus squinted up at the white-hot sky. "This weather reminds me of Kabul's in the summer—a lot like hell, but hotter and drier."

"I imagine living there is a lot like hell—first the Taliban and now the war." Roman put his camera into its case. "No doubt you're one of the people who trained and armed the future members of Al-Qaeda."

Angus shrugged. "You've got to expect some blowback if you're not willing to finish a job." He turned to Roman. "You know what the Taliban do to people like you?"

"People like me?" An edge crept into Roman's voice. "You mean photographers?"

"Nah, gays. They crush them under a brick wall." Angus grinned, but his wolf's eyes didn't change.

Tony shook his head. "Come on, Angus. The Taliban may be living in the fourteenth century, but last time I looked it was the twenty-first century here. If I told you who's gay in the NFL, you'd call me a liar."

Roman smiled at Tony. "Is that a Perazzi shotgun?"

Jean looked at Roman in amazement. His typical reaction to this sort of gay-baiting was a withering verbal attack. But now he was exercising uncharacteristic restraint. Could he possibly be getting serious about Bernie after only a day?

"Yeah," Tony said. "Ted's got a nice collection of shotguns." Tony led Roman over to a table against the house and showed him a couple of other guns, leaving Jean standing next to Angus.

He looked her up and down. His face was flushed from the heat and there was a strange gleam in his eyes that hadn't been there yesterday. "So you're the killer," he said in a low voice. "I read about it. Six .38 slugs in the chest at point-blank range, eh? He was probably dead with the first shot. Just like a woman to waste all that ammo."

Away from Ted's watchful eye, Angus was not only openly hostile, he was giving off vibes that scared Jean. Carl was a creep, but this man was something altogether different. She prided herself on being able to spot sexual predators; in fact her safety often depended on it. A woman who took chances with men had to have reliable radar. Angus made the hair on the back of her neck stand up. She held his gaze, being careful not to blink.

The hot wind blew his headdress back over his shoulder, giving her a glimpse of his maimed ear. "What happened to your ear?" she asked sharply. "Did you shoot it off by accident? Or did somebody else shoot it off on purpose?"

He shook his head. "Basal cell carcinoma. The sun doesn't like me. That's why I dress this way. The Afghans are a primitive bunch, but they know how to keep the sun off." He offered her the shotgun. "Want to shoot at a moving target?"

"No. I hate guns." She glanced at Roman. He was trying to keep a low profile, but she couldn't resist creating a confrontation. "Roman's a really good shot. Ask him." Roman gave her a narrow-eyed look.

Angus smirked. "Don't tell me those fags of yours can shoot as well."

"Of course," Roman said. "Nothing discourages gay-bashing like a well-armed queer."

"Hey, Angus," Tony said, "that's something to keep in mind the next time you push some gay guy around."

"You know how to play this game?" Angus said.

"I've done it before."

Angus barked instructions to the man operating the clay pigeon machine and the duel commenced. Jean and Tony watched from the shade of a tree. The hostility and testosterone were palpable as the two men fired in turn. Neither of them said anything beyond "pull," and neither of them missed a shot. Below her, Jean could see that a few gardeners had joined the man operating the machine. They were talking animatedly in Spanish and exchanging cash.

"Look, Tony," she said, nudging him. "They're placing bets. Who do you suppose is the favorite?"

"Hard to say. I would've put my money on Angus, since he always beats the pants off me, but Roman's pretty damn good."

As she was trying to figure out a way to climb down and ask about the odds, Chencho came onto the terrace, giving Jean a warm smile. She wondered if he'd talked to Maria.

"Hi, Chencho," Tony said. "Want to place a bet?"

"No thanks. Gloria says the Burgundy tasting will start in half an hour."

"We'll be there," Jean said. During a break in the shooting she called out. "Hey, guys. Let's call it a tie. We're tasting soon."

Roman lowered his gun. "I'm willing if you are," he said to Angus. "I have to go take pictures."

Angus wiped a sleeve across his sweaty brow. "OK. But we'll finish this before the weekend's out."

Chapter 12

Back in her cabin, Jean washed her face and put on a sleeveless light blue knit top, a dark blue silk sarong skirt she'd made, and sandals. She knocked on Roman's door and went in when he replied. He was in the bathroom with a white towel around his waist, shaking a can of shaving cream. She leaned against the bathroom doorframe. "That guy Angus gives me the creeps."

"You heard what he said about Afghanistan. And did you notice his eyes, and the way he moves? I'll bet money he was Special Forces."

"No shit. Are you sure?"

"Remember my martial arts teacher I told you about? The navy SEAL cashiered for being gay? He taught me the symptoms."

"So he could easily have broken Domingo Huerta's neck and tossed him off a building," Jean said. "But Laszlo told me he wasn't here when the waitress was stabbed. And why in the world would he kill Katharine?"

"Yet it's hard to imagine the three deaths aren't connected somehow."

"Could you have beaten Angus if the shooting match went on long enough?"

"I'm not sure. He's a phenomenal shot, but the heat was getting to him."

She watched Roman squirt out a handful of shaving cream and apply it to his face. "When was the last time you shaved twice in one day?"

"It's been awhile. But we can't have Bernie showing up at the breakfast table with whisker burn." He picked up his razor and worked carefully around his goatee.

"What's he like, Roman?"

"Somewhat bottled up and wary, as I am, but for different reasons. He tends to attract hustlers and sycophants."

"Is he HIV negative?"

Roman grinned at her through the shaving cream. "Yes, he is. He's young enough to have dodged that bullet."

"What's he like in bed?"

Roman turned back to the mirror, still grinning. "We're very good together. Let's leave it at that."

Jean was disappointed that she wouldn't get any details. "Roman, I just had a very strange experience." She told him about Maria Esposito and Pilar and Salvador. "Maria thinks I can help because Chencho told her I'm not a racist and she's read accounts of the Wingo case."

"What a tragedy. I can empathize with Salvador. My father may be a rigid, unforgiving homophobe, but he has a similar relationship with Lupe, my youngest sister. It's a common family dynamic—the stern patriarch doting on the adorable youngest daughter."

"Well, I'm the youngest in my family, and my father thinks I'm the Antichrist."

"He's probably the reason you have such a difficult time relating to men."

"That must be it," Jean said, smiling. "I'd sure like to help Maria, but I can't very well grill all the guests. If you overhear anything pertinent, let me know, OK?"

"Of course. Sounds as if the Castro Street Irregulars are back on the job," he said, using a term he'd coined during the Wingo investigation. He rinsed his razor. "Nearly everyone here wants something from you, don't they?"

"Yeah. What do you want?"

"I want you to leave so I can take a shower."

"Don't mind me."

"Be careful or I'll phone your boss and claim sexual harassment." He shut the door slowly, pushing her into the bedroom.

"See you there," she called as she went out the door.

In the wine cellar, Chencho was setting up the long table for tasting and Gloria stood at the sideboard opening wine with a counter-mounted corkscrew.

"Hi, you two," Jean said to their friendly greeting. She felt a shiver of anticipation as she read the labels—the tasting would be a vertical of twelve vintages of Domaine de la Romanée-Conti Le Montrachet, arguably the finest dry white wine in the world, going back to 1966. She put a hand on one of the bottles, pleased that it was cellar temperature. It was a crime to serve these wines too cold.

She looked more closely at the table—besides water glasses, pitchers for spitting out wine, and baskets of plain bread cubes, there were six Riedel Chardonnay glasses at each place setting. She did some quick math in her head: It was easily $5,000 worth of crystal. Pots of white orchids decorated the tables and sideboard—whoever was in charge had wisely chosen scentless flowers.

Roman arrived next. He set up his lights and took photos of the room, the table, the bottles lined up on the sideboard. Soon the guests drifted in and arranged themselves around the table. Jean sat down beside Bernie. She caught Yuan's eye as he came through the door; he smiled and started toward her, but Meide called to him and he sat next to her, giving Jean an apologetic shrug. Tony took the chair instead.

As they settled in, Chencho picked up a bottle and poured tastes into the first glass at each place, followed by Gloria with another bottle. Meide took only a tiny sip of each wine, spitting delicately into her crystal pitcher. Roman moved around the table as the group tasted through the first few wines, getting shots of the guests, and finally sat down next to Bernie to try the wines himself.

They started with the rich yet elegant 2009, which had lovely citrus and peach aromas and a mineral note on the palate. The 2004 was ripe and full-bodied for the vintage, with spicy notes of anise and pear. These two wines, like the flamboyant 2003, all needed more time in the bottle. The 1997 was pale yellow, with vanilla on the nose and rich, spicy, complex flavors. The wines were merely great until they got to 1986, which was fabulous, smelling almost like coconut, the flavors full and mouth-filling. The vintages from the seventies were less impressive, and two of the bottles were corked. The 1966, a superb vintage, had held up amazingly well. It was golden with age, but its bouquet and flavors still soared.

René spat into his pitcher. "Ah, lovely," he said. "The perfect expression of the Chardonnay grape. California winemakers are all trying to make Montrachet. They seek the toasty oak, the full fruit flavors, and the rich buttery quality. But will they ever equal this?"

"Dollar for dollar, I think they already have," Tony said. "For the price of one of these bottles, you can get ten bottles of killer California Chardonnay."

Ted chuckled indulgently. "These things don't always come down to money. There is such a thing as pure vintner's art."

"You of all people know better, Ted," Tony said. "Just about everything comes down to money."

"Indeed," Jasper said. "If it weren't for money, we'd be drinking plonk and reading about these wines in Jean's magazine."

"Thanks to our generous host, we avoid that sad fate," Yuan said, raising his glass. They all toasted Ted with varying degrees of enthusiasm and resumed the tasting.

At dinner afterward, Laszlo served a classic coq au vin, the best version Jean had ever eaten. He'd used chanterelles, and the sauce tasted suspiciously like the great red Burgundy Gloria poured to go with it, the one Jean had spotted in the cellar. Meide had chicken and salad.

Gloria served coffee and after-dinner drinks in the main living room, and soon afterward the poker foursome drifted off to the library. The wind had died down, so Jean took her glass of Cognac outside. Roman and Bernie were living dangerously, standing near the pool talking, having much too good a time. They were so engrossed in their conversation that Jean decided not to interrupt them.

Yuan came up beside her. "It seems you are not Bernie's favorite after all," he said lightly.

"Is it that obvious?"

"Well, I know Bernie is gay, and I have observed Roman and him together. And the cabins have connecting doors."

"Let's hope Ted doesn't figure it out."

"I doubt if he will. He sees only what he wishes to see."

"I've noticed that about him." Jean looked Yuan over. He smiled at her, his dark Asian eyes nearly black in the dim light. His coarsely woven linen jacket, cotton slacks, and plain T-shirt, all in shades of beige, looked good on him, and she found him very attractive. And since he hadn't been at Meide's birthday party, he wasn't a suspect in Pilar's death. Also, he certainly didn't look as if he could break a man's neck and throw him off a building.

Jean craved the release of sex, but tonight she felt drained and depressed, and annoyed with Roman for making her feel guilty about stepping out on Zeppo. If anything was going to happen, it was up to Yuan.

"You've had a very unpleasant time today," he said. "How are you feeling?"

"Pretty lousy."

"I read of the case you were involved in, so I know you have seen death before, but I also know that makes it no easier. I have seen too much of it myself."

"Where have you seen it?"

"In China, during the Cultural Revolution. But we'll not speak of ancient history. Your experience was more immediate. Come with me to the gallery. Being among fine works of art renews the spirit."

Jean looked around. To her surprise Roman and Sissy were deep in conversation at one of the tables. Bernie stood at the edge of the canyon chatting with René and Monique, who looked stunning in a simple orange dress. Everyone else had gone inside. Jean set her glass down without a word and went with Yuan into the house.

The gallery was open but empty. Yuan touched her back lightly as they made a slow circuit, looking at the displays, Jean asking questions about the pieces. She sat down on a leather bench in front of the little golden rhinoceros, still her favorite. To her surprise Yuan opened the cabinet and took out the rhino. "Would you like to hold him?"

"Won't you set off an alarm?" she asked.

"The cabinets do not have alarms, according to Meide, only the room itself. That way people can handle the art if they desire."

"What a great idea," Jean said, taking the little statue in her hands. She always wanted to touch the pieces in museums, and loved seeing the rhino's intricate workmanship up close. It felt cool and heavy; she felt a thrill at the thought that it was nearly 4,000 years old. Finally she gave it back. "You're right—it's very calming here. I feel better."

Yuan put the animal away and sat down next to her. "Good. I find great works of art relaxing as well, but they also have an unusual effect on me. If I sit with them long enough, contemplate them deeply enough, I become physically aroused. Do you find that odd?" He was very close to her now.

Jean smiled at him. "Maybe a little. But I can think of worse kinks."

"With you beside me as well, I am nearly overcome." He leaned toward her and kissed her, running his hands up and down her bare arms. His kisses were soft, delicious, meltingly erotic, and Jean felt the tension and sadness of the day lift and dissipate. He shed his jacket and she touched his smooth skin under his silky T-shirt as he caressed her. He pushed her down on the bench and gave her more of his incendiary kisses, hiking up her skirt, kissing her belly, her thighs, slipping his hand inside her panties.

"Do you have a condom?" Jean whispered.

"Yes. I have carried one since I first saw you."

Sissy's grating voice startled them from the stairwell. "So I told him if he was going to stand on principle and refuse to sell the film rights, he could find himself another agent." Jean and Yuan pushed apart and sat upright on the bench, straightening their clothes and smoothing their hair, both of them slightly breathless. Sissy, Jasper, and Ted entered the gallery, wine glasses in hand.

"Why, if it isn't Jean and Yuan," Ted remarked. "Soaking up a little culture?"

"Uh, that's right," Jean said. "We're admiring the art." She noticed that Yuan had draped his jacket over his lap. His face was a little flushed and she was sure hers was, too. But then so was Jasper's, for different reasons.

"Where's Bernie?" Jasper asked Jean. "I thought you two were spending your evenings together."

"I'm meeting him later. I came to look at the art and ran into Yuan."

"What a lucky coincidence," Sissy said archly.

Yuan stood up. "In fact, we were just leaving. Come, Jean, I'll walk you to your cabin. Bernie will be missing you."

As soon as they were out of the house, they both laughed.

"My fantasy was to make love to you in the gallery with the art all around," Yuan said. "We will save that for another time."

Things moved quickly in her cabin, and soon they were naked in the white bed, the lights on at Yuan's insistence. Jean liked his body; he was slender but not athletic, with hairless skin that smelled faintly of sandalwood. He was probably twice Zeppo's age, and it showed—he was cooler and more controlled, and he knew more tricks. Jean lost herself in sensation, forgetting the sad story of Pilar's shattered family, the image of Katharine's torn and broken body, and the pain she caused Zeppo, at least for a while.

Much later Jean turned off the lights and got back into bed, physical release giving her a sense of calm and well-being. She looked at Yuan, who lay on his side snoring softly, and smiled. He was skilled at giving pleasure, but then so was she. He was just the kind of interesting, simpatico lover she collected. When he passed through San Francisco sometime or she visited Taipei, maybe they could spend a few hours together. Of course he didn't have Zeppo's voracious appetite, but he'd do just fine until she could get home.

THE NEXT morning Jean woke to see Yuan sitting near her in a chair, dressed only in briefs, sketching in her notebook. "Don't move," he said, his eyes going from her to the paper.

"I haven't posed for anyone since college," she said. "They paid pretty well in life drawing class."

"You are an ideal artist's model—full-figured yet athletic." He flipped a page in the notebook. "Now turn onto your back. Put your left arm up over your head. That's it." He drew for several minutes in silence, the only sound pen on paper.

There was a knock on the connecting door and Bernie looked in. Jean covered herself with a sheet. "Good morning," he said. "Can I leave through your door again, Jean? There are workers outside." He grinned. "That is, if Yuan doesn't mind if I take credit for all the noise you made last night."

"Be my guest," Yuan said. "In this case, participation is its own reward. But I must ask you to wait perhaps an hour before leaving. Jean might possibly make more noise."

"Sure. We can arm wrestle to kill time." He ducked back into Roman's room.

Jean uncovered herself and Yuan finished his drawing, neither of them speaking, the tension rising between them until he put down the notebook, slipped off his briefs, and got into bed, already erect. She pulled him to her, hungry for his kisses and his skillful touch, and before long she'd dozed off again.

She woke to find him gone; she hoped he'd left when there were no lurking workers. Jean got out of bed and picked up her notebook from the floor. Yuan's drawings were really good—he'd used her black gel pen, and the heavy dark lines and spare composition were pure Picasso. She was sorry she couldn't show the sketches to Zeppo without upsetting him. Well, at least she could show Roman and Bernie.

Jean put on her red silk robe and went into the adjoining room to find Roman and Bernie sitting at a table playing backgammon. "Good morning, guys. Look at these drawings Yuan did." She handed the notebook to Bernie.

"These are great," he said, looking them over and passing them to Roman. "He did some sketches of Meide in Taipei that made her look like an Utamaro geisha. He's quite good."

"Very nice, if you like Picasso," Roman said, giving her a look of disapproval as he handed them back to Jean. "Will he be leaving through my room every morning?"

"That won't be necessary," Jean said. "He can wait until the coast is clear."

Roman rolled the dice and moved his piece. "I feel as if I'm trapped in a Georges Feydeau farce, with everyone running around slamming doors and ending up in the wrong bed."

Bernie smiled. "I think everyone's in the right bed."

"Everyone but Jean."

"Zeppo must be quite a guy for Roman to defend his interests so fiercely," Bernie said.

"He is, but Yuan's no slouch," Jean said. "He's very sophisticated. I don't have to explain things to him all the time."

Roman frowned at her. "You're a greedy, insensitive fool."

"Oh, don't start that," Jean said to Roman. "I'm not going to marry Yuan—he's just my designated fuck."

"Wendy Kroy to whatever his name was," Bernie said. "*The Last Seduction.*"

"Ha!" Jean exclaimed. "I thought you knew everything."

"Almost everything. Jean, tell me—Yuan's always so cool and proper. What's he like when he gets warmed up?"

"Very impressive for someone who's nearly Roman's age, and he's one of the world's great kissers. He's also got a quirk I've never seen before."

"Now that's saying something," Roman said.

"He's excited by great art, actually physically aroused. He's hot for me because I look like a twelfth-century Indian statue he saw in Paris."

Roman handed the dice cup to Bernie. "I've always thought of you as a Frank Thorne—you know, Red Sonja wielding a sword and spilling out of a chain mail bikini."

"You scoff. I think I'd look good in a chain mail bikini."

"You'd look good in a shower curtain," Bernie said in a fair imitation of James Cagney.

"Cody Jarrett to whatever her name was, *White Heat,*" Jean said.

Bernie glanced at his watch and stood up. "We'll have to finish the game later. Dad and I are supposed to play tennis before it gets too hot."

"Who usually wins?" Roman asked.

"He does, of course." Bernie went out through Jean's cabin and Jean sat down across from Roman.

"Just like old times, isn't it?" she said. "We go on a trip together and each find someone diverting. Although you may have found something more."

"Indeed I might. And I'm smart enough to know a good thing when I have it in my hand, unlike you."

"Roman," she said softly. "You won't tell Zeppo, will you?"

He sighed. "No, I'll spare him that."

"Thanks." Roman was one of the few people whose opinion mattered to Jean, and she didn't want him angry with her. "You know, Zeppo is still my favorite man. He just doesn't happen to be here, and I'm under a lot of stress. Don't be so hard on me."

"Most adults are able to postpone gratification for a few days."

She decided to change the subject. "What were you and Sissy discussing last night?"

"We were talking shop. She knows some of the same people I do in publishing. Apparently she handles serious nonfiction as well as true crime. Don't worry, I told her I was an editor and part-time photographer."

"Hey, what's going to happen after this weekend? Do you and Bernie have a plan?"

"As a matter of fact, we do. When the guests are gone, he'll explain it all to his father and then go back to LA for a few days to wrap things up, and after that drive to San Francisco. He'll stay with me for a while and we'll see how things go."

"That's wonderful. Isn't he afraid Ted will cut him off without a cent?"

"I asked him the same thing, but he's willing to risk it. After all, he's lived with boyfriends before." Roman smiled at her. "And he seems to have a reckless, impetuous streak not unlike yours."

"You know, all your leftist friends are going to ride you for bringing home the richest queer in America."

Roman gave a relaxed, low, easy chuckle she hadn't heard in a long time. "I'll just have to live with it."

Chapter 13

It was Saturday, the day of the Sauternes tasting. Jean went back to her room after breakfast and spent the morning studying her notes on the different vintages they'd be trying. She'd done research on the conditions of each harvest and on how the old wines had shown in years past.

Finally she called Zeppo; he was cleaning his apartment, something he did with amusing regularity. "Zeppo, it worked better than I imagined," she told him. "Bernie's coming to stay with Roman."

"Nice work, Jeannie. Roman's not the type of man who should be alone. I'm not either. I miss you."

Jean shook off a twinge of guilt. "I miss you, too," she said, meaning it. "I can't wait to see you."

"So the big tasting's today, huh?"

"Yeah. Should be memorable. And guess what else. Someone actually wants to hire me as a detective." She explained Maria Esposito's visit.

"Got any idea what happened to Pilar?"

"None at all. And no idea how her death is connected to Katharine's or to the guy at the Fairmont. This is a pretty obnoxious group, but they seem harmless except for Angus, and he wasn't here when Pilar died." She told him about Roman's shooting match.

"You guys need to get home. I know you won't leave before the tasting, but don't hang around too long after. Well, be careful, and don't find any more bodies."

"I promise."

After lunch Jean took a swim with Roman and Bernie in the smaller pool, which was mostly in the shade at this hour. When the men went inside, she stayed outside near the pool in spite of the heat; Yuan and Tony were playing bridge with Jasper and Sissy, and Jean didn't want to mingle with any of the other guests. At about four o'clock they all went to their rooms to get ready for the Sauternes tasting.

Jean had brought two good dresses: a black linen number and a cheongsam she'd made with red silk bought in Hong Kong—short-sleeved, high-necked, and form-fitting, with a deep slit up one side of the tight skirt. She chose the cheongsam; it was a little over the top, but she had long since ceased to care what these people thought of her. She put on dangly red coral and silver earrings, added a pair of red strappy sandals—flats, of course—dropped a notebook into her evening bag, and went down to the wine cellar.

The big table was set up as before, with smaller tasting glasses this time, the ones designed for Sauternes. Each place had six glasses, arranged in two groups—the Yquem would go in one group, the Chatouilleux in the other. Jean went to the sideboard where the precious bottles waited, the glass mottled with age, many of the labels torn and discolored, the wines ranging in hue from clear bright gold to deep amber. She touched one; it was cold. Gloria was letting them warm up a bit before the tasting. The oldest bottles, including the 1811s, were hand-blown, their labels barely legible. Tasting these wines might not make up for everything Jean had endured over the past couple of days, but it would sure help.

Jean pulled out the list of wines Gloria had given her so she could compare it with the labels. Collectors would be very interested in how the costly old wines were showing, and she had to make sure there wasn't a typo somewhere. According to the list, Ted owned all the bottles except for several older vintages of Chatouilleux from René, Yuan's bottle of 1945 Yquem, four vintages of Yquem from Carl, and seven assorted bottlings from Jasper. As she stood at the counter, someone came down the stairs. It was Angus; she turned back to the bottles, ignoring him.

He came up behind her, standing too close. She could feel his breath, scented with Scotch, on her neck. "Hey, sweetheart," he said. "In that dress you look just like a Southeast Asian whore, only twice as big." He brushed himself against her ass.

Jean rammed her elbow back hard in a move that had worked for her before, but his big hand was there to catch it. "Oooh," he said, mocking her. "You've taken one of those faggot self-defense classes, too, have you?"

"Get your hands off me or I'll scream," she said through her teeth.

He let her go and stood back, grinning. "Maybe you're not as tough as you think you are."

"Just stay away from me." Jean gathered her papers and went upstairs. Angus seemed to be slipping out of his benign pose into something more dangerous, as if his civilized veneer were chipping away. Maybe he'd forgotten to take his medication. She thought about complaining to Ted, but decided to wait until after the tasting.

Jean stayed in the library waiting for other guests to go past on their way to the tasting. When Yuan came along the hallway, she joined him.

His smile was warm and intimate. "You look beautiful," he said, caressing her cheek. "Red suits you. I have promised Meide that I would sit with her at the tasting. I hope you are not offended."

"Nah," she said, giving him a playful squeeze. "I survived middle school, didn't I?"

Yuan looked at her quizzically as René and Monique came by hand in hand, and the four of them went to the cellar. Roman was already there, shooting the action. Ted, Meide, and the rest of the guests joined them, and Gloria and Chencho opened the bottles. The flowers this time were huge arrangements of white calla lilies and amaryllis, with feathery greens Jean couldn't identify.

"Chencho, were you able to reach Carl?" Ted asked.

"No, sir. I tried his cell phone and his office, but just got voice mail. I left messages."

"Perhaps he's on his way here." Ted shrugged. "We'll have to go ahead without him."

They all took their places, arranging themselves more or less as they had at the Montrachet tasting, Bernie on Jean's left and Tony on her right. Gloria poured Yquem in the left-hand glasses and Chencho poured the same vintages of Chatouilleux into the right-hand ones, starting with the youngest bottlings.

Toward the end of the first flight, Jean turned around; Roman knelt behind her shooting the tasters across the table. "Hey," she said to him, "take a break and taste this flight. You can shoot more later."

"You've persuaded me," he said, sitting down on the other side of Bernie.

Bernie sighed deeply and shook his head. Jean saw a fleeting bitter expression on his face.

"What's the matter?" she asked in a low voice.

He leaned over so only she and Roman could hear him. "If I had the money Dad spent on this tasting, I'd be halfway to financing my film. It gets to me sometimes when he's so extravagant." He shrugged. "But then, it is his money."

"How is it his?" Roman said. "He earned none of it. It's a mere accident of birth that he's not picking strawberries for a living."

"Try telling him that."

Jean squeezed Bernie's knee. "Don't either of you make him mad till the tasting's over." She set to work, emptying her mind of everything but the wines in front of her, swirling, sniffing, and tasting, concentrating on color, aromas, flavors, all the history behind each vintage, carefully spitting into the crystal pitcher. The youngest wines, a pair of 2009s, were splendid. The Yquem showed myriad fruit notes, a strong aroma of botrytis, vibrant acidity, and a creamy finish. It would age for decades. The Chatouilleux was nearly as good, but lighter and less intense.

As they went back through the vintages, a few wines stood out. The 1990 Yquem was full-bodied and sweetly viscous, yet perfectly acidic, with a long future ahead of it. The 1989s from both producers were rich, sweet, and golden, the highlights of that decade. As they tasted through the 1970s, Jean marveled at the myriad aromas and flavors that could come from moldy white grapes, everything from tobacco to caramel to apricots to orange blossoms. She had to force herself to spit out the luscious wines.

Tasting wine this good was almost like sex: Both pursuits involved intense focus and total immersion in delightful sensations to the exclusion of all else. Jean smiled to herself. At least during sex she didn't have to take notes. Or spit.

René and Ted gave a running commentary, with other guests adding their impressions. Tony and Roman made a few intelligent remarks that Jean wrote down. Jasper talked a lot but said little of note, and his pitcher remained nearly empty—at this rate he'd be plastered by the time the 1811 came around. Angus was silent, which Jean found odd, since he supposedly collected dessert wines. A few times she caught him looking at her; he didn't look away, just stared unblinking with a trace of a mocking smile on his lips. She tried to ignore him.

After three flights, the tasters took a break, helping themselves to bread and cheese at a sideboard. Jean ate a bit of cheese and then sat back down at the tasting table to look over her notes.

Tony, Sissy, and Jasper stood near the sideboard, behind one of the lush flower arrangements. Jean couldn't see them very well, but she could hear them. "There are seven of your wines in this next flight, right?" Tony asked.

"That's correct," Jasper said.

"Now Jasper, tell the truth," Sissy said. "We don't actually own the bottles anymore. Ted had to buy them because my dear husband said he couldn't afford to donate them. He threatened to sell them at auction if Ted didn't shell out. Isn't that right, sweetheart?"

"That's really none of his business, Sissy."

"Don't you think all these colorful behind-the-scenes details belong in Jean's article?"

Jasper sighed heavily. "How many times can a man apologize?" He walked away and sat at the tasting table.

"You're pretty hard on him, Sissy," Tony said.

Sissy chuckled. "You should have seen him strutting around with his chest puffed out when the real estate market was high."

Ted tapped a glass with a bread knife. "Friends," he said when they'd quieted down. "Let's continue."

They all took their seats. As they moved back through time, they encountered more bottles that were flawed due to cork contamination or poor storage, but the ones that had survived were stellar, and the legendary post-war vintages—1945, '47, and '49—were magnificent.

As the tasting progressed, Jean came to a conclusion that she knew René and Ted—and her boss, Owen—wouldn't like: Chatouilleux was simply not in Yquem's league. René's wines were perfectly balanced and beautifully made, but the Yquems were consistently richer, deeper, and more complex. As she wrote out her notes, she knew few of her words would end up in the final article. Well, so be it. She'd probably never taste these wines again.

Next to her, Tony spat into his pitcher. "René, I hate to say so, but the Yquems blow you out of the water every time."

Jean nudged him. "You've got a great palate for a running back."

Ted smiled patronizingly. "Now Tony, I hope you're not letting our little financial disagreement color your responses. This tasting is bigger than Tony's Chop Houses."

"I call 'em as I taste 'em," Tony retorted. "No amount of money's going to make me shill for your lost cause."

"If I wanted a paid endorsement, I'd get someone younger and more current," Ted said sharply. "That's undoubtedly what your restaurants need."

"Gentlemen," René said smoothly, "I'm sure this is just an honest difference of opinion. Tony, we all know you have an excellent palate. Ted and I simply prefer the more artistic Chatouilleux."

Tony backed off, nodding at René. "As you say, a difference of opinion."

With reverence, they tasted the nineteenth-century vintages Ted and René had managed to collect. Jean, who decided it was time to stop spitting, found them fascinating; some of them had lost their fruit, of course, but retained a sweet, smoky, creamy quality that was quite seductive, and a few tasted decades younger than they were. The Yquem from 1847, which some critics believed to be the greatest Sauternes vintage of all time, was phenomenal, still amazingly rich and powerful, with notes of orange peel, apricot, caramel, and honey. As Jean savored it, Roman caught her eye and smiled his thanks.

Finally Gloria and Chencho ceremoniously poured the two 1811s into the glasses. To everyone's delight, both bottles were well preserved and, although they weren't as magnificent as the 1847, Jean found plenty to like: The Yquem showed raspberries, apricots, and strawberries on the nose, sweet, raisiny flavors, a velvet finish, and an elusive, haunting quality she attributed to great age. The Chatouilleux had not aged as well, and although lovely, was like a faint echo of the Yquem. No one spat out a drop.

When the tasting was finished, Gloria poured the rest of some of the wines informally. They lingered over their glasses, chatting and milling around, until one of the kitchen staff called them to dinner and they drifted upstairs.

Jean hung back and went to the sideboard to retaste one of the early twentieth-century Yquems that she'd especially liked; she wanted to expand her notes. As she swallowed a delicious mouthful of wine, someone came up behind her. She spun around, wary of Angus, but it was René.

"Jean, how can you taste Sauternes and not think of me, of our night together?" he said, taking her by the shoulders. "How can you be so cold?" He pushed her up against the table and tried to kiss her, but she shoved him away.

"How can you be such an insensitive prick? Monique's right upstairs." Jean pinched his left nipple hard enough to make him cry out, hoping she'd given him a bruise he couldn't explain. She charged up the stairs as quickly as she could in her tight skirt, and René followed her, rubbing his chest.

Laszlo pulled out all the stops at dinner. The first course was a lobster boudin in a beurre blanc, served with 1986 Romanée-Conti Le Montrachet. Breast of guinea hen in a Cabernet reduction sauce followed, with feather-light whipped truffled potatoes and sautéed baby carrots and beets on the side. Jean noticed that Meide had guinea hen, too, but without the sauce. Laszlo would be pleased. Gloria poured a 1982 Château Margaux, a superb red Bordeaux. The food was so good that everyone quickly fell into a contented, convivial mood. After a light salad course, Laszlo served an almond and apricot tart that perfectly complemented the Sauternes left over from the tasting.

The hot wind still gusted, so Gloria served coffee and after-dinner drinks in the library. Ted had Chencho make a few more attempts to phone Carl, with the same result. Soon Meide excused herself and went to bed. Jasper, Angus, Ted, and René sat down for their nightly game of poker.

"Who wants to see a movie?" Bernie asked.

"Let's watch one of your film noirs," Roman said. He and the other non-poker players followed Bernie out the door.

Jean didn't feel like watching a movie, even one she'd probably enjoy. This was her last night here, and she wanted to make it count. As the group walked down the hall toward the movie room, she fell behind, pulling Yuan into a doorway. "Let's go to the gallery and act out your fantasy," she said.

"What if we are discovered?" he whispered.

"I don't care anymore. Ted can do his worst—I've tasted the wines."

Yuan took her hand and they slipped past the library door and down the stairs, pausing for more kisses inside the gallery. Jean nodded toward the nearest leather bench. "Let's get comfortable."

"One moment." Yuan took Meide's chinchilla coat off its hanger and spread it on the bench, which he moved so it was directly in front of the jade cabinet.

Jean smiled as he unfastened the frogs at the neck of her cheongsam. She unzipped the side and pulled it off over her head, enjoying the look in his eyes as she removed her underwear and lay naked on the coat. It felt incredibly sensuous—she'd made love on fur before, but never on anything this luxurious.

Yuan undressed and joined her on the coat, his kisses inflaming her. "I love the way you kiss," she whispered.

"I know you do." As he moved slowly down over her, kissing her as he went, Jean let herself go, reveling in his skillful touch, getting a thrill that any moment someone could come into the gallery. She thought this was a perfect end to a memorable feast for the senses.

After a long lovely time, Yuan lay back on the fur-covered bench and Jean straddled him, the jade cabinet behind her, and she saw his delight as she moved before it, his eyes devouring her and the jade with equal pleasure. Each time he neared orgasm she changed speed, pulled back, or stopped altogether, waiting for him to subside, then coaxed him to the brink, only to stop again, using the strong muscles in her legs to control him. Finally he seized her by the shoulders and pushed her down onto the coat. Jean felt the soft fur caress her back as he mounted her, his ardor bringing her along, too, and he made a deep growling noise in his throat as he came.

Yuan collapsed onto her, and as she shifted slightly so she could breathe, he raised his head and smiled. "That was exquisite. How often in life does reality surpass fantasy?" He lay next to her on the narrow bench, pulling the coat around them. She snuggled against him, liking his words but knowing he was a smooth talker she might never see again after tomorrow.

They finished the night in her room. Not bad for an old man.

Chapter 14

Jean woke at dawn and decided to go for a swim, leaving Yuan in a deep sleep. Today the guests were taking a private tour of the San Diego Zoo Safari Park. Jean would have liked to go, but she and Roman were scheduled to fly home late that afternoon. She smiled at the thought of seeing Zeppo again. Yuan was a lot of fun, but she missed the emotional charge she had with Zeppo. Not to mention his twenty-four-year-old energy.

The rising sun cast long shadows across the still canyon. No one else stirred as she made her way to the big pool, adjusting her slightly damp swimsuit. A few vultures rode the early-morning currents to the south.

As Jean did her laps, a slim dark shape dove into the pool beside her—it was Monique, in a brown maillot. They paced each other for a couple of laps; Monique was a strong, sure swimmer, and soon they were racing. To Jean's surprise, Monique easily pulled away from her and soon was a length ahead.

Finally Jean gripped the side, exhausted. "OK, you win," she gasped when Monique surfaced near her. "You're really good."

"I swim almost every day. I nearly qualified for the 1984 Olympic team in freestyle."

"Then you're a ringer."

"What is a ringer?"

"That's when somebody great enters a contest pretending to be ordinary."

Monique laughed. "So I have learned a new English word. You swim very well, too. Were you on a team in school?"

"No. I stuck to track and volleyball."

Jean gazed out across the canyon and spotted a beautiful bird flying at her eye level. It looked like the injured red-tailed hawk she'd seen in the birdhouse. A bright metallic glint from Katharine's deck made Jean blink; it was the rising sun reflecting off something from behind the bougainvillea. She waited and saw the flash again. "Monique," she said, "keep swimming for about fifteen minutes. I want to check something out. I think we're being watched."

"Watched by whom?" Monique asked in amusement.

"The boy next door. Be right back."

Jean got out of the pool, threw on her caftan and sandals, and headed south around the high wall. Once Katharine's porch was out of sight, she turned back toward the canyon and crept through the chaparral. Once she got to Katharine's yard, she slipped off her sandals and sneaked onto the deck. As she'd expected, Ethan sat on the corner bench, hidden behind the screen of bougainvillea, watching Monique through binoculars.

"Boo!" Jean shouted, making the boy jump in his seat.

"Whoa, Jean," he said when he saw her. "You scared the shit out of me."

"You're turning into a real peeping Tom," she said.

"Hey, I wasn't doing any harm."

"A lot of people won't think it's so harmless. Why are you here at this hour, anyway?"

"Feeding the birds. Some Project Wildlife people are going to take them, but it hasn't happened yet." He looked at his feet, kicking at the deck with one toe. "I heard you found Katharine. Bummer."

"It was that. And Ethan, I'm really sorry. I know you were close."

He sighed heavily. "Yeah, I'll miss her. And you know what? She left her money to Project Wildlife, but she left me the house and all her stuff. It blew me away. My parents are in charge until I'm twenty-one, but I own this great place, and this land. Isn't that awesome?"

"It sure is. She must really have loved you."

"I guess so." Ethan, embarrassed, glanced at his watch. "Well, I'm outta here. I've got to meet the guys. We're going to the skate park in Escondido."

"Don't break anything," Jean said. After he drove off, she sat where he'd been, on the bench behind the dense magenta blossoms at the corner of the deck. She picked up the binoculars and looked out through a break in the foliage that had clearly been carefully clipped. She had a great view of the Lyon compound and most of the north end of the canyon. This must be where Katharine sat when she saw the gardeners burying the vultures.

As she made her way back across the canyon, on the path this time, Jean noticed several vultures circling to the south of Phoenix Garden, beyond the tennis courts and putting green. Laszlo had promised to stop salting the hills with road kill, so something must have died out there.

Jean wasn't in the mood to investigate the vultures' breakfast, so she went past the empty pool—Monique had gone—and sat in a shaded garden chair, looking out across the canyon, watching the vultures soar and dip their wings as they rode the thermals. She'd always thought them graceful creatures in flight, but now she'd seen far too many of them up close. Those birds were truly relentless. Sharks with wings.

Jean heard a commotion above her. Meide stood on a balcony a few yards away wearing a diaphanous yellow peignoir. "Teddy!" she cried, waving at the sky. "Look at the vultures. I can't stand them. Teddy!"

Ted, in a blue terrycloth robe, rushed out and put his arm around her, frowning with concern. "Don't worry, darling. I'll have someone take care of it."

Soon Chencho appeared and called to a scrawny dark man working on the roses. "Blas!" The man hurried over and they spoke briefly in Spanish.

"*Si, Señor.*" Blas grabbed a shovel and set out over the hill. Chencho waved to Jean and returned to the house.

"This place is full of vultures, vultures everywhere," Jean muttered to herself in a nasal Eastern European accent, quoting the pickpocket in *Casablanca*.

In a few moments Blas ran back, gesticulating wildly, yelling in Spanish. Jean strained to understand what he was saying, but her Spanish was pretty bad.

"Es un hombre!"

That she understood: It's a man. Jean got up and ran toward Blas. "Where?" she asked. *"Dónde?"*

"Allí!" Blas led her over the hill through the chaparral. They stopped short at a cluster of boulders that hid whatever held the vultures' attention. The shovel lay where Blas had dropped it. Jean picked it up and crept around the boulders. She ran at the vultures waving the shovel, scattering them, and forced herself to look at what was partially buried at the base of the rocks. There wasn't much left of the face, but Jean recognized the raw silk jacket and hair implants—Carl Schoonover. It looked as if some animal had dug him up and the vultures had done the rest.

Jean closed her eyes and took a deep breath, but the stench was overwhelming and she backed away quickly, dropping the shovel. "We have to call the police," she said. *"La policía."*

They ran back to the house and Chencho came out to meet them. "What's the matter?" he said when he saw their expressions.

"It's Carl Schoonover," Jean said, panting. "He's dead. Call Matt right away. I'll keep people from going out there." Chencho ran into the house as Jean and Blas crumpled into deck chairs to wait for the deputy.

Within five minutes, Matt Baeza came around the side of the house, wiping his forehead with a handkerchief, his hat in his hand.

"How'd you get here so fast?" Jean asked.

"I had business nearby."

"At the Jones place?"

Matt ignored her question. "Where's the body?"

"Over that hill, past the boulders. Blas found it. Well, the vultures found it, and he went to see what they were after."

Matt and Blas spoke Spanish as they walked over the hill. The two of them soon returned, Matt looking grim. He spoke to a deputy on his cell phone, and within fifteen minutes two more officers had arrived and gathered the Lyons and their guests together in the big living room. With Matt's permission, Jean dashed to her cabin and replaced her wet swimsuit and caftan with black shorts and a red tank top. She found Roman at one end of the room and stood close.

"What's up?" Roman whispered to her.

"Carl Schoonover's been killed," she whispered back. He put his arm around her shoulders.

Matt stood with his back to the pale slate fireplace, holding his hat. "Ladies and gentlemen," he said to the group, "I'm afraid I have bad news. Ms. Applequist and one of the gardeners discovered Carl Schoonover's body partly buried out near the big pile of boulders south of the house." He paused for the gasps and exclamations from the crowd. "We're treating this as a homicide, so I'll have to ask you all to remain here in this room until the homicide detail arrives." He introduced deputies Sheila Denslow, a stocky brunette, and Bruce Kiel, blond and buff. The two officers took up discreet positions just outside the doors to the room. Matt's phone beeped, and he stepped out of the room to answer it.

"Oh, poor Carl," Meide said, and began to cry. Ted sat with her on a white sofa, holding her protectively, soothing her with soft words.

Sissy, perched on a blond wood chair, looked at Jean. "My God, Jean. You've done it again."

"Shut up," Jean snapped. Bernie looked pale and shaken; Roman watched him with concern but kept his distance. Jean sat down next to him and took his hand. "You OK?" she asked.

"I can't believe it," he said, running his other hand over his face. "Murdered."

"Jean," Ted asked, "how did he die?"

"I couldn't tell. He was pretty chewed up by the animals."

"How ghastly," Yuan said. He looked as upset as Bernie.

"Ted," Tony said, "didn't you say Carl left you a note?"

"Yes, that's right. He said he had to go to LA to deal with a business problem."

"You recognized his handwriting?"

"Of course. It's very distinctive. He prints . . . printed in all caps, like a draftsman."

"Someone must have forged it," Jean said. "Where's the note now?"

"I threw it away. I suppose the police will want it. Chencho, go tell Deputy Baeza that I threw the note into my bedroom wastebasket yesterday. He'll have to track it from there." Sheila gave her OK and Chencho went on his errand.

"This is an outrage," Ted said, frowning darkly. "I've taken all these expensive security precautions, yet a criminal got in and attacked one of my guests."

"How do you figure that, Ted?" Tony asked. "What's more likely, that he was killed by a complete stranger or by someone he knew?"

"Tony's right," Jean said. "Most murders are committed by people who know the victim."

"Which means the killer could be one of us," Monique said softly, moving closer to René.

"That's impossible," Ted insisted. "None of you could do such a thing."

Through the living room's floor-to-ceiling windows they could see Matt leading several officers and technicians around the side of the house. A few of them spread out along the grounds near the edge of the compound, setting up the perimeters of their investigation. Ted stood to greet an officer who came into the living room.

"This is a bad business, Ted," the man said as they shook hands. "I promise you I'll get to the bottom of it."

"I'm sure you will, Wes."

Wes was around forty, average height, and obviously worked out. He wore navy slacks, a short-sleeved shirt, and a knit tie. His thinning dark hair was carefully arranged over a bald spot. Jean disliked him on sight; she never trusted a man with a comb-over.

The officer turned to the group. "I'm Detective Wes Jurado of the sheriff's homicide detail. I'll be handling this investigation. I'd like to speak to each of you regarding the death of Carl Schoonover. Chencho has given me a list of your names, so we'll call you into the library or the sitting room individually. I know if we all work together we can bring this investigation to a speedy conclusion."

One of Jurado's men appeared at the door where Sheila stood. "Detective, can I have a word?" he said. Jurado excused himself and followed the man out the door.

A few minutes later Matt came back into the room from outside. "Where's Jurado?" he asked.

"He went out this way," Sheila said, gesturing through the door.

"Thanks." Matt went in search of the detective.

Jean's curiosity was acting up again. "May I go to the restroom?" she asked Sheila politely.

"Sure, go ahead," the officer said.

Jean went out the door into a spacious hallway. The restroom was to the left, but Jean followed Matt as quietly as she could in the other direction and ducked into a side room when she heard Jurado's voice. If she kept perfectly silent, she could make out what Jurado and Matt were saying.

"You need anything else?" Matt asked.

"No, we can handle it from here," Jurado said. "Another homicide in your area, eh? Seems the crime rate's gone way up around here since you took over."

"Nah, most categories are down. Only homicide's up. I guess we can thank your twenty percent solve rate for that, Detective." Matt put plenty of sarcasm into the last word.

She heard Jurado snort. "I'm sure you have work of your own to do, officer. Try not to get underfoot."

"Yes, sir," Matt said.

Interesting, Jean thought. She stayed in her hiding place until Jurado went past her, back to the room full of suspects. Matt must have gone outside. She went back to the holding tank.

Roman's was the first name to be called. He strode toward the library, giving Jean a reassuring smile.

Jean spotted Gloria sitting on an elaborately carved bench at one end of the huge room and sat next to her. "Gloria, what's up between Matt and Wes Jurado?" she asked in a whisper.

Gloria made a face. "Wes is acting head of homicide and wants it to be permanent. He was an affirmative-action hire, so he has a lot to prove. But then Matt got into homicide in Phoenix because he's Native American. The difference is, Matt turned out to be really good and Wes is an incompetent fool. He's taken credit for Matt's investigative work more than once." She shook her head. "I believed in affirmative action until I met him."

The deputies called Gloria into the sitting room. Jean sat quietly, mulling things over, until her turn came. She was a little worried about Roman; he still hadn't come out of the library. In the sitting room she gave a statement to Jurado, who struck her as smarmy and none too bright, sticking to the facts and keeping her speculations to herself.

Laszlo put together a cold buffet for lunch, and Jean ate a delicious salade Niçoise with Monique, talking things over. As she left the dining room, she saw Matt alone in the entryway looking through a small notebook. "Matt, I have to talk to you."

"Sure." He put the notebook into his breast pocket. "Let's go outside."

They sat at a table near the small pool, the hot wind whipping around them. Matt folded down the patio umbrella before it went airborne.

"Why is Roman still in with the detectives?" Jean asked.

"They're looking hard at him, Angus MacKnight, and Tony Feola because Schoonover's neck was broken. Only those three have the training or strength to do it."

"Roman never laid eyes on Carl Schoonover until this weekend."

"Then he shouldn't have anything to worry about."

"Listen," Jean said, "I wanted to talk to you because I think Katharine was murdered." She told him about the reflection off the binoculars, and finding Ethan behind the bougainvillea. "We know Katharine kept tabs on the Lyons. What if she were watching early that morning when whoever killed Carl was hauling the body around and the killer realized he was being watched? I sneaked up on a sixteen-year-old boy with good hearing. It would have been simple for someone to get to Katharine before she could reach a phone."

Matt nodded. "I already knew she was murdered. I printed her cane—it had been wiped clean. So I called in a marker and they did the autopsy right away. Turns out Katharine was already dead when she went off the trail. Her neck was broken, too."

"A friend in the SFPD told me that the man who fell on Lyon's car at the Fairmont had a broken neck."

"Dom Huerta. I know." He stood. "Come with me."

Matt had her show him where she was in the pool when she saw the glint of the binoculars, asking what time it had been, the angle of the sun, the direction of the shadows. She led him across the canyon by the route she'd taken when she surprised Ethan, and he sat in the hidden spot and surveyed the canyon through the binoculars, as she had done. Jean was impressed by his thoroughness and gratified by the weight he gave her story.

They finally walked back across the canyon to the Lyons' house, the wind kicking grit into their eyes and making them squint. Jean tripped over a juniper root, but Matt caught her arm before she fell into a clump of cactus. As they crossed the terrace, Jean decided to try to take advantage of their camaraderie. "Since we're such a good team, can you tell me what happened at the Jones place?"

He shrugged. "Why not? It'll be on the news tonight. Your friend was right—there's a lab in the shed. We raided it this morning, but only got Farron. Honey had already cleared out. Someone must have warned her." He chuckled. "She took Mojo and her truck but left Farron."

"I don't blame her," Jean said. A lot of interesting things were going to happen over the next few days, but getting away from Phoenix Garden and seeing Zeppo outweighed her powerful curiosity. She wanted to go home right now. "Matt, Roman and I are supposed to fly home today. Are we stuck here?"

He shrugged. "That's up to Wes. Hard to say how he'll play it. You've got a better chance if I don't ask him."

"You two don't get along very well, do you?"

"Nope." He put away his notebook. "Have Ted Lyon ask him if you can leave and it's a done deal. Wes is an ambitious guy. OK, I've got to check in with my people at the Jones place. Thanks for your help, Jean." They shook hands.

Jean went into the cool, still house. The living room was empty except for Bernie, who stood gazing out a window toward Katharine's house.

Jean joined him, threading her arm through his. "Have they given you the third-degree yet?"

"Yes, but Roman's still in the library."

"Matt says Carl's neck was broken, so Jurado's paying special attention to the men who could have done it. Plus Roman's had quite a few run-ins with the police."

"Are you taking my name in vain?" Roman said as he came into the room.

"Roman, thank God. I was getting worried." Bernie gave him a hug. "Wes is just dumb enough to be dangerous."

"Everything OK?" Jean said.

"It seems so. In any case, I have an alibi." He looked at Bernie. "I hope you didn't tell them you were in Jean's bed every night."

"No, I told the truth. Somehow my father's reaction doesn't seem that important anymore." Somewhere above them a door opened, and Bernie stepped away from Roman. He shrugged apologetically. "But I don't feel like dealing with it right now."

Wes Jurado and one of his deputies came into the living room as Ted descended the stairs. "We've just about finished taking statements," Jurado said. "It looks to me like your guests are in the clear."

"Of course they are," Ted said. "Now Wes, I realize you'll need to conduct a thorough investigation, but I see no reason we can't go to the safari park for a few hours. I've arranged a special tour and a catered dinner, at great expense, I might add. Surely my guests deserve a diversion after what they've been through today."

"Well, Ted, I don't see why not. Just check in with the deputy on duty here at the house when you return. We'll come back in the morning and finish our questioning."

Jean was dumbfounded. Matt wouldn't like it that the suspects were roaming around without police supervision. Although this might mean that she and Roman could leave, too.

"That'll be fine." Ted called Chencho and ordered him to tell the guests to get ready for the excursion.

"Uh, Detective Jurado?" Jean said politely. "Will Roman and I be able to make our flight home to San Francisco later today?"

"I'd appreciate it if you'd let them go, Wes," Ted said. "Jean has had a very rough weekend."

"All right," Wes said. "I have your contact information if something comes up."

"Bernie, are you coming with us?" Ted asked.

"I'm not really in the mood, Dad. I think I'll stay here."

"Very well. You can say good-bye properly." Ted winked at Jean; the gesture was so inappropriate it startled her. He trotted back up the stairs and Jurado and his men went outside.

As Jean sat with Bernie and Roman, Yuan came down the stairs, ready for the park in cream-colored slacks and polo shirt, carrying a Panama hat. He smiled when he saw her. "Jean, there you are. I wish to say good-bye."

"Excuse me, gents." She followed him to a side room. He closed the door and they embraced, but in the back of her mind it occurred to her to wonder if he had anything to do with Carl's death.

"Meeting you has more than made up for all the unpleasantness of this weekend," he said. "I shall always remember last night."

"I had a great time, too. You have my numbers in San Francisco—give me a call if you're ever in town."

They joined the guests assembled in the entryway. Ted clapped his hands to get their attention. He'd changed his million-dollar watch for a sporty Rolex. "Let's get moving, people. We're running a little late because of poor Carl. Now, we'll take the Maybach and a limo, and Yuan's going to drive his own car. He has some animal allergies and may have to leave early. I expect we'll be back before ten P.M."

Jean and Roman made their good-byes, shaking hands all around and exchanging niceties. Monique and Jean embraced. "It was so good to meet you," Monique said, air-kissing Jean's cheeks. "Let's keep in touch."

René hugged her cautiously. "She's much too good for you," Jean whispered in his ear. "I hope she figures it out soon."

Tony gave her a bear hug and slapped Roman on the back. "If you're ever in LA, stop in and see me," he told them.

"We will," Jean said.

Sissy grasped her arm with a bony hand. "Call me and I'll help you put together a book proposal."

"Sissy, you are the last person on earth I'll ever call." Jean turned away from her.

"You'll change your mind."

Meide, in a pale lavender dress and broad-brimmed hat, approached Jean. She'd exchanged her stilettos for Mephisto walking sandals. "Jean," she said, taking her hand, "I'm sorry you have had such bad luck here at my house."

"Not your fault," Jean said, eager to see them leave. "Thanks for your hospitality. And don't miss the live condor exhibit." Meide smiled uncertainly.

Ted seized Jean's hand. "I look forward to reading your article. And thanks for everything."

To Jean's relief, the group finally went out the door to the waiting cars. Everyone waved, but Roman frowned after them. "Under the circumstances, I can't believe Ted would insist on going on this excursion. Also, why does Jurado do whatever he asks?"

"It's simple," Bernie said. "Wes Jurado wants to run for sheriff and he needs my dad's support." He started for the cabins. "Let's get out of the heat."

They headed for Roman's cabin, and Bernie phoned the kitchen for a bottle of Cristal Champagne in a silver ice bucket. Jean opened the bottle and served wine into three Riedel sparkling wine glasses.

"It doesn't seem to bother Ted much that his friend was murdered," Jean said, sipping the wine. It was cool, complex, and delicious, the perfect antidote to Ted.

"Why should it?" Bernie said. "He lives in his own world. September 11 barely fazed him." He sat on the bed hunched over, his Champagne bubbling away on an end table. "I can't get over it, though. What a horrible thing, to have your body eaten by vultures."

"The Parsis in South Asia dispose of all their dead that way," Roman said. "Zoroastrian doctrine prohibits them from contaminating earth, wind, or fire with corpses, so they leave bodies out to be eaten by vultures."

"That's fascinating," Jean said. "When I die, that's what I want you to do with my remains."

"Nonsense. I'm donating your body to science so they can isolate the cause of your overactive libido."

Bernie looked up angrily. "How can you two joke around at a time like this?"

Roman put his glass down and sat next to Bernie, putting his arms around him. "We're not making light of what's happened. Sometimes joking around is all one can do to survive."

"I'm sorry, Roman. I'm just not used to so much death." Jean discreetly slipped through the connecting door to her room. She sat in a white chair thinking things over as she finished her glass of bubbly.

Chapter 15

Jean looked around the cabin. Her suitcase lay on the bed, packed except for a few last-minute items. She had time for one more errand before she and Roman had to leave for the airport.

She went into the house through the kitchen. It smelled heavenly, like chiles and chocolate. Laszlo stirred a deep brown sauce, whistling tunelessly as he watched a small TV on the counter. "Jean, take a look," he said, nodding toward the conflagration on the screen. "On top of everything else, we got a couple wildfires going here in North County, one in Harmony Grove and the other over near Bonsall."

"Are they nearby?"

"Nah, miles away. But until now it's been a pretty good year, fire-wise. These are the first big ones we've had. The guy on the news says they're probably both arson."

"What kind of wacko sets fires in this weather?"

"Hey, this is arson season. Pyromaniacs get a lot of bang for their buck this time of year." He tasted the sauce. "OK, that's ready. You know the deputies who were stationed here? Sheila and Bruce? They hadda leave so they could help deal with problems from the fires—traffic, evacuations, livestock, all that shit. The whole apparatus is spread pretty thin right now."

"It'd be a good time to rob a bank," Jean said.

"You think like a felon. Want a taste of this? It's mole sauce. I'm serving rabbit mole tomorrow night." He gave her a spoonful.

"Mmm. I'm going to miss your cooking, Laszlo."

"Want me to make you something before you go?"

"Thanks. I'll take you up on that in a few minutes." She looked at the list on the bulletin board. Yuan had been assigned the dragon room.

Jean went upstairs to the guest rooms. There was something she had to do before she left: search Yuan's room. What did she really know about him? That he was supposedly a friend of Meide's dead brother and that he was an expert on Chinese art who could copy anything. In his drawings of her he'd mimicked a great artist perfectly. It would be easy for him to forge a simple thing like Carl's handwritten note. Even though he hadn't met Carl before, she couldn't shake the idea that his smooth, cool persona might be hiding something else. Although she doubted if he could break someone's neck, he could be working with someone else. She had to put her mind at ease before she left.

As Jean walked along the hall, she heard a muffled explosion in the distance. She knew there were lots of military installations in San Diego County, and a friend who lived in San Clemente often complained of artillery practice at Camp Pendleton that rumbled for miles. She looked out the nearest window, but there was no more noise or other disturbance, so she quickly forgot about it.

The dragon room was larger than her cabin, with the same white furnishings and Chinese art. She checked out the bathroom, picking up the bar of soap on the edge of the bathtub. Sandalwood. In the soft leather Dopp toilet kit on the counter were shaving cream, razor blades, two vials of Asian medicine whose labels she couldn't read, condoms, and a couple of American over-the-counter drugs—Advil and an unopened box that held motion-sickness patches. He'd told her that he often got seasick, especially once on the Yellow Sea crossing from China to Japan in the wake of a typhoon.

She moved to the bedroom, searching quickly through the clothes in the drawers and closet. The labels were mostly

Chinese and European. Under a stack of men's briefs, she found three sketches on lined paper torn from a spiral binder. They showed a lovely woman with long curly hair sleeping naked on a bed, partially covered by a sheet. A bottle of wine with an odd triangular label and two partly filled glasses sat on the nightstand. The headboard was half of a big Western wagon wheel. The pencil drawings were softer and more representational than the ones he'd done of Jean, Toulouse-Lautrec rather than Picasso. She put them back in the drawer.

There was nothing else out of the ordinary about his clothes, so Jean pulled his brown leather luggage down from the top of the closet and put it on the bed. His big suitcase was empty, even the side pockets. The valise, obviously well used, looked like a large old-fashioned doctor's bag. She popped the top open. Nothing in there either. Something about its shape seemed strange—it was deeper outside than inside. She measured with her hand and realized the difference was nearly three inches. It had a false bottom.

Excited, Jean ran her fingers around the inside of the valise. There was a small fabric tab in the middle of one edge. She tugged on it and uncovered a dense foam pad that just fit the floor of the valise. She pulled that up, too. There was another pad underneath, but this one had shapes carved into it, each one different and somehow familiar. Jean counted them; there were twelve. She realized the pad had been cut to hold the Han jade zodiac figures.

Jean sat on the bed, stunned, putting things together in her mind, getting a headache from her conclusions. She'd have to put everything back and phone Matt Baeza right away. As she stood up, Yuan walked through the door, putting something into his pants pocket. Jean saw a flash of metallic blue. He was as surprised to see her as she was to see him.

"What are you doing here?" she demanded.

"I am asking you the same thing."

Jean realized she was in deep shit. If push came to shove, she was sure she could get away from him; they probably weighed about the same, and she had taken several of Roman's self-defense classes.

He walked past her and looked at the dismantled valise, the carved foam underlayer still exposed. "I wish you had not done this, Jean," he said, his voice soft and regretful. "Your blunder will have serious consequences."

Jean knew she should make a run for it, but couldn't restrain her anger or curiosity. "You're running a con, aren't you? You've got Meide and Ted thinking you're an old friend of the family. I'll bet you never even met Meide's brother."

"No, never. But he was the darling of the Taipei press."

"You conned me, too."

"I desired you, so I said what you wished to hear. Don't play the seduced maiden, Jean. I gave as good as I got, as you Americans say."

"I won't argue with that. You're an expert at pleasing people, aren't you?"

"I give people what they want. Meide wanted a new big brother and Ted wanted a new and interesting toady. And in the end, I will get what I want from them."

"The Han jade. But since there's no way you could ever fence it, you must already have a buyer."

"Of course. There is a collector who wants the jade above all things and is content to keep it hidden, to be seen only by himself."

"Why didn't you steal it the first night? Why hang around all weekend?"

"To taste the wines, of course. And to have you in the gallery."

"It's too late to sweet talk me, Yuan. You must have done this before. What did you think would happen when Roman gave your picture to the police? How could you run another con if everyone knew what you looked like?"

"The world is full of rich fools who own great art they do not understand, people Frank Lloyd Wright called mere janitors of their possessions. In any case, once the jade is sold, I need never venture out again."

"You killed Carl, didn't you? Katharine saw what happened, and you killed her, too."

"I have never killed anyone. I abhor violence."

"Then you had help. What did Carl do? Did you have his neck broken just because he was an asshole?"

Yuan gazed past her for a moment, then brought his eyes back to her face. "He recognized me."

"From where?"

"From many years ago. I didn't know him until he spoke about the past. He must have lost a hundred pounds and he was no longer bald. He wanted me to cut him in. I thought I should, but I was persuaded otherwise."

"Persuaded by whom? Whoever killed Carl and Katharine? And probably Domingo Huerta and Pilar, too, although I don't know how you managed that."

"Huerta overheard my partner and me talking and became suspicious. He intended to warn Ted Lyon that we were planning to rob him."

"Who's your partner?"

A rough hand slapped a wide piece of tape over Jean's mouth and someone very strong pinned her arms to her sides. She looked down at the leathery, splotchy hands—Angus. She tried to stomp on his instep, but he lifted her off her feet.

"What kept you?" Yuan said. "I've been stalling for several minutes."

"I was right outside. I wanted to hear what she had to say. She's too smart by half."

Jean's struggles were getting her nowhere. Angus bent her arm behind her. "Settle down," he ordered, "unless you want me to break something." He hurt her enough to make her stand still.

"Did you kill that waitress?" Yuan asked him.

"Figure it out," Angus said impatiently. "By the time we checked into the Redskin Hilton she'd been dead more than a month." He tightened his grip on Jean's arm, making her eyes water. "Anyway, I'd never use a weapon on a little piece like that. How do you want to play it now, Casanova?"

"Give me a moment." Yuan put the liners back into the valise. He grabbed a stack of white hand towels from the bathroom, dropped them into the valise, closed it, and picked it up. "Jean, you have really disrupted things. I had planned to wait for the window of time when you had gone to the airport and the Lyons were not yet back. But we must move things forward now. These fires have been most helpful in drawing the police away—we needn't create our own diversions. Where is Roman?"

Angus snorted. "In his cabin, buggering his boyfriend."

"Well then, we shall hope to avoid him."

"Don't worry about that faggot," Angus said. "I can handle him. What about her? Do her here?"

"No, bring her with us. We shall leave her in the gallery when you disable the doors. She can raise no alarm from there, and by the time they manage to free her, we will be out of the authorities' reach."

"We should off her now."

"No, Angus. It's out of the question. Please do as I say this time."

Angus shrugged. "Have it your way." He made Jean walk in front of him as they followed Yuan out the door and along the hall, Angus gripping her elbow in a way that made her dizzy with pain. "Come on, sweetheart. You're lucky Yuan's such a pussy." He gave an ugly, high-pitched laugh. "He won't butcher the steer, but he'll sure eat the steak."

Yuan frowned back at them. "I see recent events have excited you. We both know what can happen when you become what the Americans call blood simple. That is why you must let me make the decisions from now on."

"As long as you don't think with your dick again."

"You have no right to complain of my deportment. You did not intercept Huerta until he was nearly at Lyon's side.

And you showed very poor judgment when you dropped his body on Lyon's car."

"I was just going to toss him into the street, but then I saw that car right next to the building. Thought I'd give his lordship something to think about." He eyed Jean. "If I'd known what a pain-in-the-ass bitch your girlfriend was going to be, I'd have waited till she was in the fucking car."

"I am grateful that you spared her," Yuan said.

They went downstairs to the gallery and Angus pushed Jean into a tall wooden chair next to a glass tabletop display of antique fans. She thought of trying to run past him, but was afraid of what he'd do if he caught her. He took a roll of duct tape out of his pocket and secured her forearms to the arms of the chair, cutting the tape with a large, nasty-looking pocketknife.

As Angus knelt on the floor to tape her legs together, Yuan set his valise on a bench and opened the jade cabinet. "I never should have let you talk me into killing Schoonover," he said. "It would have been less costly to cut him in."

"And I never should have let you talk me into staying here so goddamn long."

"In retrospect, you are right. We should have done our business and left at once. But the wines were extraordinary, and so was Jean." Yuan took the false bottom and pad out of the valise and carefully placed the zodiac figures into their foam cradles.

Angus finished taping Jean's legs and stood up, looking her over, a glint in his pale eyes. "You won't get any more of this," he said to Yuan. "Why not let me have some fun?"

"No. Leave her alone."

"I won't hurt her." He leaned toward Jean. "Much," he whispered. She recoiled as he squeezed her bare throat and slid his hand down over her breasts. She worked at the tape on her mouth; if she could get it off, she'd bite him to the bone.

"Come on," Angus said. "I've kept my pants zipped through this whole thing, as promised, which is more than you can say."

"There is a difference. My sex life does not involve any felonies."

"I'll give you another three percent," Angus said.

Yuan turned and looked at Jean with an expression of measured speculation, filling her with cold dread.

Angus licked his lips. "Five percent."

Yuan regarded her for a few more seconds. "Will we still make our rendezvous?"

"I guarantee it. Starting early gives us more time."

"Very well. But wait until I've finished here. I don't wish to see it. And don't do any permanent damage." Yuan turned back to the jade.

Jean strained desperately against her bonds, but was taped so tightly she could barely move. She thought about the self-defense tricks Roman had taught her, planning what to do, struggling to stay calm. If Angus really were Special Forces, all her amateur skills would be useless, especially since he was armed. Jean felt her eyes fill with tears of rage and frustration. She took a few deep breaths—if her nose got stuffed up, she might suffocate.

What would prevent Angus from killing her once Yuan was gone? She was sick with fear at the prospect of being raped, but now she faced the very real possibility that she was about to die. She'd never felt so helpless before in her life. Jean willed herself to stay angry and not slip into panic.

"I know what you're thinking now, girlie," Angus said. "Do I fight and maybe get hurt, or do I go along? I tell you what—I'll enjoy it a lot more if you fight." He gripped the neck of her dress and used his knife to slit it to the waist, exposing her plain black underwire bra. Her stomach lurched at the sight of the erection pressing against his pants, and she fought against the bile rising in her throat. If she vomited, she'd suffocate for sure.

"Angus," Yuan said sharply. "Wait until I have gone."

"Whatever you say, Bwana." Angus closed the knife and dropped it into his pants pocket, then took off his sport coat and laid it on a nearby bench. "But hurry up. I don't like to keep the lady waiting."

Yuan finished packing the jade and moved to other cabinets, where he took out small portable treasures—silk scrolls, snuff bottles, the golden rhino—wrapping them in white towels. Finally he snapped the valise closed. "Now I must pack a few things. Meet me at the car when you're finished." He looked at Jean, who put everything she had into her eyes, begging him not to leave. "I am sorry, Jean," he said, "but the one thing I abhor more than violence is poverty." Yuan turned to the stairs as Angus advanced on Jean, grinning. He'd have to take off the tape to get at her, and she steeled herself, ready to strike out as soon as she was free.

The faint sound of musical, tuneless whistling drifted in from the stairwell—Laszlo must be somewhere nearby. Jean realized this was her only chance. She used her toes to push the chair over backward into the tabletop cabinet behind her, hoping she wouldn't be cut to ribbons. The chair made a gratifying crash as it broke the glass top, and she ended up leaning back at a forty-five-degree angle, the chair supported by the cabinet's base.

"You'll pay for that, bitch," Angus said. He hooked a finger under the center of her bra and pulled, righting the chair.

The whistling had stopped, and she heard the murmur of male voices. Then Laszlo said, "I'll check it out." Yuan froze in his tracks and Angus spun toward the stairs.

Jean breathed out, weak with relief, as Laszlo ran into the gallery, stopping abruptly when he saw Jean and the open cabinets. "What the fuck?" he exclaimed. "Hey, Roman," he shouted over his shoulder. "Get your ass down here."

In a moment Roman trotted down the stairs and stopped near the door, taking in the scene. "We seem to have interrupted a heist and a rape," he said, loosening his stance. "Step away from Jean, Angus."

Angus grinned at Roman. "I guess we'll finish it now." He patted Jean's cheek. "Don't worry, sweetheart. This won't take long."

Laszlo rushed toward Jean. "Laszlo," Roman said, slipping off his loafers, "keep Yuan from leaving. We'll free Jean in a moment." He met her eyes and she nodded her consent.

"You got it." Laszlo moved back toward the stairs, blocking Yuan's escape route, rubbing a fist into his palm. "Stay put, lover boy."

Yuan, looking thoroughly alarmed, backed up against the wall, clutching his valise.

Angus took the knife out of his pocket and snapped it open. He held it like an oar, palm down, the blade sticking out to the side with the sharp edge forward. "You fucking faggot," he said, a malevolent gleam in his eyes, "I'm going to split you like a chicken."

Roman said nothing. His breathing was deep and slow, his movements minimal. Jean had seen him fight in matches and exhibitions, and recognized his intense focus and concentration. His eyes darted quickly around the room, and she knew he was looking for a weapon. The nearby chairs were too big to use, and all the heavy vases and bronze pieces were inside glass cabinets. There were no lamps, just track lighting. And Angus was moving fast. He closed the distance between them and made a sharp jab at Roman's torso with the knife. Roman jammed his stiffened left arm, palm open, inside the curve of Angus's right arm, forcing the knife away. Before Angus could deliver a punch with his left hand, Roman brought the edge of his right hand down hard on Angus's collarbone and smashed his left knee with a stomping kick. The sounds of impact were sickening, dull splats and cracking bones.

Angus gave a strangled cry and crumpled to the floor. It was over in seconds. Jean stared wide-eyed at Angus. His breath came in gasps and his grimacing face was beet red. He clutched at his broken collarbone, grunting in agony. The knife lay a few feet from his twisted leg, the blade smeared with blood. Laszlo gave a low whistle. "Hot damn," he said.

Roman didn't skip a beat. He went over to Jean and pulled the tape off one wrist. She flinched as arm hair came off with it. Blood dripped onto the beige carpeting from a cut on the outside of his left forearm. "I'm going to let you take the tape off your mouth, because that'll hurt," he said softly. "OK?"

She nodded again.

"Roman, behind you!" Laszlo shouted.

Roman spun around. Angus had pulled himself the short distance to his knife and held it by its tip, poised to throw. As he released the knife, a deafening explosion filled the room. Roman fell to his knees and pitched sideways at Jean's feet, the hilt of the knife protruding from his left thigh. Across the room Angus sprawled on the pale carpet, his head a pulpy mass. Bernie, at the foot of the stairs, lowered a shotgun, passed it off to Laszlo, and hurried to Roman's side, kneeling down, his face contorted. "Oh my God, Roman," he said, reaching for the knife.

Jean tore the tape off her mouth with her free hand, crying out as hair and skin came with it. "Leave it in," she ordered.

Bernie stared at her as if she were insane. "Why?"

"If you take it out, things that are holding together might start leaking. I read it in a mystery."

"She's right," Roman gasped. "Leave it in."

"Roman, I'm so sorry," Bernie said, touching his shoulder.

"For saving my life?" Roman said through his teeth. "If that shot hadn't thrown his aim off, he would have hit something important." He'd broken into a sweat, and blood soaked his slacks around the wound.

Jean struggled to pull the rest of the tape from her arm and legs, forcing herself to concentrate on one thing: getting help for Roman. She glanced at Laszlo. He stood near the stairs, training the shotgun on Yuan, who hadn't moved from his spot against the wall and still clung to the valise. Jean saw shock and fear in his eyes. "We have to call 911," she said.

At the top of the stairs she heard voices—Gloria and Chencho. The two froze halfway down the stairs when they caught sight of Laszlo holding the gun. "We heard a shot," Gloria said.

"It's all over," Laszlo said. "Call 911—Roman's hurt."

"Chencho, do it," Gloria said as she entered the room, gasping at the sight of Angus's body. She knelt next to Jean. "What's going on?"

"Angus and Yuan were ripping the place off," Laszlo said. "Angus threw the knife at Roman just before Bernie blew him away. Nice timing, Bern."

Jean sat on the floor next to Roman, her heart pounding, her stomach in a knot. She didn't think the knife had hit an artery, but then her knowledge of anatomy was somewhat specialized. "Roman, should we put a tourniquet on you?"

"Yes. Use a belt."

Bernie took off his brown leather belt and carefully tightened it around Roman's thigh above the knife.

"Does it hurt?" Jean asked.

"Only when I breathe."

Bernie made a sound that was half laugh and half sob. "Jake Gittes to Russ Yelburton," he said. "*Chinatown*."

Jean gently stroked Roman's face—his dark skin was clammy and paler than usual. "Gloria, get that fur coat off the rack. We don't want him to go into shock. And see if you can find something for the cut on his arm."

Gloria did as Jean asked, bringing another jacket to put under his head and a white bar towel. Jean bound the cut on his arm, which wasn't deep, and made him as comfortable as possible.

Gloria looked at Jean's sliced up dress. "Who did that to you?"

"Angus. He had plans, but the cavalry arrived in the nick of time."

They heard someone running along the hall, and in a moment Chencho pounded down the stairs, eyes wide with fear. "We have to get out of here," he told them. "The whole mountain's on fire."

"What happened?" Gloria asked.

"I smelled smoke upstairs and when I called 911 they said someone blew up the meth lab at the Jones place. The fire's out of control and it's moving this way."

"That must have been the explosion I heard earlier," Jean said. "What about the paramedics?"

"The explosion messed up the road. They're sending a helicopter for us. We have to get Roman out to the lawn."

"Oh man," Bernie said. "Can this get any worse?"

"The trick will be getting Roman up the stairs," Laszlo said.

"I can walk, with help," Roman said, his voice constricted with pain.

"Hey, Jean. Here you go." Laszlo set the shotgun down, took off his white chef's coat—revealing a gray Patti Smith T-shirt underneath—and helped her into it. The sleeves were too short and it smelled of garlic and cigarettes, but it covered her torn dress.

"Thanks," Jean said.

Bernie stood and faced Yuan. "OK, Yuan, if you cooperate and don't try to run off, we'll get the police to cut you some slack."

"Very well," Yuan said.

"Like hell we will." Jean stood and walked up to Yuan, her fear for Roman fueling her rage. "You son of a bitch!" With the last word, she slammed the heel of her hand into his nose as hard as she could. He dropped the valise and staggered back, blood spurting down his face and onto his cream-colored shirt.

Bernie came up behind her and pulled her gently by the shoulders. "Enough, Jean."

"Let go of me."

"We can't carry him out, too."

She faced him. "Listen to me, Bernie: Angus killed Carl and Katharine and Domingo Huerta. He and Yuan were running this con together. And Yuan just gave Angus permission to rape me for a bigger cut of the take."

"My God." Bernie hugged her. "Jean, I'm so sorry."

"What a piece of shit," Laszlo said, shaking his head. He took Yuan's chin in his hand, making him flinch, and looked closely at Jean's handiwork. "Nice punch, Jean. You broke his nose." He handed Yuan the kitchen towel that hung from his back pocket, then turned to Jean and Bernie. "We can deal with him later. Let's get this show on the road."

"Right," Bernie said. "Jean and I will help Roman up the stairs. Meanwhile, who else is here?"

"The kitchen staff has the day off," Laszlo said.

"The house staff, too," Gloria said.

Bernie nodded. "OK, but we'd better check. Gloria, search the house. Laszlo, you and Chencho search the grounds. Hang onto the shotgun, Laszlo. Meet us on the lawn."

"You got it," Laszlo said. "What about Yuan?"

They looked at him coldly; he dabbed at his smashed nose with the towel, his eyes watery and wary. "He'll follow us," Bernie said. "If he tries anything I'll let Jean finish him off."

"No need for that," Yuan said, sounding as if he had a bad cold. "I shall cooperate, as promised."

There wasn't time to argue, so Jean turned to the task at hand. "Make him bring that valise," she said. "It's evidence."

Jean and Bernie uncovered Roman and helped him stand. He stifled a groan, teeth clenched. They draped his arms over their shoulders and walked him slowly toward the stairs. Yuan followed with the valise.

The ascent was agonizing, each step a struggle, and Jean was afraid Roman would faint before they got to the top. The level floor was easier going, and soon they stepped out onto the terrace, all of them sweating and panting with effort, the stain on Roman's slacks growing in spite of the tourniquet. The smell of smoke was strong.

Out on the lawn Laszlo, Gloria, and Chencho stood together looking over the top of the house. A man in a khaki uniform sat at their feet, his head in his hands. Jean recognized him as the security guard from the front gate. She saw dried blood and a big bruise across the side of his shaved head.

"Hank, what happened to you?" Bernie asked.

"That asshole MacKnight knocked me out and taped me up, right in the kiosk."

"Chencho found him," Laszlo said. "I think he's got a concussion."

"Anyone else?" Bernie said.

"Not that we could find."

"Roman," Jean said, "do you want to sit down?"

"No. It'll be too hard to get up again."

Tall plumes of gray-white smoke billowed from the other side of the house, and they could hear planes circling and the occasional siren. A low heavy thrumping sound came closer, and they backed up as a small helicopter darted through the canyon and landed on the lawn, the wind from the rotors adding to the hot, harsh air buffeting them.

Bernie helped Roman toward the helicopter. "What's your name?" he asked the pilot, who'd pushed the door open.

"Jack Padia."

"I'm Bernie Lyon. What's the situation, Jack?"

"The fire's moving uphill fast, toward the house. We're shorthanded—most of our aircraft and personnel are deployed at the other fires. Help's coming from Orange County but it's not here yet. I can only take four of you, and that's pushing it. I'll have to come back for the rest."

Jean started to realize the danger of their predicament. She met Bernie's eyes and saw it was dawning on him, too.

"Take these two wounded men and the ladies," Bernie told the pilot. "We'll catch the next bus."

"What about him?" the pilot said, gesturing at Yuan. "He's hurt, too."

"No," Bernie said. "He'll stay with us." He took the valise from Yuan and handed it to Gloria. "Give this to Matt. Tell him it's evidence."

Jack helped Bernie and Jean lift Roman in; they managed it without decapitating anyone on the whirring blades. Roman rested on one of the seats, half reclining so his wounded leg stuck straight out in front of him. Hank took the other seat and Gloria sat next to the pilot. Jack was right—there was space on the floor for only one more person.

"Come on, lady," the pilot ordered when Jean hesitated. "We're in kind of a hurry here."

Jean had been watching Chencho's terrified face as he struggled to appear brave. "I guess this is where I find out if I really am a feminist," she said, stepping back. "Take Chencho—he's younger."

"Are you sure?" Chencho said. "I . . . I can wait."

"I'm sure," Jean said. "Go ahead, get on."

"*Gracias*." Chencho smiled in grateful relief and climbed into the copter.

"Goddammit, Jean," Roman said, his face contorted with pain.

Jean threw him a kiss. "See you soon, Roman." Bernie, standing beside her, threw a kiss, too. The pilot waved and took off over the canyon.

Bernie put an arm around Jean's shoulders. "You're a good man, sister."

"Sam Spade to Effie Perrine," she said, watching the copter sail away through the blowing smoke. "*The Maltese Falcon*."

They turned back toward the house, and Jean was horrified to see how far the fire had come. She could see flames licking up from the far side of the compound. A deep roaring noise filled her ears. The entire sky was a dusty orange color, the sun a flame-colored disk. She'd heard about fires so fierce that they made their own weather, and the searing wind that whipped around them, changing direction every few seconds, was uglier than any Santa Ana she'd ever felt.

"Christ almighty," Bernie muttered. "The whole place is going to burn." He took a deep breath. "OK, we've got twenty minutes or so till the copter comes back. Let's save what we can. Everything's insured, but the only irreplaceable stuff in the whole barn is the good Chinese art, and we can't save it all. Yuan, I want you to come down to the gallery and tell us what's worth hauling out of here. Look on it as part of our deal."

Yuan's nose had stopped bleeding, but the entire center of his face was swollen and purple. "Very well."

Laszlo gave Bernie the shotgun. "I have to get some things."

"Me too," Jean said.

"Go," Bernie said. "Meet us in the gallery."

Jean ran to Roman's cabin, where Clive's camera bag sat on the bed, already packed up. She took out everything but the cameras and put the bag over her shoulder. She opened Roman's suitcase and dumped it on the floor—there was nothing he couldn't replace except his notebook. She put it into the camera bag.

In her room she collected her notes, wallet, birth control pills, a small jewelry case, and her cell phone and packed them into Clive's bag. The red cheongsam lay across the top of her suitcase; she stuffed it in, too. It had taken her hours to sew the frogs on right. She thought about changing her torn dress but didn't want to waste time.

She ran down the stairs to the gallery. Someone had put a tablecloth over Angus's head and torso, for which she was grateful. Bernie had gathered four empty suitcases, and he and Yuan ran back and forth from the cabinets, filling the cases with rolled-up scrolls and textiles, small ceramic pieces, and other treasures, Yuan telling them what to save and what to leave. Jean joined in, forcing her fury down, avoiding eye contact with Yuan.

"What about these?" Bernie said, gesturing toward the Tang ceramics.

"No. They are second-rate and too large to carry. Take those smaller Song vases and the Ming blue and white. The bronzes and Ming furniture present a problem: They are among the finest pieces, but much too heavy."

"Why don't we put the bronzes in the pool?" Jean asked.

"That is an excellent suggestion, Jean," Yuan said. "Underestimating your intelligence and ingenuity has been my undoing, it seems."

She ignored him. It was either that or scratch out his eyes. "Bernie, I know your movies are replaceable, but what about your photographs?" she said.

"Replaceable. The originals are in LA."

"Let's put the really good wine in the pool, too." Jean's eyes rested on Angus. "You know what else?" she said to Bernie. "Use Roman's camera to shoot a few frames of the body. Just in case it burns."

"Another good idea." Bernie dug through Clive's bag and took out one of the cameras. Jean pulled the tablecloth off Angus, looking away from him. "Jesus," Bernie said, but he moved around the body, shooting several exposures.

As Bernie handed the camera to Jean, Laszlo trotted down the steps empty-handed, his face and clothes streaked with soot. "We have to get the fuck out of here. The cabins near the entrance are on fire, including mine, and it's spreading fast."

"Why isn't the sprinkler system slowing things down?" Bernie asked.

"It ain't working is why," Laszlo said. "I tried to rinse off in the kitchen and there's no water pressure. The explosion must have busted a pipe."

Bernie shook his head. "This is unbelievable."

"Well, believe it. Let's book outta here. Fuck all this art."

Yuan surveyed the cabinets. "We have already packed most of the finer pieces."

"We'll have to leave the wine, too. OK, let's go." Bernie fastened all the suitcases, and each of them picked up a case and a bronze piece that Yuan selected. Once upstairs, they dropped the bronzes into the pool and went out on the lawn, putting down the suitcases. The air was so hot it was difficult to breathe. The hard, shifting wind blew the acrid smoke into their faces, making them cough and squeeze their eyes closed.

"Where the fuck is that copter?" Laszlo said.

"Let's find out." Jean pulled out her phone. Miraculously, there were two bars of service. "Whom do we call?" she asked.

"Lemme have that," Laszlo said. "I'll find Matt. He'll know what's up." He made a couple of calls and soon was dialing Matt's cell phone number. "Hey Matt, it's Laszlo. We're playing croquet on the lawn here while we wait for your boy to pick us up. Gloria and Roman get there OK?" He listened for a while. "Uh huh. . . . No shit. OK, I'll get back to you. You got this number."

Laszlo handed the phone to her. "Well, we're totally fucked. Matt says the copter barely made it out of here because of the wind. Almost blew into the canyon wall. The wind is worse now, so he can't land here again."

"What do you mean?" Yuan said. "He must land here."

"It ain't gonna happen. So Matt says we got two really attractive options: Either we get in the pool and hope we don't die of smoke inhalation when the fire goes over us, or we walk out by way of Katharine's and hope the fire doesn't catch up with us. They'll send a truck for us. If we make it."

An especially strong gust of wind blew up, surrounding them with swirling smoke, ashes, and embers, making the top branches of the big sycamores toss wildly. "Let's get in the pool while we decide," Bernie said, raising his voice above the wind. "If we walk across, we should be wet."

They picked up their suitcases and moved fast toward the pool. The slender palms behind the cabaña were bent almost double by the wind. Jean dropped her baggage, slipped off her shoes, and dove in—the cool blue water felt heavenly after the inferno outside, and she drank several gulps of it, chlorine and all, soothing her parched throat. When she surfaced she saw that the three men had climbed in by the steps in the shallow end.

Jean felt she must be having the longest adrenaline rush of her life. Despite the danger, this time she didn't feel helpless. Far from it—she'd been watching the fire and thought they had a chance. "I vote for walking to Katharine's," she said. "Look at the fire: The wind isn't driving it this way—it was just going uphill. We can make it."

"Let's do it," Laszlo said. "I don't wanna get poached alive."

"I think it would be safest to remain in the pool," Yuan said.

"You don't get a vote," Laszlo told him.

"OK, we'll walk across," Bernie said. "Let's call Matt and tell him what we're doing." He frowned at Jean. "The phone's still in your pocket, isn't it?"

"Uh, yeah." Jean took out the dripping phone and punched a few buttons. It was dead. "So sorry. Don't you have a cell?"

"In my room, which is now on fire. Let's hope Matt figures it out and sends the truck."

"I'm damned if I'm gonna carry any of Ted's shit across with me," Laszlo said.

"Agreed," Bernie said. "We may have to move fast."

They climbed out of the water, put their shoes on, and dropped the four suitcases into the deep end of the pool. Jean picked up Clive's camera bag, lengthened the strap, and looped it over her head and one arm. She took a last drink of the bad-tasting water. As they set out across the canyon on Ethan's path, a cyclone of sparks engulfed the big trees and they exploded into flames, raining embers over the terrace and into the pool. The four of them broke into a run.

Chapter 16

Jean led the way as they dashed across the canyon, Clive's bag banging against her hip. Laszlo and Yuan followed and Bernie came last, still carrying the shotgun. The wind was less intense in the canyon, and for the moment blew toward the fire.

They slowed on the climb to Katharine's yard, Laszlo and Yuan panting. Jean looked back at Phoenix Garden—half the buildings and the two big trees were completely engulfed in flames. Embers drifted into the canyon, but none had ignited the chaparral yet. The smoke billowed hundreds of feet in the air, blocking out the sun. It was dim as twilight.

Jean shifted the camera bag. The chef's coat was nearly dry and had gotten stiff and scratchy. Roman's dried blood stained one side of it.

They heard a car's engine as they rounded the house. In the driveway, a familiar figure in shorts and a Muse T-shirt got out of a blue Hyundai.

"Ethan!" Jean cried. "Am I glad to see you."

Ethan stared wide-eyed at the inferno across the canyon. "Whoa. I saw the smoke and wanted to check on the birds. I didn't know the fire was so close."

"How about a lift outta here, kid?" Laszlo said.

"Sure, no problem."

"Do you have a cell phone?"

"Yeah," Ethan said, "but it doesn't work up here."

"Can we make a phone call from the house?" Bernie asked.

"It's shut off."

Ethan looked at Yuan's smashed nose. "What happened to you?"

"He walked into a door," Laszlo said.

Ethan shrugged. "Well, there's nothing I can do about the house, but I have to save the birds."

Jean glanced at Bernie, who nodded. "Do it fast," he said.

"Wake up, people," Laszlo said. "If the wind shifts, we're barbecue."

"They'll burn if I don't free them." Ethan put on Katharine's heavy leather gloves and ran into the birdhouse. He brought the birds out one at a time, holding them gently against his body, and set them free. The Cooper's hawk bolted away from him like a shot. The great horned owl and the red-tailed hawk lingered briefly, hopping on the ground, perching on nearby trees, finally flying away. In spite of her fear, Jean appreciated the raw beauty of the moment.

Ethan entered the birdhouse a final time and brought out a cage covered with a white cloth. "We've got to take the barn owl with us—he can't fly," he said. "Let's get out of here." They climbed into the small car, Bernie in the front seat with the shotgun propped against the door and the birdcage on his lap, and the other three squeezed in back, Laszlo in the middle.

"We have to let people know we're OK," Bernie said. "And we have to find our friend Roman. He was hurt and taken out by helicopter."

"There's an emergency operations center at the high school," Ethan said. He drove them out Katharine's long dirt driveway and onto a side road that curved away from the mountain, down to the main road and toward town. The wind shook the small car. Fire vehicles sped by them in both directions.

They pulled into the high school parking lot, which was full of cars and official vehicles. Several horse trailers were parked at one end; three saddled horses and a llama were tethered to a chain-link fence. The Maybach and a white limo sat at the far end of the lot. Ethan maneuvered past the green stucco classroom buildings toward a big, brightly lit gymnasium; they could see the rescue helicopter parked on the football field behind the gym.

"Things are set up in here," Ethan said. "Come on, I'll show you." They piled out of the car, leaving the owl behind.

The gym looked like what it was: the center of a disaster area. Near the entrance, harried emergency workers dealt with a milling crowd of evacuees. At one table a woman dispensed coffee, sandwiches, and doughnuts. Exhausted firefighters rested on cots or mats on the floor. Half the room held tables, chairs, and cots full of civilians, adults and children, surrounded by whatever belongings they'd managed to carry out.

At the far end of the gym, voices rose in argument. "He's my only son!" a man cried. "I'll buy the helicopter if you want. His life depends on it!"

Jean craned her neck. She could see Ted striding frantically back and forth waving his arms before a large, impassive, soot-streaked man in yellow protective gear who blocked the back door. Matt Baeza stood to the side, watching the confrontation.

"Oh shit," Bernie muttered. He hurried toward Ted.

The large man scowled at Ted, arms crossed. "You can buy the whole damn fleet and you'll still need a pilot," he said angrily. "I wouldn't let any of my men fly in this wind if *my* life depended on it."

"I'll have your job, you idiot!" Ted shrieked, his voice breaking. "If he dies because of your cowardice, I'll kill you myself!"

"Dad!" Bernie called, running toward Ted. "Dad, I'm OK."

Ted spun toward him. "Bernie!" he cried, embracing his son fiercely, sobbing. "Dear God, I thought you were dead. I couldn't bear it. I thought you were dead."

"I'm fine," Bernie soothed him, hugging him.

There were smiles and a smattering of applause among the onlookers. The large firefighter shook his head. "Good thing he wasn't armed," he said to Matt. "He'd have hijacked it."

Matt spotted Jean and navigated through the crowd. "Am I glad to see you," he said with relief when he saw the group. "I was afraid we'd lost you."

"Ethan drove us out from Katharine's," Laszlo said.

"Good work, son," Matt told the boy. "Now call your mother. She's worried." Ethan took his phone outside.

"Any of you get too much smoke?" Matt asked.

"I don't think so," Jean said. "The wind blew it away from us most of the time."

"Well, if you start to cough or get a headache or get short of breath, there are medics on duty. Everybody else get out?"

"Everybody alive," Jean said.

Matt nodded, eyeing Yuan's nose. "Mr. Wang, you're under arrest. Before I take you to the station, see the medic." He looked around the room. "Sheila!" he bellowed. The stocky female deputy came over. "Mr. Wang's under arrest. Read him his rights and watch him while he gets his nose seen to."

Sheila, a hand on her revolver, led Yuan to a nearby door that had a white banner with a red cross tacked above it. Yuan went along without a word.

"I'll need statements from you both, and Bernie, too," Matt said to Jean and Laszlo. "Gloria told me some of what happened."

"Matt, where's Roman?" Jean asked.

"At Palomar Hospital in Escondido. He didn't want to go until he found out what happened to you, but that French doctor insisted."

"You mean Monique Chatouilleux?"

"Yeah. A deputy intercepted Lyon and his friends at the safari park and brought them here. We put her to work since we were shorthanded for a while."

"How bad is he?"

"The doc said he'd be fine once he got to a hospital."

"Did you get the knife from his leg?" Jean asked.

"Yes, I did. Military issue."

"There's a shotgun in Ethan's car that you should take, too. It's the one Bernie used on Angus."

"I'll do that."

"Gloria OK?" Laszlo asked.

"She's fine," Matt said. "I took her home so she could be with her boys. Her neighborhood's not in danger."

"Can I make a call to a friend in Davis?" Jean asked. "My phone drowned."

Matt nodded. "Sure, but make it quick."

Jean took his phone outside and called Zeppo. If he'd seen the news, he'd be frantic. To her intense frustration, his cell was turned off. "Zeppo," she said to his voice mail, "I'm OK and Roman's injured but OK. I'm on a borrowed cell phone. Mine's drowned. I'll call again." She went back into the gym and gave Matt his phone.

"Look, Deputy," Laszlo said, "I need to wash off in the worst way. And Jean could use a shirt or something. Angus cut up her dress."

Matt looked at her with concern. "Did he hurt you?"

"He just scared me," Jean said, patting his arm.

Matt walked to a box of clothes behind the sandwich table and came back with a blue T-shirt, handing it to Jean. "There's a locker room over there. Go get cleaned up. I'll want the dress later so don't throw it away. I'll get you an evidence bag before you leave."

She and Laszlo went into the girls' locker room and washed off the soot at small white sinks, drying themselves with stiff brown paper towels. Jean tossed the chef's coat and put the blue T-shirt over her ruined dress. The shirt bore a picture of a slot machine crossed out by a red diagonal line in a circle. She glanced at the camera bag at her feet. There was always the red cheongsam, but somehow that seemed like overdressing.

Jean stood before a dingy mirror. "I look ridiculous."

Laszlo came up beside her. "You got a lot of red around your mouth where the tape was, but otherwise you look great. Not my type, but great."

Jean grinned at him. "What's your type?"

"I go for a darker, more compact model. Like Salma Hayek. That's another thing I like about this place. You got Latinas everywhere."

"Come on," she said, picking up the camera bag. "Let's talk to the cops."

Matt waited for them outside. "Before I take your statements, why don't you check in with the people from Phoenix Garden? They've been worried."

"I'll pass," Laszlo said. "I need a smoke."

"Haven't you had enough smoke for one day?" Jean said.

"Wood smoke just doesn't hit the spot," he said. "Anyway, those people wanna see you, not me. I'll bum a cigarette and go out back."

"I'll take your statement when you're finished, Laszlo," Matt said. He directed Jean down a hall to a cluttered room that held all the detritus of a school office. Seated on chairs and desktops or milling around were the surviving Phoenix Garden guests.

Monique spotted Jean first and embraced her. "Ah, Jean. We were so worried."

People crowded around Jean, and Tony gave her a fierce hug. Sissy and René wisely kept their distance. Jasper sat on a windowsill drinking from a silver flask.

"How did you all get here?" Jean asked.

"A sheriff's deputy found us at the safari park and told us about the fire," Monique said. "And when we lost contact with you, we feared the worst."

"I can't believe what I'm hearing," Tony said. "We treated those men as friends."

"Believe it," Jean said. "They had us all buffaloed. Where's Bernie?"

Meide, who had clearly been crying, sat in a desk chair. Ted, calm now, knelt near her, holding her hands. "Washing off the soot," he told Jean. His eyes brightened as he looked past her. "Here he is."

Bernie got the same treatment, hugs and soft words. He extricated himself and put an arm around Jean's shoulders. His collar and short sleeves were slightly damp. "You doing OK?" he asked.

"Yeah, fine. You?"

"I'll live. How's Roman?"

"He's in the hospital," Monique said. "I spoke to his doctor a few minutes ago, and his surgery went well."

"Gloria told us how it ended, but how did it start?" Ted asked. "What on earth happened to Angus?"

"I killed him with a shotgun," Bernie said quietly, gripping Jean's hand.

"Was it self-defense?"

"No," Bernie said. "Defense of a loved one. He was about to throw a knife at Roman." He took a breath. "Jean and I were never lovers, Dad. It was always Roman. I'm sorry we deceived you."

Ted moved closer and took Bernie by the shoulders. "I just had the fright of my life, son. I'm sorry, too. I'll never again try to force you to be something you're not." They hugged.

Jean smiled; here was another good thing to come out of this catastrophic weekend.

"You tell the story, Jean," Bernie said. "I don't really know how things started."

Jean leaned against a desk and gave a quick version of the day's adventures, drawing gasps and expressions of sympathy and horror from her audience. "Now you tell me something," she said to the room in general. "What were Yuan and Angus doing back at Phoenix Garden?"

"When we were looking at the okapis, Yuan started sneezing, supposedly from his allergies, and had to leave," Tony said. "Angus said he'd had enough sun and went with him. Obviously the whole thing was planned. But they didn't reckon on you busting up their play."

"If it weren't for Roman and Laszlo, they'd have scored." Jean glanced around. "Hey, where's Chencho?"

"Getting some dinner," Ted said. "I can't expect my guests to consume donated tuna sandwiches."

"What happened between you and Angus, Bernie?" Tony asked.

Bernie looked decidedly paler and shakier than when he'd come in. "Roman and I spent some time in his cabin, and it was getting late so he went to find Jean. I followed a few minutes later to say good-bye. I heard Angus and Roman arguing in the gallery, and it sounded serious, so I went after one of Dad's guns. When I finally got down there, Angus was about to throw his knife. I shot him. Look, I need to sit down. It's all starting to hit me."

Tony pushed a desk chair forward and Bernie collapsed into it. "You saved Roman's life," Tony said, clapping him on the shoulder. "That's what matters."

Sissy approached Jean, her eyes feverishly bright. "Jean, forget Martin Wingo—you have to write the story of Phoenix Garden. Did I say three hundred grand? I think we're talking seven figures here. It'll be like one of those old-fashioned murder mysteries set in an English country house, but with a terrific contemporary edge. And it'll all be true."

Jean seized the front of Sissy's black T-shirt and pulled her forward until they were eye to eye. "Sissy, if you say another word to me, I'll break *your* nose."

Sissy extricated herself and took a couple of quick steps back. "You'll change your mind."

Jean was too tired to deal with Sissy. "I have to give a statement to the sheriff's deputy," she said abruptly. "See you all later."

As she hurried down the hall, someone behind her called her name. She waited while Meide caught up, eyes red and face streaked with tears; Jean noted that she looked no less beautiful for it. She seemed much smaller and more vulnerable without high heels.

"Jean, I feel responsible for the danger you were in," Meide said. "I'm very sorry that these men I invited to my house hurt Roman and threatened you."

"I don't blame you, Meide. They were experienced con men. They fooled us all."

"I know you had a lover, too, and Sissy says it was Yuan."

Jean sighed. "Yeah."

Meide took her hand. "His betrayal of you was worst of all. For a man who has been your lover to treat you in that manner—I can't imagine how you must feel. If there's anything I can do, you only need ask."

"Thank you so much, Meide." Jean was impressed with Meide's perception; she realized that aside from Roman's injury, Yuan's betrayal was the thing that disturbed her most.

Jean went back to the gym in search of Matt. Instead, she found Ethan surrounded by a crowd of children. He'd brought the barn owl in, and the beautiful little bird perched calmly on his glove while he showed the children its damaged wing and talked animatedly about its habits and diet. Katharine was right—he did have a gift for the work. Jean caught his eye, and he put the owl back in its cage and came over to her.

"Hey, Jean. How's it going?"

"Not bad." A commotion outside drew Jean's attention. "What's up?" she asked.

"Somebody freed the horses," he said. "They're trying to round them up before they wander into traffic."

Jean went to the door and looked out. Most of the horse trailers were open and empty, and several horses trotted aimlessly around the dusty parking lot. People dashed back and forth in the hot wind, some leading captured horses, others chasing loose ones. Near the fence Matt and Sheila were trying to put a rope on the llama.

Laszlo came up beside her. "What the fuck's going on?"

"Someone let the horses out," Jean told him.

"Why would anyone do that?"

"Good question," she said. Matt brought the llama under control and handed its rope to another deputy. "Matt!" Jean called. "I need to talk to you."

Matt and Sheila, both harried and sweaty, crossed the parking lot to the door. "What is it?" the deputy said, wiping his forehead with a bandanna.

"Where's your prisoner?"

"I left him with Manny, the paramedic," Sheila said. "The painkillers knocked him out. We can take him to the sub-station and book him now. I'll go get him." She went into the medical room and returned right away, looking stricken. "He's gone. Manny was tending to a horse bite and he slipped out. I'm really sorry, Matt."

"Who you looking for?" Ethan asked.

"Wang Yuan," Sheila said.

"The Chinese guy with the broken nose?" Ethan said. "He's outside."

They all turned to him. "When did you see him?" Matt asked.

"When the horses first got loose. I was getting the owl out of my car and I saw him walking across the football field."

"Why didn't you tell someone?" Sheila demanded.

"What for?" Ethan asked, putting plenty of adolescent insolence into his tone.

"He's under arrest," Matt said.

"Oh. I didn't know. Sorry."

"Sheila, move your butt," Matt said, clearly disgusted with her. "Get the other deputies and meet me at my car. Ethan, show me where he was."

"Matt," Jean said. "I think Yuan's leaving by boat. He gets seasick, and when I searched his room I found motion sickness patches in his bag."

"Then he has to travel thirty miles to the coast. We can still run him down." He punched a number into his cell as he strode out the door.

CHAPTER 17

Jean walked back to the office where Ted and his guests waited. So Yuan had escaped. Who had let the horses loose? Had Yuan taken advantage of a prank, or had someone done it deliberately to create a diversion? Maybe Yuan did it himself. In any case, he'd never make it to the coast; the broken nose and black eyes would make him easy to spot.

The group turned toward her as Jean entered the office. She looked around. Most of them ate sandwiches and drank from Champagne flutes. Ted, Meide, and Bernie sat in chairs next to one of the desks, while Tony, Monique, and René clustered around another. Sissy and Jasper leaned on a windowsill, eating and sharing the silver flask. "Have you all been here since I left?" Jean asked.

"More or less," Bernie said, "except for bathroom and smoking breaks. Why? What's up?"

"Someone let the horses loose and Yuan slipped away in the chaos. They're searching for him now."

Tony scowled. "He'd better hope I don't find him first."

"Do you think one of us is in cahoots with Yuan?" Jasper asked brightly. He sounded drunk.

"The possibility had occurred to me," Jean said.

Ted snorted. "That's preposterous. None of my guests would—"

"Have something to eat, Jean," Meide interrupted gently.

Jean realized she was starving. On the largest desk, Chencho presided over a lavish buffet. He'd procured sparkling wine, beer, and the makings for gourmet sandwiches. There was even a silver ice bucket for the bubbly. Jean made herself a sandwich of chèvre and tomato on brioche and grabbed a glass of sparkling wine. "Ted," she said, "if you want to make big points here in Valle de los Osos, why not shell out for some fancy food for the broad masses?"

Ted nodded. "That's a good idea. I hadn't thought of it. Chencho, see to it. Have them send over some of everything."

"Right away, Mr. Lyon." Chencho grinned at Jean.

Laszlo had declined to join the Phoenix Garden crowd, so Jean brought a beer and a roast beef sandwich out to him in the gym.

The food and wine revived her. Since Matt was chasing Yuan, she knew she was in for lengthy interrogation by Wes Jurado and his homicide crew. Sure enough, Jurado soon arrived and she spent the next several hours in various gym offices telling her story and answering questions. The detective was pleased to hear that Angus had taken credit for tossing Domingo Huerta off the Fairmont; undoubtedly he'd score points by solving that murder. Jean told him who to call in the SFPD to convey the information—her old pal George Hallock. The inspector would be pissed that she had indeed gotten involved in the investigation.

Jurado surmised that Huerta had somehow overheard Yuan and Angus talking about the planned heist and hoped to get a reward from Ted for telling what he knew. Jean thought the detective was probably right, for once. But where could Huerta have encountered the two of them so long before the tasting?

Occasionally Jean would cross paths with other members of the group who were being questioned as well, and she was delighted to see two catering vans deliver fine food and drink to the evacuees and worn-out firefighters in the gym.

Jean turned Clive's cameras over to a police technician; besides the shots of Angus's body, they'd want the photos of Yuan and Angus. Rumor had it that most of Phoenix Garden had burned, so there would be little evidence left.

Jurado finally let Jean, Bernie, and Laszlo go, sending them out to the parking lot. The air smelled strongly of smoke, and white ash rained down like snow. Ted and the other guests had long since left, but Chencho waited in the limo. Jean and the two men got in, all of them exhausted, and they headed over the mountain to Escondido.

"There's some domestic bubbly open in the fridge," Chencho said from the driver's seat. "The local liquor store doesn't have much of a selection."

"No problem." Bernie poured them each a glass. "Here's to survival."

"I'll drink to that," Laszlo said, and they clinked glasses. Jean leaned back on the white leather seats, too talked out to discuss things any further.

"Mr. Lyon got you rooms at a motel in Escondido," Chencho said. "He thought you'd want to be close to the hospital."

"Take Laszlo to the motel, but Jean and I want to go to the hospital right away," Bernie said.

"It's past visiting hours," Chencho said.

Jean leaned over to see the dashboard clock and was amazed to see it was nearly ten o'clock.

"We'll go anyway," Bernie said. "I'll make them let us in."

Chencho pulled up at the Felicita Inn, an ordinary-looking motel on Centre City Parkway. Here the air was smoky as well and everything was covered with a light dusting of ash.

"Hey, Jean," Laszlo said. "What a rush, huh?" He leaned over and kissed her on the cheek, then got out of the limo.

"Sweet dreams," Jean said.

"I'll check on the room arrangements," Bernie said, getting out, too.

When they were alone, Chencho turned in his seat. "Jean, I want to thank you for what you did back there, letting me get on the chopper. I . . . I was really freaked out."

She smiled at him. "No big deal. We all got out, didn't we?"

"That's the second time you've saved me. I owe you."

"Don't worry about it." The bubbly was making her feel human again. It was one of her favorites, a Roederer Estate

Brut from Mendocino County, and Chencho had no reason to apologize for it. As she sipped wine, putting her feet on the camera bag, she sighed deeply; she longed for Zeppo, but not for the usual reason. She wanted him to hold and comfort her, to soothe her with his calm, forgiving presence. It hurt to think that it would probably be days before she'd see him.

Bernie got back in the car. "Everything's A-OK. They're expecting us, too. Apparently we're lucky to have rooms. All the motels are booked up for miles due to the evacuations."

"I'm sure your dad had something to do with our good luck," Jean said.

"No doubt," Bernie said.

"Hey," Jean said as Chencho drove them downtown. "Do you think your father's for real?"

"Yes, I do. He's never said anything remotely like that to me before."

"Do you realize what it could mean? Besides getting his blessing to be with Roman, maybe you can finance your movie."

"I haven't thought that far ahead. I'm feeling pretty shell-shocked."

"Yeah, me too," she said, taking his hand. They rode the rest of the way in silence.

"This is the place," Chencho said. Palomar Hospital was a big modern structure in the center of town. Bernie and Jean went in through the emergency room, relatively quiet on a Sunday night.

Monique had told them Roman was on the fourth floor. Bernie tracked down the nursing supervisor and used a combination of charm and his father's clout to finagle a few minutes with Roman. They walked down the dimly lit hall to his room. An old man lay in the bed nearest the door, snoring loudly; Roman's bed was next to the window. He seemed to be asleep.

Bernie leaned over Roman and gently stroked his head until Roman opened his eyes.

"Bernie," Roman said, "and Jean. Thank God." He pulled Bernie's head down and kissed him.

Jean hugged him, feeling his black whiskers against her face and his broad, muscular shoulders under the flimsy hospital gown. He'd always seemed invulnerable, and now here he was, laid low because of her recklessness. "Sorry it took us so long to get here," she said lightly. "We've been getting the third degree." She sat next to him on the bed, careful not to bump his wounded leg. A white bandage covered his left forearm.

"Tell me what's happened," Roman said.

"Well, we all got out, Ted had a life-changing scare, and Yuan escaped," Jean said.

"That's it in a nutshell," Bernie said. "How are you doing?"

"I was lucky, it seems. He missed the artery, thanks to you." Roman adjusted his bed so he was sitting up.

"You were absolutely amazing in that fight," Jean said.

Roman smiled at her. "Angus's mind-set worked in my favor. He was overconfident because he saw me as a theorist and himself as a practitioner. And on top of that, I was a fairy. He thought it would be easy. But I underestimated him when I turned my back on him. I thought he was in too much pain to do anything. I should have known better."

"You were preoccupied with saving my honor," Jean said. She added softly, "Thanks, Roman. Things would have gotten really ugly if you hadn't shown up."

"However did you get yourself into that situation, Jean?" Roman asked. "I've never known you to let a mere man get the better of you."

"It's a long story, and we've only got a few minutes. The nurse will throw us out soon."

Bernie stood. "Go ahead and tell him. I'll provide a distraction. I'm going to see about getting you a private room, OK, Roman? Dad can foot the bill."

The old man in the neighboring bed gave a deep, rattling snore. "This is one time I won't object to a little Lyon money and influence," Roman said.

Bernie went in search of the nursing supervisor.

"After everyone left for the zoo and you and Bernie were otherwise occupied, I got the bright idea to search Yuan's room," Jean said. "I didn't really trust him." She explained what had happened, knowing he'd want to hear everything, no matter how painful.

Roman frowned, concentrating on her words. After she was done, he lay for a while in silence. "You realize Angus would have killed you," he said finally.

"Oh yeah. That's why I was so glad to see you." Jean stood up and walked to the window, looking down on the parking lot. "He scared the hell out of me, but it wasn't personal; I'm a loudmouthed female, and that was enough for him. Angus was nothing but your garden-variety psychopath. What bothers me is Yuan. How could a man I was so close to physically sell me out for money? How could there be no shred of emotional attachment?"

"You've been compartmentalizing sex and emotion all your adult life," Roman said. "Yuan is simply better at it than you are."

She turned around to face him. "What, I'm supposed to cleave unto Zeppo, forsaking all others?"

"You're supposed to respect him enough to behave like an adult."

"Don't you lecture me," she said sharply. "You've screwed twice as many men as I have." Jean bit her lip, regretting her words at once.

Roman looked at her with sad, tired eyes. "Yes, I probably have. Now that I've retired from competition, are you trying to even the score?"

"I'm sorry, Roman. I'm mad because I feel so stupid and guilty. Now I'll have to tell Zeppo everything."

"And he'll forgive you, as he always does. When are you going to wake up?"

Jean took a deep breath. "Roman," she said, sitting next to him, "I don't want to fight with you. I'm sorry you got hurt because of me."

His expression softened. “I can hardly blame you for that. It was an amazingly unfortunate confluence of events.” He took her hand. “You’ve been through quite a bit today, haven’t you? But I never worry about you snapping back. You’re indomitable.”

“Don’t be so sure. If I can’t get Zeppo on the phone soon, I might actually break down and cry.”

“You haven’t talked to him yet?”

“I left a message hours ago. I drowned my cell.”

Roman stroked his goatee. “It occurs to me that it might be worthwhile finding the woman in Yuan’s drawings. Do you think you could describe her to a police artist?”

“I couldn’t describe her very well, even though I could probably recognize her. Her eyes were closed and her face turned partly away. The drawings were impressionistic.”

“Post-impressionist, if it was Toulouse-Lautrec,” Roman said.

“What I don’t get is why Angus and Yuan were close enough to Valle de los Osos for Huerta to overhear them long before the tasting.”

“I’m convinced Angus was Special Forces. The things he said about Afghanistan, his predatory nature, the professional way he fought, it all adds up. The point is, he would have come here before the main event to reconnoiter. No Special Forces operative would enter an area cold if he could help it.”

Jean thought about it. “They’d have to stay far enough away that no one would recognize them later, but close enough to run into Huerta. Where?”

“We’ll work on it later.” Roman yawned and lowered his bed. “I seem to be wearing out. Another disadvantage of old age.”

Bernie came back into the room accompanied by the nursing supervisor, a short muscular man with a shaved head who looked like a former marine. “It’s all set,” Bernie said. “Mr. Kendall here will move you to a private room.”

“Thanks. See you two tomorrow.”

They took the elevator to the lobby. "Roman's amazing," Jean said. "Even in a hospital gown he looks good."

Bernie chuckled. "Yeah, I noticed."

They walked slowly out of the hospital. Jean's relief was quickly giving way to exhaustion; once she'd gotten hold of Zeppo, she'd take a long shower, get into bed, and sleep for two days. She glanced at Bernie, who looked as bad as she felt; he gave her a tired smile.

As they approached the glass doors, she could see Chencho in the parking lot next to the limo arguing with two men in shorts and T-shirts. In the dim light it took her a moment to recognize the taller man.

"Zeppo!" she cried, running out the sliding door. He turned and smiled, rushing toward her, opening his arms. She hugged him tightly, loving the feel of his arms around her.

"So you do know these guys," Chencho said. "I thought they were a couple of pushy reporters."

"Jeannie," Zeppo said, holding her face in his hands, "are you OK?"

"I'm fine. I'm so glad to see you. How did you get here?" She belatedly noticed the man with Zeppo. It was Clive Deegan. "What's he doing here?"

"I saw the fire on the news and tried to call you and Roman, but couldn't get through," Zeppo said. "Then I called about a thousand fire department and sheriff numbers, but no one knew what had happened to you and Roman. I was going crazy. Then my phone died and I missed your call. So I drove to Sacramento and got on a plane. At the San Diego airport I ran into Clive and we shared a rental car. We finally talked to the right deputy and he said Roman was here. When we saw the limo we assumed it was Lyon's. What's Roman doing in the hospital?"

"Angus threw a knife into his leg, but he'll be fine," Jean said.

"The guy from the shooting match?"

"Yeah," she said. "He's dead. Turns out you were right—there was something dangerous going on."

"Jesus, Jeannie. What the hell's been happening?"

"Later, I promise," Jean said. Clive and Zeppo seemed a very odd couple. "How do you know each other?"

"Met at Roman's when I was giving camera lessons," Clive said.

"I saved your cameras," Jean told him, "but the police took them. They say you'll get them back in a couple of days."

Zeppo looked past Jean. "You must be Bernie. I'm Zeppo, and this is Clive."

"Zeppo, I've heard a lot about you," Bernie said as they shook hands. "And Clive. So you're the one who taught Roman to impersonate a photographer."

"That's right. Looks like I didn't do him any favors."

Bernie grinned. "But you did me a big favor, in spite of everything."

"Save the details for later," Clive said. "I want to get moving. OK if I take the car, Zeppo? You can get a ride with Jean."

"Sure," Zeppo said. "Just be careful."

"Where are you going?" Jean asked.

"Valle de los Osos to get some shots of the fire. According to the news it's still out of control."

"You're crazy to go near it," Jean said.

Clive raised an eyebrow at her. "You want to go along? Make a real reporter out of you."

"No thanks. I've had enough fun for one day. If you happen to make it out alive, we'll be at the Felicita Inn."

"See you there. Oh, and don't forget to notify the Pulitzer committee." Clive waved and took off in the rental car.

Chencho dropped Jean, Zeppo, and Bernie at the motel and headed for Rancho Santa Fe, about fifteen miles west of Escondido; the Lyons and the rest of the Phoenix Garden crowd were staying at a resort there.

Jean's suite was decorated in Southwestern style, the predominant colors turquoise and tan. She collapsed on the queen-size bed before the door was shut. "Remind me to call my parents and my editor tomorrow. I wonder how the magazine will handle this."

Zeppo slipped off his shoes and lay down beside her, putting his arms around her, his big feet hanging off the bed. Jean snuggled into him, inhaling his familiar delicious scent. "God, I'm glad you're here," she said.

"You want to talk about it?" he said softly, nuzzling her hair. "Or wait till morning?"

"I know you'd rather hear it now." She was too tired to remember what she'd already told him, so she went over the whole story, relating the discoveries of Katharine's and Carl's bodies and the final terrible hours at Phoenix Garden for what seemed like the hundredth time. Zeppo sighed and shifted when she told him about sleeping with Yuan, but he didn't let go of her.

When she was done with her story, he got up and looked at her reproachfully. "Mind if I say I told you so?"

Jean sighed. "OK, you were right—but the wines were incredible."

"You almost got raped and killed. What if Laszlo and Roman hadn't found you? What if Angus had kicked Roman's ass? What if Bernie hadn't showed up with a shotgun?"

"I know exactly how close it was. You should have seen the fight—Roman was scary. I had no idea he could move that fast or hit that hard."

"Jeannie, I know you'll do what you want no matter what I say, but next time will you please think twice before you put yourself in so much danger?"

"Truly, I had no idea how much danger I'd be in. Who'd imagine that a Sauternes tasting could be so hazardous? The worst thing I ever got at a tasting before was a hangover." Jean yawned. "I'm absolutely exhausted. Let's go to sleep. We'll talk more tomorrow."

"You smell like smoke," Zeppo said. "Shower first." He removed her shoes, then pulled her up and took off her T-shirt and dress.

"There's an evidence bag in my purse," she told him. "Put the dress in it. For the deputy."

He did as she asked, helped her out of bra and panties, and guided her into the bathroom.

Jean looked at herself in the mirror over the sink as Zeppo adjusted the water in the shower. Her face, hair, and arms bore traces of soot, her eyes were bloodshot, and the skin around her mouth was red and irritated. She sighed, realizing she'd gotten off lightly. But Roman hadn't. "I made some really bad decisions back there," she said.

"You got worked over by a couple of pros." Zeppo pushed the yellow plastic shower curtain back for her.

"That's what I told Meide. Somehow it's not much consolation." She stepped into the warm water, leaning against the cool yellow tiles, her head under the stream, feeling too tired even to wash herself.

As he often did, Zeppo seemed to read her mind. She heard a rustling of clothes, and in a moment he pulled the curtain aside and got in the shower with her, standing behind her. Without a word he picked up the little bottle of motel shampoo, poured some into his hand, and lathered her short hair.

She closed her eyes, enjoying the feel of his long fingers on her scalp. He adjusted the showerhead and rinsed her hair. "Zeppo, I'm so sorry for sleeping with him. I know how much it bothers you, even though you never say anything."

"Yeah, it bothers me. I hate thinking about you with someone else, but I'm also nervous. I mean, look what almost happened." He reached out to the towel rack for a washcloth and a small bar of beige soap. He gently washed her face, shoulders, breasts, arms, working his way down.

"Roman says you never complain because you're afraid I'll dump you. I promise not to dump you unless you get a sex-change operation."

Zeppo laughed. "No worries. My HMO would never pay for it."

"I'll try to be better," she said, feeling a slight stirring in spite of her fatigue as his hand moved over her.

"I can't complain too much. If you weren't pretty casual about who you sleep with, you never would have slept with me."

"Oh Zeppo—"

"Obviously there's a lot more to it now, but that first night I was really glad you were such a tramp."

"Watch your mouth, boy."

"Why can't you masturbate? That's what I do."

"It's not the same and you know it. I need the whole package. Preferably yours." She turned and put her arms around him, feeling his erection against her.

Jean closed her eyes and leaned into him. "A few minutes ago I didn't think I was up for it."

"You're always up for it." He gave her a deep, insistent kiss.

"Let's get into bed," Jean whispered. "I'm too tired to screw standing up."

They rinsed off and dried each other on the rough white towels. In the bedroom, Zeppo pulled off the Navajo-print bedspread and they climbed in. The white sheets were cool on Jean's skin, and Zeppo's body against hers was warm and electric. Exhaustion made her uncharacteristically passive, and she let his loving hands erase the taint of Angus's touch, and especially Yuan's. The contrast between her terror and rage of a few hours ago and the way Zeppo was making her feel now was overwhelming. Roman was right—there was plenty to appreciate in Zeppo, and she'd been taking him for granted. She'd never realized before how important it was that every word he said and every move he made were true.

Chapter 18

Jean woke briefly in the early morning when Zeppo opened the door and spoke to someone. She'd dozed off by the time the door was shut. She woke again to the tantalizing smell of coffee. Zeppo, in a white terrycloth robe, sipped from a Starbucks cup and read a newspaper by the light of a table lamp.

"Hey," she said, "good morning."

"Good morning yourself." He got up from the chair and sat on the bed.

"New robe?"

"Yeah. That guy Chencho brought two of them, plus clothes for you, plus breakfast. Compliments of Ted Lyon."

Jean sat up and eased him back onto the bed, opening the robe. She straddled him and ran her fingers through his curly red chest hair.

"It's good to see you feeling frisky again," he said. "Although I also liked it last night, when you were putty in my hands."

"Now you're putty in mine. It's all part of my new Appreciate Zeppo Program."

He chuckled. "I surrender."

Later that morning, Jean showered and put on her new clothes. Chencho had wisely chosen loose black drawstring shorts, since he hadn't known her size, and a red T-shirt. Her underwear reeked of smoke; she'd have to buy some new clothes today. At Zeppo's insistence she called her parents in Indiana, careful to downplay the dangers she'd faced, and Kyle, her editor, who was amazed by her tale. He promised to call back once he and Owen decided how to cover it.

Jean drew back the curtains and opened the window. The wind had subsided, and the air, though still smoky, was a good twenty degrees cooler than yesterday. "Hey. It's cooled off."

Zeppo opened the door. "Feels more humid, too. That's got to help with the fire." He turned on the TV and they watched with horrified fascination as a deep orange wall of fire crawled over the parched landscape like a moving wound. The Valle de los Osos fire was out, but the Harmony Grove and Bonsall fires were still out of control. The Bonsall fire had moved into Camp Pendleton, and the fire line was twenty-five miles long. So far 50,000 acres had been blackened, 300 homes had been destroyed, and five people had died—a couple and their child caught in their car as they tried to evacuate, an old man who'd had a heart attack watching his house burn, and a firefighter killed by a falling tree. Authorities were counting on the cooler weather and lighter winds to help their firefighting efforts.

Jean and Zeppo had finished Ted's coffee, croissants, and juice by the time one of Wes Jurado's men came by to pick up her ruined dress. He sent Zeppo outside and then asked Jean some follow-up questions. When the detective left, Jean poked her head out to look for Zeppo. He stood in the shade of a big eucalyptus tree in the central courtyard with Clive and Laszlo. Ashes covered every surface like dirty powdered sugar.

"Hey, Jean," Laszlo called. "How's it going?"

"A whole lot better than yesterday." She crossed the grass and joined them. "So, Clive, I see you survived the night. Get any good photos?"

"You bet I did. Singed my eyebrows a bit, too. Laszlo's been filling me in on recent events. I don't blame you for staying home last night. It sounds pretty rough."

"It was that. Have you been watching the fires on TV? Makes me glad I live where it's foggy all the time."

Laszlo nodded. "Yeah, it's pretty ugly. That's the downside of living in paradise."

"Where's Bernie?" Jean asked.

"He went to see Teddy," Laszlo answered. "Said he'd be back by lunchtime so you two could visit Roman."

"OK, good," Jean said. "According to the news, the Valle de los Osos fire is out. I sure hope it didn't burn Katharine's house."

"Which?" Clive asked.

"There's a house right across the canyon that belonged to the old woman who was killed," Jean said. "Why don't we go check it out?"

"There's a great view of Phoenix Garden from there, too," Laszlo said. "Might make a good photo."

Clive drove them in the rental car back over the hill to Valle de los Osos. Laszlo used Ted's name to get through the various checkpoints authorities had set up to discourage looting and lookie loos. They passed ravaged hillsides and the ruins of houses and businesses just off the main road. Fire crews moved around in the burned areas, watching for flare-ups. The smell of smoke was strong on this side of the pass.

Jean couldn't see any flames, but to the north, heavy gray smoke from the dying fire shared the sky with a few wispy clouds. Laszlo directed Clive to Katharine's. To Jean's great relief, the old adobe house was untouched. The fire had gotten only about a third of the way across the canyon. At the edge of the blackened chaparral, she could see wide, irregular swaths of orange fire retardant, no doubt dropped from a plane.

They walked around the house and stood in drifts of ashes on the deck, gazing across the canyon at the charred remains of Phoenix Garden. All the outbuildings and most of the main structure were gutted. Part of the wall that surrounded the house still stood, but it was blackened and cracked, and the wrought iron gate had buckled. A few scraggly gray trees were all that was left of the lush landscaping.

"Do you think it's safe to go over there?" Jean asked. "I'd really like to see if anything survived the fire."

"As long as we stay clear of the structures we should be fine," Zeppo said. They crossed the canyon on Ethan's trail.

The pool looked like a thick black tar pit, and a huge sycamore branch had fallen squarely across the shallow end. A few vultures sat in what was left of the big trees.

"Goddamn," Zeppo said. "It looks as if it's been carpet bombed."

Laszlo gave a low whistle. "Good thing we didn't stay in the fucking pool, huh, Jean?"

"Uh, yeah." As she surveyed the devastation, the warm, comfortable feelings she'd been getting from Zeppo were giving way to cold anxiety. She stood close to him, and he put his arm around her. "I don't think this phoenix will be rising from its ashes," she said.

"Teddy's got more money than God," Laszlo said. "He can have an ice palace here if he wants it."

"Speaking of Ted, we should call him," Jean said. "He needs to send someone here right away with a truck to pick up the suitcases and bronze vases in the pool."

"He'll need an armored truck if this stuff is as valuable as Yuan says it is," Laszlo said.

Clive, grinning broadly, set a tripod on the edge of the pool deck and attached an expensive-looking DSLR camera with an enormous lens. "This is fantastic," he said as he took dozens of shots, moving the tripod around, finally detaching the camera and switching lenses for more shots. "Once-in-a-lifetime stuff. The light and the angle couldn't be better."

Jean watched him with amusement. "I'm glad someone's enjoying this. You always were perverse."

When Clive was finished, they hiked back over to Katharine's deck, where Clive took more photos. They finally drove back to the motel. The rest of Jean's day was taken up with a visit to Roman, who felt much better, and a trip with Zeppo to the mall for some new clothes. Jean and Zeppo ate dinner at a pretty good California cuisine restaurant with Bernie, Laszlo, and Clive. Bernie told them that Ted already had hired a crew to retrieve his treasures from the pool.

After dinner they returned to their room and turned on the TV news. Zeppo had brought a map from the rental car so they could follow the two fires' progression. The Harmony Grove fire was nearly under control. Santa Ana winds from the high desert no longer drove the Bonsall fire west-southwest; now the wind off the ocean drove it east, where it had jumped six-lane Interstate 15. People who had thought their neighborhoods spared as the fire blew past them were now being evacuated.

Late the next morning Clive knocked on Jean and Zeppo's door and gleefully announced that the wire services had picked up several of his images. The *U-T San Diego* ran three full inside pages of color photos, mostly his: harrowing nighttime scenes of the fire consuming trees, buildings, and cars; fire crews dwarfed by towering flames; close-ups of panicky evacuees and their terrified livestock; firefighters at the end of their endurance. The front page featured Clive's shot of the Lyon compound's smoldering shell in its moonscape of ashes, stumps, and drifting smoke. In the charred, skeletal remains of one of the big sycamores, a vulture stretched its wings, giving an air of menace and malevolence to the whole scene.

Jean looked at the images with wonder. They were truly great photographs. "Damn," she said to Clive. "Finally, you were in the right place at the right time."

Around five, Matt Baeza knocked on Jean's motel door, dressed not in uniform but in jeans and a plaid shirt. Jean surmised that this was an unofficial visit.

"You want a beer?" Zeppo asked after she made introductions.

"Sure, thanks." Once they were settled in chairs, sipping cold Mexican beer that Chencho had supplied, Matt cleared his throat. "I've got some news. But first I have a proposition for you, Jean. Wes Jurado cut me out of the investigation, and I know he's not asking the right questions. So I'm doing some snooping around on my own. You were there the whole weekend and got to know the players. I want you to tell me a few things honestly. And keep it to yourself."

"Why would you trust me?"

"I called the SFPD and talked to the investigating officer on the Martin Wingo case, George Hallock. He says you're smart and you can keep a secret."

Jean saw an opportunity to fulfill her promise to Maria Esposito. "It's a deal, if Zeppo can stay, too."

Matt shifted uncomfortably. "Uh . . . some of this is about Wang Yuan."

"Zeppo already knows about him," Jean said. "Hallock would tell you that you can trust him, too."

"OK, then." He took a breath and let it out. "We think Wang hiked cross-country around the roadblocks, then at some point he got a ride. A Mexican fishing vessel docked at Oceanside Harbor for emergency repairs set sail six hours after he got away, without repairs. We're not sure how he paid the toll."

"Hey, wait a minute," Jean said. "When Yuan came in while I was searching his room, he was putting something in his pants pocket, something metallic and blue. It may have been Ted's watch. Matt, did Sheila frisk Yuan after she arrested him?"

"No, she didn't. But how far is a watch going to get him?"

"As far as he wants to go. It's a Vacheron Constantin worth a million and a half. Ted wasn't wearing it when they left for the safari park."

Matt pursed his lips. "I'll see if I can find out if it's missing. Maybe Ted kept it in a safe. Meanwhile, we know Honey Jones blew up her lab. She's the only one with keys to the shed, and several people saw her speeding through town right after the explosion. Witnesses also say a truck like hers was seen near Harmony Grove just before that fire started, and a local man saw Mojo near the origin point of the Bonsall fire. It looks like she set those to draw the crews away so she'd have a better chance of burning the Lyons out. She's also being charged with five homicides."

"Have they caught her?" Zeppo asked.

"Yeah, a couple of hours ago, trying to cross into Mexico at San Ysidro. A border patrol officer had to shoot Mojo."

Zeppo leaned forward. "If she hadn't come back to blow up the lab, she would probably have escaped. Why did she have such a hard-on for Ted Lyon?"

"Her family once owned all the land around there. They lost it over the years through bad investments and stupidity. Lyon picked up a big chunk of land cheap when her father went bankrupt. She blames him for the family troubles." Matt drank more beer.

"As far as the jade goes, I talked to Lyon and did some research," Matt continued. "The figures were brought out of China just ahead of the 1949 revolution by a former KMT general who'd had them in his family for centuries. He settled in Taipei and got friendly with Mrs. Lyon's father. The general died a few years ago, and his heir is more into vintage cars than Chinese art. When Lyon showed up on a buying spree, he saw the jade, made an offer, and took it home. The pieces have never been on the market. The point is, no photographs of them have ever been published. But the foam in the valise was cut perfectly to hold the figures."

"So someone had to take photos beforehand," Zeppo said. "There was an inside man."

"Exactly. We know Carl Schoonover was in a deep financial hole. He was paying alimony to two ex-wives and business wasn't good. He closed his Beverly Hills office several months ago but didn't tell his friends. His fiancée dumped him because he couldn't pay her bills. He didn't tell his friends that, either.

"Now, Lyon says the gallery was left open only when there were houseguests. Wes Jurado thinks Schoonover was the inside man, that he took photos of the jade when he was here for Mrs. Lyon's birthday and passed them on to Wang Yuan. Then they had a falling-out and Angus MacKnight broke Schoonover's neck. Katharine Murdoch saw MacKnight burying the body, and he broke her neck, too."

"What about Pilar Ochoa?" Jean asked. "Does Wes think Carl Schoonover killed her?"

"Yeah. The theory is that she saw something that night—maybe Schoonover taking pictures of the jade—and he killed her early the next morning. What I want to know is, do you have any reason to think it happened some other way?"

Jean thought about it. "Yes, actually. Once when we were in the gallery, Carl scolded Ted for leaving it open. He complained that the Lyons weren't using their expensive security system. And when I asked Yuan why he had Carl killed, he said it was because Carl recognized him from a long time ago. Also, I got the impression that neither Yuan nor Angus knew who killed Pilar." Jean took a sip of beer. "It doesn't make any sense. If Carl was their partner, why wouldn't he tell them what he'd done?"

"Maybe he was afraid they'd off him for being dumb enough to let Pilar catch him messing with the jade," Zeppo said.

"Could be," Matt said. "Maybe that's why they killed him, because he was a liability. They would reason that if he got arrested for Pilar's murder, he'd hand them over to get a better deal." He thought for a few moments. "Tell me about the other guests," he said to Jean. "Anyone else hurting for money?"

"Nearly all of them," Jean said. "Jasper and Sissy lost a lot of money in the real estate crash. They were so broke they lost their summer home, and Jasper made Ted buy the bottles he brought to the tasting. I overheard Tony ask for more money for his restaurants, and Ted turned him down. Tony was at Meide's birthday party, but he seems to be a great guy." Jean sighed. "Although it turns out I'm not a very good judge of character."

"Aren't his knees too messed up for him to carry Katharine's body so far?"

"Not really," Jean answered reluctantly. "He limps a little, but I saw him move pretty fast once."

"What about the French couple?"

"As far as I know, the Chatouilleux family is doing fine. His wines are selling well, and she's a doctor."

"I can do some checking on them," Matt said. "Wang and MacKnight must have been working on this thing for more than a year. We know MacKnight and Lyon made contact online about ten months ago, and Wang called Mrs. Lyon in Taipei about a month after that. The wine tasting was already in the planning stages—Lyon was buying up old vintages at auction, and your magazine and the other wine mags ran some articles about it. All MacKnight and Wang had to do was learn enough about wine, genealogy, and Mrs. Lyon's brother to pass, then get friendly so they'd be invited to the tasting."

"I got the feeling Yuan knew quite a bit about wine," Jean said.

"So he only had to study the brother."

"Were those their real names?" Jean asked.

"No. We don't know who they were yet, but it's only a matter of time. There were no useful prints on the knife, but we'll have dental records for MacKnight once the place cools down and we're able to go in and get his body. There are prints all over the jade and the other art that was in the valise. We're running them now, comparing them against the prints of all the guests. Any we can't identify must be Wang's, since you saw him handle the stuff."

"What about Domingo Huerta?" Zeppo asked.

"I think Wes has this one right. Huerta must have overheard MacKnight and Wang say something about their plan. We don't know where or when it happened. But Huerta was a regular at most of the bars around here. I spoke with Roman, and I agree with him that MacKnight and Wang must have checked out the area before this weekend. Huerta undoubtedly overheard the two during their reconnaissance mission. Also, if I can find out where they stayed, I might get a handle on who the inside man was."

"But how would they know Huerta overheard them?" Jean asked.

"I think he must have approached them and asked to be paid off to keep quiet, and they refused. Before they could off him, he somehow slipped away and decided to try to get money out of Lyon. So MacKnight followed him to San Francisco."

"That sounds reasonable," Jean said. "That last day, Yuan scolded Angus for letting Huerta get so close to Ted." She finished her beer. "So what'll you do now?"

"Keep asking questions. I know someone here in town must have seen something the morning Pilar was killed. I just have to ask the right person. And I need to find where the two of them stayed when they were casing the area." He stood. "Thanks for all your help."

They shook hands, and Jean and Zeppo watched from the open doorway as he drove away. The sky was still a dull orange-gray, and Jean wondered if she'd ever get the smell of smoke out of her nostrils.

"I'm sure glad he's not after me for something," Zeppo said.

Jean put her arms around Zeppo's waist. "Me too."

ON THE flight home the plane wasn't full, so Jean and Zeppo had three seats to themselves. Roman and Bernie planned on flying to San Francisco as soon as the doctors OK'd Roman to travel. Ted had offered them the use of his Cessna.

Since it was already late afternoon, Jean bought a gin and tonic and Zeppo had a beer. As they sipped their drinks, they mulled over the information Matt had shared. "Given the fact that he told Ted to lock the gallery, I don't see how the inside man could be Carl Schoonover," Jean said.

"He could have been covering his tracks with Ted. Maybe he knew Ted wouldn't lock it up no matter what he said."

"That's possible." Jean squeezed a tiny wedge of lime into her drink.

"But if it wasn't him, who could it have been?" Zeppo asked. "Tony Feola?"

"I hope not. I like him. He was hurting for money, but if Ted had agreed to another loan, he wouldn't have needed to steal anything. I can't see him planning the crime and then asking for money."

"Unless he was putting up a front for Ted's sake."

"Maybe," Jean allowed.

"Who's left? The happy couples?"

"Yeah, but the Chatouilleux family has plenty of money, and I can't see Jasper or Sissy being involved with a scam like this. Jasper's a serious drunk and Sissy's totally caught up in her own world."

"What about the help?" Zeppo said. "They had a lot of servants and gardeners, right?"

"Oh yeah, dozens. I only got to know Laszlo, the chef; Gloria, the sommelier; and Chencho, Ted's assistant. They seem like upright citizens, except for Laszlo. But he didn't act like a coconspirator there at the end. He helped us."

"There's always the family."

"That's a long shot," Jean said. "I don't know much about Lydia, the daughter, except that she's an animal rights nut. Anyway, I'm sure Matt Baeza has checked out the family."

Zeppo tried and failed to stretch his legs in the cramped seat. "I don't think we have enough information yet," he said. "If you want, we can do more digging."

Jean rubbed her eyes. "Not right away. I just want to think about something else for a while." She took a big drink, and they spent the rest of the trip talking about anything but Phoenix Garden.

CHAPTER 19

Back in San Francisco, Jean's life settled into a normal routine, or what passed for normal two weeks before Halloween. She'd have to go to San Diego for an inquest, but that wouldn't be for a few weeks. It was a pleasure to breathe cool, smoke-free air again.

Kyle, her editor, had told her to write up events at Phoenix Garden as a straight news story. The article would run in the December issue of *Wine Digest*, late relative to all the TV and newspaper coverage, but Jean had the advantage of being the only reporter with an inside track. She was proud of the article; she'd related most of the pertinent information without getting too personal, and it sure had a bang-up finish. Jean felt like Al Michaels, the sportscaster who'd come to San Francisco for the 1989 World Series and ended up doing days of live earthquake coverage.

The police had given Roman's photos back, and they'd turned out to be quite good. Her magazine would run some of Clive's photos as well. Carol, the art director, selected an image for the last page of the layout that could be deleted if something important happened before press time and Jean had to write a new ending.

Anticipating big newsstand sales, Owen had ordered 200,000 copies printed instead of the usual 60,000. It was their biggest issue ever; since the magazine had an exclusive story to sell, the ad people broke all records. Jean planned to ask for a long-overdue raise after the issue hit newsstands. The Sauternes tasting was relegated to a two-page sidebar, and Ted had lost interest in vetting it, so it would run as Jean wrote it, with Yquem declared the clear winner. She'd been in e-mail contact with Monique, who didn't care one way or the other about the tasting, but René was furious, much to Jean's delight.

All told, the fires had caused seven deaths and burned more than 100,000 acres, 753 homes, and dozens of outbuildings. Jean had read all she could about the fires, marveling at how much destruction one crazy person with a book of matches could cause if the brush was dry and the wind high.

At Phoenix Garden, Ted's wine cellar had miraculously sustained only heat and smoke damage, and most of the bottles were salvageable. The art Jean and the others had saved by sinking it in the pool had survived with minor damage, but nearly everything in the gallery had burned or melted. Ted had indeed stored his expensive watch in a fireproof safe, which had been recovered. The watch was, in fact, missing. Jean figured Yuan would know just where to sell it so it couldn't be traced back to him. There was no word yet on Angus's and Yuan's true identities. The police had given back Jean's notebook but had kept Yuan's sketches. She didn't care—she never wanted to see them again.

This year the Halloween party of choice was to be at the home of Jean and Roman's cross-dressing friend Lou Kasden. Their costumes had to be good; Lou's gang set a very high standard. Jean had started sewing Zeppo's costume before she'd left for Phoenix Garden and it was almost finished, but she hadn't settled on her own until returning home. Roman would usually have gone on patrol for Bash Back for most of the evening, protecting the revelers from gay bashers, but his wounded leg meant he could relax this year. With Bernie's help, he had quickly progressed from wheelchair to cane, but still refused to wear a costume.

Jean had never felt closer to Zeppo. He missed a few days of class to stay with her at first, but they soon got back to their usual schedule: He'd arrive at her apartment on Thursday or

Friday and leave Sunday night. He never seemed to tire of discussing what had happened in Valle de los Osos, which she appreciated, since she couldn't let go of it. She was sure the inside man was still on the loose.

Jean was getting to know Bernie, whom she liked more and more. Ted had been as good as his word; he'd restructured the family incentive trust into a standard trust that paid out a much larger sum than before, and he had created an account for production of Bernie's film, *Night Sweat*. Bernie planned to go down to LA after Halloween and start casting. He had a meeting scheduled with John Cusack. Jean had read the script and thought it was terrific, true neo-noir.

Bernie did have certain rich-boy tendencies that Roman teased him about—he spent too much on clothes, was sometimes impatient with clerks and waiters (although he tipped heavily), and didn't do housework unless reminded.

Jean's only gripe was that Zeppo seemed reluctant to hang out with Bernie and Roman. She thought she knew why: Zeppo was a little jealous of Bernie. She didn't complain, though; it seemed a minor issue that would resolve itself in time.

Soon after their return to San Francisco, Bernie called Jean at work and asked her to have lunch with him. They met at Zuni Café, on Market Street a few blocks from her office. Today he wore an Armani sport coat, a butter-yellow Lorenzini silk shirt, and dark brown slacks, with John Lobb shoes that Jean knew had cost at least a thousand dollars.

Bernie gave her a kiss as they were shown to their table. "Great dress," he said. "Did you make that, too?"

"Yeah." She smoothed her red dress, a copy of a Dolce & Gabbana sheath she'd seen in a magazine. "You look like a billion bucks."

"Thanks," he said. "I'm buying lunch, so go crazy."

"Don't think I won't." She looked over the menu. Bernie was very generous, a characteristic Jean appreciated and didn't mind taking advantage of. "Let's have some bubbly."

Bernie ordered a bottle of Billecart-Salmon Brut Rosé. "I'm glad you don't mind if I treat sometimes. Roman will barely let me buy him a cup of coffee. He says I'm only allowed to get him a Christmas present and a birthday present."

"Did you know his birthday's on Halloween?"

"Yeah. That's why I wanted to see you. I have a plan, but I need his measurements."

"No problem. I've made him lots of clothes." Jean raised an eyebrow. "He's nearly the same size he was the day I met him seventeen years ago."

"That figures. He exercises like a maniac, even with a hobbled leg."

"Tell me about it. He makes me cycle up Twin Peaks three times a week and I still can't beat him to the top." The waiter brought their food, a salad with shrimp and baby beets for Jean and a grilled portobello sandwich for Bernie.

Jean ate a shrimp. "So how are you two getting along? Is the honeymoon over yet?"

"Far from it. Roman is the sexiest, most beautiful man I've ever known. Wait till you see him in the costume I'm getting."

"What is it? Tell me—I can keep a secret."

"I want to surprise you, too. But I will say it's connected to his Latin roots."

"He'll love that. Back when he used to dress up for Halloween, he came as Che Guevara one year. And you should have seen him as Montezuma, with a huge feather headdress and a shaved chest. He stopped traffic."

"He's full of contradictions. Everything in his house is William Morris or arts and crafts, and the only remotely Hispanic thing he has is that wonderful little Juan Gris oil. Not to mention, his favorite music is three hundred years old and German."

"So he's eccentric. Would you change anything about him?"

Bernie grinned. "Not a thing. The better I know him, the more I admire him. He's made it alone, with no help at all from his family. He's supported himself since high school, all through college, too, and meanwhile he founded Bash Back and did all that work for AIDS. It makes me feel so lame and dependent, as if I haven't grown up yet."

"I know what you mean. Zeppo is the same way. They're both completely self-reliant and self-made. Did you read about Zeppo's being acquitted on technicalities of killing his sister-in-law?"

"Yeah. I read everything remotely connected with the Martin Wingo case."

"The press never mentioned that his family thought he did it and had him committed to an institution for two years," Jean said. "He hasn't spoken to any of them since."

"Jesus. He seems so well adjusted. Does he have a dark side I've never seen?"

"No, not at all. He's conflicted about his family, of course, but he's the sweetest man I know. And after all he's been through, little things don't faze him."

"I don't think he likes me much," Bernie said.

"He likes you fine. He's just jealous of the time Roman spends with you. They used to hang out together and ride bikes, go hiking, see movies, things like that. Don't worry—he'll get over it. Zeppo's a very reasonable guy, but every now and then he does act his age."

Bernie sipped his wine. "He doesn't really seem like your sort of man. I'm surprised you're not with someone sleek and dangerous, like Roman but straight."

"Zeppo's dangerous in his own way. Hey, what are you going to wear? Need some help?"

"No thanks." He narrowed his eyes at her. "You'll suggest something and I'll go for it, only to find as I walk into the party that Roman's dead lover came to their last Halloween bash in the same costume."

"Mrs. Danvers and No-Name, *Rebecca*," Jean said with a grin.

When not a scrap of food or drop of wine was left, she promised to e-mail Roman's measurements to Bernie and went back to work.

JEAN, INSPIRED by Roman's comment that he thought of her as Red Sonja, decided to dress as the red-headed warrior for Halloween. She rented a long red wig, a sword, and a chain-mail bikini, and put rawhide laces on a pair of flat sandals. The outfit was perfect, silver mail over opaque gray fabric, and it provided more coverage than a bikini. The lightweight aluminum sword came with a black fake leather scabbard. The bright red wig fell past her shoulders.

Roman had invited Jean and Zeppo to his house to have a drink before the party. They were late arriving at Roman's, since Jean's costume had inspired in Zeppo a lust that wouldn't be denied. Finally Jean put on her wig, fastened her sword, and threw on a coat. Zeppo wore a paint-spattered smock and loose rough cotton pants that Jean had made him, along with size thirteen and a half wooden clogs they'd found in a gardening shop. A white bandage over one ear completed his ensemble. He'd been growing his beard for a few days so he'd look suitably scruffy.

At Roman's, Jean took off her coat. Bernie's delighted reaction was nearly as gratifying as Zeppo's had been.

"Red Sonja," Bernie exclaimed. "It's perfect. You look fabulous."

"Very fetching," Roman said. "You're going to have waffle patterns all over your voluptuous parts by the end of the evening."

"Nothing wrong with a little texture," Zeppo said.

"And you're Vincent van Gogh," Roman said. "I hope you never have to mutilate yourself for love."

Roman was dressed in his usual night-on-the-town outfit: unstructured jacket, polo shirt, and pleated slacks, accessorized now with a black cane. He still limped, but Jean could discern progress every time she saw him. Bernie wore a beautiful 1930s-style cream-colored three-piece suit with a vintage tie and two-toned shoes. His hair was cut short and combed straight back. He was the perfect Depression-era dandy.

Jean looked him up and down. "You're a blond to make a bishop kick a hole in a stained glass window."

Bernie laughed. "Marlowe, internal monologue," he said. "*Farewell, My Lovely*."

"Perhaps thirty years ago he was," Roman said. "He's far too old for most bishops now."

"Nice suit," Zeppo said to Bernie. "Who are you supposed to be?"

"Give me a minute." Bernie went into the bedroom and came out with a large white bandage taped to his nose and a cream-colored fedora on his head. "OK, who am I?"

"Jake Gittes," Jean and Zeppo said together. "*Chinatown*."

"Look at the three of you, all bandages and canes," Jean said. "The walking wounded."

Bernie poured everyone a glass of Cristal. "OK, now it's time for Roman to open his birthday present." He led them to the bedroom, where a big black gift box, artfully tied with gold ribbon, sat on the bed.

Roman removed the ribbon and opened the box. Inside, nestled in tissue, was something black and gold. He took out a short black satin jacket lavishly decorated with gold embroidery, beads, sequins, and tassels. "My God," he said in amazement. "It's a *traje de luces*."

"A what?" Zeppo asked.

"A suit of lights. A *torero's* costume. It looks like the real thing." He laid the jacket and a black bicornered hat on the bed. As Jean and Zeppo oohed and aahed, he took the rest of the outfit out of its box: high-waisted knee-length pants, also covered with embroidery and beads, a white shirt, narrow black tie, red sash, pink tights, and black ballet-style shoes. Finally he pulled out a short red cape with fancy epaulets.

Jean sat on the bed and examined the suit. The workmanship was unbelievably complex and intricate. "It's beautiful. Where in the world did you get it?"

"Madrid," Bernie said, enjoying the effect his gift was having. "I ordered it from one of the top matadors' tailors."

Roman grinned at Bernie. "It must have cost a fortune."

"Of course it did," Bernie said, grinning back. "It usually takes eight people a month to make, but this was a rush order. And how crass of you to mention money at a time like this."

"You're right. Sorry. *Muchas gracias.* Well, it seems I'm going to wear a costume after all. Everybody out."

The three of them went into the living room to wait, full of pre-party excitement and good cheer. They finished the Cristal, and finally Roman emerged.

Jean blinked at him; he was absolutely gorgeous. The suit of lights fit him perfectly and he wore the cape on one shoulder, like the pictures of matadors she'd seen. He'd shaved off his goatee, too; she hadn't seen him clean-shaven in years. "Rudolph Valentino," she said. "*Blood and Sand.*"

"The cane works with it," Zeppo said. "You're a matador who got gored by a bull."

Bernie stared at Roman, lips parted, a glazed expression on his face. "I'm positively weak in the knees."

"It's been awhile since I had this kind of an effect on an audience," Roman said, swirling his cape. "Come on, let's go to the party."

~

Bernie had arranged for a limo so they wouldn't have to deal with driving or parking. They adjusted their bandages and weaponry and piled in, and the chauffeur navigated slowly over the hill to Noe Valley, past throngs of costumed partiers—a very creditable Satan with huge bat wings, a gaggle of women in elaborate steampunk attire, Osama bin Laden deep in conversation with a giant chicken, the inevitable nuns on roller blades. Roman rolled down his window and waved at two big men in black and purple Bash Back sweatshirts—part of the Halloween patrol.

Lou's house was a modern, characterless stucco box a few blocks from Jean's apartment. Lou was known for his relentless dance mixes that included everything from Motown classics to eighties punk to hip hop to the latest dubstep. As Jean and her escorts got out of the limo, they could hear the beat of techno dance music. They passed a handful of exiled smokers on the front stoop.

While Roman held court near the refreshment table, Jean and Zeppo joined the crowd on the dance floor, a sea of feathers, sequins, and leather. They took breaks to drink beer, eat hors d'oeuvres, and greet old friends. They edged their way to the kitchen around midnight, sweaty and parched, to get more beer. Lou was there in a funereal black 1890s frock with a huge feathered hat, pouring himself a glass of sparkling wine.

"Are you two having a good time?" Lou asked. Jean could tell he was fairly drunk.

"You bet," Jean said. "This is your usual fabulous party, Lou. Did you see Bernie dancing? Isn't he great?"

"Isn't he just perfect?" Lou said. "And both of them negative. Now they can practice forgotten techniques of unsafe sex." He poured a few drops of cassis into his glass.

Jean looked hard at Lou. "What's the matter with you? Aren't you happy for Roman?"

"Oh yes, I'm happy. Ecstatic. Rhapsodic. The comely pauper goes to the ball and ends up marrying the prince. It's just like a fairy tale." He sipped his kir royale.

"You're jealous," Zeppo said in surprise.

"Jealous," he repeated. "You might say that. I've been in love with Roman since the first night I met him."

"I can sympathize," Zeppo said. "I was crazy about Jean for months before I tricked her into jumping me." Jean squeezed his hand.

Lou stroked Zeppo's cheek, smiling. "Silly boy. Jean's easy compared to Roman. All you had to be was a straight functioning male between the ages of eighteen and eighty. Roman's impossible. He only likes a certain type of clean-cut, corn-fed man. He'd never go for a nelly queen like me. I can't blame him, really. I'd never go for me either. He's never taken me seriously."

"That's not true. You're one of his best friends."

Lou waved a dismissive hand. "Always a buddy, never a bride. Well, I have to go make sure nobody's having more fun than I am. Later, children." He drifted out of the kitchen.

Jean and Zeppo looked at each other. "Wow," Jean said. "That was news to me. Do you think Roman knows?"

"No, I don't. Like you said, to him Lou's just a good friend." He shook his head. "Poor Lou. I remember what that was like, feeling so hopeless and frustrated all the time. I hated it."

"If I'd known what a stud you were, I would have jumped you much earlier."

They grabbed beers from an ice-filled cooler and headed back out to the dance floor.

Chapter 20

Jean woke the next morning with a headache. She turned toward Zeppo. He was still asleep, lying on his stomach, his face turned away from her, his pale freckled back uncovered. She'd just decided to wake him by kissing along the length of his spine when she heard the downstairs buzzer. She glanced at the clock—it was nearly noon. Zeppo didn't stir, so she got up and put on the red silk robe he'd given her to replace the one that had burned, with a phoenix instead of a dragon on the back. Peering out the window, she saw Laszlo on the stoop. She hadn't heard from him since leaving Escondido. She buzzed him in, stepping out into the hallway.

Laszlo came up the stairs carrying an old nylon garment bag. He was puffy-eyed and unshaven and smelled of sweat and cigarettes. His green T-shirt said "Too dumb to live in New York, too ugly to live in LA."

"Laszlo? What are you doing here?" She didn't have to ask how he'd found her—she was easy to find online.

"Jean, hey. You're looking great. Sorry to bother you so early. Listen, can I take a shower?"

She frowned, sleepy and irritated. "A shower? Here?"

"Yeah. See, I was crashing on a friend's sofa in Alameda and his wife didn't like it. Last night they went to a Halloween party and got drunk and had a big fight about me staying there. So I split."

"Why don't you check into a motel?"

"I'm flat broke. Look, can I come in?"

"OK, but give me a minute. It's a studio apartment and there's a naked man in my bed."

"Thanks, Jean. I really appreciate it."

Jean went back inside and gently woke Zeppo. "Good morning, big boy."

"'Morning, gorgeous." He rolled over and pulled the covers back, exposing his slim torso. "Come here."

The warm bed, his tone of voice, his sleepy smile—not to mention his erect member—beckoned to her. She sighed. "Can't. Laszlo's outside."

"Well, shit. Better let him in." He got up and put on his robe.

When Zeppo was decent, Jean opened the door.

"Sorry to be a bother," Laszlo said, "but I have to get cleaned up. There are a couple of guys over in Oakland I can hit up for a loan, but I've gotta look like I don't need it, you know what I'm saying?"

"I guess so," Jean said.

"How about some coffee?" Zeppo asked.

"Sure, thanks."

Jean motioned Laszlo to a chair and Zeppo went into the tiny kitchen. "Why are you broke?" she asked.

"That fire really fucked me up. My cookbooks and the computer with all my recipes burned, and my knives. Plus I lost a lot of inventory—three hundred hits of E, a pound of good dope, two ounces of blow, and five hundred dollars' worth of meth."

"Isn't there anyone else you can stay with?"

"Not on this coast. My sister says I can come live with her in Jersey City, but I can't do that. There are a lot of pissed-off people back East as well."

"What's that all about, anyway?" she asked.

"It was a fucked-up drug deal—I got away with a little money and everybody else did time. Since this mess has been in the news, I've hadda lay low, not call any of my connections. I mean, I'm practically homeless here."

The fog in Jean's head lifted slightly. "You got the meth from Honey Jones, didn't you? You're the one who warned her."

Laszlo gave her a guilty look. "Yeah. OK, I really blew it. I thought she'd just get outta there ahead of the deputy sheriff. How was I supposed to know she'd nuke the whole county?"

"You nearly got us all burned to death."

Laszlo sighed heavily. "So sue me."

"You know, Bernie says Ted's fully insured. He'll get a huge settlement on this thing, and part of it is yours. Anyway, I'm sure he could pay you off right now out of petty cash. He's been very generous reimbursing me for everything I lost in the fire."

Laszlo took out a cigarette and toyed with it, averting his eyes. "No way I'll get a dime from him."

"Why not?"

He hesitated. "See, Gloria really screwed things up for me. She told Ted I was selling some of his goods on the side. If all this hadn't happened, he was gonna call the sheriff after the guests left. As it is, he just told me to get lost and not use him as a reference."

"Why would Gloria do that? She doesn't seem like a vindictive person."

"Well, I . . . uh . . . I actually was selling stuff, and she caught on. It wasn't much—a few cases of wine, a few steaks, a few lobster tails Teddy wouldn't eat anyway." He put the unlit cigarette behind his ear. "Hell, he can afford it."

Jean shook her head. "Sounds as if you screwed things up all by yourself."

Zeppo put three mugs of black coffee on the low table and sat next to Jean. "Where's all the money you made selling the stuff?" he asked.

"I hid it in my cabin, with my stash. I tried to get it out, but by the time I got there it was already on fire. Is there any cream?"

"Just low-fat milk." Zeppo got the carton from the kitchen and handed it to Laszlo. "What about the money from the drug deal?"

Laszlo poured milk into his coffee. "I spent that long ago. I'm not good with money."

Jean raised an eyebrow. "No shit."

"That's why I need to get cleaned up. Once I have a couple of grand, I can invest in some product and look for a job. So how about that shower?"

"Of course," she said. "You were great under pressure—positively chivalrous. The bathroom's in there. But you'd better not steal anything."

Laszlo put up his hands. "Hey, don't worry, I'll behave. I saw what you did to Wang Yuan." He grinned at Zeppo. "You're a brave man."

"She's mean, all right, but she hardly ever leaves marks on me." Zeppo went to his suitcase and took out some clothes. "Jeannie, I'm starving. How about if I get Mexican take-out?"

"Sounds good. You want something, Laszlo?"

"Sure, that'd be great. Anything but chicken."

LASZLO, CLEAN and shaven, joined Jean and Zeppo at the table for fish tacos, pork tamales, and Mexican beer. He'd used Jean's iron to press slacks and a striped dress shirt, and looked quite presentable.

"This isn't bad," Laszlo said between bites. "That's one thing that was cool about Valle de los Osos—really great Mexican food."

"So Laszlo," Zeppo said, "did Matt Baeza question you?"

"Oh, yeah. First that putz from homicide grilled me good, and then Matt came around and asked a whole different set of questions. I don't think they're working together. They don't get along."

"I noticed that," Jean said.

Zeppo finished a taco. "OK, now I want you to tell us the stuff about Wang and MacKnight that you didn't tell the cops."

"What for? You a detective?"

"Just a talented amateur," Zeppo said. "You know about Jurado's theory that Carl Schoonover was an inside man, that he was partners with Wang and MacKnight?"

"Yeah, I read about that."

"Jean has her doubts about it. She thinks the inside man's still out there. Also, we think Wang and MacKnight were scoping out the area before they came to Phoenix Garden. That's when Dom Huerta overheard something that made him run to Ted Lyon in San Francisco."

"What do you want to know?"

"What did the staff say about those two? What did they like to eat? What did they complain about? Things like that."

"Sure, why not?" Laszlo leaned back and wiped his mouth. "I only spoke to Wang Yuan a couple of times, when he was telling me how great my cooking was. Usually that's what you get with the Chinese—they love good food. He was a polite, formal kind of guy. Tina, my sous chef, and the maids thought he was cute. That's about it. Remember, it was his first visit to Phoenix Garden. Who knew he was such a dick?"

"What about MacKnight?" Zeppo said. "Did he ever talk to you?"

"Nah. I was the help—he treated all of us like lower forms of life."

"Think about it. You must have heard what the other help said about him."

Laszlo thought for a few moments. "OK, let's see. He complained about the sun all the time, and the heat. He groped a couple of maids. He bragged about winning a lot of money at pai gow poker, and it bugged him that Tony and the rest of them didn't like to play it. I heard him say that he could always drive a few miles and find a game."

Jean frowned. "Find a game where?"

"Probably at one of the Indian casinos," Laszlo said. "They got them all over San Diego County."

"Oh, sure," Jean said, nodding. "There are two right in Valle de los Osos." She sat up straight. "Hey, I just remembered something. On that last day, Angus said Pilar died before he and Yuan checked into the Redskin Hilton."

Zeppo rubbed the coppery whiskers on his chin. "The Redskin Hilton, huh? If it wasn't Washington, DC, maybe they stayed at one of the Indian casinos while they waited for game time."

"I bet they didn't stay close to Valle de los Osos," Laszlo said. "Someone local might have recognized them later."

"Wherever they stayed, it was probably on Huerta's regular route," Jean said. "He had to run into them somehow."

"What about the casinos that are farther away?" Zeppo asked. "Do they have hotels attached, like in Vegas?"

Laszlo shrugged. "Some have hotels, resorts, spas, entertainment, the works. But some are pretty low rent and people stay in motels."

"Laszlo, didn't you tell me that Huerta liked to play slots?" Jean said.

"Yeah. The sucker's game."

"I'll bet Huerta overheard them at one of the casinos." Zeppo squeezed Jean's knee. "This could be a real lead. We should call Matt Baeza."

"I'll do that," Jean said.

Laszlo stood up. "OK, I'm off across the bay to troll for cash. I tell you what. If you let me leave my stuff here, I'll cook dinner."

"It's a deal," Jean said instantly. "Will you make coq au vin?"

"No way I'm cooking chicken."

"I'd eat vulture au vin if you put it in that sauce."

"Nah, predators taste like shit," Laszlo said. "I'll surprise you. Hey Zeppo, obviously you're not a vegan or a vegetarian. You got any other eating disorders?"

"I'll eat anything," he said. "We're going to a movie later, but we'll be back here around dinner time."

Laszlo took the door key Jean offered and left.

Zeppo grinned at Jean. "Alone at last."

IN THE afternoon, Jean called the Valle de los Osos sheriff's office; Sheila Denslow, the deputy who'd let Yuan escape, answered.

"Sheila? This is Jean Applequist. Is Matt there?"

"No, he's out. Can I help you?"

"I've got some information for him. How can I reach him?"

"You can't," Sheila said sharply. "Matt's on vacation until next week. He took Gloria and her boys camping to the Anza-Borrego desert. He has his cell phone, but it's my job if I bother him for anything less than a Martian invasion."

"Come on, Sheila. I won't tell him you told me. I really need to talk to him."

"No way. He's still pissed about Wang. I got suspended for two weeks without pay."

"This is important. I might have a lead about the Lyon thing."

Sheila snorted. "Forget it. Officially he's off the investigation. If you bother him for that and it gets back around, I'm dog food. Call Wes Jurado." She read off a number.

Jean hung up. "He's on vacation and Sheila won't give me his number," she said to Zeppo. "What now?"

"Let's check the web." He booted up her computer. "OK," he said after a few minutes of clicking and typing, "we've got eight Indian casinos in the county. The Valley View Casino and Harrah's Rincon are right in Valle de los Osos, so he probably didn't stay at either of those. Barona, Sycuan, Viejas, and Golden Acorn are way south and east. Closer in are Pauma, about eight miles north of Lyon's place, and Pala, about twenty miles north. And there's one right across the Riverside County line in Temecula called Pechanga. Most of them advertise pai gow poker on their websites, and of course they all have slots."

"Do you know how to play pai gow?"

"Sure. It's where you're dealt seven cards and make two poker hands. The object is to beat the dealer's two hands. It can get pretty complicated."

Jean regarded him with amusement. "What, you're a card shark?"

"I played a lot of cards in the nut house. A Korean kid taught us pai gow."

"Why was he there?"

"Cutting himself. Hey Jeannie, let's you and me go down there tomorrow and ask around. Maybe we can find where they stayed. We'll make it a road trip." He leaned close to her and said softly, "We can drive your Porsche."

His attitude seemed strange; if she didn't know him better, she'd think he had an ulterior motive. But right now Jean was eager to accommodate him, and anyway, it sounded like fun. "OK, let's do it. We'll visit Ethan and see the condors."

Jean and Zeppo went to the Castro Theatre to see a revival of *Asphalt Jungle* and got back around six. When they unlocked the door to Jean's apartment, they were greeted with the enticing aromas of paprika and garlic. They could hear Laszlo's tuneless whistling coming from the kitchen.

"Hi, Laszlo," Jean called. "How'd you do?"

He stuck his head into the room. "Really great. I'm solvent again."

"What's cooking?" Zeppo asked. "It smells incredible."

"Something my mom used to make. Goulash with potato dumplings. Plus there's wilted cabbage with caraway and a tomato salad."

"Five hours ago he was homeless and now he's serving us a Hungarian feast," Zeppo said. "I like the way you operate, Laszlo."

"You'll like the taste even more. And watch out, Jean, I sharpened all your knives."

The fabulous dinner put Jean into a happy, overfed stupor, and she gave Laszlo a warm hug as he left. On Sunday morning she and Zeppo retrieved her red Porsche Carrera from Roman's garage and got on the road.

During the long trip down Interstate 5, they filled the time with thoughtful speculation about their quest, comfortable silences, playful groping, and occasional hilarity, interspersed with good blues from Zeppo's iPhone and bad country music on the radio. Near Coalinga they ate at one of Tony's restaurants; the décor and service weren't bad for the Central Valley, but the food was pricey and unimaginative. The weather was breezy and cool, and the only heavy traffic they encountered was LA's eternal snarl.

They crossed into Riverside County on Interstate 15 at about three thirty, exiting the freeway just south of Temecula and driving a couple of miles to Pechanga, a big adobe-colored hotel and casino decorated with Native American motifs and statuary.

They'd agreed that Jean would wait outside while Zeppo went in with copies of Roman's photos of the Phoenix Garden guests; she'd been in the San Diego papers after the fire and didn't want to be recognized.

Jean waited in the car, watching people come and go, most of them older and none of them prosperous-looking. Gambling was one vice she didn't have; she couldn't understand the appeal of throwing money away for entertainment. She threw a lot of money away herself, but at least she had something to show for it: a fast car and memories of great trips and fine meals and delicious bottles of wine. A cool breeze blew up and she put on a denim jacket. It was quite a contrast to the hellish weather of less than a month ago.

In about forty-five minutes, Zeppo came out and got in the car. "That was weird," he said. "I can't remember the last time I was in a public building that smelled like cigarette smoke."

"Yeah, the Indians are a sovereign nation, so they don't have to abide by California laws." She poked him in the ribs. "Come on, spill."

"I spent some money but didn't get much information," he said. "A few of the staff recognized the photos from the news. They knew Domingo Huerta—he used to come here sometimes. I don't think Angus was ever here. But Matt Baeza was, about two weeks ago, asking the same questions."

"No shit. I wonder how he figured it out."

"He probably questioned the Phoenix Garden staff and found out about Angus and his thing for pai gow poker."

"Let's keep going anyway, since we're here. Pala's next, right?" Jean got back on the freeway and drove south. A sign proclaimed this stretch of road as the Avocado Highway. Early rain had put out the last of the wildfires, but the land on both sides of the freeway was scorched black from the Bonsall fire. A few gutted homes and businesses were visible from the road. Jean searched the wasteland for green shoots but saw none; they'd come with the winter rains.

Jean turned inland on two-lane Highway 76, which wound through rocky hills dotted with citrus and avocado groves, produce stands, widely scattered houses and trailers. The rural poverty was appalling, especially on the Indian reservations, and Jean realized how important the casinos must be to these people. She wondered how much of the money they actually saw.

In the late afternoon light, Jean and Zeppo caught occasional glimpses of Palomar Mountain in the distance. The fire had been stopped short of Pala, and soon the blackened landscape gave way to dusty greens and browns.

They passed a huge greenhouse full of poinsettias and corrals containing horses, cattle, and even a few bison. Pala Casino loomed on their right. It was a pinkish-beige stucco hotel almost as big as Pechanga. No Native American motifs here—this place took its architectural inspiration from Las Vegas.

Jean went inside with Zeppo so she could use the bathroom. On her way out, she passed the bar, which was filling up with thirsty gamblers. She stopped to read a poster at the bar's entrance that offered a special tasting of wines from nearby Temecula, giving brief descriptions of the wines. Under any other circumstances, Jean would have gone in and tried them—she wasn't that familiar with the wineries in this Southern California appellation and didn't like holes in her wine knowledge.

She read the descriptions of the different bottlings, getting into wine geek mode for a moment. A few of them were Rhône varietals, which Jean thought would probably do well in this hot, dry climate. The Isosceles Cellars Syrah, billed as the new winery's first bottling, sounded especially interesting. Isosceles. Something nagged at the edge of Jean's brain.

She looked around the huge casino for Zeppo, finally spotting his mop of red curls in a corner of the restaurant. He listened intently to a young Native American man in a busboy's outfit. That looked promising. She went outside to wait in the car.

Zeppo came out in fifteen minutes and climbed into the passenger seat. "I used the tried-and-true technique of finding the lowest-paid employee and slipping him fifty dollars. He said Angus was here all right, but he didn't stay in the hotel. He'd come in and play pai gow poker, drink Scotch, and scare the waitresses. Says he saw Yuan a few times but he didn't gamble. Dom Huerta was a regular."

"Good work. Hey, there's such a thing as an isosceles triangle, right?"

"Sure. It's got two equal sides and two equal angles. Why?"

"Remember I told you about the triangular label on the bottle of wine in Yuan's drawings of the curly-haired woman? I just read that there's a winery in Temecula called Isosceles Cellars. What if the bottle was from there? What if the woman has some connection to the place?"

"Let's take a look." He poked at his iPhone. "They're pretty small-time, based on their website. OK, here's the label."

Jean took his phone. The screen showed a bottle you could order if you joined their wine club. Its label was a familiar tall, teepee-shaped triangle. "This is the same label, I'm sure of it. Should we go over there now?"

Zeppo worked on his phone again. "They're about twenty minutes away and they're open till six. Let's do it."

Jean took Highway 76 back to Interstate 15 and drove north to Temecula. She'd read that a temperate wind from the coast blew through nearby mountain passes, cooling the inland Temecula Valley just enough for wine grapes to prosper at its twenty-five or so wineries. She had seen photos of the area that showed the valley's clear blue sky filled with colorful hot-air balloons, part of an annual wine and balloon festival.

Most of the wineries were scattered along both sides of Rancho California Road east of the freeway. They passed Callaway Vineyard and Thornton Winery, large, long-established operations whose wines Jean had tasted, and smaller wineries unknown to her. Tourist traffic was light at the wineries this late in the season. Harvest was long over, and the leaves on the rows of vines showed golden fall colors in the fading sunlight.

Isosceles Cellars was a tiny operation about half a mile up a side road. Architectural details on the stark modern structure echoed the triangle motif. Neatly trellised immature vines surrounded the building—the winemaker must be buying grapes from other growers. No restaurant here, just a small tasting room attached to the main building. There was only one other car in the parking lot.

"It's actually good that it's small and off the beaten track," Zeppo remarked. "Increases the chances that she has something to do with the winery, since otherwise it would be unlikely that she'd get her hands on such an obscure bottle of wine."

During the drive they'd debated what to say, and had come up with a plausible if somewhat feeble story. It was going to be tough describing the woman, since Jean had only a vague idea of her age and no clue about her coloring. At least her hair was distinctive.

The modest tasting room contained a counter to one side scattered with tasting glasses and a few bottles of the Syrah. A glass-fronted cooler against one wall held bottles of white—an Isosceles Chardonnay. A slightly plump middle-aged woman in a T-shirt bearing the triangular label smiled at them from behind the counter. Her pleasant face was weather-beaten and her graying dark hair pulled back in a low ponytail. "Welcome to Temecula's newest winery," she said cheerfully. "Would you like to taste our wines?"

"Not today, thanks," Jean said. "I wonder if you can help me. I'm looking for a woman I met at a wine tasting over at Callaway a couple of months ago. I work for *Wine Digest*, and I'm doing a color story on people working in the wine industry here. I took her info but I lost my phone and all my contacts. I think she said she worked here. She's in her thirties, nice looking, with long curly hair."

"You must mean Vanessa Morse," the woman said.

"That's the name," Jean said. "I knew it began with a 'V.' "

"She worked here in the tasting room this summer," the woman said. "Tourist season. Now it's just my husband and me."

"Is this your winery?" Zeppo asked.

"That's right. My husband is a retired professor of mathematics. Hence the name. He always dreamed of making wine, so here we are."

"Do you know where we might find Vanessa?" Jean asked.

"She lives in town. I don't feel right about giving out her address, but I could give you her cell number."

"That would be great," Jean said. "Thanks." She pulled out her cell and typed in the number the woman read from her own phone. Zeppo bought a bottle of Syrah and they went back out to the car, where Jean made the call.

"Hello?" The woman's voice was soft and low.

"Is this Vanessa Morse?"

"Yes?"

"My name is Jean Applequist. You don't know me, but I think we have something in common—Wang Yuan."

There was an intake of breath and a long silence from the other end. Jean gave Zeppo a thumbs up. This must be the right woman. Finally she spoke. "What do you want?" Jean could hear wariness and fear in her voice.

"I just want to ask you a few questions about him." Jean paused. "I was his lover, too."

"How do you know about me?"

"I saw the sketches he made of you and followed the triangular wine label. Don't worry, I'm the only one who saw the drawings. They burned with the rest of Phoenix Garden."

"Did you say Jean Applequist? I saw you on the news. You're some kind of reporter."

"Not a news reporter. I work for *Wine Digest*."

Again there was a silence. "I'd like to talk to you, but I don't want any of it on TV or in the papers. I have kids."

"No problem—I only write about wine."

"OK, there's a place called Rosarita's not far from my condo, just off Ynez Road. I'll meet you there in half an hour."

Zeppo got directions online and Jean drove to Rosarita's, a big, brightly lit cantina in a strip mall. Inside, the ceiling was hung with tacky piñatas and the walls with velvet paintings, but the place smelled heavenly, like chiles and roasting meat.

"I'm starving," Zeppo said. "Let's eat here."

Jean realized she was hungry as well. They got a table in the crowded restaurant and ordered Mexican beer, a carne asada burrito for Zeppo, and a couple of chicken tacos for Jean.

In about twenty minutes, as they worked their way through the delicious food, a woman came into the restaurant alone and looked around. Jean was pretty sure it was Vanessa Morse. She stood up from the table, caught the woman's eye, and beckoned.

"You're Vanessa?" Jean said, shaking her hand. "I'm Jean, and this is my friend Zeppo." Vanessa's handshake was soft and hesitant.

Jean studied Vanessa with interest. The fine lines around her eyes and at the corners of her mouth meant she was older than Jean had thought, close to Yuan's age. She had the same lovely delicate features and mature curves he'd caught in the drawings. Her luxurious curly hair was a glossy light brown, her eyes dark brown. She smiled uncertainly at Jean.

"Please sit down," Jean said. "Do you want something to eat?"

"No thanks. I've had dinner."

"How about a drink?" Zeppo offered.

"Some wine would be nice." She glanced at the bar, where a board listed wines by the glass. "The Ponte Meritage, please." Zeppo collared a waiter.

Jean eyed Vanessa's jeans, old blue sweater, worn canvas purse, and Payless shoes. This was not a well-off woman. Not a self-confident one either, based on her shy manner and body language. She wore no wedding ring, but a circle of pale skin on her left ring finger indicated she'd only recently taken it off.

"Thanks for coming," Zeppo began. "How closely have you been following the news about Wang Yuan?"

"I've read everything I could find."

"Then you know what went on at Phoenix Garden and what happened that last day?"

"Yes, at least as much as was in the news." The waiter brought her a glass of the red blend. She turned to Jean. "That must have been a terrible experience for you."

"It was that."

"I'll bet it was pretty hard on you to learn what Yuan was capable of," Zeppo said. "Do you mind telling us how you know him?"

"Why do you want to know if you're not going to write about it?"

"It's bothering us because we think the police are wrong about who the inside man was," Jean said. "We're trying to trace Yuan's movements before he got to Phoenix Garden. Finding where he stayed might even help the police catch him."

"Police?" Vanessa said in alarm. "You didn't say anything about the police."

"Hey, don't worry," Zeppo said. "If we learn anything useful, we'll just tell a friendly sheriff's deputy we know in Valle de los Osos. He's not working with the task force. He doesn't need to know how we found out. Come on, wouldn't you like to see Yuan caught?"

"I'd very much like to see him caught. But not enough to risk anyone finding out about me."

Zeppo slid two hundred-dollar bills out of his wallet and laid them on the table. Jean was glad to let him deal with bribes; she never had any idea how much to offer.

"I'd be happy to pay you for your time," he said.

Vanessa eyed the bills, biting her lower lip and frowning. "OK," she said finally. "But you can't ever tell the police about me. My daughters are fifteen and seventeen. They can never know I'm connected to any of this."

"We give you our word they never will from us," Zeppo said.

Vanessa took a deep drink of her wine. "All right then. Several months ago he came into the tasting room at Isosceles when I was working. He called himself John Kim. Said he was Korean. It was a slow day, nearly closing time, and he was the only customer."

"Go on," Zeppo said.

"He was so good-looking and charming, and I was lonely. I'm recently divorced." A blush crept up her slender throat to her face. "We drank a bottle of wine together. It never should have happened, but . . . the things he said, the way he said them—"

"You don't have to explain," Jean said gently. "That's how he got to me, too."

"He wanted to go back to my place, but that was out of the question. My girls were both home. So we went to his motel. May I have another glass of wine?"

Zeppo ordered one from a nearby waiter. "What motel was that?"

"The Hitching Post, over near Pala. We . . . we were interrupted by banging on the door. It was that man Angus MacKnight. I never heard the name he was using then. Yuan went next door with him and they had an argument. I could hear some of it. MacKnight accused Yuan of bad tactics and thinking with his dick. I heard Yuan soothing him." Her wine arrived and she took a healthy sip.

"Finally Yuan came back and laughed it off," Vanessa continued. "He explained that MacKnight was his business partner and they were supposed to be working, but that he'd talked him into going gambling instead. I heard MacKnight leave. I was upset, but then Yuan used that silver tongue of his to restore the mood. I fell asleep afterward and he made those drawings." She sighed. "I was so flattered. Later I learned who they really were and realized the danger I'd been in. They could have killed me. I mean, look what almost happened to you." She shivered. "It's enough to put you off sex forever."

Zeppo gave Vanessa's shoulder a comforting squeeze. "Hey, don't dwell on it. They were professional con men, and they're both out of the picture now. Anyway, you've helped us a lot. We know which motel they stayed in, and no one ever has to know how we found it."

"It was actually good to talk about it. There's no one else I can tell." Vanessa drained her wine and glanced at her watch. "I have to get home. My youngest is having a sleepover."

Jean and Zeppo had finished their meals as she talked. The waiters were all singing "Happy Birthday" in Spanish to someone at a big table in the far corner of the restaurant, so Zeppo went up to the cashier to pay the bill.

Vanessa gazed after him. "You're lovers, aren't you?"

"I guess it's obvious."

"He's forgiven you for Yuan." It wasn't a question. "You're a lucky woman."

"I know I am," Jean said.

"My husband of nineteen years divorced me because I slept with an old boyfriend at my twenty-fifth high school reunion. I was drunk at the time, and I hadn't had sex with my husband in over six months. I did everything I could to make it up to him, but he couldn't get over it. Yuan was my first lover since then." She gave Jean a sad, regretful look. "Lately every time I have sex something goes horribly wrong."

Jean patted her arm. "Don't let it put you off. You've been incredibly unlucky. That can't last." Vanessa was drunk enough to be confessional and her nose had reddened slightly. "Hey, you OK to drive?"

"I'm fine. I live right around the corner. Anyway, wine's the only fun I have anymore."

In the parking lot, Jean and Zeppo said good-bye and watched Vanessa drive away in an old Dodge Neon.

"That's a sad woman," Jean said. They got into the Porsche. As she drove, she told Zeppo the story of Vanessa's divorce. "I sure hope she meets a decent man soon," Jean said, squeezing Zeppo's hand.

HALF AN hour later Jean turned the Porsche into a driveway under a brown and yellow neon sign that read "Hitching Post

Motel." Beyond the parking lot was a tan stucco L-shaped building with twenty or so yellow doors. A big swimming pool cast an eerie blue-green light onto the building. Half a dozen cars sat near the doors.

A woman with long straight blonde hair smiled as they came into the reception area, decorated with lassos, bulls' horns, and other western props. She was in her early twenties, with pale blonde lashes and brows. Her blue and green flowered blouse was too tight over her full figure. "Can I help you?" she said.

"Hi," Zeppo said. "We're reporters working on a story about the fire at the Lyons' place."

Her vacant blue eyes grew big. "Are you with TV?"

Zeppo leaned his elbows on the counter. "Nah, we work for *Wine Digest*. The story's about the wine cellar that almost burned up."

"Oh yeah?" The woman was fast losing interest.

"What's your name?"

"Rhonda Navarro."

"I'm Jay Zeppetello and this is Jean Applequist. I wonder if you'd mind looking at a few pictures. We're trying to find out where some people were in the weeks before the fire."

"My husband would know about that. I wasn't working then." She smiled and gestured to something behind the counter. Jean leaned over to look; a baby was fast asleep in a carrier on the floor, wrapped in a blue cotton blanket. "Toby was born around that time."

Jean smiled. The baby had thick brown hair and skin several shades darker than Rhonda's. "He's beautiful. Your first?"

"Yeah. He was so big I had a C-section, so Mickey—that's my husband—had to run the motel by himself for like a whole month. He said the police came here and asked him stuff about those people."

"What did he tell them?"

Rhonda shrugged. "That they stayed here and used different names. I don't really know what else. You can ask him.

He'll be in first thing tomorrow." She brightened up. "You want rooms? I can let you have a couple of nice ones with queen-size beds for fifty-four ninety-nine each, plus tax."

"One room will be fine," Jean said. She and Zeppo registered and moved the car to the space in front of their room. Jean gasped as she opened the yellow door and saw the bed. "That's it. That's the wagon-wheel headboard from Yuan's sketches."

Zeppo put an arm around her shoulders. "So we've found the Redskin Hilton. But if the cops were already here, I doubt we'll get anything new."

"Let's spend the night and talk to Mickey anyway. Maybe you can weasel something out of him. You're a lot more persuasive than the average local deputy sheriff."

The motel room was definitely low-end, but the towels were big and everything was clean. They opened the bottle of Isosceles Syrah and poured it into squat plastic cups, talking over the possibilities and sipping the wine, which was a trifle overripe but better than Jean had expected. She'd have to keep an eye on the winery. They got into bed early.

The knowledge that Yuan had been here, if not in this bed then in the same motel, distracted her as they made love. Zeppo sensed her mood and took things slowly. Jean reached above her head and gripped the spokes on the headboard, but that made her think of Yuan again. She wondered if he'd have handed Vanessa over to Angus as readily as he did her.

"What's the matter, Jeannie? You're not with me."

"I don't know. This place makes me nervous."

"It's the bed, isn't it?" He reached up and gently disengaged her hands from the spokes, entwining his fingers with hers, lowering himself down on her. "Don't think about him," he said, slipping in and bringing her instantly back to the moment. "Think about me."

Chapter 21

"The sheriff's deputy asked me the same thing," Mickey Navarro said, leaning on the reception counter as he flipped through the photos Zeppo handed him. "I seen some of these other people in the news, but I never saw anybody visit the two guys who stayed here. That's what I told the deputy."

"Which deputy?" Zeppo asked. "The homicide investigators?"

"Yeah, but they came later. First it was that big guy works over in Valle de los Osos. Baeza." Mickey handed the photos back. He was a tall, bony young Native American man with acne and beautiful brown eyes. He wore jeans and a yellow button-down shirt with "Hitching Post Motel" stitched on the pocket. "How come you want to know about them two if your article's on wine?"

"We were working on the wine angle and decided to do a little snooping," Zeppo said smoothly. "We thought we could maybe sell the story to a bigger magazine."

"Uh huh. Well, sorry I can't help. I didn't see nothing besides them coming and going."

"Did either of them ever bring a woman here?" Jean asked. "A pretty one with long curly hair?"

"I didn't see one, but that don't mean it never happened. I was real busy then, plus I was worried about Rhonda and Toby in the hospital."

"How long were the men here?" Zeppo asked.

"About a week," Mickey said.

"You're a friendly guy," Zeppo said. "Did you ever talk to them?"

"Nah, not really. Usually I like talking to the guests. That's the fun part of running a motel. But those two weren't friendly at all, just stayed in their rooms. They never even used the pool that I know of, even though it was really hot."

"Do you and Rhonda own the motel?" Zeppo asked.

"Yeah," Mickey said. "We got it for nothing because it was in foreclosure. We're doing OK. Even with the big hotel at the casino, people always want someplace cheap to stay, but nice."

"You think the casino is a good idea?" Jean said.

He looked at her as if she were crazy. "Are you kidding? It's a great idea."

"So you told the deputies all there was to tell?" Zeppo said.

"Sure. I've got nothing to hide."

Zeppo took a small stack of twenty-dollar bills out of his wallet and laid it on the counter.

"What's that for?" Mickey asked.

"I was thinking you might have held something back. Something that could help us."

Mickey hesitated, eyeing the bills. "How much?"

"Depends on the quality of the information. I could go as high as two hundred."

Mickey looked from Zeppo to Jean and back again. "Well, there is one more person you could ask."

"Who?" they both said at once.

"My brother Hector. He came and helped out when Rhonda was in the hospital so I could be with her sometimes. I didn't tell her he was here cause she doesn't want him around. Thinks he's bad news."

"Is he?" Jean asked.

"Yeah, pretty much."

"Did the deputies talk to him, too?"

"Nah, he's on the run. The cops are looking for him."

"What for?" Zeppo asked.

"They think he's involved in a car-theft ring up in LA. Everybody thinks he's in Mexico, but he's been staying around here at his girlfriend's place."

"Would he talk to us?"

Mickey stroked his chin, looking at the bills. "Maybe, if there was something in it for him. And if you promise not to tell where he is."

"We'll keep it to ourselves," Jean said. "We're only interested in these two guys."

"OK then. I'll call him and see."

Zeppo paid Mickey two hundred dollars, and he arranged for Jean and Zeppo to visit Hector at his girlfriend's place in Pauma Valley. He gave them detailed directions, and they packed up and got on the road.

It took half an hour on a curving mountain road to get to the tiny town of Pauma Valley, in the hills north of Valle de los Osos. They passed Casino Pauma, right at the foot of the mountains. It was much smaller than the other two casinos, with no hotel. Jean turned onto a narrow two-lane road that wound up a steep, rocky hill covered with chaparral and cactus, finally coming to a rutted dirt road. Dust coated the Porsche by the time they pulled into the yard of a well-maintained green and white trailer in a grove of live oaks. Off to one side, a small brown horse watched them from a corral attached to a red barn.

A tall man in baggy shorts and a black T-shirt stood at the edge of the driveway, arms crossed, eyeing them warily. He was an older, heavier, slightly dissipated version of Mickey. An elaborate tattoo of a rattlesnake wound around his right forearm. Jean and Zeppo got out and introduced themselves.

"I'm Hector," the man said. "Mickey says you two are OK, but first let's see the color of your money."

Zeppo took out his wallet and handed over several bills. "Half now and half when we see if you can help us," he said.

Hector counted the money and pocketed it. "OK, then." He walked over to the Porsche. "This is a sweet ride. Love the 2005s. At the time, this baby had the largest engine Porsche ever put in a street-legal vehicle. What's your top speed?"

"I've had it up to one twenty-five," Jean said. "I get a lot of speeding tickets."

"It'll go a lot faster than that." He stroked the Porsche lovingly. "I guess writers get paid a lot, huh?"

"No way. The car was a gift."

"Some gift."

A slim young Native American woman came out of the trailer. She was dark and pretty, with long thick hair and no makeup. She wore a blue denim skirt and a white eyelet top, and looked unexpectedly wholesome and innocent. She smiled shyly. "Hi. I'm Suzanne."

Zeppo introduced them. "Were you at the motel when Hector was helping out?"

"No, I was at work most of the time. Are you really a writer?"

"Jean here is a magazine writer."

"That's great. I want to be a writer someday. I work at the library in Temecula and I read a lot," she said as she led them to a grouping of aluminum lawn chairs in the shade of a big oak.

Hector stood behind Suzanne's chair possessively, gently massaging her shoulders, making her smile. "So show me what you got," he said.

Zeppo handed him the stack of photos and he sat down next to Suzanne. He flipped through them, pausing over one. "Yeah, I remember these two dudes, the ones who stayed at the motel." He continued through them. "Oh, hey. I recognize this guy, too. He came to see them one time." He turned the photo so Jean and Zeppo could see it.

Jean looked at the face in the photo, feeling a sharp twist in the pit of her stomach. "Are you sure? Maybe you saw him on TV."

"Sure I'm sure," he said, nodding. "We don't get TV up here—no cable, and Suzanne doesn't want a big satellite dish in the yard. The guy drove a 2007 Edo Lamborghini Murciélago LP640. Incredible machine. Only the second one I've ever seen. He parked it back up the road, but I heard that rumbling engine and went to look. Some rich fuck."

Suzanne rolled her eyes. "Excuse Hector's language."

He grinned. "Sorry, babe."

"You recognize anybody else?" Zeppo said, not meeting Jean's eyes.

Hector looked through the stack again. "Nah, just the blond guy."

Jean felt cold, as if she were in shock.

"Well, thanks for everything." Zeppo handed a few more bills to Hector and stood to go. When Jean didn't move, he took her hand and pulled her up.

Suzanne frowned as she watched Jean's reaction. "This is important, isn't it?"

Zeppo nodded. "Could be."

"You're going to tell the police, aren't you? And then they'll come up here after Hector."

"No," Zeppo said. "We promised Mickey that wouldn't happen. Now that we know who it is, we'll find some other way."

"You better mean that, *vato*," Hector said. "We don't want any trouble."

Zeppo steered Jean to the Porsche and helped her in. He got in the driver's side. As they drove out the dirt road, Jean saw Suzanne staring after them, still frowning.

"The Navarro brothers seem to be lucky in love, unlike Vanessa," Zeppo said.

Jean was having trouble formulating a coherent sentence.

"I'm sorry, Jeannie," Zeppo said, resting a hand on her knee. "I wish it was anybody else."

His words brought her out of her funk. She looked at him in wonder. Suddenly everything odd he'd said and done over the past few weeks made perfect sense. "How long have you suspected him?"

"Since the beginning. He had the best motive of anyone."

"Why didn't you say anything to me?"

"I wanted to be really sure because I knew you wouldn't believe it. You're too emotionally involved."

"Oh, Zeppo. I thought you were jealous of the time Roman spent with him. I should have known better."

"You know I want Roman to be happy."

"How could Bernie do that to his father? How could he bring those vultures into his home?"

"Look what his father was doing to him: using blackmail to force him to change his sexuality. Imagine if someone you loved tried to force you to be a lesbian. How would that feel? He couldn't get financing through the usual channels for the same reason—the script was too gay. Bernie's personal life was fucked up and his career was stalled. He must have felt cornered."

Jean didn't understand his tone. "Are you trying to justify what he did?"

He hesitated. "There's more. You won't like it."

"How can it get any worse?"

"I think Bernie killed that waitress," he said softly.

Jean looked at him, stunned. "He couldn't have."

"Think about it. He was the only one of the three conspirators who was at the house when she died. He must have taken photos of the jade so Yuan could make a carrier. All he had to do was take digital shots and burn a CD. Remember you told me Pilar had a crush on him and always tried to talk to him? What if she was following him and saw him take the photos? And you said where she was killed there were no signs of a struggle."

Jean thought it through, testing his analysis against all her nagging doubts about Wes Jurado's neat solution. No matter how hard she tried to reason a way around it, Zeppo's scenario made too much sense. "Oh, Zeppo," she said finally. "What are we going to do?"

"How about we bag the zoo and drive straight back?"

"Yes, right now." A fresh wave of anguish rolled over her as she realized what this would mean to Roman. "I wish Phoenix Garden had burned to the ground before I ever set foot there."

Chapter 22

Jean and Zeppo arrived in San Francisco in the middle of the night and went to her apartment, where they slept fitfully for a few hours. In the morning, Jean called in sick, and they got to Roman's house about ten A.M. Tuesday.

Bernie, in jeans and a black and purple Bash Back T-shirt, let them in, surprised but happy to see them. He led them back to the kitchen and they sat at the table, which held a mug of coffee, a partially eaten bagel, and the newspaper. The back door was open, and a cool breeze came through the screen. It hurt Jean to see how at home Bernie seemed, how well he fit into Roman's life.

"Where's Roman?" Zeppo asked.

"Out buying cigarettes. I threw his away a few days ago, and he's got a jones this morning. Want some coffee?"

"No thanks," Jean said. "Bernie, we need to talk."

"What about?"

"Phoenix Garden," she said. "I'll get right to the point: Carl wasn't the inside man, was he? You were."

He blinked at her, startled. "That's preposterous. Are you out of your mind?"

"We've been to San Diego County," she said. "We found a witness who saw you visit Yuan and Angus at the Hitching Post Motel, where they stayed before they went to your father's."

"That's impossible, because I was never there."

"Bernie, he picked out your picture," Jean said. "He even saw your car. How do you explain that?"

"I don't have to explain anything," Bernie said indignantly. "God, are you so jealous of my relationship with Roman that you'll try this pathetic ploy to sabotage it?"

"I'm the one who set the two of you up, remember?"

"You just wanted to get Roman laid, and you got more than you bargained for when I moved in with him." Bernie leaned back in the chair. "Do the police know about this so-called witness?"

"Not yet," Jean said. "But all I have to do is phone Matt Baeza."

"Wait a minute," Bernie said quickly. He took a breath. "Matt has a grudge against my father. He'd love to stir up trouble for him."

"That's bullshit," Jean said. "All he wants to do is find Pilar's killer."

"This is the most outlandish thing I've ever heard. You two are fucking crazy."

"Nah, it actually makes a lot of sense," Zeppo said. "You gave Yuan and Angus the background they needed on your family, all about Meide's brother and your father's research on your mother's ancestors, the MacNaughtons. You photographed the jade. You set the horses loose after the fire. And you killed Pilar Ochoa."

Bernie stood up, his posture defiant. "Are you calling me a murderer?"

Zeppo nodded. "Yeah, we are."

"So if you've made up your minds, why did you come here? Why didn't you go straight to the police?" He narrowed his eyes at them. "This must be a shakedown. How much do you want?"

"Don't fuck up more than you already have," Jean snapped. "If it weren't for Roman, you'd be under arrest by now. For his sake, we decided to come here first. Since you're offering money, I'd say we're right."

"This is outrageous. If you say these things to anyone else, I'll sue you for slander."

"Let's run it by Roman," Zeppo said. "See what he thinks."

"No!" Bernie exclaimed. He gave them a pleading look. "Don't do this. Roman and I love each other."

"But he doesn't know you scammed your father and killed an innocent woman in cold blood," Jean said, her voice rising.

He snorted. "Pilar wasn't innocent."

"She was innocent of greed, betrayal, murder—all the things you're guilty of."

Bernie looked at Jean. "You've killed."

"That was self-defense!"

"So was this. And if I'd never killed anyone before, I might have hesitated with Angus. I might have been too late, and Roman would be dead. Do you realize I saved both your lives?"

"If it weren't for you, Angus and Yuan wouldn't have been there in the first place." Jean caught a movement out of the corner of her eye and looked toward the screen door. A dark shape stood just outside. "Roman," she said. "How long have you been there?"

"Long enough." He opened the screen and came in, leaning his cane against the wall. "Bernie, you're working on the wrong side of the camera," he said, his voice as soft and cold as a snowdrift. "That was the best acting performance I've ever seen."

Bernie turned to him, fear and alarm on his face. "I wasn't acting with you. With my father, yes, but never with you."

"But you were. You played the part of the misunderstood rich boy who finally found true love. Evidently I don't know you at all."

"Roman, I've been looking for a man like you all my life," Bernie said, his voice strained. "If I'd met you first, none of this would have happened. But I felt so empty and frustrated. I knew it wouldn't work out with my boyfriend, again, and my career was going nowhere. And all I needed was money."

"Wang Yuan and his merry band of mercenaries, thwarted by the Castro Street Irregulars." Roman seized Bernie by the shoulders. "How could you betray your own father and then kill for money? How could you move in here after that and insinuate yourself into my life?"

"Roman, I'm so sorry."

"Sit down," Roman ordered, releasing him. "You're going to tell us everything." He leaned back on the counter, arms crossed, his expression stern and unrelenting.

Bernie slumped in his chair. "You don't know what it's like, being so close to all that money but unable to touch it. Dad's disgustingly healthy. And now he'll have other heirs—Meide's disgustingly healthy, too."

"Why didn't you kill Ted before he impregnated Meide, or before he married her?" Jean asked. "That would have solved your problems."

"I could never hurt him. I love him, and I owe him too much." Bernie ran a hand through his hair. "I swore to myself that if I didn't have my film in production by the time I turned forty, I'd do something about it, but I didn't know what to do. Then Yuan approached me. He knew amazing things about us already—he even knew about the family incentive trust and how desperate I must be. I just filled in the details for him." Bernie's voice had taken on a pleading note, as if he were begging them to understand and forgive.

"What happened with Pilar?" Zeppo asked.

"She saw me in the gallery photographing the jade. Yuan wanted detailed pictures with a scale. He was going to make the carrying case, and it had to be just right—the pieces are so ancient and fragile. I put two rulers on the bench at right angles, as he instructed, and took them out one at a time, turning them so he could see every dimension. Pilar came in, saying she was looking for dirty glasses and dishes. She was looking for me, of course. She always followed me around. She didn't have any idea what I was doing, but she was such a chatterbox. Once the jade was gone, she would have told what she saw, and Matt Baeza would have found out, and my father, too.

"I thought it over that night, and in the morning I waited for her near the restaurant where she worked. I called to her from the woods. She came right over, smiling. Afterward I went through her purse so it would look like a robbery." He shivered. "Killing her was the hardest thing I ever did in my life. I still have nightmares about it."

"I'm sure that'll make a lot of difference to her family." Jean looked at him with contempt. "I'm surprised you didn't send Angus after her. He'd have enjoyed it."

"Yes, and he would have raped her first. At least I saved her from that. I didn't want her to suffer. I even looked at a medical text in Dad's library so I'd know where to stab her."

"How thoughtful of you," Roman said. "Not to mention that Angus would certainly have killed you if he knew how sloppy you'd been. He'd reason that a soft rich kid like you would roll over if you were arrested."

"I thought of that, of course. In the end I had to kill her—there was too much at stake."

"Exactly how much was at stake, in dollars and cents?" Zeppo asked.

"I don't know the total sum, but they promised me two million dollars, and I was the junior partner."

"And you made up an investor so you'd have an explanation for where the money came from," Jean said. "What about Dom Huerta and Katharine and Carl?"

"I didn't know Huerta's death was connected until Yuan arrived for the tasting and told me. Apparently Huerta was passed out behind a dumpster outside Pala Casino. Yuan and Angus didn't see him there, and he woke up as they stood nearby discussing a change of plan on how to get the jade to the buyer. The fool demanded that they pay him off and Angus said no. Then a garbage truck pulled up near where they were standing, so Huerta was able to slip away and get out of the casino and on a bus before Angus could catch him. Then when Katharine died, I thought at first that she had fallen. But when you found Carl's body, I realized Angus must have killed them both, too."

"I know he killed Katharine because she saw him with Carl's body, but why did he kill Carl?" she said.

"I asked Yuan that after you found the body. He said that years ago he stole some Persian miniatures from a man in Florida. Carl was at the same house party and recognized him at Phoenix Garden. He demanded they cut him in, so Angus killed him. He wasn't going to let a witness slip away twice." Bernie shook his head. "I didn't mean for anyone to die. That was never part of the deal. Things just got out of hand. Angus was like a wild animal. Yuan could barely control him. When I saw him threatening you, Roman, I didn't hesitate."

"I'm eternally grateful," Roman said. "It occurred to me later that fetching a shotgun when you heard us arguing was an overreaction, but I was too besotted to think critically. Now it makes perfect sense—you realized the plan was shot to hell and that Yuan would be much easier to deal with in the aftermath than Angus."

"And when you and Yuan were alone in the gallery, I'll bet you told him to play along until you could help him escape," Jean said.

"Something like that."

"I wondered why you kept apologizing to Jean and me," Roman said. "Now I know."

They sat in silence for a few moments, rage and indecision filling the room. Finally Bernie shifted in his chair. "So what happens now? Are you going to break my nose, Jean? Or is Roman going to break my neck?"

"Get out before I do," Roman said.

"Roman, please." There were tears in Bernie's eyes and a catch in his voice. "I'm so sorry. I regret all of it, more than you know. I love you."

"That's rather beside the point, isn't it?"

Bernie gave an ugly sob, weeping openly now. "How can you push me away like this after what we've meant to each other? You have to forgive me."

"Now you're overacting," Roman said.

Bernie wiped his face with a white cloth napkin from the table. "Are you going to tell the police?"

Roman shrugged. "I haven't decided what to do. I need to think. Call me tomorrow."

"I'll come over."

"No," Roman said. "I don't want to see you again. But I'll let you know what I decide."

"Wait a minute," Jean said. "You can't let him go. He might escape."

"He won't as long as he thinks there's a chance I'll forgive him," Roman said. "Isn't that right, Bernie?"

"Yes, I swear it. I'll do anything you ask." Bernie stood for a moment, about to say more, but Roman's scowl stopped him.

Bernie went into the bedroom. They heard him opening and closing closets and drawers.

Jean got up, too upset to sit down, and faced Roman. "You're going to let him walk?"

"I don't know what I'm going to do," he said, his voice strained and husky.

Bernie came into the living room with two Louis Vuitton suitcases. "Roman—" he began.

"Good-bye, Bernie," Roman said. Bernie turned on his heel and walked out the door.

Jean turned to Roman. "Goddammit, I don't want a *Third Man* ending, where you try to help him get away even though you're through with him. I want a *Maltese Falcon* ending, where he takes the fall for what he's done."

"This isn't one of your black-and-white movies, Jean," Roman said wearily. "This is real life."

"How can you let a cold-blooded killer leave like that?"

"Do you have any idea what will happen to a man like him in prison?"

"You mean being gang-raped by three-hundred-pound felons? A fate worse than death? I don't believe there is a fate worse than death, and he's responsible for the deaths of four people."

"Five, if you count Angus," Zeppo said.

"I don't count Angus," she said. "Killing him was a public service."

Roman rubbed his eyes. "I can't argue with you right now. All I ask is that neither of you does anything until I think it through. Please. Bernie was right about one thing—I love him."

There was so much pain in his voice that Jean relented. "OK, Roman, I promise. I'm sorry." She longed to touch him and comfort him, but knew he wouldn't want her to.

"I promise, too," Zeppo said. "We'll give you as long as you want."

"Thank you." Roman turned and took a full bottle of Jack Daniels from a high cupboard. "I never believed in killing the bearer of bad news, but I now understand the impulse. Please leave." He got a glass from the drying rack and poured himself a healthy slug.

Jean and Zeppo slipped out the front door and stood in the garden between Roman's house and Beau's. "We have to get someone over here," she said.

"I think he wants to be alone, Jeannie."

"Remember I told you about the man he loved who died?"

"Sure. Perry. Roman talks about him sometimes."

"Right after Perry died, Roman got drunk and put his fist through a wall in his bedroom. Broke four bones in his hand."

"Oh. Then I guess we'd better call someone."

Jean tried to think of someone who truly cared for Roman and whom she could trust to keep quiet. The name came to her at once—Lou Kasden. She sat on a bench at the base of a big shade tree and pulled out her cell phone. Lou answered.

"Lou, we've got a major situation here," Jean said. "Can you come over to Roman's right away?"

"Whatever is the problem? Has Zeppo gone queer?"

"This is serious, and just between us. It turns out Bernie *is* too good to be true. He was the inside man in the robbery, and he killed that waitress I told you about."

"Mother of God. Are you going to tell the police?"

"I don't know. Roman begged us to let him go, for now. We really haven't decided what to do. Everything's very complicated."

There was a brief silence. "And Roman's into the Bourbon."

"Yeah. He threw us out because we broke the news to him, but I don't want to leave him alone. Will you stay with him and keep him from hurting himself?"

"Honey, I'm already there."

Chapter 23

Jean and Zeppo, feeling thoroughly wretched, left as soon as Lou arrived. Zeppo had to return to Davis the next day, since he'd already missed so many classes. Jean went back to work and accomplished practically nothing.

Lou stayed with Roman for a couple of days until things stabilized. He was still keeping an occasional eye on him and had called Jean a few times to say Roman was doing badly and hadn't decided what to do about Bernie. Lou told her he'd confiscated the suit of lights before Roman could cut it up, and hoped it would bring a good price at the next Bash Back fund-raising auction.

On Friday Zeppo drove in from Davis and met Jean at the bar in Max's café, the restaurant nearest her office. She arrived first, and instead of her usual glass of wine, ordered a Rémy Martin.

Zeppo sat on the stool next to her. "That was a rough week," he said.

"I'll say. I can't concentrate on my work and my coworkers are getting annoyed. And I can't tell anyone what's wrong. I've thought of pleading post-traumatic stress disorder."

"I know what you mean. There was really no point in going to any of my lectures." He ordered a draft beer.

"Roman's asking too much. I mean, how long can we sit by and let—"

"Jeannie," Zeppo interrupted, nodding toward the TV above the bar. "Look."

Jean raised her eyes to see a stock photo of Bernie smiling into the camera. She strained to hear the announcer:

". . . arrested at his father's suite at the Fairmont Hotel in San Francisco. Authorities confirm that he has been charged with the murder of Pilar Ochoa, a waitress who sometimes worked at oil billionaire Theodore Lyon's San Diego County home. She was stabbed to death in August. Theodore Lyon has issued a statement saying he has complete confidence in his son's innocence." There was a shot of Ted, Meide, and a young woman who could only be sister Lydia at a press conference. Lydia had the family coloring and bone structure, but her dowdy thrift-shop clothes looked deliberately anti-Lyon.

Jean gripped Zeppo's hand. "I guess Matt Baeza's back from vacation."

"You know what else?" Zeppo said. "Roman's going to think we did it." He stood and tossed some money on the bar. "We'd better get over there right away."

They retrieved Zeppo's car from the garage under Opera Plaza. "Matt must have found Hector and Suzanne," Jean said.

Zeppo pulled into the stream of rush-hour traffic. "It's more likely that Suzanne found Matt."

"What do you mean?"

"She's smart. I bet she did research on the case at the library and figured out who Bernie was and what it meant that Hector saw him. She realized this was a way for Hector to cut a deal on the stolen-car rap."

Jean stared at him. "You knew Suzanne would do that, didn't you? That's why you told Roman you'd give him all the time he needed—with her help, Matt would figure it out first."

"Once I met her, I thought it might go down that way. But Matt has to have some other evidence, too, something really damning, to get a warrant for a Lyon. He can't make a case just on Hector's testimony."

"You're right about that," Jean said. "I sure hope Suzanne didn't tell Matt that we were there first."

"If she did, we'll hear from him."

They parked in Beau's driveway and went around through the garden gate. Roman answered his door. One glance at his face and Jean knew he'd assumed the worst—the look he gave them made her stomach hurt. "Roman," she said quickly, "it wasn't us. We didn't tell anyone."

"It's true," Zeppo said.

Roman stared at them, still scowling. "Very well, I believe you." He started to shut the door.

Zeppo put out his hand and caught it. "Let us in," he said softly.

Roman stood silent for a few moments, then turned abruptly and went into the house, leaving the door open. Jean and Zeppo followed him into his office. On the small television tucked into a bookshelf, a CNN announcer discussed the stock market. Roman muted the sound and flopped onto the sofa, near a tumbler of ice cubes and amber liquid on the coffee table. Jean sat nearby and looked more closely at him. His eyes were red from lack of sleep and he hadn't shaved recently. It was obvious why he'd never grown a full beard—he looked like a terrorist from Central Casting.

"We heard a local news flash that he'd been arrested," Zeppo said, sitting down next to Roman. "Have you found out anything else?"

"No. I heard it on the radio and turned on CNN. Reports have been sketchy." He rubbed his heavy black whiskers. "If indeed you two had nothing to do with this, then Matt Baeza must be responsible. It's hard to believe that Wes Jurado and his Keystone Kops could have stumbled on the truth."

"We thought the same thing," Jean said. "At least now we can stop fighting about it, Roman. It's out of our hands."

"Not entirely," Roman said under his breath.

"You're going to help Bernie jump bail, aren't you?"

"I'll make my own decisions now. You've done enough damage."

"Come on, Roman," Zeppo said. "It's not Jean's fault you and Bernie hit it off so well. Without her, Angus and Yuan would be living it up in some posh Asian hotel right now and Angus would be assaulting the maids. And Bernie would be making his movie on stolen money, at least until Matt Baeza caught up with him."

"And I wouldn't give a rat's ass whether Bernie lived or died," Roman said harshly, glaring at Jean.

"If you want to blame someone, blame me," Zeppo said. "It was my idea to go to San Diego and find the witness. After that things were beyond our control."

Roman turned his glare to Zeppo. "Why have you taken such a morbid interest in these proceedings?"

"Because a woman was murdered. My sister-in-law's killer got away with it. I don't want that to happen again. And you seem to be forgetting that Jean was almost raped and killed and you were almost stabbed to death because of Bernie."

Roman sighed deeply. "No, I'm not forgetting that. It's one of the things that makes these revelations so agonizing."

Zeppo put a hand on Roman's knee. "Tell me, Roman, would you rather have gone on living with him and never know?"

"Sometimes I think the answer to that is yes," Roman said, his voice husky with emotion. "Sometimes I want to have things as they were, no matter what he's done. But in my lucid moments, I'd rather know." He leaned forward and cradled his head in his hands. "This is worse than having him die."

Zeppo moved closer and put his arm around Roman's shoulders. That was another thing Jean loved about Zeppo—he was unselfconsciously affectionate with his male friends, even his gay male friends.

Jean touched Roman's arm. "I wish it could have turned out any other way."

Roman looked up. "I know you do. And of course I realize intellectually that neither of you is to blame. But I still must insist that you don't interfere."

Jean wanted to argue more, but she had never before seen Roman in such bad shape. "I won't do anything to endanger you," she said finally.

"Me either," Zeppo agreed.

"Thank you. That's all I can ask. Now go away. I'm not fit for company right now." He picked up the tumbler and took a drink.

"Hey," Zeppo said, his voice gentle, "remember when you told me not to wallow in self-pity, even if it's justified? Now I'm telling you. You're drinking way too much."

Roman's expression softened and he put the glass down. "I suppose I should practice what I preach. But I would like to be left alone so I can try and get some sleep."

Jean started toward the door, but Zeppo hesitated.

Roman gave a faint smile. "Don't worry, you needn't phone Lou. I won't have any more Bourbon tonight."

"OK, but call us if you get thirsty."

"I will."

Outside, Jean stood beside Zeppo's car, unsure of what to do next.

"Now that I've talked him out of getting drunk, how about we find another beer?" Zeppo said.

"Good idea."

They walked the few blocks to Eighteenth Street and went into Il Castrato. Jean had a Cognac and Zeppo an Anchor Steam beer. In the background, a tenor and a soprano sang a mournful duet.

"I've never known you to wallow in self-pity," Jean said as they settled at a window table. "When did Roman tell you to stop?"

"When do you think?" he said. "Whenever you were with another man."

She took his hand. "Oh Zeppo, I—"

"Forget it. We've got bigger problems now."

Jean took a drink of Cognac. "They can't possibly grant bail. Bernie's too much of a flight risk."

"Yeah, but then there's always the Lyon clout. If he gets the right judge, who knows?"

"If that happens, we'll have to keep a close eye on Roman so he doesn't get himself arrested, too."

"That'll be a real challenge. He's a crafty dude."

"I know," Jean said. "Maybe Lou will help us. God, I'll be glad when this is over." She finished her drink, feeling even worse than she had before Bernie's arrest.

THE NEXT day Jean's phone rang while Zeppo was out getting breakfast. To her alarm, it was Matt Baeza.

"Hi, Matt," she said. "Are we in trouble?"

"You ought to be," he said crossly. "I know you and your friend talked to Hector Navarro and kept it to yourselves. I also know you bribed Mickey to get to Hector. How'd you find the motel, anyway?"

Jean had a white lie ready. "Old-fashioned legwork. We must have tried a dozen motels before we got lucky. How'd you find it?"

"Same way."

"Sorry we didn't call you," she said contritely.

He sighed. "Don't worry, I'm not going to pursue it. If you hadn't gone out there, Suzanne never would have come to me and I wouldn't have focused on Bernie. He was low on my list of suspects until I talked to Hector. Anyway, I know why you didn't tell me—because of him and Roman. I imagine Bernie moved out of Roman's place because of what you found out. This must be pretty rough for all of you."

"Yeah, it is." Jean relaxed into her chair, relieved. "Any trace of Yuan?"

"None. We can't even trace the boat he left on. Finding him will take time. But none of the prints on the jade belonged to the other guests, so we're assuming they're all Yuan's. Bernie must have wiped the jade clean after he took photos. Those prints should help us get a lead on Yuan."

"Is Wes Jurado going to take all the credit this time?"

Matt chuckled. "Nope. The brass scheduled a press conference for tomorrow, and I'll be answering questions about the investigation."

"So you're finally going to be a star."

"No way. The last thing I want to do is spend the rest of my life working homicide. I'll be happy to get back to breaking up bar fights and finding stray horses."

They ended the conversation on a friendly note, and Jean relayed the exchange to Zeppo when he returned with bagels, lox, and cream cheese.

Within a week, one of the investigating officers picked up Bernie in San Francisco and transported him to San Diego County. Jean phoned Roman a couple of times, but he was still depressed and withdrawn and didn't want to see her or Zeppo. She decided to keep her distance and let him heal in his own time; he'd call sooner or later. At least Lou was keeping an eye on him.

She and Zeppo agreed not to tell the police what Bernie had admitted to them unless the case against him looked weak, since they didn't want to get into trouble for not cooperating sooner, or get Roman into trouble for trying to help a murder suspect flee the country. Jean knew that the information about Yuan stealing the Persian miniatures in Florida years ago might help identify him, so she promised herself that if no one had traced him within a couple of months, she'd write an anonymous note to Matt Baeza.

One rainy evening as Jean was reading a mystery at home after work, she got a call from Lou. "How's Roman doing?" she asked.

"I wouldn't know," he said. "He's avoiding me, which isn't like him at all. So I've been following him."

"Why, Lou. Just like a real detective."

"Honey, I'm the girl of a thousand faces. Anyway, he just went to the Fairmont and up to the Death Star suite. But here's the strange part: I asked my friend who works at the Tonga Room and he said there's no one staying there now but the Dragon Lady."

"You mean Meide Lyon? Why would he meet her?"

"Haven't the foggiest."

Jean was getting the beginning of an idea that she didn't like. "Lou, where are you?"

"On the J Church, on my way home."

"Let's meet at that Chinese place on Twenty-Fourth Street."

Jean got her umbrella and walked down the hill to the restaurant, which was just starting to fill up for dinner. She sat at a small round table in the bar area and ordered a glass of Chardonnay. The place smelled deliciously of garlic and ginger. As she sipped her wine, a man approached her, smiling as if she should know him. He was not quite her height and slim, with short spiked brown hair and hazel eyes, in jeans and a soft leather jacket splattered with rain. He was good-looking and very familiar.

"Hey, baby," he said. "How'd you like to buy a boy a drink?"

"Lou! I didn't recognize you."

He sat down. "Don't the waxed eyebrows give me away?"

"If I met you at a party, I might even give you a tumble."

"We all know how discriminating you are. Now what about that drink?"

"If you order a kir royale, it will give you away."

He gestured at her wine. "Is that any good?"

"Too flabby. Try the Sauvignon Blanc."

Jean looked at him more closely as the waiter took his order, fascinated by his new incarnation. He had several holes in each ear, but now wore only a single turquoise stud. "That's not a wig, is it? You cut off your hair."

“It was pretty damaged from all the coloring, so I thought I might as well start over. And how else could I hope to follow Roman without getting spotted? He may have his flaws, but he’s not dumb.” The waiter delivered his wine and he took a drink. “Come to think of it, he has no flaws.”

“Roman might go for you dressed like this. You look positively clean cut and corn fed. Have you ever tried it?”

“What’s the point? He knows what I am. The question is, why is he meeting Meide?”

Jean leaned toward him and lowered her voice. “You know what must be happening? Meide and Roman are planning to get Bernie out of the country if he makes bail. She has the money and he has the know-how.”

“Why would she do that?”

“She’ll have her baby in a few months. I’m sure she wants Ted fixated on her child, not spending all his time and money on Bernie’s trial and endless appeals. If she and Roman manage to get Bernie to a country with no extradition treaty, that’s the end of the problem. He’ll be an exile. Ted can visit him in Timbuktu or wherever, but he’ll never be number one son again.”

“If that’s so,” he said slowly, “then I think I’ll have to resign from the Castro Street Irregulars. I want Bernie gone as much as she does.”

Jean put her glass down sharply. “You think he should get away with murder just so Roman will be alone and lonely, and maybe you’ll have a shot at him?”

Lou looked at her coldly. “I’ll never have a shot at him. Use your pretty, empty head: You know how he despises the prison system, and you know he never does anything halfway. If Bernie is found guilty, do you think Roman will listen to ‘I Will Survive’ a few times and forget about it? He’ll get drunk and agonize over it for a while, and then he’ll break down and drive to San Quentin or Chino every weekend with a carton of cigarettes and a homemade cake. He’ll be as involved as Ted in the various legal appeals. Before you know it, he'll be spending all his time teaching self-defense to incarcerated queers. No one rich ever gets the death penalty, so it will go on for decades. Is that how you want Roman to spend his life?"

Jean finished her wine, wondering if she had enough cash for a Cognac. "No, of course not. But I don't want Bernie to go unpunished for what he did."

"Isn't exile enough punishment? Living in some backwater with no gay bars and no Wilkes Bashford, and all the movies are in Arabic or Korean? Roman will get over him eventually if that happens."

"Exile is not enough punishment for stabbing a woman to death with an ice pick for money," Jean said heatedly. "Wherever Bernie goes, he'll live a sweet life in a mansion with twenty servants and a private plane. I want him to do time."

"Well then," Lou said, "I'm afraid you and Zeppo will have to play avenging angels without my help. Roman's mental health is a lot more important to me than getting even with Bernie." He stood. "Thanks for the wine. It's too grassy and lacks fruit."

Jean watched him walk away, wondering if she'd have any friends left besides Zeppo by the time Bernie went to trial.

Back in her apartment Jean ate takeout Chinese food, poured herself a glass of good Chardonnay to make up for the plonk at the bar, and made a few phone calls she'd been putting off. After her conversation with Lou, she felt like talking to someone sympathetic. She called Laszlo first; he was as surprised as she'd been by Bernie's arrest, and they discussed it for quite a while. He'd found an apartment in South San Francisco and was still looking for honest work. She declined his offer of primo Ecstasy at a good price.

She reached Tony at his flagship restaurant in Santa Monica. "Tony, it's Jean Applequist."

"Jean, I've been meaning to call you. This business with Bernie must be hard on you, and especially on Roman."

"Yeah, it is. Roman's really messed up."

"It's a damn shame. This whole thing sure makes me a lot less likely to trust people."

"Me too," Jean said. "How's business? I know you were having some financial troubles."

"We got a loan from another source and the new TV ads are running. Have you seen them?"

"I don't watch much TV." Jean had a sudden flash of inspiration. "Hey, you know what? I ate in one of your restaurants recently and thought it was OK, but not great. I think you need to jazz up the menu."

"Yeah, I've been told that before."

"Are you on good terms with Ted these days?"

Tony chuckled. "Not exactly. He hasn't spoken to me since I told him that Bernie might really be guilty."

"I know he is," Jean said.

"That's what I thought. I saw how Ted treated him, and I can sure see why Bernie would slip a cog and start to believe he was entitled to get money out of his father any way he could. But killing that girl was crazy. He must have been desperate and stupid all at once. When I said that, Ted got furious. All those years of trying to force Bernie to go straight, and now Ted thinks he can do no wrong."

"Ted never could get it right," Jean said. "But about your restaurants: Remember Laszlo Harady, Ted's chef? He's unemployed now. He and Ted had a falling out."

"Laszlo, huh?" There was a pause. "Now that man can cook, and I know he used to run some big operations."

"Would it bother you if he'd had a little trouble with the law?"

"You forget I spent nine years in the NFL. Give me his number."

Jean felt better as she hung up, as if she'd accomplished something positive. Her next call was to Maria Esposito, Pilar's aunt who ran the bridal shop. "Oh, Jean!" she said. "I've been thinking about you since the arrest. None of us can believe it was Bernie Lyon. He seemed like such a nice person."

"That's what I thought, too. But they have the right guy. I'm sure of it."

"Well then, thank God. Did you help Matt solve it?"

Jean didn't want to take any credit for the current situation. "He uncovered most of it himself. How's your brother doing?"

"Salvador's better. He's eating again, and working. It will help him a lot to hear they've really got the one who did it."

"Then I'm glad I called, Maria. Keep in touch."

"Thanks, and God bless you."

Jean felt very far from blessed, except in one area. The stress and pain of the past couple of weeks hadn't made a dent in Zeppo's libido. She looked forward even more to his visits now, since the only time she wasn't worried or angry or miserable or all three was during sex. Cycling always gave her an endorphin rush, but the rainy weather had curtailed that outlet. Sleep helped, of course, but for the first time in her life, she was experiencing insomnia. Come Friday she'd be guaranteed hours of oblivion, measured out over their long weekend together.

Jean craved his companionship more and more. She'd now seen him in way too many high-pressure situations and had never known anyone else who handled adversity as well as he did. When the going got tough, Roman might drink too much and she might throw temper tantrums, but Zeppo always remained calm and centered. She also found herself amazed by how sharp he was, especially the way he'd realized early on that Bernie was the inside man and adroitly planted the seeds of his arrest.

She dialed his number, the last call of the evening, so she could hear his voice before going to bed.

Chapter 24

Ted's influence and money did get Bernie out on bail—ten million dollars. There was an uproar in the media, since a witness had seen Bernie's car hidden in a grove of trees in Valle de los Osos the morning of Pilar's murder and the police had searched Bernie's suite at the Chateau Marmont in Los Angeles and found a well-hidden CD with images of the Han jade. But the deed was done and Bernie was free, as long as he stayed in San Diego County. Since his release, reporters had staked out various Lyon properties and those of family friends, but so far he remained elusive. Jean updated her article to include Bernie's arrest; there were a couple of weeks before press time in case she had to do another rewrite.

After the bail hearing, Jean called Roman and Lou a few times at both home and cell numbers, getting nothing but voice mail, so the next Saturday she and Zeppo used her keys to check Roman's house. A quick search revealed that his old leather suitcase, toiletries, and favorite jacket were gone. On the kitchen table lay a note in Roman's handwriting to Nick, a man Jean knew from Bash Back, instructing him how to water the plants. Jean phoned Nick, who said that Roman was out of town indefinitely but reachable by cell phone. Next she phoned the San Diego chapter of Bash Back, and a helpful woman told her that Roman was indeed in the area and had scheduled a series of planning meetings over the next week.

"He's there, all right," Jean told Zeppo. "Why do you suppose the receptionist was so forthcoming? You'd think if

Roman were plotting Bernie's escape, he'd want to stay out of sight."

"He must be up to something. We shouldn't complain—this way it'll be easy to find him."

They locked up, dashed through the cold drizzle, and got into the red Porsche. "Zeppo," Jean said, leaning on the steering wheel, "the closer we get to the end game, the more I realize I'm not such a hard-ass after all. I want Bernie punished, but I can't do whatever it'll take to bust him if it means getting Roman or Lou arrested."

"Yeah, I've been thinking the same thing. If we have to choose between catching Bernie and saving Roman and Lou, I'm with you. But if we're going to do any good at all, we have to get down there now. The preliminary hearing is scheduled for next Wednesday, and if Bernie's going to run, it'll be before then."

Jean started the car and backed out of the driveway. "What about your classes?"

"Midterms are over, and I'll bring my laptop and have friends e-mail me lecture notes."

She turned up the hill toward Noe Valley. "Roman must know we'll follow him."

"Sure, but he thinks he's smarter than we are."

"Isn't he?"

"Maybe one on one, but not when we team up. Then nobody can outsmart us."

"OK," Jean said, "first we need to outsmart Kyle. I know I'll get a subpoena one of these days and have to go south, but right now I'm out of vacation and sick days."

"Tell him you have to be there to finish the article. That's actually true. If Roman and Bernie try something, you'll have a whole new ending, whether we stop them or not."

She smiled and ruffled his hair—the humidity put his coppery curls into tight corkscrews, and his beard was growing in curly, too. "I'm glad I'm not doing this alone." She pulled her hand back to shift gears. "Of course, if I were doing this alone, Bernie would have gotten away with murder."

"You never know—Matt might have found Hector all by himself."

They went back to Jean's apartment, spent the afternoon packing, and left midmorning Sunday. Bad weather made the trip slow, and they stayed the night at a motel in Buttonwillow rather than drive through the Grapevine section in the dark and rain. Jean called her office Monday morning, explaining to a cranky Kyle that she was already gone, and they got to San Diego before two o'clock, checking into a bed and breakfast near Balboa Park that Zeppo had found on the Internet. The room was comfortable in spite of the fussy Victorian décor, with lavender chintz covering nearly every surface. The next step was to find Roman.

The day was cold by San Diego standards and rainy, so they dressed in jeans, sweaters, and waterproof jackets. Since they had no idea where the chase would take them, they filled a cooler with water, energy drinks, supermarket sushi, and bananas. Zeppo brought binoculars and even a deck of cards.

Jean drove to the Bash Back office, a storefront on Fourth Street near Robinson in Hillcrest, circling to find a good vantage point. The area was mixed residential and commercial, with lots of well-maintained bungalows and mature trees. They parked across the street and about a block down from the office, behind a panel truck that bore the logo of a nearby furniture store. As long as the truck stayed put, they were partially hidden from anyone entering or leaving the office.

They waited for a couple of hours, talking things over and wiping off the foggy windows periodically. Five people went into the office and two came out, but there was no sign of Roman. Zeppo seemed content to wait, but Jean grew restless; she had never understood how real detectives could stand to spend hours on stakeouts. Of course, the Red Bull she'd drunk didn't help matters.

As Zeppo leaned forward to see out the front window, Jean ran her hand up and down his back. He turned and kissed her. She put her arms around him underneath his jacket, getting as close to him as she could in the bucket seats.

He pulled back and looked into her eyes. "Remember how much trouble we got into the last time we tried to have sex in a car?"

"This time we'll just make out," she said. "No touching below the waist."

"If you say so." He slipped his hands under her black sweater, unhooking her bra and pushing it above her breasts. Soon the windows were completely steamed up.

A sharp rap on the passenger-side window startled them and they pushed apart. Jean refastened her clothes as Zeppo rolled the window down. Roman stood outside, holding a black umbrella and scowling at them. He'd shaved and wore only a goatee.

"I see you've foolishly gone on a stakeout with no chaperone," he said. "I've been expecting you. Thanks for being so obvious—this is a rather conspicuous car."

"Roman, we're just—" Jean began.

"I know exactly what you're doing," he interrupted. "You're hounding me so I can't help Bernie. Well, I'll make things easy for you. My next stop will be the Bash Back office down the street, where I plan to spend a few hours. Then I'll have drinks at a friend's home near First and Spruce and dinner at Kemo Sabe on Fifth. I may go out clubbing after that, but I'm not sure where, so you're on your own. If you lose me, you can pick me up again at the Cabrillo Motel on University, room 207."

"Roman, listen," Zeppo said. "This isn't all about Bernie. We're trying to keep you from doing time."

"Better me than Bernie. At least I could live with it." He turned and limped to the office.

"Oops," Jean said. "The Castro Street Irregulars screwed up. We should have rented something nondescript."

Zeppo stroked his red beard. "He's not trying to shake us and he's keeping a pretty high profile. That means he won't go near Bernie. In fact that's probably the plan: Roman stays visible so the press will follow him, and we will, too, and meanwhile Bernie slips away. So there's only one thing to do—find Bernie."

"How can we, if the entire national media can't? I read that the *National Enquirer* is offering a hundred grand for his whereabouts, and I'm sure plenty of other magazines and TV stations would pay, too."

"We know something they don't—that Lou and Meide Lyon are in this with Roman. All we have to do is tail one of them until they lead us to Bernie."

"It'll be tough locating Lou," Jean said. "I don't know who any of his friends are down here."

"Meide's a better bet. Ted keeps holding press conferences declaring Bernie's innocence and she's always right there with him. I read on the Net that they're staying at the Park Hyatt Aviara in Carlsbad, north of here. So we go back on stakeout." He grinned at her. "But no more fooling around, OK?"

"We'll be like saints," she said, crossing herself. "And tomorrow we rent a boring car."

Back in their room at the bed and breakfast, Jean arranged the containers of sushi on a round table covered with purple flowered linen while Zeppo looked up the Aviara on his laptop.

"OK," Zeppo said as he clicked around the site. "It's a pricey resort near the beach. Has a spa, golf course, gym, four restaurants, the works. It's going to be tough getting past security at a place like that, and there are probably several entrances."

"Shit. Why couldn't they stay in a Motel 6?"

"The biggest, baddest room is the presidential suite, so we can assume the Lyons are there."

"Let's see it," Jean said, coming over to stand behind him. The photos showed luxurious, vaguely Italianate décor.

"Look, here's a floor plan." Zeppo clicked. "See, a master bedroom and a couple of spares."

"One for Lydia and one for the help. I wonder if Chencho's with them."

Zeppo turned and gave her a look. "You're a genius. If he is, that's our in. He owes you big time, doesn't he?"

"He thinks he does, which is all that counts. I know how to find him, too—Maria Esposito is a friend of his." Jean got her phone from her purse and called the bridal shop. "Maria," she said, "this is Jean Applequist. I need a favor. Do you know Chencho's cell number?"

"Sure," Maria said. "Let me look it up."

"How's Salvador doing?"

"Not so well. It really upset him that they let Bernie out on bail. He's afraid that someone with that much money will flee the country."

"We think so, too," Jean said.

"His wife's worried about him—he's taken some time off work, but he stays away from the house all day and won't say where he's been." She read off Chencho's cell number and they said good-bye.

Jean phoned Chencho. "This is Jean, but don't say my name," she said when he answered. "Are you in Carlsbad with the Lyons?"

"Yeah. How'd you know?"

"Are they there with you?"

"Nearby."

"Get away from them and phone me as soon as you can. We need to talk." He called back within half an hour.

"Jean, how are you?" His voice sounded warm but cautious.

"Doing fine. Listen, I'm in San Diego—can we meet somewhere?"

"Uh . . . I don't know. I mean, things are really tense here right now."

"This is important, and it won't take long. I'll drive up to Carlsbad."

"I guess so. OK, go north on Interstate 5 and cut over to the Coast Highway, to South Carlsbad State Beach. You'll see the mouth of a river with big stones piled on either side. Park just north of there along the beach. Meet me at around five P.M. I'm driving a silver Audi."

"I'll find you." She said good-bye.

"Let's move," Zeppo said. "We have to get a different car." They rented a beige Nissan Sentra at the airport and drove north on Interstate 5 through rain and rush-hour traffic to Carlsbad.

Zeppo used the car's GPS and directed Jean to Chencho's beach. The parking strip along the sand was nearly empty, and Jean pulled in next to a silver Audi. Chencho got into the back seat of the Sentra. He wore his usual uniform of white shirt and khaki slacks, and today he had a navy sport coat over it.

"Hi, Chencho," Jean said, turning around. "Thanks for coming. You remember Zeppo." Zeppo reached over the seat and shook hands.

"I can't stay long," Chencho said, his round face creased with worry. "Mr. Lyon needs me."

"I'll get straight to the point," Jean said. "I know Ted's convinced that Bernie is innocent. What do you think?"

"He could never do a thing like that," Chencho said, shaking his head. "Matt must have made a mistake."

"It's no mistake," Jean said kindly. "You know Matt's too good for that. Zeppo and I talked to the witness who saw Bernie at the motel with Angus and Yuan. After that Bernie admitted to us that he did it."

Chencho looked at Zeppo, who nodded. "I . . . I don't know what to think," Chencho said, working his hands together. "If he really did it, that'll break Mr. Lyon's heart. I've been with him three years. I know most people don't like him, but he's always been really good to me."

"I'm sorry he'll be hurt, but Bernie did stab Pilar to death for money, and it's because of him that Dom Huerta, Katharine, and Carl were murdered and Roman and I were almost killed," Jean said. "The reason I wanted to see you is that we think Bernie is planning to jump bail. That means he'll get away with everything."

Jean waited as Chencho struggled to sort out his loyalties. "So what do you want from me?" he said finally.

"We think Meide may be helping Bernie leave the country without Ted's knowledge," Zeppo said. "What's your take on that?"

Chencho thought about it. "It could be. Mr. Lyon's been busy with lawyers all the time, and Mrs. Lyon goes out shopping a lot, but she never has very many bags when she comes back. I mean, usually she's buying clothes and shoes and jewelry and now baby things all the time, but not lately. If she wasn't pregnant, I'd think she was having an affair."

"Chencho," Jean said, "do you know where Bernie is?"

He met her eyes. "No, I don't. Only the Lyons do. It's a big secret. Even the lawyers don't know. They talk to him on Skype."

"Will you help us find him?"

"How?"

"The next time Meide decides to go shopping, will you call us? We want to follow her and see if she really is setting things up for Bernie to escape. If she's not, she'll never know we were there."

Jean could see an agony of indecision on Chencho's youthful features as he mulled it over. "You promise no one will ever know I told?" he said.

"We swear it," Jean said.

He nodded. "OK, then. I'll do it."

Jean gave him one of her business cards with her cell phone number written on the back. "Thanks, Chencho. We can't stop Bernie without your help."

"I have to get back." Chencho hesitated, his hand on the door latch. "I liked Bernie. He seemed like a great guy. But only a monster would do what he did." He got out and slammed the door.

CHENCHO MADE the call just before four o'clock the next afternoon: Meide had ordered her car brought around. That morning Jean and Zeppo had packed a picnic lunch and again parked at South Carlsbad State Beach near a public restroom, stretching their legs with strolls along the water, managing to keep their hands off each other most of the time. They drove to the intersection Chencho specified and waited until a new white BMW rolled past. Meide wore big sunglasses and her hair was tucked into a beige cloche hat; Jean would have missed her if she hadn't been watching for the car.

They pulled into traffic, keeping their distance as Meide got on the two-lane Coast Highway heading south. She was a terrible driver, slow and unsure, which made her easy to follow. The rain had stopped but the day was overcast, and the gleaming white car stood out.

The drive was beautiful; heavy gray clouds merged at the horizon with the pewter sea, and the rough white breakers were some of the biggest Jean had ever seen on the California coast. Out in the water, a few hardy surfers in full wetsuits took advantage of the storm tide.

In the small beach town of Leucadia, Meide turned right from the left lane, cutting off the car beside her. "The woman's a menace," Zeppo remarked.

Jean turned to follow. "I imagine she usually has a chauffeur."

The white BMW was parked right around the corner beside a Chinese restaurant with red plastic lanterns hanging above the door, between a liquor store and a tattoo parlor. Several other cars were parked along the street, none of which Jean recognized. She drove slowly past. "Looks as if Mrs. Lyon is slumming."

"Maybe the food's great," Zeppo said. "Park across the street, near that shop."

Half a block down, Jean made a U-turn and pulled into a spot in front of a store offering antiques and seashells. They watched Meide get out of the BMW and walk to the restaurant. She wore a well-cut taupe maternity dress and carried a small purse. Jean was amused to see that her ankles were slightly swollen and her shoes had low sturdy heels.

After about fifteen minutes, Zeppo got restless. "I'm going to see who's with her." He rummaged in the trunk, returning with a navy blue watch cap and sunglasses. Jean helped him with the cap, stuffing his hair out of sight. He turned up his coat collar and put on the sunglasses. "How do I look?"

"Like a six-foot-five redheaded geek in disguise."

He kissed her and got out of the car. She watched him walk past the restaurant, buy a newspaper from a machine in front of the liquor store, and saunter back.

"Jackpot," Zeppo said, getting in and pulling off his cap and glasses. "Meide's having potstickers with Lou."

"How's he dressed? Male or female?"

"Full drag," he said. "Wig, makeup, loud dress."

Jean took his hand. "We're getting close. Let's hope you're right about no one being able to outsmart us."

Chapter 25

Jean and Zeppo sank down in their seats as Lou and Meide left the restaurant together. He wore a shiny black raincoat and matching hat over a bright yellow dress and a dark brown shoulder-length wig. They conferred briefly before Meide got into her car and left. Lou unlocked the door of a small blue rental car; he looked around before getting in, but his eyes didn't linger on the Sentra.

Jean pulled out behind Lou, who took the Coast Highway going south. He drove through Leucadia and the more upscale Encinitas. After Encinitas they were right on the coast again; a railroad track ran along the highway on the inland side. Just past Cardiff State Beach, a hill scattered with trees and high-end houses rose up between the road and the ocean.

Lou turned right onto one of the streets that ran into the hilly enclave and Jean followed. As they drove closer to the sea, the houses got larger, grander, and more widely spaced. There was so little traffic that Jean was forced to hang back a few times. Finally they lost Lou completely. Jean stopped the car and turned off the engine, but they could hear nothing except the surf and the distant hum of highway traffic. "What now?" she said.

"We've only passed a few driveways since we last saw him. Let's see if he turned into one of those. Pull in here." On the right was a small park with two picnic tables and a redwood jungle gym. The only other car there was an old white Econoline van. "Won't we get busted for wandering around in a neighborhood so ritzy they don't even have sidewalks?" she said.

"It's only two blocks." Zeppo pulled binoculars out of the glove compartment and looped them around his neck. "We can say we're bird-watchers and we've spotted a rare tropical vulture."

"Yeah, that'll work."

They donned camouflage rain ponchos over jeans and sweatshirts and walked back to the area where they'd last seen Lou's car. Jean looked up at the gathering clouds; it wasn't raining now, but it would again before long.

The first house they came to had a locked entry gate between stone pillars and a sophisticated intercom system. They peered through the wrought iron rails but saw no sign of the blue car. Jean noticed that a puddle in the driveway was undisturbed by tire tracks. At the next house, on the east side of the street, a construction van blocked the driveway and a green plastic tarp covered part of the roof. A skinny Latino gardener in a hooded yellow rain slicker clipped the boxwood hedge along the road. He didn't look up as they passed.

The third house was tucked beneath a rise on the west side of the street. They couldn't tell if anyone had recently driven over the gravel driveway. "Let's climb up and see what we can see," Zeppo said. They crawled up a muddy embankment, pulling themselves along by grasping vines and tree trunks, and at the crest lay on their stomachs on a thatch of eucalyptus leaves between two rhododendron bushes.

From their perch it was a ten-foot drop to the driveway below. Lou's car was parked in front of a huge, ultramodern house of poured concrete and glass. Past the house was a narrow yard overlooking the ocean bluff. The surf was loud and the air smelled of salt spray. A light was on somewhere inside the house, and as they watched, another light switched on upstairs.

"Jeannie, we found him," Zeppo whispered. "This place is perfect—it looks like a bunker, and it's got the sea on one side and a hidden entrance on the other. I wonder who owns it."

“Some rich fuck,” Jean whispered back. They hunkered down to wait. Drops fell from the canopy of eucalyptus trees above. Jean felt a cold dampness seeping through her jeans and up her sleeves, but adrenalin kept her warm.

Some twenty minutes later, the front door opened and Lou walked out in his yellow dress and raincoat, followed by Bernie in a heavy turtleneck sweater and jeans, carrying a Louis Vuitton suitcase. It was nearly dusk and Jean strained to see in the failing light. Bernie looked as if he'd lost weight since she'd last seen him. Lou popped the trunk and Bernie stowed his luggage. The two men stood next to the blue car talking in low tones; Jean couldn't make out their words.

Zeppo pulled the binoculars from under his poncho and focused on the scene below them. After a few moments he handed the glasses to Jean. “Notice anything unusual?”

She took a look. Lou's feet were out of sight behind the car, but he must be wearing really high heels; he was taller than Bernie. She adjusted the focus. “Shit!” she exclaimed in a low whisper. “That's not Bernie—that's Lou. Bernie's the one in drag.”

“Come on.” Zeppo scooted down the embankment where the drop to the driveway was only a few feet, and Jean followed him. Bernie was in the car and Lou stood at the front door, one hand on the knob, ready to go in. Jean and Zeppo were about to jump down onto the gravel when a figure in a hooded yellow rain slicker approached Lou from the other side of the house. Jean realized it was the gardener they'd seen earlier. Zeppo grabbed her arm and pulled her back.

“You're him,” the gardener said, his voice loud and rough. “You're the *maricón* who killed my little girl.” He had a heavy Spanish accent.

“Oh fuck, it's Salvador Ochoa,” Jean said to Zeppo.

“No,” Lou said, pressing himself against the door. “No, it wasn't me.” Jean was near enough to see terror in his eyes. Salvador pushed his hood back and gestured with his hand. He held a midsize revolver.

"You're Bernie Lyon—I seen you on TV," Salvador said. "You killed my Pilar just like squashing a bug. Now you're going to die, too."

Lou glanced at the car, where Bernie sat frozen. "No," he said. "You've got the wrong guy."

"You're a lying coward." Salvador took a step toward Lou, gun raised.

Bernie opened the door of the car and got out, pulling off the hat and wig. "Stop," he cried. "I'm Bernie Lyon. I'm the man you want."

Salvador strode toward Bernie, his dark, deeply lined face twisted with hatred and revulsion. "You're no man. You're some kind of freak." He fired three times. Bernie jerked spasmodically as each shot hit him, and fell backward onto the gravel. Salvador turned and ran up the driveway and out to the street.

Jean and Zeppo jumped down to the drive. Lou got to Bernie first and knelt next to him, pulling the black raincoat open, his face a mask of horror and alarm. "Mother of God." He glanced up as Jean and Zeppo knelt on Bernie's other side. "We have to call an ambulance."

The pallor of Bernie's face made his lipstick and blush seem clownish. Blood soaked the front of the yellow dress, but he was still breathing. Jean glanced at Zeppo; he sat back on his heels, face ashen and eyes closed. She'd forgotten how much the sight of blood upset him. "Hey," she said, touching his arm.

He rubbed his face with both hands and swallowed hard. "I'm OK. How bad is it?"

Jean tore open the dress and pushed aside the blood-soaked padded bra. All three bullets had hit Bernie square in the chest, and one of them looked as if it must be near his heart. "It's bad," she said. An indistinct sound escaped Bernie's lips, and Jean leaned over him. "It's OK, we'll get you a doctor," she said. "Lou, call 911." He didn't stir.

"Roman," Bernie breathed, and then something changed behind his eyes and Jean knew he was gone. She pressed two fingers against his neck but found no pulse. He lay utterly still.

"He's dead," she told them, gently closing his blue eyes.

"Oh my God," Lou said. "What am I going to tell Roman?"

Jean, horrified by the situation, examined Lou. He'd dyed his hair honey blond and his makeup had been applied to give the illusion of a longer jaw and a broader nose. From a distance he really did resemble Bernie. "Were you just going to stand there and let him shoot you in Bernie's place?" she demanded.

"I don't know," Lou said, shaking his head slowly, his voice trembling. "He didn't have to do it. All he had to do was sit in the car and say nothing and that man would have shot me. He saved my life." He started to cry, his artfully applied makeup running down his cheeks.

"Lou, pull yourself together," Jean commanded. "We have to call an ambulance, and before it arrives, our stories have to be straight."

Lou rubbed his eyes and blinked at them. "What are you two doing here?"

"Lou," she said sharply. "What was the plan?"

He got up, staggering. "I . . . I can't tell you. I promised Roman."

Jean shook him by the shoulders. "Listen, this game is over. Tell me what was going down or you and Roman will do time, and not in the same cell."

Lou pulled away and leaned over, his hands on his knees, and took a few deep breaths. "Bernie was going to drive my rental car to the Fashion Valley mall. There's another car there waiting for him. Then he was supposed to drive to the LiuCom airstrip and get a helicopter that would take him to a ship."

"LiuCom? Is that Meide's father's company?"

"Yeah. He was going to Indonesia, where there's no extradition treaty."

"What about you?"

"I'm supposed to walk around in front of the picture window. The cops have been doing intermittent surveillance from a house nearby."

Jean thought this over. "What if you got picked up in this outfit?"

"I'd say Bernie wanted to see Roman without the paparazzi hanging around, so he asked me to switch clothes and stay here for a night in case anyone was watching. I was going to be an innocent dupe. No one does the dizzy drag queen like me."

"You'll have to go with that story, lame as it is," Jean said. "Call 911 right now."

As they headed indoors it started to rain. Zeppo took off his poncho and laid it over Bernie's corpse. They followed Lou into the house, where he picked up a sleek black phone and made the call. The three of them sat on black leather couches that faced an enormous picture window. With a corner of her brain, Jean realized the spare modern décor was stunning and the view spectacular: clouds, light rain, the storm-driven sea below, the nearby cliffs lined with wind-tossed palms.

"Now Lou, there are still a few loose ends," Zeppo said. "What were you and Meide talking about at the Chinese restaurant?"

"She wanted me to tell Bernie some things about what to do when he got to Jakarta. We had to talk in person in case the police were tapping their phones. Is that how you found Bernie? By following me?"

"Yeah. What's in the suitcase?"

"Overnight gear, as far as I know. Roman told Bernie not to carry anything with him that would suggest he was about to blow town."

"We'd better leave it in the car. What about us?" Zeppo asked Jean. "Why are we here?"

"Lou told us where he was staying and we followed him so I could interview Bernie for my story," she said. "We waited in the bushes because we weren't sure if Bernie was here. Lou, where are you staying?"

"With a friend in Hillcrest, at 62 Sandpiper Lane."

"OK. God, we're all going to sound like utter morons. The San Diego police are a lot sharper than Wes Jurado. Now we have two more calls to make." Jean took out her cell phone and punched in Chencho's number. "Chencho, it's Jean," she said when he answered. "Listen: Bernie's dead. Salvador Ochoa shot him and ran off. I'm here with Lou and Zeppo waiting for the cops. You'll have to break the news to Meide and Ted."

She heard him gasp. "What . . . what . . ." he stammered.

"They'll find the records of our phone calls to each other. Say I was looking for Bernie but you couldn't tell me anything. I promise not to mention your help with Meide."

"Jesus, this'll kill Mr. Lyon."

"We'll talk later." She hung up and looked at Lou. "Now you're going to call Roman. I don't want him hearing about it on the radio."

Lou took the phone and punched an autodial number. "Roman, I've got really bad news. The father of the murdered girl shot Bernie. He's dead." Lou closed his eyes, pain etched on his face as he listened. "I'm so sorry, Roman," he whispered. "We'll call you when we can. Jean and Zeppo are here, too." He listened for a moment, then said good-bye and turned to glare at the pair. "He thinks the killer followed you here. Did he?"

"Absolutely not," Jean said. "He was lurking down the street when we arrived."

"You'd better hope you can convince Roman."

They could hear sirens closing in. Zeppo came over to Jean and put his arms around her. "It's going to be a long night," he said.

Chapter 26

The Encinitas sheriff's station released Jean, Zeppo, and Lou just after midnight. The rented Sentra was in police custody for now. As they stepped outside, a white Prius pulled up in front of them. Roman was at the wheel, his expression dark and full of grief.

"Get in," he ordered. Lou sat next to Roman, and Jean and Zeppo got in the back. "Any problems?" he asked Lou as he pulled into sparse traffic on the rain-slick El Camino Real.

"No," Lou said. "Since there's no question of any of us having shot him, they seemed to buy our story."

"What about Salvador Ochoa?"

"Nothing yet. They're looking for the white van Jean and Zeppo saw."

"Where are we going?" Zeppo asked.

"Back to my hotel," Roman said. "We have a few things to discuss."

Jean leaned close to Zeppo, physically and mentally exhausted, glad she didn't have to talk to Roman right now. She was deeply sorry for what he was going through and at the same time furious at him for endangering Lou. She also felt real anguish about what was going to happen to Salvador and what it would do to his family. There didn't seem to be any end to the pain Bernie had caused.

Inside Roman's suite, they sat in overstuffed chairs and sofas set around a hideous wood and glass coffee table. Roman ordered drinks and assorted sandwiches from room service, then sank into the sofa next to Lou.

Jean leaned forward in her chair. "First let's get one thing straight: Salvador didn't follow Zeppo and me. One of the detectives told me that the neighbors say he's been hanging around near the bunker for two days. Each of the neighbors thought he was working for somebody else. He was obviously just waiting for Bernie to come outside."

"So it's a coincidence that he died the day you found him," Roman said.

Jean stood up. "Yes, it is a coincidence. How dare you accuse us of getting him shot. You're the one who put all this in motion. Setting a killer loose was your idea." Zeppo reached out and took her hand, gently pulling her back into her chair.

"Salvador must have followed me on one of my earlier visits," Lou interjected. "I must have been sloppy."

Roman put a hand on Lou's knee. "You're the last person I blame. All you've done is help me."

"Which brings me to my main question," Jean said. "What the hell were you thinking, Roman? You almost got Lou killed."

Lou frowned at her. "Leave it alone, Jean. I made my own choices."

"Lou, don't you get it? If Bernie had been a second slower getting out of that car, you'd be dead."

"Which brings me to *my* main question," Roman burst out angrily. "Why didn't one of you stop Salvador?"

"I admit I pulled back when he waved the gun," Zeppo said. "I've been shot, and I never want that to happen again. I especially don't want it to happen to Jeannie."

"Come on, Roman," Jean said. "Are you blaming us for not tackling a crazy man with a loaded gun?"

Roman slumped back on the sofa. "If only I'd been there. I could have stopped him."

"Oh, you'd have killed Salvador?" Jean said. "What a perfect ending that would have been."

"I'd have disarmed him, or talked him out of it. At least I'd have done something."

"It all happened really fast, Roman," Zeppo said. "Salvador was way over the edge. I doubt even you could have done anything."

There was a knock on the door and Roman let in the room-service waiter. No one spoke while he pushed in the cart and set it up. When he left, Roman served Lou a glass of sparkling wine and himself Bourbon on the rocks from a bottle on the dresser. Zeppo poured Jean a snifter of Cognac and opened a beer, then loaded a plate with sandwiches. Jean watched Lou nibble at a sandwich; with his makeup worn off and his hair tousled, he no longer resembled the dead man.

Zeppo swallowed a bite. "Who owns the bunker?"

"A Bash Back donor," Lou said. "He's a rich, high-profile closet case. Roman happened to know he was in Europe and he lent us the house." He sighed. "Of course, once the press figures things out and links him to Bash Back, he'll be out of the closet, like it or not." Someone knocked on the door. "Are we expecting anyone else?"

"No," Roman said. He set his drink down and went to the door, putting the chain on and opening it a couple of inches.

"May I come in?" It was Meide Lyon's voice. Roman unhooked the chain and let her in. Meide, wrapped in a knee-length hooded chinchilla coat, embraced Roman. "I am deeply sorry for what has happened," she said. "I loved him, too, you know."

"I know." Roman helped her out of the coat. Underneath she wore a long-sleeved black knit maternity dress and jade jewelry. "Meide, this is Jean's friend Zeppo. Please sit down."

Zeppo pushed another chair into their circle and Meide sat. Her eyes were red and puffy and her expression miserable.

"Would you like something to eat or drink?" Lou offered.

"No, thank you, Lou. I cannot stay long. Ted needs me. Bernie's death has crushed him. The doctor gave him a sedative. Lydia is with him now, but I must return before he wakes up."

"Why have you come, Meide?" Roman asked. "You shouldn't be driving around alone at this hour."

"Chencho brought me. He's waiting downstairs. He knows nothing of our efforts, so I told him I wished to offer you my condolences."

Jean and Zeppo exchanged a quick glance.

"The chief of police came to see Ted and explained what happened," Meide said. "I know you and Zeppo were there, too, Jean. I assume it was to stop Bernie from leaving. I have come to ask a favor. If we had been successful and Bernie was safe in Indonesia, Ted would be upset but would eventually realize it was for the best. But now he can never know that I was trying to help Bernie escape. It is clear that the killer must have followed me or Lou." She took a handkerchief out of her Fendi bag and dabbed at her eyes. "If we had not visited Bernie, he would still be alive."

"Don't blame yourself," Jean said. "Salvador Ochoa was very determined. If he hadn't managed to find Bernie before the trial, he would have gone after him during the trial."

"But then he would have had policemen protecting him," Meide said. "If Ted learns I was responsible, I don't think he will ever forgive me. I know Roman and Lou will not speak of it, and I ask you never to reveal what you know about our plans. I am willing to pay you."

"That won't be necessary, Meide," Jean said. "We were going to keep quiet about it anyway. We don't want to see Roman or Lou in prison. But I would like to satisfy my curiosity. Why exactly did you want Bernie gone?"

Meide laced her fingers together atop her belly. "I read all the papers that the lawyers brought, and I believed Bernie was guilty. Despite what he did, I could not bear for him to go to prison. If that happened, Ted would suffer, too, and would take little joy in my child. I wanted Bernie to be free and comfortable, even if it was far away. But instead, I was an instrument of his death."

Zeppo leaned forward. "You know, there's one place money could really help. Why not give a couple of million to the Ochoa family? The mother and sons had nothing to do with all this, but look what they've lost. And now they'll have to pay a lawyer to defend Salvador. You could do it secretly—that way it wouldn't look like an admission of Bernie's guilt."

"That's a very good idea," Roman said. "It would compensate them in a small way for what they've been through."

"I shall do it," Meide said. "I have my own money." She pushed herself up out of the chair. "I must get back to Ted. Thank you." Roman helped her into the fur coat and she left.

"Now she'll spend the rest of her life worrying that Ted will find out," Jean said. "Old Bernie just keeps on giving."

"Shut up, Jean," Roman snapped, his scowl returning. "I'm sick of your snide, nasty remarks."

"Lay off her, Roman," Zeppo said so sharply that they all looked at him in surprise. His face was flushed with emotion; Jean had never seen him so mad. "Chencho said it best: Bernie was a monster. A lovable monster, but a monster nonetheless. He caused all kinds of pain and destruction. You fell for him, which was your screw-up. Now you've compounded it by thrashing around trying to save him, and in the process, endangering the people who love you. I've tried to ride this out with you, but I can't do it anymore. Bernie's better off dead, and the sooner you accept that, the sooner you'll come to your senses." He stood up and took Jean's hand. "Let's go, Jeannie."

Jean let him pull her up and they went out the door without another word. There wasn't anything left to say.

Chapter 27

The day before Thanksgiving, Jean left work early to clean her apartment; Zeppo would arrive soon. They hadn't heard from Roman since that night in San Diego nearly three weeks ago, and although Zeppo was still angry at him and didn't want to talk to him or about him, Jean really missed him. She suspected Zeppo did, too. She hated this silent treatment—she wanted the two of them to have it out, then kiss and make up. She and Zeppo had reconciled with Lou, and they were going to his house for Thanksgiving dinner. Jean loved surprises, and she and Lou had taken steps to move things along.

In any case, now there was something besides sex to cheer her up: The issue of *Wine Digest* with her Phoenix Garden article, updated to include Bernie's death, had hit the newsstands a few days earlier and had sold out nationwide in twenty-four hours. Owen had been on the phone all day negotiating with the printer about overtime pay so they could get another 100,000 issues printed by early December. Their website hits had gone up by a factor of a thousand. Owen hadn't given her the raise she asked for, but in Jean's opinion, she'd gotten something better.

The authorities hadn't yet captured Salvador Ochoa, and the search had widened to Mexico and Central America. Jean had spoken several times to Maria Esposito, who'd recently told her that Salvador's wife and sons were holding up, and that after much discussion, they'd decided to accept Meide's monetary gift.

Yuan was still at large; several law enforcement agencies, including Interpol, were looking for him, but given his resources and connections—not to mention the Vacherin Constantin watch he'd stolen, which hadn't turned up either—the authorities weren't hopeful.

Jean wasn't looking forward to her various court appearances in San Diego. At least when she went south, she could visit Ethan, Tony, and Laszlo, who was now the executive chef of the Tony's Chop House chain.

The downstairs buzzer rang and Jean jumped up and hit the button, hoping Zeppo was early and had forgotten his key. She opened the door; to her disappointment it was Clive Deegan, accompanied by a young Asian woman in jeans and a black and white striped sweater.

"Jean," Clive said, "this is Helen Tang from the *Chronicle*."

"Goddammit Clive, you know I don't want to talk to any reporters!" She tried to slam the door.

He put a big booted foot in her way. "That's right, start screaming before you know what's going on."

Helen grinned, watching them. "Still a few sparks, I see." She stuck a hand out. "Hi, Jean. Clive asked me to come over and talk to you. I promised him I wouldn't try to interview you."

Jean shook the offered hand warily. Helen's was one of the few local bylines she recognized; Jean had enjoyed her stories over the years, most recently the articles about Phoenix Garden, and had sent her an anonymous tip once, for which Helen had thanked her by phone when events revealed who the tipster must be. "Talk to me about what?"

"I'm doing an investigative piece for the Sunday magazine about Wang Yuan. The police have found out who he and Angus MacKnight really were. Clive thought you'd like to know before you read it in the paper."

"Why, Clive," Jean said, "who knew you were such a sensitive guy? I'm sorry. Come in and sit down." Jean regarded Helen Tang as she settled into a chair. She was short and slim, with a broad, intelligent face. Although she was probably in her late twenties, there was a wide gray streak in her shoulder-length black hair.

"I loved your article in *Wine Digest*," Helen said. "Pretty good hard news story for a wine writer." Her smile told Jean she was teasing.

"Thanks. You want a glass of wine? I just opened a Beaujolais Nouveau." They both accepted and Jean poured the fruity red wine.

"The police traced Wang Yuan through the fingerprints on the jade," Helen said. "His real name is Zhang Jinshan. He was born in Beijing in 1962, an only child. His father was a museum curator and his mother was a professor of literature. During the Cultural Revolution, they were sent to the countryside and forced to work in the fields. His father died within two years. He and his mother escaped to Hong Kong, and she worked in sweatshops there until she died, too. Zhang was fifteen at the time. He lived on the streets of Hong Kong for six years and finally got on a boat for San Francisco, where he lived for a few years and worked in an antiques shop.

"In 1984 he showed up at a house party in Osaka posing as a Chinese art consultant and stole a famous set of erotic netsuke. That's his modus operandi: He uses his charm and knowledge of art to get invited to a wealthy person's house, then swipes something he's been commissioned to steal. He has also been linked to the theft of some Persian miniatures from a house in West Palm Beach, Florida, where Carl Schoonover was a guest, too, so he wasn't lying when he told you Schoonover recognized him."

"That sure explains why he's so obsessed with money," Jean said. "Sounds like a rough childhood. Why wasn't he ever caught?"

"He works all over the world, and apparently not very often. The art he steals is really high-dollar, so his fees last him for years."

"He told me he'd never have to work again after he sold the jade. Did they ever find out who ordered it stolen?"

"No. There aren't any leads on that one."

"What about Angus?" Jean asked.

"They traced him with dental records. His real name is Roy Walker, born and raised in West Texas. He was Army Special Forces. In the 1980s he served in Afghanistan, and after that he worked with the contras in Nicaragua. When he got back stateside, there was a series of rapes near Fort Benning, Georgia, where he was a Special Forces instructor, and he was arrested. He killed an MP and escaped. After that he was a mercenary all over Africa and the Middle East. Looks as if Walker and Zhang met sometime in 1994, because later that year they both spent the weekend at the home of a Venezuelan oil executive and left with his collection of pre-Columbian jewelry."

Jean was fascinated in spite of the revulsion she felt for both men. "I can't wait to read the article."

"It's been great fun doing the research. My editor thinks there's a book in it. Zhang is an amazing and complicated guy." She touched Jean's arm. "I don't mean to make light of what happened to you. It's just such a great opportunity for me. And I speak Mandarin, so I can use sources other reporters can't."

"I understand completely. I know a relentless agent if you need one."

"If I do write a book, can I talk to you again?"

Jean liked Helen and was intrigued by the idea of finding out more details of Yuan's life. Of course, she didn't have to tell her everything. "Sure. Give me a call."

"Thanks, I will. I really appreciate your time, Jean." Helen and Clive stood.

"Thanks, Clive," Jean said as she let them out. "Maybe there's hope for you yet."

"I thought you two would hit it off," he said. "A couple of pushy broads, not to mention fellow members of the sisterhood of the prematurely gray."

Helen grinned. "The prematurely gray who aren't fighting it. That's a much more exclusive club." She shook Jean's hand and left with Clive.

Zeppo arrived about an hour later and she told him about Helen Tang's visit as they ate dinner and drank Beaujolais Nouveau.

"It's scary to think about how close you and Roman came to getting killed by Roy-Angus," Zeppo said. "He was even more dangerous than you suspected. That makes it even more amazing that a couple of amateurs like you and Roman prevailed."

"Having seen him fight, I don't think Roman counts as an amateur."

"How about if I make dinner next time, Jeannie?" Zeppo said as he finished his overcooked chicken and undercooked potatoes. At least the salad was edible.

"Be my guest. I'm no Laszlo Harady."

"So Thanksgiving at Lou's tomorrow, huh?" Zeppo said. "He serving a traditional dinner?"

"Yeah. He's promised us a homemade feast. We just have to bring wine."

Jean selected *Touch of Evil* from Netflix and they spent a cozy evening watching film noir. Jean did her best not to think of Bernie.

~

THE NEXT day the weather was clear and cool, so Jean and Zeppo took an easy bike ride through the city to Golden Gate Park. The streets were quiet on this holiday morning. After their ride they lolled around Jean's apartment watching football until five o'clock, when they walked over to Lou's bearing two bottles of Beaujolais Nouveau and a cold bottle of Veuve Clicquot Brut Champagne.

The house smelled just as it should, like roasting turkey and warm spices. Lou took their wine offerings to the sideboard, his coral-colored caftan and long dangly gold earrings flowing out behind him. His short hair was spiky and his makeup tasteful. "Let's start with some bubbly," he said, easing out the cork and pouring wine into three tall flutes. "Here's to love," he toasted. They clinked glasses and drank.

Jean looked around the spacious room. The artful centerpiece on the chrome and glass dining table was made from colorful autumn leaves. Zeppo looked at the table, and Jean noticed it was set for four. He cocked his head to listen to the music. It wasn't Lou's usual dinner party fare, soft jazz, but one of the Brandenburg concerti. Zeppo looked sharply at Jean. "Roman's here, isn't he?"

"Yeah," she said. "Sorry to spring this on you."

Roman came out of the kitchen wiping his hands on a long white chef's apron. "Hi, Jean. Hello, Zeppo. Lou has convinced me that it's time we cleared the air."

Zeppo made a face. "So I'm supposed to apologize for talking out of turn?"

"No," Roman said. "I'm the one who needs to apologize. I've behaved very badly, endangering those I love in an attempt to save a man who didn't deserve it, and blaming you two for my failings. I'm sorry."

Jean put down her glass and threw her arms around Roman. "I forgive you," she said.

Lou was all smiles, but Zeppo hung back, looking skeptical. "As easy as that, huh?"

Roman released Jean and faced Zeppo. "Look at it this way," Roman said. "What if Jean had committed a crime and was in danger of going to prison for years? Is there any limit to what you'd do to save her?"

"When you put it like that, no," Zeppo said. "Although Jean would never betray anyone or commit that kind of murder."

"I know she wouldn't," Roman said. "Forgive me for falling in love too quickly with a man I didn't know well enough. At my age, too."

Zeppo sighed. "OK. I guess I can forgive you, too."

The rest of the evening passed in a convivial mood, with Zeppo gradually warming up to Roman. Lou and Roman had prepared a fabulous dinner of roast turkey with cornbread stuffing, mashed potatoes and gravy, shredded Brussels sprouts with pancetta, and brandied cranberries. It all went beautifully with the Beaujolais Nouveau. By the time Lou served homemade pecan pie, the four of them were back to their old camaraderie.

"I have a surprise," Jean announced. "Owen claims he can't give me a raise because times are tough in the magazine world, this latest issue notwithstanding. But he did give me four weeks of vacation a year instead of two."

"That's great, Jeannie," Zeppo said. "Now we can take a trip over Christmas break."

"That's what I want to do. But since I couldn't afford to go anywhere and my car insurance was breaking me, I did something rash." She paused for effect. "I sold my car."

The three men stared at her open-mouthed. "You sold the Porsche?" Lou asked in astonishment. "But you love that car."

"I love to travel, too, and it seems I can't have both."

"I should have suspected," Roman said. "I wondered where you were parking—it hasn't been in my garage all week."

Jean grabbed her purse from a nearby coffee table and pulled out four airline folders. "Here's how I spent part of it: We're going to Italy for Christmas. In a month the four of us will be sitting on a veranda in Calabria drinking Cirò."

"Jeannie, that's fantastic," Zeppo said. "I've never been farther than Mexico or Canada."

"Then it's about time."

Lou clapped his hands. "What fun! I love Italian men."

"Will you go, too, Roman?" Jean asked.

He smiled. "Of course. It'll do me good to get out of town. And I can't think of three people I'd rather travel with."

After a while Jean and Zeppo, feeling thoroughly stuffed, said warm good nights and walked back to her apartment.

"Whew," Zeppo said. "I'm glad this thing with Roman is resolved. It was really bugging me."

"I thought it would be a good idea to take Roman somewhere diverting and completely unconnected to Bernie."

"Good move inviting Lou. He's been through a lot himself."

Jean unlocked her door and they went into her apartment and flopped on the sofa. "It's ironic when you think about it," she said. "This whole thing played out just like film noir. The dashing hero falls hard for someone who turns out to be poison. The hero does stupid things for love and the lover dies in a tragic screwup. Who knew a clean-cut rich kid could be such a classic *homme fatal*?"

"But it's not pure noir, is it? Our sidekick subplot has a happy ending." Zeppo put his arms around her and gave her a soft, slow kiss.

"A smutty ending," Jean said, pushing him down on the sofa. "My favorite kind."

Epilogue

On a chilly afternoon in late December, as Jean searched through her closet and debated what to pack for the trip to Italy, a FedEx man delivered an odd package. It was a heavy cardboard cylinder about two and a half feet long and maybe four inches in diameter. The tube was covered with customs stickers and labels in both English and Chinese. The return address was Hong Kong. No name.

Jean cut the tape off the plastic cover at one end and looked inside. It appeared to be a rolled-up scroll, well padded with bubble wrap. She pulled the scroll out and unrolled it on the bed. It was unmistakably Chinese, a red stone rubbing on a white ground mounted on faded black silk. The rubbing was an exquisite rendering of a woman in a full skirt riding on a camel and wielding a sword. She wore an elaborate headdress and what looked like armor on her arms and torso. A male attendant followed behind, carrying a tall standard. The rubbing was splotched with age.

Jean pulled all the bubble wrap out of the tube. A plain white note card fluttered to the floor. She picked it up—to her astonishment, it was in her own handwriting. It must be from Yuan—he had seen her handwritten notes in the notebook when he drew her portraits.

She read the card. "This is a stone rubbing of a Tang princess from a tomb in Changan, near Xian. The Tang Dynasty existed from 618 to 907 A.D. The Tang were Han, but are a leading example of Sino-barbarian synthesis. Their vibrant art is often symbolic of the dynasty's warrior ethos. Tang people, and especially women, were free of the subsequent strict mores of the Song and Ming dynasties. Tang women rode horses and camels and did not bind their feet." There followed a line in Chinese.

Jean sat down on the bed and gazed at the scroll, wondering idly how much it was worth. She had no idea what to do with it. She found it beautiful and would love to keep it. On the other hand, it was from Yuan, and she knew he was smart enough not to leave any clues to his whereabouts in the packaging. Still, she should turn it over to the cops. But first she needed to know what the entire note said.

Jean grabbed the card and ran down to Twenty-Fourth Street and into the Chinese restaurant. A middle-aged Chinese woman at the hostess station smiled in recognition. Jean recalled her name was Martha.

"Want to order takeout?" Martha asked.

"Not today, thanks. I have something I need translated from Chinese. Would you mind looking at it?"

"Sure, no problem." Martha took the card and read the Chinese characters under her breath. "OK, this means 'I salute you. We will meet again.' "

"Thanks." Jean walked slowly back to her apartment. Did Yuan imagine she'd ever want to see him again? He couldn't possibly. Was he simply trying to scare her? Or was it a real threat? After all, she was responsible for the death of his partner and the total destruction of his plan to steal the jade. Not to mention his broken nose. She suddenly felt cold—she had run out without a jacket.

Jean rolled up the scroll and put it back in its cardboard sleeve, along with the note. She shoved it behind boxes at the top of her closet. She didn't want to deal with it right now. It could wait till she returned from Italy. She'd talk it over with Zeppo and Roman once they got to Calabria.

She went back to her packing, anticipating the trip ahead, trying not to think about looking over her shoulder for Yuan's slim, sandalwood-scented shape for the rest of her life.